SHIELD

GREENSTONE SECURITY

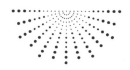

ANNE MALCOM

SHIELD

Greenstone Security #2
Anne Malcom
Copyright 2018

DEDICATION

For those wild children, who live hard and love harder.

AUTHOR'S NOTE

I've been waiting for this book for a long time. Maybe since the beginning. I've wanted to write it since the beginning.
But they weren't ready.
Things needed to happen.
And they did.
This story took a lot of work because this story has happened in the background of all the books in the Templar universe, before Gwen and Cade started it all.
Because here's a secret—Gwen and Cade didn't start it all.
Rosie and Luke did.
No one knew.
Not even them.
I know a lot of people have wanted to read their story, and I really hope it's all you expected and more.

Anne
xxx

*Also, you can read this book as a standalone, but I would

recommend reading *Still Waters* first. If you want the complete reading experience, and love MC, I'd also read my Sons of Templar series before this.

PROLOGUE

ROSIE

AGE FIVE

Most doomed romances didn't actually know they were doomed at the beginning. I mean the *very* beginning. Before the tragedy. In that Hollywood mega zoom-in moment when their eyes meet and lasting—and more often than not, fatal—love is born. First comes love, and then comes all the rest of the shit.

This is in *most* cases.

Romeo and Juliet, Heathcliff and Catherine... and I don't know any more, come to think of it. I flunked English.

Anyone who knows me knows I'm never going to fit into the category of 'most cases.'

Or maybe I'm the ultimate fucking cliché. The girl who strives so hard to be extraordinary that she meets the masses doing the exact same thing. Falls for love right where she shouldn't. Just like the rest of them.

1

Whatever.

I knew it was doomed before it even began. The second I saw him.

I was five. First day of school. Yep, it's that fucking pathetic. Even more so because he didn't even know I existed at that point, and many points after.

Total fucking cliché.

I knew who he was. Even at five, I knew the line drawn in the sand. The one splattered in blood.

Dad dropped me off at school, with me riding on the back of his motorcycle. My dad was the president The Sons of Templar MC.

Not many people had stark, in-detail memories of their five-year-old selves. Normally it was a mix of images, some memories muddled with make-believe. Recalling it was like staring at an interior TV screen. Maybe because moments with my father could've been held in my hand, treasured because moments and memories were all I had left.

Maybe it was because then, precisely then, was when my life stopped being my own.

"Now, baby, what do you do if anyone gives you trouble?" Daddy asked, his knees clicking as he bent down so I could see his eyes smiling, even if his face didn't.

Daddy didn't smile around other people. Bad for his image, he said.

I didn't get that. A bad image was like a photo of someone who looked bad. And even when he wasn't smiling, my daddy never looked bad. I thought my daddy was the most handsome man *ever*.

I grinned, holding up my fist, squeezing it tight so my nails cut into the insides of my palm. "I give them a knuckle sandwich," I said.

Daddy chuckled, rustling my hair. "That's right, my princess. No one fucks with my girl."

I was laughing too, happy I'd made Daddy laugh. I collected

2

that sound, and it made me smile whenever I was the reason Daddy chuckled. His laugh stopped when he focused on a car.

I looked at the car too, uninterested, until I got a look at *him*.

He was dropped off in front of us, in a policeman's car—his daddy wore a uniform. With a great big badge on it.

I barely knew how to tie my shoes, but I knew the police were *bad*. We didn't like the police, and they didn't like us.

I also knew the look that darkened Daddy's face.

It meant someone was in trouble. A lot of it.

I'd seen that look a lot, though never directed at me. Mostly it was directed at the men in the club if they did something to 'fuck up.' I knew *fuck* was a bad word from the way it sounded in the air, harsh and wrong. I heard other mommas yell at their kids who said it in the grocery store. But I didn't have a momma, not to take me grocery shopping at least, and no one yelled at me when *I* said it. No one had ever yelled at me.

I was the princess. That was what my brother Cade called me. And Daddy.

But I'd never really felt like much of a princess. And I knew I really wasn't when I caught sight of the older boy getting out of the police car. The second I saw his blond hair, his beautiful face, his clean clothes, I knew. *He* was the prince. The real one, like in the movies. The good guy.

I looked down at my boots, the smallest ones at the Harley Davidson store and they were still a little big. Daddy said I'd grow into them. Another reason why I knew I wasn't a princess—they always wore froufrou dresses and a lot of pink, and their hair was *always* in lots of pretty braids.

I didn't wear pink. Pink was for pussies, as Uncle Steg said, so I always wore all black. Like my brother, Cade. Black was my favorite color in the whole world. My hair was always curly and crazy; I didn't know how to braid, and neither did Cade or Daddy. Sometimes Daddy would brush it and tie it up into the ponytail I had it in right now. But my hair wasn't straight and shiny like

ANNE MALCOM

Barbie or princesses; it was curly and wild, and some of it was always escaping from my hair bobble.

I didn't mind that.

I didn't want froufrou, or pink or Barbie. I didn't *want* to be a princess.

I wanted to be a warrior like my daddy. Like my big brother.

Until that moment outside the school, on my very first day. When I saw the prince. Then I wanted very badly to be the princess he saved from the bad guys and rode away with to live happily ever after.

The problematic thing was the bad guys were my family. The ones I loved with all my heart. If you wanted to get technical, I was a bad guy too. Maybe the worst of them all.

The bad guys didn't get a happily ever after.

As it happened, neither did princes.

4

CHAPTER ONE

ROSIE

AGE SIX

"Why can't I be like them, Daddy?" I asked, nodding toward the men roaring away on their motorcycles.

Daddy ruffled my hair. "Because even for a Fletcher, six years old is too young to be on a motorcycle," he said, his voice smiling. "But don't worry, kid. Soon as you can reach the pedals, you're on a bike. It's in your blood."

I smiled too, but I also frowned because that wasn't what I meant. "No, why can't I be in the club too? Like you." I tugged at the leather he always wore, so much so that it was a part of my daddy, just like his gray eyes and his smile voices. "Is it because I'm a girl?"

Daddy grabbed my chin. His eyes weren't smiling. "Simple answer? Yeah, baby, it's 'cause you're a girl. 'Cause my pops lived in a time where women didn't have much say in anythin' and he quite liked it like that." He paused, and even though he was looking at me, I thought he might've been seeing something else. "Still like that now, I guess. Society is moving on in that respect, but our club doesn't move with society. Our club just *is*. Not many rules, but the ones we got ain't gonna change. I'm sure of that. Not while I'm around, at least." He looked at Cade, who was helping Uncle Steg with a car. "I have a feelin' your big bro might shake things up a bit, though. Maybe after I'm gone." There was both a smile and a frown in his voice.

I slipped my hand into his.

Daddy looked down, staring at my teeny tiny hand. He squeezed mine, not too tight, just right, then smiled.

"You're gonna shake things up more than a bit, my little princess," he said. "I already know that. Which is why even if the club wasn't the way it is, I wouldn't have you wearin' a cut, following rules. There ain't many, but there's enough to tell you to be a certain kind of person. My Rosie will never let anyone tell her what kind of person she is. You're my caterpillar. You're gonna grow wings, baby. And you're gonna soar and be the only version of you in this whole world. I know you'll be the heart and soul of this club. In more ways than one. But you're destined to be somethin' different. Somethin' bigger."

AGE THIRTY

Something magical happens when you separate from someone you love and it's someone you shouldn't. When it's too totally Fucked Up—Fucked Up requires capitals because of the sheer consistency of that phrase in my life—to ever work. When there're a million and twelve reasons why it won't. You know it when you're together. Even when those little cracks of sunshine peek through the darkness that is un-destined love, disguising themselves as happiness for a fleeting moment, even then you *know*.

You make your plans to end it. You convince yourself that you'll be okay. It'll hurt, of course. It won't be easy to walk away with a broken heart, but you'll do it. You've broken things before and you've survived. You know the pain will be crippling, but you're also sure you can do it.

Self-preservation and all that.

So you leave.

Walk, run, crawl. Whatever it is that gets you out the door so you can commence the process of repairing yourself. Or re-breaking everything he fixed because you can't be whole without him; you only know broken, can only survive broken.

Then it happens, once you actually do it. All those reasons, those concrete barriers to true and lasting happiness that had seemed so unsurpassable before they melt away. The reasons, all one million and twelve of them, don't seem so important anymore.

Because of the magical thing that happens when you leave someone when you don't want to. When you leave someone because you know it's ultimately the best thing for both of you, even though in your entire life you've always known that the best things for you have never been *right* for you.

You forget all the bad. The blood trickles down the drain, not leaving a trace of the wounds you sustained while together. Making you forget they even existed, convincing yourself that you imagined them. The only ones left are the new ones, so raw and painful that they have to be real. The ones that, in the empty air of loneliness, cut even deeper than the ones you couldn't handle before. The ones that made you leave. The ones that you perhaps imagined.

Then it gets even more Fucked Up. You find yourself craving that exquisite pain you had before.

With him.

It had been unbearable, but it was easier to experience than the stifling empty air that yawned ahead of a life without him.

Even if I was never really *with* him.

"Please fasten your seat belts and set your electronics to airplane mode before stowing them safely," a professionally pleasant voice requested over the intercom.

That was easy since I'd tossed my phone in a trash can two connections back. Right after I'd bought a one-way ticket out of the country. It wouldn't do very well disappearing if I had a big fucking homing beacon in my pocket declaring where I was going.

Which was why my phone was buried amongst discarded sodas and soggy airport sandwiches.

Which was why I used my fake passport and stolen credit cards.

This was not my first rodeo.

My brother may have gone legit, and good for him. He could join the fucking Boy Scouts, bathe in his new, almost law-abiding life.

I excelled at breaking the law. When your brother is the president of an—until recently—outlaw motorcycle gang, you found the law didn't pay much attention to the younger and seemingly harmless little sister. I utilized that, even though it killed me. Kurt Cobain had once said, "Thank you for my tragedy. I need it for my art."

I couldn't sing for shit, but I did make an art out of breaking the law and not getting caught. The boys could learn a few things from me, if they decided to go dark side again—unlikely—and listen to a female—even more unlikely.

I was a better criminal than all of them put together.

Not that any of them, including my brother and his club, otherwise known as my family, would ever know. The only thing they'd know was that the flighty and unpredictable Rosie had disappeared.

Again.

Hopefully that would be all they focused on. And hopefully no one inspected my now-abandoned house with a blue light.

They wouldn't. They were used to this by now.

It wasn't their first rodeo either.

Sure, Cade would go all stoic, perhaps break a couple of chairs, maybe even send someone to check my usual haunts: Las Vegas, Mexico, the Dominican Republic.

Maybe.

And he wouldn't be overly worried when no one found me. He knew I could take care of myself. He taught me to. Well, taking care of my physical self. Emotional self was a shit show. Another Fuck-Up.

He'd sit back on his throne and wait. Plan on yelling at me when I eventually got back, toting a new guy or a new tattoo and a thousand new stories. He'd think about that for a hot minute, then focus on the wife he worshipped and the children he adored.

My finger twitched thinking about them. My beautiful niece and nephew.

My throat burned with the knowledge that I wouldn't be seeing them for a long time, of all the things I'd miss of their lives.

"The crew are pointing out your exits, in case of emergency."

I didn't glance up. I'd already selected my exit in case of emergency. It was this fucking plane. If it went down, so be it.

I clenched my fists against the one armrest I had. The asshole in the middle had his meaty clams claiming both on either side, and most of my personal space as well, so his sweaty skin brushed on my bare arm when he moved. Normally, I would've called him out. Calling out assholes was my favorite hobby.

But I was kind of in the middle of one of my not-so-favorite hobbies.

Ruining my life.

"Cabin crew, be seated for takeoff," the harshly accented voice of the captain replaced the soft and calm one of the attendant.

I've made a huge mistake. The ultimate Fuck-Up.
I was pushed back in my seat and the roar of the engine filled my ears as we ascended, lifting from American soil.

Well, it was too fucking late now. Besides, the only mistake bigger than leaving was staying.

SIX MONTHS LATER

"Una cerveza, por favor."
I paused, my mind running over the events of the day. The horror. The blood. The death.

Just another day at the office.

"And a shot of Patrón," I added in English. I could've said it perfectly well in Spanish—I was near fluent at that point—but it felt nice to speak my native tongue, a way of holding onto an identity that was slipping away. That I was trying to shed at the same time I was clutching at it to store for later, like a sweater I could slip back into once I'd left this season of my life behind.

But like when you gain a few too many pounds, regardless of if you lose them again, the sweater will never fit right. Just like when you change too much from who you were before—you would never fit back into your old life.

The cold beer slid along the bar, a lemon sticking from the neck of the bottle—not because it was trendy, but because it kept the flies away from the rim. A water glass filled with clear liquid that was so not water joined it.

It was what I liked about this country. They knew how to drink.

Then again, most of the population were living in poverty and subject to political upheavals, corruption and violence—a heavy hand was medically necessary as a prescription to cure this thing called life. A bullet was another, just about as common.

"En la casa," the bartender told me with a sneer that I think he was trying to fashion into a grin.

On the house.

I raised my brow, not grinning, and slammed cash down on the bar. "Despite the fact that putting anything heavier than a couple of raindrops on the roof of this particular house would cause it to collapse, I pay for my own drinks," I replied, evenly meeting his lecherous gaze. "Tends to help bartenders punching way above their weight from getting the wrong idea."

I picked up the glass, letting the harsh liquid slide down my throat and soothe some of the burn that had been present for months, ever since I left.

Since I ran away.

From Amber.

From my family.

My girls.

Him.

But I wasn't allowed to think of that. Those blue eyes, those sculpted muscles, or that kiss.

That fucking *kiss.*

No, I had to focus on the shield. That shiny, squeaky-clean piece of metal that was now tarnished and blood-splattered.

Because of me.

I blinked the blue eyes out of my mind and focused on the hardened, muddy brown, and mean ones of the bartender.

The gaze tried to tell me that he wasn't used to rejection. I had to think the opposite was true. He had a moustache that only Tom Selleck could pull off, and it had pieces of his last meal trapped in the wispy stands. Broken capillaries on his cheeks gave away the fact that he sampled his wares more than a little. Prison tattoos snaked across the soft skin of his arms, exposed by a filthy wife beater, a hairy paunch sticking out from the space between it and his belt buckle.

I wasn't exactly at my best, in ripped jeans and scuffed combat

11

boots, my tight tank only slightly cleaner than his. I only had a swipe of mascara on my eyes, for business purposes more than anything else, and I'd grown out my chocolate curls to a length that cried out for multiple styling products. Which I didn't have. They were all littered on my bathroom counter at home. Along with the broken pieces of the old me. My current makeup collection consisted of old mascara, a cracked lipstick and an empty tube of concealer.

The wardrobe situation was even more dire.

So un-Rosie-like.

Which was kind of the point.

But even with all that, I was nothing to sneeze at. I wasn't afraid to admit that I had a bit of that natural beauty thing going on. On a good day, I had *a lot* of it going on.

That day, and the ones before, and most likely the ones proceeding it, couldn't and wouldn't be characterized as 'good.' Happiness made a woman glow with natural beauty; heartbreak and pain did something too. Magnified her beauty in a hard way that almost hurt to look at, but made her more endearing nonetheless.

I snatched the cold bottle of beer, my hands dampening from the condensation running down the chilled glass in the sticky room.

"The right idea," I clarified, "would be to make sure you and your buddies figure something out."

I glanced around the dirty and poorly lit room, a fan laboring at the ceiling to circulate the smell of hot body odor and cigarette smoke. Men and a handful of women were scattered around the tables, most lingering in the shadows. The men were more or less different versions of the bartender, some a little more attractive but with a meanness radiating around them that I recognized immediately.

That and the hard and cruel beauty of the women who were with them told me I was in the right place.

"That none of them think I'm looking to exchange free drinks for… anything," I continued. "That's if they actually *like* holding onto their manhood." I winked at the scowling toad in front of me, whirling on my boot to find shadows of my own.

They'd come.

They always did.

And then my job began.

CHAPTER TWO

ROSIE

AGE SEVEN

Death isn't something kids understand. It's some black cloud that drifts in and out of their lives, perhaps when some barely known great aunt gets swallowed up in its embrace. They witness it from afar, feel its chilly grip drifting past. But most children, the lucky ones, they forget that fleeting coldness and sense of terror; the cloud drifts away with the winds of youth brushing it quickly by, replacing it with whatever new toy was around, the best places to ride their bikes, the best way to escape the newest bully.

For *most* children.

I was not, nor had I ever been, a normal child.

Death wasn't a disembodied cloud, drifting far above my innocent head. It didn't just brush me and then move away. Death was always a thing, a personification that had always existed.

Like Santa Claus.

But instead of the red jolly man, the black and imposing thing did not come giving gifts. That menacing presence came and snatched things off me. Little pieces here and there, leaving empty spaces in the mosaic of my family.

Always violent. The endings of the men patched into the Sons of Templar were not anticlimactic, withering away in old age and senility.

No, it was always a rapid and violent end.

I was spared some of the violent endings.

Some were inevitable.

Like the time, right after my first day at school, when I'd been sitting on Dad's workbench, swinging my boots, sucking on a lollipop and daydreaming of that boy I'd seen. Then my magical daydreams of princes and princesses and all those simple fantasies that can only be made in youth were snatched away with the screeching of tires and shouts and chaos.

There was always chaos.

"Rosie, baby, stay there and don't move until I say," Daddy shouted, dropping his tools with a clatter and sprinting toward where the black van had stopped. It was parked funny.

I wasn't focused on how Evie would yell at the grown-ups for blocking the parking lot because there was more than that to focus on.

Red.

Blood.

It stained the cracked concrete of the parking lot.

I blinked, just in case I was seeing something that really wasn't there. Like how I had been just seeing that boy smile at me and say hello and take me for a ride on his horse even though he'd never smiled or talked to me.

But it stayed.

And it got worse when I saw the blood was coming from Sonny.

He wasn't moving.

He was staring at me.

But not in the way he did when he pulled a penny from my ear. There was no sparkle in his eyes. No twinkle. There wasn't *anything* in them.

My lollipop tumbled to join Daddy's discarded tools on the ground, where the blood would eventually creep up and swallow it away.

That was only the first, and most dramatic, time.

When I'd met the man called Death.

It didn't happen often, but I saw him more than Santa Claus.

He had been taking pieces from the mosaic of my life, but I managed to glue what remained together, still smile and pretend to forget about the thing called Death.

That was until he grabbed me by the throat and smashed every piece of my mosaic apart.

It was when he took Daddy.

I didn't see the glassy stare of Death replace the fond gray gaze of my father like I had with Sonny.

I wished I had.

It would've been bad. Horrifying. Terrifying.

But it wouldn't have been—couldn't have been—as bad as Evie walking woodenly toward me. Like a zombie. Like a stranger wearing her skin and impersonating her almost perfectly.

Almost.

"Rosie, it's your father," she said, the rough husk somehow disappearing from her voice. It was the audible version of cardboard.

My stomach dropped, in a hideous and unbearable way, and it didn't stop dropping. Like a pebble tumbling into the black depths of a well.

"He's dead," she choked out, her shaking hands pulling me into an uncharacteristic embrace. "Your dad's dead."

Evie didn't hug. She wasn't like the other moms: she didn't bake, didn't dress in pastel, didn't join the PTA.

16

would recognize as his father's silent battle between his job and his moral responsibility.

"I'll always keep you safe. Whatever it takes."

And he did. Luke and his mom were safe, happy, content. He would walk down the street with his father, watch him greet everyone, most people by first name—he took the time to do that kind of stuff. Amber was small, and there weren't any bad guys, so he had the time.

He didn't know when it stopped. That hero worship thing, that boasting to his classmates that his daddy kept the whole of Amber safe.

Maybe it was when Luke began to understand the politics of the town. Who really ran it. Not his father with his uniform and moral responsibility but the motorcycle men, with the tattoos and that something else that Luke wouldn't see as morals.

He didn't know when the hero worship started to fade off. But he knew when it disappeared completely.

He'd often ride with his father in his cruiser after school, when his mother was at book club or working at her part-time job at the library. He loved it at first, riding up front, watching his dad at work.

But he was older now, and he didn't quite know if he liked watching anymore. He didn't quite like what he saw.

He'd been pissed that day that he couldn't go shoot hoops with his friends. He couldn't escape this horrible feeling creeping up on him like a bad tuna sandwich that his dad wasn't the man he thought he was.

Then he got the call on the radio telling him to go to the compound. The one on the outside of town where the bikers lived. His dad's jaw went hard and he raced out there, lights and everything. Before that, he usually only put them on when Luke begged him. Or if someone was going just a little too fast on the road outside town.

His dad usually didn't give them tickets, just warnings. Luke used to think that was cool.

Now he wasn't so sure.

"You need to stay in the car, Luke," his dad ordered in a voice Luke didn't quite recognize.

Luke didn't answer, because they were screeching into the clubhouse and he saw blood. A lot of it. And a dead body.

His father saw it too.

"Luke, do not move and do not look."

Luke squeezed his eyes shut, not just because his dad ordered but because he didn't want to look. No way.

But he couldn't help it.

When he heard the car open and close, and muffled voices and radio noise, he opened them again. His father was looking down at the man with the blood. Talking with the men.

He waited for his father to do more than look and talk.

He was waiting a long time.

He didn't know what made him move his gaze.

And then he saw her. She was swinging her legs, with boots much too big for her hanging off them. He didn't think she was doing that for any reason other than she must've been doing that before.

Before the man and the blood.

Luke saw her face. It was the girl from school. Cade's pretty sister who didn't look at all like she belonged to this. Luke watched her. Watched innocence seep out of her like water from a fast-emptying bathtub. He watched the hurt that didn't even seem to fit on such a small face take over.

He clenched his fists on top of his knees, itching to clasp the door handle. To do something to help her.

His dad would help her. It was his job. He kept people safe.

He'd somehow keep her safe.

Because he was watching her, that frozen moment of when a little girl had something sacred stolen from her in the backyard of her childhood, Luke did not see that his father had finished the conversation with the men.

Not the bleeding man, of course. That man wouldn't be having any more conversations.

He didn't notice until the car door opened, slammed closed and his father started reversing out of the lot. Luke whipped his head around, hating that he had to leave the girl. He focused on his father's hard-jawed profile.

"What are you doing?" he demanded.

His father didn't look at him. "Taking us home."

Luke gaped at him. "You're not doing anything?" he spluttered. "You're not helping them?"

You're not keeping her safe? was what he didn't say.

There was a long silence, long enough for his father to direct them out of the parking lot and back onto the open road. Long enough for Luke to realize that he didn't even get one glimpse of that little girl.

One last glimpse.

Because the next time he saw her, she wouldn't be a little girl at all. She'd be changed, matured beyond her years, something ripped from her soul that would ensure the absence of carefree happiness.

"Yeah, I'm not doing anything," his father murmured, little more than a whisper. "And that's how I'm helpin' 'em." The last part was barely audible.

"What are you talking about?" Luke's harsh adolescent yell somehow didn't seem as loud as his father's muted whisper. "You have to help! That's what you do. That's your *job*."

His father finally looked at him then. Luke thought he glimpsed something like shame, but it was quickly replaced by something just as unfamiliar.

Anger.

"No, son. My job is to keep Amber safe. Keep you and your

mother safe. That's exactly what I'm doing. I'll hear no more about it."

"But—"

"I'll hear no more about it!"

Luke flinched at his father's cruel tone. He didn't want to be quiet. He wanted to yell, scream at his father that he was doing it wrong. Being wrong. Beg him to at least take him back so he could do something for that little girl.

But he did none of those things. Instead he folded his arms across his chest, staring out the window and trying to blink away the tears that inexplicably rose behind his eyes.

No, Luke could not remember when he started respecting his father less. But he could remember when he stopped respecting him altogether.

That moment right then.

And he'd always thought it'd been because of the injustice of letting outlaws make their own justice, which turned out to be revenge. Thought it was encouraging lawlessness.

Or maybe he'd forced himself to think that.

Because it was actually none of that.

It was because he'd driven away from that little girl before Luke could do anything.

Before Luke could protect her.

PRESENT DAY

ROSIE

I was roughly yanked out of the bed of truck that I'd been hurled into an hour before. My arm caught on a protruding piece of metal, sharp pain followed by the warmth of blood radiating from my bicep.

I didn't flinch, keeping my body slack as they muttered to each other in Spanish. My eyes stayed squeezed shut, but I keenly took notice of my surroundings: the smells, the crunch of gravel, not dirt, beneath their feet.

They didn't know I was awake. Nor that I could understand how they were arguing over who would "fuck the mouthy American first."

Of course, they counted on me still being unconscious for that particular rape. They'd make sure I was awake for the rest of them. They'd try not to hurt me too badly, or bruise my face. Couldn't damage the merchandise before they sold me.

Then I'd be raped again. But it would be by someone different. Someone richer, most likely. Maybe I'd get brutalized on a private jet, surrounded by beautiful things. But a woman may as well be surrounded by filth—she always would be at the moment a man took something brutally that should never be taken. That was never his to take.

In the States, back home in *civilization,* there is a reported rape every six minutes. That's just what's reported. Here, who the fuck knew. Who the fuck knew how often a woman had that innocence, which she didn't even know she had, stolen.

She'd know she'd had it the second it was taken. The absence of it would eat her up inside.

Which is why I'm here. To hopefully take it right back.

Along with their manhood if it was a slightly less shitty day.

It didn't look like it was going to be difficult. The idiots didn't even notice me swapping out my dosed beer for the one I'd stashed in the corner behind me. I always chose a seat with a view of the door and my back to a wall. A little of my brother's advice sticking, or just common sense in this particular line of work.

I let myself be groped and roughly tossed around, gritting my teeth when the dirty paws of some animal cupped me between my legs. Even though I was prepared, even though I knew I was in control, it didn't make that moment any less degrading, didn't mean it didn't take a tiny slice of my dignity from me. Every time it happened, I was back in that room—*he* was touching me, violating me. It was almost too much in those few seconds before I got a hold of myself. And I did. Remembering that I couldn't stop what happened to me in the past, but I might be able to do something for someone else who hopefully would never know what I did for them.

The stench of sweat and human waste was thick enough to choke on in the room they planned on being their house of pleasure and my house of horrors. I could taste the sorrow and the pain of the women who came before me. Or maybe I was imagining that because I knew those women were lost. No matter what I did now, they would be lost.

There was money to be made, after all—trafficking in human beings was the third biggest business in the world. Almost one million people were trafficked among international borders annually. Eighty percent of them women, half of them children. And of that almost one million people, eighty percent were trafficked for the purpose of sexual exploitation.

They were gone the second they were put in this room. The second they took a sip of the drink laced with rohypnol, GHB, or ketamine, or a cocktail of all three.

Not me.

I was already lost in a different way, in a way that meant I could at least prevent someone else being taken, even if I couldn't save the ones who'd come before.

My bones and muscles protested with the way they handled me, but it was good, because them being rough gave me the opportunity to press a button stitched into the thick leather cuff at my wrist without them noticing.

No sound came when I pressed it, but I knew what it did.

I had about seven minutes, give or take, depending on how much of a distance Lucian kept when he followed us from the bar.

I'd run into them by chance, him and his team. It was the first time people like these assholes had tried to drug me. Lucian and the boys came in to try and save me. My captors were all dead by the time they arrived, guns drawn.

I grinned at them. "Sorry, boys. You snooze, you lose."

And it began. They were all ex-military, all here for reasons that weren't important to anyone but themselves. They were here to escape something. And it just so happened that the best way to escape something was to kill people who deserved to die. Our operation was just that, traveling around Venezuela mostly, with me as the bait.

Which was what I was right then.

I lost a handful of breaths as I was hurled onto broken and cold concrete, the impact winding me. I stayed still, braced against the pain. I was used to it.

I mentally scheduled myself in for a tetanus shot and maybe a round of penicillin to be safe. I immediately changed the maybe to a definite when rancid breath kissed my cheek and an equally rancid tongue ran along my face.

"Cunt tastes good," he declared in Spanish.

Out of the corner of my eye, I saw a flash of black as a figure entered the structure that could be roughly classified as a shack. After I kicked the man with the knife off me, breaking his neck in one swift movement so he collapsed gracelessly at my feet, I glanced up and found my initial guess of a newcomer was correct.

A very familiar one at that.

His icy eyes regarded me levelly, thick tattooed arms crossed as he leaned leisurely against the wall, not speaking, not interfering, just watching.

"Perra!" a voice snarled.

My attention moved from the newcomer to another attacker. I skirted the body at my feet to dodge the knife that was hurtling toward my neck. My dodge meant that I sank my own penknife into the man's own neck before he knew what was going on.

His eyes widened in grotesque surprise, a wet gurgling noise coming out of his mouth. I held his frantic and desperate gaze, keeping my grip tight on the handle of the knife.

"Yeah, you didn't expect to meet your end in this room, did you?" I hissed at the small amount of darkness remaining in his eyes. If you looked really closely, you could see the evil draining out of him, sinking into the soil, searching for a new home and a new landlord. His warped and ugly soul would follow and meet a man named Lucifer. I hoped.

Or maybe that was just my mind taking creative license in the midst of murder. My teachers always said I had an 'active imagination.' And 'problems with authority.'

They weren't exactly wrong.

I held his eyes a beat more. "It's been a profound honor killing you. If only it had been a lot sooner and your death a lot longer." I sighed. "But a girl can't get *everything* she wants."

Another thick and wet sound escaped from his body as I yanked the knife out, then stepped away from the spurt of blood that came with the gesture.

"Hit the carotid artery," a flat voice observed. "Nice."

My would-be attacker turned victim collapsed ungraciously on the ground, the smell of fresh excrement filling the already rancid air.

I screwed up my nose.

People shat themselves when they died, something they did not show you in the movies. Then again, good always triumphed over evil in the movies, and the girl always rode off into the sunset with the hero.

This particular girl rode off into the sunset alone to make sure her particular hero stayed far away from her. She'd already turned him into the villain; no use ruining what remained of his life.

I whirled, shaking thoughts of referring myself into the third person out of my head. I was already half crazy, I so didn't need to go full Charlie Sheen.

I glared at the owner of the voice.

"Yeah, I know how to kill someone. I'm not in kindergarten," I snapped, then regarded him, tilting my head and holding my scowl. "You didn't feel like, I don't know, *helping* me?"

Gage looked at me, then at the two bodies at my feet, with a blank, unblinking gaze.

"You didn't exactly need help," he replied, digging in his pocket. "And I'm rather attached to my balls. Don't like the thought of you ripping them out because I decided to get all chivalrous and help you kill a man. Feminism and all that."

He put his smoke between his lips, the flicking of his Zippo replacing the quietness of death that hung in the air. I'd quickly gotten used to that, though it didn't mean I liked it. Death was ugly, whichever way you spun it. Killing someone evil didn't make you good. It did exactly the opposite. Murder was murder.

Gage wasn't wrong. Him helping me would've been the most annoying thing he could've done, apart from just being here in general. Any other man in my brother's club would've rode in, guns blazing, testosterone overdosing, determined to save the girl they saw as their little sister.

Not Gage.

He was the exception to the rule.

He was the exception to a lot of rules.

I took the smoke he offered me, even though I didn't particularly want it.

I needed it.

Just like after getting laid, you needed a smoke after killing someone. A bowl of pasta wouldn't go astray either. Neither would an orgasm. But I wasn't looking to Gage for that. Even if he did brave the 'no touch' rule Cade had plastered all over me, I didn't think even I had enough kink in me to handle all of *that*.

Murder, sex, and food. The basis of life. They all worked together in some kind of twisted threesome.

"You found me," I observed, taking a long and unpleasant inhale.

He grunted in agreement.

If it was anyone else, I would've been surprised. In regular circumstances, I excelled at hiding my tracks. My most recent exit had been under more than regular circumstances; therefore, I more than excelled at hiding my tracks.

But like I said, Gage was an exception to a lot of rules.

"You going to tell my brother where I am?" I asked, blowing out another plume of smoke while wiping my knife on the thighs of my jeans.

Gage regarded me, and I squirmed under his gaze. He was one of the very few people who made me uncomfortable when he looked at me. His glassy stare always seemed to push right through whatever mask or costume I was wearing at the time and see the ugly truth. Gage lived the ugly truth, his past dark and twisted and full of things that would even give me nightmares. I didn't even know the details—I could just tell. A piece inside that had fallen off, been ripped out. And they may operate the same by appearances, but there was something wrong in there.

The kind of wrong that Jeffery Dahmer and Charles Manson had. But Gage channeled his in different directions. Not the 'right' ones, by far, but what was right anyway?

"No," he said in answer.

That time I was surprised. "No?" I repeated, dropping my smoke and crushing it amongst the blood and dirt at my feet. "You came all this way, to this shithole in the middle of the jungle, spent all this time on what I can only assume is my brother's request, and now you say you're not going to tell him? Bullshit."

Gage didn't move, didn't blink. Like a shark. Except if sharks stopped moving, they died. I didn't know of anything that could kill Gage.

"Your brother didn't send me."

"Yeah," I spat sarcastically.

He shrugged. "Believe what you want." His tone communicated the fact that he couldn't care either way. "I was curious."

I gaped at him. "You came to Venezuela, in the middle of rebel-owned territory, dirtied your boots, just because you were *curious?*"

The corner of Gage's mouth turned up, the closest he'd come to a smile. "In case you hadn't noticed, haven't had much cause to get my boots or my hands dirty with all this straight-and-narrow stuff we've got going on." He glanced down to where a trail of blood had pooled at the toe of his motorcycle boots. "I like getting dirty."

It was comical how uncomical that statement was coming out of his mouth. It wasn't sexual. Not by a long shot. It was cold and calculated.

I crossed my arms and his glance flickered for a second to my chest, where I'd unintentionally pushed up my boobs. It only stayed there for a moment, then moved up to my eyes, uninterested.

I wasn't offended. I was used to it. Gage barely looked at any woman with any real interest. Sure, he'd fuck a club girl if the occasion arose, but he wasn't really interested. Like the way a man might regard a freeze-dried meal when he had nothing else to eat —yeah he'd have it, but only out of need, not out of actual want.

"You were curious," I probed.

"Yep," he agreed. "'Course, I knew you're prone to goin' walkabout, but this time felt different. Had some time on my hands, checked out your place." He gave me a look. "You did a good job of cleanin' up, babe. Almost perfect. Most likely anyone else, save a cop with a black light, wouldn't have noticed anything. I'm not anyone else."

No, you're not. A bitter taste of dread climbed up my throat. Not for me, of course. Gage would never say a word to a soul to

31

rat me out. Definitely not to the cops, and it seemed not even to my brother. He was loyal. To family. To me. But not the cop who had spent the last decade trying to bring down the club.

I'd unwittingly handed him the evidence that would do what Cade had been wanting to do for the last decade.

Bring Luke down.

I struggled to keep my composure, watch Gage for any signs that he knew. But that asshole had the poker face to end all poker faces. We could've been talking about motorcycle parts for all he gave away.

"And you didn't run to Cade," I said, a statement, not a question.

He shook his head. "Not exactly my style. Would've, if I had any inkling you were in trouble. Well, a different kind than usual," he added. "But had a pretty good idea you were alive." He gave me a pointed look. "You are. Will say I'm impressed."

I raised my brow. "Impressed?"

"Your current line of work." He nodded to the bodies at my feet.

Of course he would be impressed with anything that had to do with blood and murder.

"Curiosity satisfied, and you're not telling Cade?"

"You left for a reason. I'm guessing a good one?"

I nodded.

"Then no. I understand what you're doin'. Maybe not the specifics, but enough to know that it was the only choice you had. Runnin' away from demons is a hard job. I'm not the one who's gonna make you face them. Doesn't work that way. You gotta face 'em yourself."

I tilted my head. "And you've faced yours?"

He laughed. A throw back your head, hold your belly kind of laugh. "Why do you think I chased you? Chase the blood? I'm the best runner there is, darlin'."

I gaped. The small glimpse I had into Gage's past, not exactly with the words but the way he said them, the way they sat heavy in the air. His thousand-yard stare. It was like staring directly into a black hole. My demons were infants compared to his, and I shivered at the thought of just what was chasing him. Despite the bitterness of the air, I wanted to know more, but the gun raised to Gage's temple kind of stopped our heart-to-heart.

Gage didn't move, didn't flinch. He continued smoking his cigarette, slowly, casually, as if he didn't have a worry in the world. "You may want to lower that, friend, in case you're attached to your head."

I glanced at the four men training semiautomatic weapons on Gage. They'd obviously noted that I'd neutralized any and all other threats.

"It's okay, guys, he's... a friend," I said calmly. A woman always had to stay calm when in a room full of men with guns. They were children who just needed their mom to firmly tell them what to do. "Guns down."

It took a second for the words to puncture, but they did. Three of them lowered their guns.

The handgun at Gage's temple remained. Lucian eyed him with a thick and distrusting glare. He wasn't an idiot, knew a threat when he saw one. Though he was stupid to think that he was going to come out on top, or even that his connection to me might stop Gage from killing him. Gage was loyal to an extremely small group of people. Everyone else was disposable.

"Lucian," I warned.

His emerald eyes flickered to me, keeping the gun raised for a beat longer, like a petulant child might to remind the mother that it could, then lowered it. He didn't even get it to the holster at his hip before Gage moved in a blur. When they both came into focus again, Gage was holding Lucian's gun to his temple.

The rest of the team scrambled for their weapons, eyes panicked. I rolled mine and sighed audibly. Gage wasn't even breathing heavily, his almost-finished smoke still hanging out of the corner of his mouth.

"I don't like guns waved at my head by people who don't know how to use them," he said.

Lucian glared. "I know how to use it."

Gage smiled. "You knew how to use it, I'd be dead."

CHAPTER THREE

ROSIE

AGE FIFTEEN

A group of kids were hassling some girl in the halls. Calling her names, tossing her backpack to-and-fro so she couldn't catch it.

It pissed me off. A lot.

Mean for the sake of mean. There was no excuse for being a shitty person when you had no reason. Sometimes life gave you a shitty deck, and to play that deck you had to be kind of shitty too. But never to innocent people.

I snatched the bag out of the air, scowling at the hair-sprayed teenager I didn't know the name of. I didn't care to.

"You're such fucking clichés, aren't you?" I glared at the group, giving a gentle look to Aimee, the small and quiet girl they'd been tormenting. I handed her back her bag. She took it gratefully with a shaky smile.

"This is none of your business, Rosie," one of the jocks said. "What do you care?"

"Call me crazy, but I care when I see idiotic clones tormenting someone for daring to be individual because they're so fucking insecure that they don't know what else to do. How about you go shower with your buddies and pretend not to be checking out their asses while you plan your next date rape?" I asked sweetly. "And if I hear you're hassling Aimee again, I'll blow up your BMWs... with you inside them."

A small smile danced at the corner of Aimee's lips and she pushed her hair behind her ear self-consciously, not realizing how pretty she looked. I hoped one day she'd learn that for herself. That someone told her that.

I could tell the little *Cruel Intentions* club wanted to say something back. Wanted to snatch back the power they thought they had in this school. But they wouldn't. Not when they knew my threat wasn't empty. Not when they knew the motorcycle club that ran the town would burn their houses to the ground if they did anything to me.

Not that I needed them. I could take care of myself. Rather well, thank you very much.

"What are you waiting for? Shoo, clones." I made a motion with my hands and one of the jocks actually flinched, like he thought I would hit him or something.

Cowards.

That's what those who picked on others were. The weakest of us all, trying to hide it by preying on someone else.

They scuttled away rather quickly.

I winked at Aimee, who was watching their retreat in awe.

"You okay, babe?" I asked her, softening my voice.

She smiled. She really was beautiful. "Yeah, thanks, Rosie. That was, um... you're not really going to blow up their cars with them inside them, are you?" she whispered nervously.

I laughed. "No, of course not."

She visually sagged.

"I'll make sure they're not in them. Promise." I did a Girl Scout salute.

She laughed nervously. "You don't need to do that because of me. It's not a big deal."

I lost my smile. "It is a big deal. Because they made you feel small, didn't they? For no reason other than they're jealous and ugly creatures. No one should make another human being feel like that. Just... don't let them, okay? You're so much better than them."

Aimee's face changed at my words, seeming to not know what to do with them. That hurt me. She obviously hadn't had much experience with compliments, which meant her parents were A-grade assholes. I just had a club of men who broke the law for a living and I still had experience with love and support.

This was a majorly fucked-up system.

The system being life.

"Thanks," she said finally.

The bell tolled and I inwardly groaned at my upcoming Calculus final, then decided to ditch. What use was Calculus going to give me in the real world?

None.

"I've got to get to class," Aimee said, her eyes darting around at the rapidly emptying halls.

I nodded. "Sure, yeah. Just let me know if they give you any trouble again, okay?"

She nodded and smiled again. "I don't think they will, but thanks."

I smiled and watched her walk away, hoping this world wouldn't grind her down and hating that I already knew it prob-ably would.

I had experience in that.

"You know, you should probably make sure you don't have any

37

witnesses when you threaten murder and arson," an amused and deep voice said from behind me.

Every cell in my body froze. The only voice that could do that to me. Make my stomach roil so the PB&J I'd had for lunch churned unpleasantly in my stomach. I wasn't like that with anyone. Which was saying a lot since I had a motley group of murderers and ex-cons as my constant company and babysitters.

Not that I needed to be babysat anymore.

Hadn't since I was seven years old.

But a motley group of murderers and ex-cons was more protective of me than a minister and his wife were of their treasured daughter. I'd bet their treasured daughter wasn't a virgin, like this biker princess. In fact, I had it on good authority that Lila, the preacher's daughter, was pretty much as far from a virgin as a fifteen-year-old could be.

Like I said, fucked-up system.

I whirled around on my heel, trying for casual. My eyes met steel first—the shield pinned on top of his perfectly pressed uniform, which covered his perfectly defined pec. My gaze traveled upward, noting the cords in his throat, the movement of his Adam's apple when he swallowed, the square and smooth jaw, always perfectly shaved. Then I got to the eyes. The ones that were the perfect shade of turquoise. If you asked me what my favorite color was in public, I'd say black, like my coffee and my soul. If you really asked me, I'd say turquoise with flecks of green, like Luke's eyes. Of course, I'd never say that out loud.

Usually on the occasions I'd met those eyes, they were as hard as actual turquoise. Now they were liquid stone, twinkling with amusement.

That told me that there was no one else around, the halls empty. I knew Luke would never look at me with anything resembling affection if he had witnesses. He had a reputation to uphold, after all. And so did I, for that matter.

Fraternizing with the enemy wouldn't do well for either of us.

But that wasn't what made my heart fracture the ribs containing it when our eyes locked. Maybe it was part of it, the fact that he was forbidden. Different. But it was more than that. He was everything I couldn't have. Everything I wasn't.

And a lot of other things I couldn't explain. Couldn't pinpoint.

I struggled to compose myself, structure a cheeky smile on my face. "Well, a girl's gotta find fun where she can in this Podunk town," I said with a lightness I hoped didn't sound as forced as it was.

Luke returned my smile, crossing his arms across his chest. I tried not to focus on the way his biceps flexed when he did that. I failed. I was a teenager with a mess of hormones, after all. It wasn't just boys who had sex on the brain. It was girls who had barely been kissed thanks to everyone in a sixty-mile radius being too scared of their brother's wrath to even touch her.

Though I wasn't interested in *boys* touching me.

"Hmmm," he pondered, the vibration of that sound in the air creating goose bumps on my exposed arms. "So you didn't do that in order to stop bullies from hurting a shy and fragile girl?" he asked playfully, his eyes hardening slightly.

"Who me?" I asked, pointing at my chest with faux dramatics.

I didn't miss the way his eyes flickered, for less than a second, to my exposed cleavage.

I developed early, and dressed 'provocatively,' to quote the principal, so I was used to boy's gazes flickering there. But not *men's*.

I swallowed roughly. "Never," I said, breathless. "I'm the *bad* girl, remember? I blow up things for fun. You won't tell on me, will you? Rat me out to the cops?" I paused, focusing on his badge. "The *other* cops."

He furrowed his brow, smile disappearing with my insinuation, my subtle reminder for him, and me, of our respective positions on either side of the law.

"I'm guessing if someone's BMW does go down in flames,

you'll have no knowledge and an airtight alibi?" he said by way of answer.

I grinned, megawatt and completely fake. "Ding, ding, ding!"

He regarded me. "You're different than them, Rosie. You always have been. I don't want to see you get hurt. You're a good person."

The words, the seriousness of them, punctured me. Right in the stomach. For all the wrong reasons.

I cocked my hip, my own brow furrowing. "No, I'm not different than them. And I'm not ashamed of that. Because it means that I'm not the same as everyone else, all of these people." I waved toward the empty halls. "The people you *serve and protect*. The people who torment innocents because it's fun and most likely that's what their parents do to them. Good is a construct, *Officer*. Just like bad. They don't exist. Not in my world, at least. Like I said, I'm just trying to get out of this alive. Have some fun."

He stared at me a long time after that. Really looking. Really seeing. Or maybe it was a trick of the light. A hallucination brought on by the fantastical hope that life might actually be like all those books and movies. He even opened his mouth, preparing to say something... real. I could feel it, the way the air was charged with someone electric.

But then it fizzled as he shook himself back into the uniform that held him and his worldview together.

"Fun and trouble aren't usually mutually exclusive for most people," he said instead.

I hid my disappointment well. Oscar-worthy, I reckoned. "Well, I'm not most people."

His eyes twinkled again. "I've noticed."

"Have you really?" I asked, my façade breaking to whisper those three words.

They did something, those words. Hit him somewhere.

His response was silenced by the buzzing of the radio at his hip. I didn't hear the words coming out of it, but they killed the moment.

He lifted it to his mouth, eyes still on me. "I'll be right there." He put it back on his hip. "I gotta go."

I nodded. "Going to enforce the law." The words did what they were meant to do, opened the chasm that separated us, that always would.

He eyed me. "Try to stay out of trouble."

I smiled. It hurt. Near crippled. "Not sure that's possible. You do that *so* much better than me."

His eyes hardened, and he gave me the brisk professional nod that was customary when were in public.

I hid my swift intake of breath when that nod hit me physically.

He turned, leaving, then glanced back at me, eyes liquid once more. "Yeah, Rosie. I have to," he said so lightly that I was afraid I'd imagined it.

That would've been it.

You know, the movie moment when it all clicks for the couple that was meant to be, destiny or whatever lined up for them and they started the romance that Hollywood and Disney were built on.

Except I was a Fletcher. By extension and definition, an outlaw.

Not Hollywood.

Definitely not Disney.

I blinked after him, the air still tasting sweet and clean from his presence. My heart thundered from my ribs so hard that I put my hand on my chest just to make sure it hadn't broken the skin.

"You like him."

The voice was so unexpected from the hallway I thought was empty, I jumped. And I didn't jump. Ever. Nothing could scare me at that point.

My scowl went toward a flushed and beautiful—despite being

makeup-free—face, blonde hair wild and tumbling down Laurie's back. She was grinning, her eyes light with her perpetual happiness.

"You like testing to make sure I have a heart condition?" I snapped.

Her grin didn't waver. "No, I think someone already did that." She nodded toward the closing door.

I bit my lip and started to walk in the opposite direction. "I have no idea what you're talking about."

She wasn't perturbed as she walked with me, pushing her arm through the crook of mine. "Oh I do. You *like* Luke."

I snapped my head toward her. "I don't like Luke."

"Babe, I know you. I've known you since you ate glue and beat up boys you liked. You didn't punch him, but I still know you're smitten."

"I don't like Luke," I repeated. "Because I *can't* like Luke." My tone was defeated, sad, bordering on pathetic. I didn't like that. I wasn't pathetic.

Laurie's smile disappeared and she stopped walking, causing me to as well. "What are you talking about, Roe?" she asked. "Of course you can like him. In fact, you don't get much choice in who you like. That's the fun in it." Her eyes went dreamy and I knew she was thinking about Bull. She'd been obsessed with him since she'd bumped into him at the club. She *fell* into him and he caught her. Literally.

If I hadn't seen it with my own two eyes, I wouldn't have believed it. It was like one of the movie meet-cute moments that made you so sick you threw popcorn at the screen knowing it could never happen in real life.

But it did happen.

The world stopped for the two of them right then. I almost felt it stop spinning as they locked themselves in a little world that existed here and yet someplace altogether different.

Bull felt it too. I knew it.

I also knew he wouldn't act on it. Not until Laurie was old enough. Much to her frustration.

But he'd protect her. Be there for her. Ensure that beautiful smile stayed on her face. And I loved that. That I could pass the torch to him and know he'd never let it go out. That's what we all had an unspoken agreement about. Laurie was a rare person who was untouched by the world's evil, naïve and so genuinely good you knew that something in this ugly world so rare had to be preserved. Maybe it was because I'd seen so much ugly that I didn't want to think of Laurie having to experience that.

So yeah, I got why she was confused.

"I can't like him, Lo," I said gently. "And you can never mention this. We weren't meant to be. We can't be. He's the enemy."

Laurie screwed her face up. "He's not the enemy. He's *Luke.*"

"He's the law," I said simply. "The club do not mix with the law."

"You're not the club," she said, confused.

I sighed. "Yes I am. That's all I am."

She reached out and squeezed my hand. "Oh, Roe, you're so much more than one thing. You're everything, all squeezed into one. And you deserve to like who you want. You deserve to be happy. It shouldn't make a difference just because he wears a badge."

"It shouldn't," I agreed. "But it does."

Laurie may not have believed in the barriers that were between me and my feelings, but they became clear and unsurpassable later. When I was back at the clubhouse that night, when I was hanging out, focusing on not doing my homework while Lucky talked me through the installation of a small but effective car bomb.

I didn't do empty threats.

"What the fuck, Rosie?" Cade twirled the barstool I was swinging on so I came face-to-face with his steely glare. The angry bark was scary enough—he'd perfected it as soon as he'd gone through puberty, at ten—but he only really liked it when he could pair it with his signature death glare. Perfected also around the age of ten.

They stopped working on me around a week after that when I figured my brother could be scary to everyone but me. His one and only soft spot, even if soft for him was marble.

I utilized it.

I fluttered my eyelashes in an innocent look I'd perfected. "What? It's not like I *plan* on anyone being in the car when I blow it up."

Lucky pushed off his seat. "I plan on having children, or at least being a huge whore until I'm eighty, so I'm leaving before Cade can do anything about that," he muttered, then scuttled off.

Unexpectedly, Cade didn't even glance at Lucky.

"You talked to Crawford today," he bit out.

I tilted my head, something pooling in my stomach at the knowledge in his gaze. "Um, he was wandering around the halls. It's a small place, so we conversed. It's a job hazard." I went for flippant, casual. "Plus, how would you even *know?*" I asked with narrowed eyes.

Even though he was twenty-one now—just like Luke—Cade had dropped out and started prospecting the moment he turned sixteen. Not exactly club policy, but an exception was made for the children of founding members and adopted children of current presidents.

Hence the chilled beer sitting in front of me.

Not that Cade would let anyone walk away with all their teeth if they insinuated that Steg was anything more than his president. He hated him with something I didn't understand. Steg was the only father I knew.

"Are you spying on me?" I accused.

He didn't blink at the sharpness in my tone. "I'm looking out for you."

"I can look out for myself," I snapped, crossing my arms.

Cade raised a brow, silently reminding me of all the trouble I'd landed in so far. Most of which I'd gotten out of without help. "Not when the club has shit going down. And not when you're talking to the enemy."

I scoffed. "Luke is hardly an enemy, Cade. Get out of the Middle Ages. Just because you don't like him doesn't mean I can't talk to him. You know, being *polite*. I know they don't teach manners in caveman biker badass schools—you're too busy specializing in grunts, death stares, and waterboarding."

He didn't like my humor. "You're not polite to Crawford, Rosie."

I rolled my eyes, hopping off my stool and intending to saunter off and get the last of the instructions off Lucky. "Whatever."

Cade clutched my arm, stopping me from moving, the grip bordering on painful. That in itself shocked me enough to freeze.

Cade was what could be considered a violent man. A fully patched member of the Sons of Templar MC was required to be a violent man.

But never had he put his hands on me. Never.

He yanked me forward so his gaze was all I could see. "I know you like to push the limits, Roe. Break the rules. Trouble is your thing. I get it. Scares the shit out of me since your version of trouble is blowin' up cars, not sneaking a beer." He eyed the one at the bar. "But fuck, I approve. It's you. I'll never stop you from being you. But this is the limit you aren't pushing. One rule you can't break. Crawford is the law."

"He's not, Cade. He's just Luke," I said on a whisper.

"No he's not, and you know that," he clipped. "The second he put that uniform on, he was comin' for the club. Ain't worried about that. We can handle that. But anyone who comes for our family, they're an enemy. We don't talk to the enemy, we don't smile, and we don't be fuckin' *polite*. A member would be excommunicated if they were *lucky*, Roe. Not many lucky Sons." He gave me a long look. "You get spoiled here. We love you. Steg loves you. You're not his blood but he considers you so. But even blood won't matter if he sees betrayal. And that's what he'll consider it. It's my job, first and foremost, to protect you, Roe. I'll die doing it if I have to, but I can't protect you from the club. You need to know this isn't teenage girl bullshit. This is serious."

Every word had a taste to it. Bitter and ugly and it seeped into my bones. Because he knew somehow. My secret. The one I'd harbored since that day ten years before.

The Luke secret.

And though I wasn't your normal teenage girl, I still had teenage girl fantasies. Like somehow Luke would see through everything and see *me*. And it would work.

But here it was, brutal, ugly, and heartbreaking evidence from the one man who would rather die than hurt me. But that's what his words did, each of them little tiny slices in my fantasy, slices that were making my eyes water they were that painful.

He shook me a little, his eyes softening. "Tell me you get me, Roe."

I stared at him. At the realization that the life that was meant to revolve around freedom from the prison of society was just another cage. One I would never escape because I loved my captors more than life.

"Yeah, Cade. I get you."

PRESENT DAY

Things after Gage finally lowered his commandeered gun and organized chaos resumed—Gage punched Lucian in the nose, of course, and then the rest of the team had to restrain Lucian —were tense.

Gage's exit was welcomed by everyone except me, especially Lucian.

He slammed the door of my tiny bedroom so hard, I swore the rickety hotel we were staying in shook. I reasoned anything more than a stiff breeze would likely cave in the roof, though the roof coming down on me wouldn't exactly be the worst thing in the world right now.

"What the fuck was that, Rosie?" he yelled. "More accurately, *who* the fuck was that?"

I peeled the bottom of my shirt upward to discard the dirty and bloodstained tank on the floor. "An old friend, like I said," I replied, not reacting to Lucian's temper. He was somewhat of a hothead.

He snatched my wrist and wrenched me around to face him. "I need more information than an *old friend*," he demanded. "Did you used to fuck?" His words, like Lucian himself, were harsh and uncouth.

He could be kind when he wanted to be, or when he needed to be, but he just wasn't wired for proper human emotion. Which made him perfect for the job and perfect for me. You had to be a little—or more likely a lot—broken to survive this life. And even then it wasn't a guarantee. In the six months I'd been here, I'd seen the worst of humanity I'd ever experienced. My thirty years living with an outlaw motorcycle club was nothing compared to this.

Sure, my family killed people. But not without cause. It was a twisted code, but it was underpinned by an equally twisted sense of humanity.

That didn't exist here. Human life worked as a currency. It was a dangerous thing when death became a part of life, made it all too easy to pull the trigger. That should never be easy. No matter how many times you did it.

I'd already made peace with the demons I'd add to my collection from the two lives I'd ended today. It was when you *stopped* collecting demons that you transitioned into the real monster. I didn't know whether I was looking forward to or dreading that.

Maybe I was already a monster.

I met Lucian's empty eyes and laughed. "No, I haven't fucked Gage. Like I said, he's an old friend. That's all I'm telling you, and that's all you need to know. We don't do personal, remember?"

He yanked me closer. "I sleep in your fuckin' bed. That's pretty personal."

I didn't flinch. "No. *We fuck.* Both for our own reasons that have nothing to do with each other. I'd say that's the furthest from personal you can get. And the second it becomes different for you, you can sleep somewhere else."

I wrenched my hands from his grasp to step toward my sleep aid—a half-full whisky bottle. The murky liquid sloshed into the chipped glass sitting on the table beside my bed. I downed the liquid quickly so I couldn't taste how warm and shitty it was. Once I swallowed, I turned to eye Lucian, who was still glaring at me. "You touch or talk to me like that again, I'll put my knife through your temple," I promised, slamming the bathroom door shut.

It wasn't empty either.

None of my threats were. Not anymore.

Killing was like tattoos: done once, it's painful and scary, but afterward it's almost addicting. The scars of it lasted the same amount of time as tattoos too. In other words, forever.

Just like heartbreak.

I couldn't figure out if it'd started or ended that day in the halls of Amber High fifteen years back. And here, in the middle of Venezuela, in the middle of an argument with another man, in the middle of an escape from these very memories, they came back to me, the halls as vivid and stark as they were had it happened yesterday.

I remembered it. Luke's fresh uniform, his unlined face. The butterflies smashing at the bottom of my stomach. Laurie's gentle romantic hope. Cade's harsh and inescapable reality.

My inescapable reality.

I surfaced from my memories with an audible gasp, clutching at the sides of the dirty sink in my bathroom. My head sank onto my chest that was rapidly rising and falling as if I'd run a marathon. And I had, of sorts. A marathon through the years, visiting my past failures.

My chocolate hair fell around me like a waterfall. I pushed it away and yanked my head up, regarding the stranger in the mirror. She blinked her long lashes at me, cheeks flushed and eyes somehow empty and full at the same time. Without makeup, she looked younger, almost like that girl in high school. But her features were sharper, face almost gaunt due to the unintentional diet she'd been on. It was hard to enjoy crappy food when corpses routinely filled your vision as you chewed.

Corpses she'd created.

She blinked again, that time a lone tear trickling down her face.

I wiped at my cheek furiously, both me and the girl in the mirror glaring at each other, accusing each other of that fatal weakness.

"Get your shit together," I ordered her.

I stared hard. The mop of hair was the last of what remained of who I had been before. A mess of chocolate curls, sprinkled with honey highlights. Why was I clinging to it?

He looked at me, then lifted his arm to push away some errant hair that was masking my face, as it tended to do at this length.

I held my breath as he did so.

He tucked it behind my ear, pausing at the contact between our skin, eyes locked on mine. Seemingly reluctantly, his hand went back down to his side.

"Like your hair long," he murmured.

Once again, I yanked myself out of the shark-filled waters

known as my memories much the way a lifeguard would snatch a drowning woman from the unyielding ocean.

He liked it long.

My gaze landed on a pair of scissors discarded on the sink.

I didn't hesitate. I snatched them and began hacking at my locks.

CHAPTER FOUR

ROSIE

AGE SEVENTEEN

I couldn't put my finger on when things changed for Luke and me. Like *really* changed. Morphed from a handful of almosts. Almost glances, almost declarations. All the almosts added up to nothing.

Because almost didn't mean shit.

Almost dying? You're still living.

Almost living? You're still dead.

Almost pregnant? You're not pregnant, go have a cocktail.

I grew into a woman. He noticed. I knew he noticed because I grew into a woman, and a woman knew when a man noticed her.

Once—a time I'd never told someone about, not even Lucy— he caught me and some guy making out in his car on the outskirts of Amber. We'd met at a party, and he didn't know my family, which meant I had a real chance at finally giving up my V-card.

My brother's promise to kill anyone who touched me seemed to stick with any fuckable guy in town. I took what I could get.

Things were getting to *almost* sex when a blinding light illuminated the cheap and cliché act. When the door opened and the half-naked guy was wrenched out of the car with a violence I was all too familiar with, I was sure it was my brother. I scrambled out of the back seat, forgetting I was just in a bra and unbuttoned cutoffs.

"Hey! Do you have to—"

But it wasn't a leather cut and a bike. It was a uniform and a cruiser.

And Luke, beating the shit out of my would-be deflowerer.

The cop, Luke, beating up a minor.

"You"—thump—"little"—thump—"piece"—thump—"of shit," he grunted, punches enunciating his words.

"Luke." My voice was soft, though it punctured his violence as if I'd screamed it.

In the headlights of his cruiser, I saw him drop the half-naked teenager to the ground, looking from him to his hands, dazed, as if he was wondering what they'd done when Luke had left the building.

Andy scrambled up, bleeding from the nose. "She was consenting, I swear," he babbled through the blood. He pointed at me. "Babe, tell him you wanted—"

"Get the fuck in your car and drive off," Luke growled.

He scrambled to do exactly that.

I was gaping at Luke, all traces of the night's shots wearing off to see him in stark reality. Though being sober didn't provide any more sense of logic to the situation.

His eyes moved from his fists to me—more accurately, my exposed chest. "Get your shirt on and get in the car," he ordered, voice so rough it was barely recognizable.

I blinked. "Luke—"

"Now!" he yelled.

I jumped, as if I wasn't used to people shouting at me, as if they didn't do it on an almost daily basis. *They* did. Luke? Never.

I snatched my shirt, yanking it over my head, most likely ruining whatever was left of my hair and makeup. Andy had already started the car and was regarding me with panic, as if he was considering driving away even though the door was open and half of me was still in the car.

"Get in, Rosie, before he decides to lock us up," he demanded.

I was about to do as he instructed when the savage version of Luke stopped me.

"Not with him. With me," he ordered.

I froze for a split second, fear and joy mixing in my stomach even worse than tequila and red wine.

On autopilot, I leaned back and shut the car door. Andy didn't hesitate in roaring backward the second I did so, blowing up dust with his hasty escape. Good thing I didn't give him anything I couldn't get back. Guy was a douche.

"Not a word. In the car," Luke said, reading my mind as I glanced up at him to ask him what the fuck was going on.

I blinked again. "Front or back?"

He ran his hand through his hair in frustration. With himself or me, I wasn't quite sure. "Jesus, Rosie, the front."

I quickly darted to the door he opened. It slammed as soon as my butt was in the seat. I regarded the radio and police parapher-nalia like an alien on a foreign planet.

The air thickened as Luke got in and slammed his door shut. The moment of silence between us, the first time we'd been truly alone, was both beautiful and terrifying.

"Seat belt," he barked.

I glanced at him. "Seriously?"

He clenched the steering wheel in answer.

I did as requested, something extremely rare for me.

He reversed out of what was known as the second-best make-out spot in Amber. I didn't go to the first because it was closer to town and had a higher chance of getting me caught by whoever Cade had gotten to stalk me tonight.

We didn't speak for the longest time, the car too full of quiet for one of us to add words to it. Too full of questions and answers and almosts. The radio wasn't even on: there wasn't the space for music.

I watched Luke's profile the entire drive through Amber, the lights illuminating his stiff jaw and granite features every now and then. I didn't even realize he was taking me right back to the party before we were almost there.

"Why are you taking me back here?" I asked, tearing through the air in the car.

He didn't answer.

He didn't need to.

Of course he couldn't exactly drop me off at home, saying, "I just beat the shit out of the guy sucking face with Rosie and stopped her from having her first time in the back of a car with a douchebag like so many other girls."

If it was anyone else, they literally could've dropped me off and said that, verbatim. They would've gotten a pat on the back and a beer for their troubles.

Anyone but Luke.

There would be no pat, certainly no beer. Just a lot of fucking questions as to why the man who considers the law to be set in stone would so easily break it for the first daughter of a club he was intent on bringing down.

That's what I was asking myself. Too afraid to ask him. Too afraid of the answer.

He pulled over a block away from the party. Even through the closed windows, I could hear the thumping base and screams of inebriated girls.

"Breakin' this up in fifteen. You'll want to move on before

then," he said, his voice both rough and flat at the same time as he stared straight ahead.

"Why?" I whispered, deciding to conquer my fear.

He wrenched his eyes to me. "Because you're better than that, Rosie."

It was meant to be soft, but it hit me like a punch in the chest. I unbuckled my seat belt, glaring. "Thing is, Luke, I'm not," I spat. "You're so intent on making me good, even if it's just in your mind. *Especially* if it's just in your mind. Maybe that makes you sleep better at night, I don't know, but stop trying to make me into something I'm not so it suits you better. It's fucking bullshit!" I narrowed my eyes at him as well as I could in the dim light. "I'll tell you a secret. My brother and all those men with rap sheets as long as my Sephora receipt... all those *criminals*. Those outlaws?" I paused, letting the venom in my voice penetrate. "They've got nothing on me."

I spat the last part out, jamming all my bitterness and sadness into it, before jumping out of the car and slamming the door shut. I didn't look back as I stomped back to the party, where I would drink five more tequila shots and wouldn't be gone by the time the cops showed up.

Luke was not among them.

I hated that I let myself wait long enough to look for him.

To hope.

Hope was deadly.

ROSIE

PRESENT DAY

Four months passed after Gage left and things went back to whatever version of normal I'd constructed. Not that I'd ever, since birth, experienced something close to normal. I had convinced myself that it was good, great. The only thing worse than death was normalcy. Nine-to-five, white picket fence, two-point-five kids and a golden retriever.

But Gage's visit, his words had shaken some of the cupboards of my minds so hard that the skeletons came out.

Not the bodies, of course. All of those were out in the open, except one. Crime and murder wasn't something I had to keep a secret from my family, even now when things were as close to the straight and narrow as they'd ever be—that being a definite curve away from anything resembling normal society.

My skeletons were different. The ones I even hid from myself. That shameful yearning for the white picket fence, the dog—heck, maybe even the kids. The whole package. The fairy tale. With the man who represented all of that, the safety and order.

Luke.

But his version of safety and order was destroying the thing he considered a threat to that.

The Sons of Templar.

One hell of a Catch-22.

One of the many, many reasons that I shouldn't think of that. Couldn't. But didn't a girl always want what she couldn't have?

I downed my tequila, warm and cheap, but you couldn't find anything else around here. It did the job. Kind of.

I twirled a piece of metal in my hand. An extremely dangerous one. Not a knife, or a gun. Worse than that.

A cell phone.

I'd purchased it in one of those shitty electronic shops that smelled of cigarette smoke and were packed to the gills with rudimentary rip-offs of all of the big names. It worked well enough. I was fingering the one thing I didn't discard along with my phone. My SIM card.

Inserting it into the phone would mean that my old life would come tumbling back in, would mean that Cade, or even Luke, could find me. If he was actually looking for me, which was doubtful, if our last meeting was anything to go by.

Because of—or in spite of—tequila, my mind went there. To the last place it should have.

The past. With Luke. With my family. With everyone.

It stayed there for a long time.

I emerged from the past much like a person would surface from the water after almost drowning: breathless and gasping for air. Swimming around back there wasn't healthy.

I tipped my head back and welcomed my shot of tequila.

I'd lost count of how many.

Not enough or too much, obviously, with my little trip down memory lane.

I regarded the SIM card. I was fucked now, so why not make it another signature Rosie Fuck-Up?

I inserted the card, waiting for the screen to light up. Which it did. Missed calls, voice mails, texts. The list was long; I guessed I should've counted myself lucky to have that many people caring about me. That many people who loved me.

> **Gwen:** *Hey, sis, so the hubby is a little worried about you. And so am I. I need a drinking buddy. Your nephew is entering the terrible twos, and Amy is pregnant and can't drink. Which means she's almost worse than the toddler. Okay, she's definitely worse than the toddler. Please come home. I miss you and love you.*

Gwen: *And by a little worried, I mean Cade has broken four pieces of furniture.*

Amy: *Everyone's having babies. And now Brock wants one. Despite the damage it will do to my vagina. I need backup. Not just for the vagina stuff.*

Ashley: *Hey, my love. I know why you needed to go, even though you never said anything. I get it. Just remember you have an entire family that loves you. That needs you. You're the crazy glue that holds us all together.*

Polly: *My sister is lost without you. Which means I'm lost without you. She moved to LA. You were supposed to do that together. Come home.*

PS. I'm in love and his name is Jared.

Bex: *I'm betting you've already ditched your phone, because you don't want to be found and you're not an idiot. What you did for Gabriel and me, for the club, there are no words. I know what it cost you. Heal, then come home. You've got a wedding to be in, bridesmaid. You can wear anything you like. As long as it's not fucking pink.*

Mia: *Hey, honey. Know you're out doing your thing. Being you. Your family is a little worried, and us girls are battling toddlers trying to get out alive. We need you to dole out the drinks and keep us insane.*

Lily: *Hey, Rosie, I don't know if you'll get this, and if you do, I'm sure it's lost in between all Cade's text versions of frenzied grunts, lol. But I just wanted to tell you that I'm pregnant too! Asher won't let me find out what it is. He wants a surprise. I hate surprises. Must be something in the water around here. Maybe it's a good thing you left, morning sickness sucks.*

Lucy: *I've sent a thousand and twenty-one texts and left as many voice mails but I'm still going to send a*

*thousand more. You're my best friend. No matter
what. Even though you leave me behind without a
word to navigate this shit show called life without my
partner in crime. It's your fault if I get locked up
because I don't have you to drive the getaway car.*
Cade: *Get back home. Now. This isn't fucking
funny, Roe.*
Lucky: *Hey, honey boo boo, come home please. I'm scared
Cade will shoot me. Also I'm worried about you,
little sis.*
Evie: *Steg here, don't have a darned cell phone and don't
get this texting shit. But we love you, girl. Don't
hesitate to call home if you need backup. Though
know you're strong enough to figure it out alone. Just
remember, you don't have to. You have a big family
with bigger guns at your back.*
Luke: *I'm looking for you. I'm not stopping. I fucked up,
letting you leave. I'll go to the ends of the earth to find
you. And I won't let you go this time.*

Each and every single one of those messages hit me somewhere in my soul, leaving it in little more than tatters when I read what I missing out on, what I was causing. It was physical, my yearning for all of them. Which I'd been ignoring, blocking.

Luke's message hit me square in the chest. Simple. Not saying much but saying everything at the same time.

There were dozens more of the same as I scrolled through. I decided to move to the flashing icon of my voice mail. There were a lot of those too, but I was already torturing myself, and it didn't look like I was going to stop until I hit bone.

I may have craved Luke with a fierceness that I could barely survive, but that wasn't the only kind of love that held me together. My family was everything to me; therefore, their absence in my life had a yawning chasm where my heart was supposed to be. And my girlfriends? Not having them? It was almost as bad as not having Luke. Because they were my true soul mates. So hearing Lucy's voice was like phantom pain in a missing limb.

"Rosie, this is my twelve hundred and fifty-fourth message," she joked, her voice saturated with a false lightness. "And I'll leave twelve hundred and fifty-four more until you call me back." I smiled a little, her words echoing the text she'd sent. "Tell me where you are. I'll come and pick you up from the Dominican Republic, Australia, even Wisconsin." I choked out a little laugh at that. "Just let me know my best friend is okay, please. I need you." My laugh was stolen by the single tear that rolled down my cheek hearing the hurt in her voice. A loud sigh followed. "Just call me, okay? I—"

Instead of whatever threat she was going to make if I didn't call her back, I heard a swift and bone-chilling intake of breath. Even through a shitty connection, thousands of miles away, I could hear the fear in my best friend's gasp. I could taste it, because her fear was my own.

"Lucy," I yelled, forgetting momentarily that this was a message, that whatever was happening had already happened. I could only listen, a spectator in the past.

"Please be okay. Please," I begged as crashes echoed through the phone.

"Now don't do anything stupid like run, darlin'. I'd hate to have to kill you before we get to play with you."

Then the line went dead. Nothing more. I yanked it from my ear, looked at in in horror, and then slammed it down on the table.

"No!" I screamed as bottles and glasses shattered to the ground.

No one around me even looked up from their drinks.

I stood, snatching my phone with the screen I'd shattered, my chair scuttling to the ground as I pushed it back.

I prayed it would still work to book me a flight back home and to my best friend. I prayed even harder that she was okay.

But God had never listened to me before. Why should He start now?

CHAPTER FIVE

ROSIE

AGE TWENTY-ONE

W hen you're young and stupid—and old and stupid,
for that matter—you ruin your life when you're
drunk.

Which was precisely what I did on the night of my twenty-
first birthday. I'd partied a heck of a lot before that, so it wasn't as
wild as you would've thought. There was a big party, of course,
but I mainly just sat with Bull and Laurie and watched their
happiness. Not with jealously exactly, but seeing how different
they were, how much they shouldn't fit and how perfect that
made them, it made me drunkenly decide that if they could do it,
we could.

So after I'd been dropped home by the designated sober
prospect, I got into the car and drove to the station. Yes, drinking
and driving was supremely stupid, but what happened afterward
was arguably more dangerous.

I parked crookedly outside the station. It was the middle of the night and everyone else was gone.

Luke wasn't.

I'd known that because we'd driven past on the way home and seen the light shimmering from the shadowy building. No one but Luke was that dedicated to their job as a small-town police officer.

The front door was locked, of course. I picked it with a rogue bobby pin.

"The only Templar who would break *into* a police station," I muttered to myself as I walked down the dark hall.

My heels clicked loudly in the eerie quiet; it would've been creepy, if creepy and scary weren't what passed for normal in my world. The only creepy thing, even through my drunken haze, was what I was about to do. There was a small, sober voice prattling in the depths of my brain, commanding me to snatch up my self-respect and hightail it the fuck out of there.

Drunk Rosie never listened to Sober Rosie.

Shit, Sober Rosie never listened to Sober Rosie.

So I kept walking, glancing around at the cookie-cutter desks, some scattered with files, other freakishly clean. Posters here and there. I was surprised to see Gage on one.

Wanted.

"Hmm, interesting," I muttered.

I wasn't surprised that he was running from something, but I *was* surprised that the police were in possession of this and he was yet to be arrested. Then again, as long as Bill was sheriff, we were unlikely to be arrested for anything. As long as Cade kept delivering him fat envelopes every month.

It was when Luke took the reins that we had the trouble.

And there I was, running right into trouble.

What's new?

The light in his corner office was brighter now, offending my eyes that had become accustomed to darkness.

My soul had too.

And there was I seeking out the light when I wasn't designed for it, nor used to it.

I didn't hesitate at the door because if I hesitated, it would've been over. Hesitation was for cowards and sober people. I was neither.

Luke was bent over a black folder, concentrating so hard that he obviously hadn't heard the not-so-stealthy break-in. He did hear the creak of his door opening. He wasn't one to hesitate either, his gun up and pointed at my forehead in a matter of seconds.

Most people's immediate reaction to having a gun pointed in the region of their brain might be to scream, cry, plead and definitely hold up their hands in the universal "don't shoot me" gesture.

I did no such thing.

The only thing I did was reach into my purse and slip out a cigarette, put it between my lips and light it up. I took a leisurely inhale.

Not that I even *liked* to smoke. It made my clothes smell like shit, fucked with my teeth and may or may not give me cancer. It was something I was trying out. Plus, it went with my look. I was wearing tight leather pants with some third-hand Manolos, towering me high above my regular 5'7, and a see-through blouse that showed off my lacy red bra. My hair was straight—it took about two hours to do that—and tumbling down my back. My red lipstick left an imprint on the white filter as I took the smoke from my mouth.

"Jesus, Rosie," Luke yelled, letting his gun clatter onto his desk.

I took another inhale, mainly to hide my nerves. "Nope, it's just me. Don't think the other guy's been seen in a few thousand years, and even if he was in this neck of the woods, he wouldn't be hanging out with me." I watched him glance down at the file he'd been so focused on, snap it closed and shove it in a drawer. I wondered idly about that, for about a second. "He'd most likely be in here with you, Luke. The saint."

I wandered into the room, glancing around with interest. It was clean. Neat. Obsessively so. Framed photos spaced evenly, diploma on the wall.

"You know I'm not a saint, Rosie," he gritted out.

I focused on him, raising my brow. "Oh really? Because you're pretty sure who the sinners are in this 'burb, and I thought only saints had the authority on sinners. The rest of us can't see the grass for the trees, being sinners and all."

He glared at me, then at the plume of smoke. He was out of his seat and in my face in seconds, my cigarette out of my mouth in the same time.

"You can't fucking smoke in here," he growled.

He didn't leave my atmosphere immediately, holding my lit cigarette with the red lipstick kiss on the end, watching me.

"You're not a sinner," he murmured. "And I'm not a saint."

"What makes you so sure?" I whispered.

The moment lasted longer than it should have, giving me butterflies of hope.

"Because saints don't want things that they can't have," he said finally.

And before I could grasp onto that moment of hope, hold it in my hands and use it as proof that coming here—drunk or not—was a good idea, he was gone.

Luke rounded his desk, stabbing my smoke out on a scrap piece of paper before throwing it in the trash. He stayed on that side, keeping the piece of furniture between us like a shield. From my feelings or his, I wasn't sure. I just knew it wasn't working for me. There was no shield thick enough for that.

"What are you doing here, Rosie?" he sighed, crossing his arms. He looked me up and down, and that time really *looked*. He couldn't really look in public. Or that's what I told myself. Not that he wouldn't. Or didn't want to. That truth would make me all the more pathetic.

I entertained the idea that now that it was just us, with no one to hide from, real hunger danced in his gaze.

But then it was gone.

Maybe with just us, there was so much more to hide from.

"How'd you get in?"

I smirked, a good ploy to distract from my hurt. "The front door was open."

Luke frowned. "It was not."

I shrugged. "It is now."

"Jesus, Rosie, you broke in?"

I looked around. "You keep mentioning this guy. Can I just not see him or something?"

"This isn't a joke, Rosie," he clipped. "You broke into *a police station*." He looked at me again, but it wasn't the Luke look. This was the Deputy Luke look. "You're drunk."

I eyed him. "It's the middle of the night and I broke into a police station. You think I'd do that sober?"

He looked at me for a long time. "How did you get here?"

That was not the question I expected him to ask. I expected a lecture about the laws I'd broken, not to do it again, yada yada yada.

Knowing that telling him I drove would not be a good idea, I shrugged. "Flew in on my broomstick."

Luke's glare deepened to the point that one could possibly call it pure fury. "You fucking *drove?*" he roared, not buying the broomstick thing.

That time he forgot the shield between us and rounded the desk.

His hands were biting into my shoulders and he shook me a little.

"Are you fucking out of your mind?" he shouted. Right in my face. No more Mister Nice Deputy. No more Mister Deputy at all.

This was Luke, pure and simple.

But not simple.

Because this was the rage of that night he'd wrenched the guy out of my car. The rage that didn't make sense. Because rage like that was only roused when you cared about someone. A lot.

"Most of the time!" I yelled back, deciding that I was a little raging too.

Luke didn't let go of my shoulders with my returning shout. Instead he shook me again, just on the edge of violently. "Driving fucking drunk is stupid and dangerous, Rosie. Fuck. Don't you have people to drive you home? The one thing your brother does that I agree with is that he doesn't let you drive drunk, and he even failed at that," he seethed.

I narrowed my eyes. "Let's get one thing clear, buddy. No one *lets* me do anything, I do what I want."

"Including wrapping your car around a fucking pole and then making me come and find your dead fucking body?" he hissed.

"My car is in the parking lot, unharmed. And I'm very much alive, as you can tell," I snapped.

My gaze was pointed at his hands which were bordering on painful. His eyes followed but his grip didn't loosen.

"Yeah, you're alive," he said. "For now. You keep pushing it, Rosie. The boundaries. The rules. One day, they're gonna push back. And I don't want to ever fucking see that day."

I blinked at him. "And why is that, Luke?" I whispered. "Why is it that you're so passionate about my well-being when I'm just another dirty *outlaw*?"

He flinched at my words, the quiet tone that screamed loud, too loud, with my emotions. Alcohol made me honest. Too honest.

He stayed silent and still for a moment until he stepped back, erected the shield between us once more. "You're not dirty," he murmured. "I never have and never will think that."

I eyed him. "You sure about that?"

67

He eyed me right back. "Never been more sure about anything in my life."

I swallowed whatever that sentence did to my emotions. "Apart from your determination to ruin my family, right? You're pretty sure about that."

Luke's face darkened. "Rosie," he warned. "We can't get into this. You shouldn't be here."

I stepped forward, backing him into his desk. "But I am here," I said, confidence or stupidity fueling me. "I'm here, and no one else is, and I'm not going anywhere until—"

"Until what, Rosie?" His voice was ice.

I stuttered on his response, on his demand of an explanation, an uttering of what had been, for years, unmentioned.

On my side, at least.

Maybe it was all on my side.

I lost all my bravado, my confidence, sobering in the worst way, shrinking down into a vulnerable girl who didn't want anything more than him, *the guy*, to love her.

"You know what," I whispered, unable to say anything else. Anything else would be too risky, to real to reveal, even without my few inhibitions.

Luke looked at me for a long while, as if reading the unsaid words, like I'd written them in the air. "You want me because I'm the one thing you can't have, Rosie. It's not real," he said, not unkindly.

The tone may not have been unkind, but what did that matter when every word was a blade?

"*Real?*" I whispered, choking out the word. "I've had a brutal and continuous education on real, Luke. I'm not a child. I don't live in fantasies, don't entertain myself with them. I'm all about real. So trust me, I didn't *want* to feel this for you. I didn't trick myself that forbidden romance would be exciting or passionate or magnificent. That's the fantasy. But the real? The real is fucking ugly. Because it's not what I can't have. It's what was never mine in the first place." The words tumbled out though I had no intention of saying them.

Not even in the most perfect of circumstances would I have done it. And this definitely wasn't the most perfect of circumstances. But I said them anyway, like a drowning person scrambling for that life raft that they knew had a hole in it but hoped beyond hope might somehow save them anyway.

"Rosie," he whispered, barely audible. "It's not. We're not. *I'm* not right." His own words tumbled out, much fewer than mine, trickling almost incoherently, painfully.

I was proud for the way I tilted my chin up and for the fact that my eyes stayed dry.

"No, you mean *I'm* not right," I corrected. "I'm not right for your image. For your lifestyle. For the *good guy.*"

"Fuck, Rosie, no," he pleaded, stepping forward as if to touch me.

Self-preservation kicked in at this point and I stepped back before his fingers could grasp mine.

"Yes, Luke," I snapped. "You're clinging to your mold, and admitting anything about me, acknowledging me, will ruin it all, I'm sure." My voice turned cold. "It's what people don't realize. In life, you don't actually have to act a certain way, dress a certain way, live a certain way. It's a big and brilliant fucking con by the Man that has us thinking so. The only reason I see them, the strings that are attached to 99 percent of people on this planet, is because of where I live. Where I grew up. In the 1 percent. And I know what you think of that. Murderers, rapists, criminals. Whatever. Scum of the earth, right?"

I laughed. "Well, that's okay, because that 99 percent? That's exactly what *they* are. They just hide it when they put on their fucking suits every day. Everyone's pretending, for each other. It's comical when you think about it. Yeah, there's laws you don't break. I kind of get that one. But then there's the invisible ones about how to dress, where to live, what age to pop out a spawn, what shit to spout at cocktail parties. That's the shit I don't get. Most people act like it's the gallows if they step out of it. This great big lie called life. People live it and don't even realize they've wasted it. Never made it theirs. I'm not going to do that. I'm going to make it mine. And I'll fuck up. I'm good at that. But I'd rather fuck up a life I've designed than perfect something someone else controls."

I took in a strangled breath after yet another word vomit. I didn't even know if I could blame alcohol for this. It was years of pent-up emotions, of unsaid words, unshed tears, all packaged into one rambling speech.

He stared at me, at my words, as if they were floating around in the air.

"Different time, different life, we woulda been perfect." His raspy voice was full. Of regret, of hope, and of resignation.

"We only have now. We only have this life," I whispered, my heart breaking. "Imperfect is all there is. It's all I need. I know it's not the same for you. You need perfect. Not me."

Luke was just staring at me, still—shocked, maybe.

But he didn't say anything.

I didn't wait to see what new and careful way he'd structure his words to break my heart.

"Don't worry. In regard to you, I think I've made enough Fuck-Ups to last us both a lifetime." I turned on my heel and intended on stomping out, hopefully waiting until I was at home to shed the tears that were prickling the backs of my eyes.

"Rosie."

One word gave me pause. Hope.

This is it. What happens in the movies. When you thought all was lost, it was really just the climax needed to show you that the guy, the good guy, would never let the girl he really loved walk away.

I turned.

He held his hand out. "I need your keys. I can't let you drive. I'll give you a ride."

I was impressed that I stayed upright.

"They're in the ignition," I shot back, voice ice. "Do what you like with the car. And no way on this earth would I accept a ride from a *cop*. I'll call one of the boys. You know, the big bad outlaws whose lives you're making it your mission to ruin?" I paused. "Yeah, my family has my back. And you ruin their lives, mine goes with them. But you already knew that, didn't you?"

Then I left.

And it hurt.

A fucking lot.

But I walked, head held high, face dry, heart broken.

Not enough women got medals for doing that. And I knew they did it. Every day, women did it.

And they all deserved fucking medals.

Because no way a man would be strong enough to make that walk—and in heels, no less.

LUKE

AGE TWENTY-EIGHT

He stood there for a long time after she left. A long fucking time.

He wasn't sure if it was by choice or not.

But he did. Like a fucking coward. Didn't do anything. Didn't say anything. Just fucking stood there. Going over every single thing she'd said. Every single thing he should've said.

Fuck, her face when she turned and he asked for her keys. That would be something he'd have to answer for when he met his maker. Turning that beautiful hope into beautiful heartbreak. The most painful kind of beauty. The kind you appreciated, marveled at, but would kill the fucker who made such a creature have to deal with that pain.

It was him.

He was the fucker.

He wasn't going to say shit about the keys. He'd intended on telling her that they weren't a fantasy, that he was hers, that somehow, in this fucked-up world, she'd managed to make everything else less important.

But he didn't.

Because he was a coward.

Not just because he was a cop.

And not for the reasons she believed. No, it had nothing to do with him and his opinion of where she came from. Where she came from made her who she was. He didn't want to respect the club for turning her into that, but fuck if he did.

No, he'd closed his mouth for *her*. Because he knew that if he gave her what she wanted in that moment, he'd take away everything she'd need in the rest of them.

Her family.

The ones who would do anything for her.

Except accept him into that family.

That would be the price. The choice for her. He'd never put her in that position. Never hurt her like that.

His aim was to prevent hurt.

But he'd created it.

And he'd have to live with that.

Somehow.

ROSIE

PRESENT DAY

Luckily, I always carried my passport—one of them, at least—on me at all times in case of emergency or boredom. That meant I could hop in my battered and almost falling apart Jeep and speed straight through the chaotic streets of Caracas, toward the airport.

Road rules were nonexistent here, apart from the singular one of don't die. I didn't have to worry about something as asinine as getting pulled over while I dialed my phone and put it to my ear.

I'd already tried Lucy.

Four times.

It barely rang before an immediately familiar fury greeted me. "Rosie, where the fuck—"

I swerved around a stationary taxi, the driver shouting at someone across the road, then shouting at me as I took out a side mirror. A honk from the car I was about to plow into on the other side had me swerving back into my lane.

"Save your swearing, shouting or synchronous series of caveman grunts for another time, bro," I shouted above the traffic noise. "I need to know about Lucy. Tell me she's okay." It was more of a plead than anything else.

There was a pause. One that told me everything I needed to know and made sure I left my heart on the bottom of the road as I sped away toward the airport. I was so focused on making it through the streets that I forgot to guard against the memories, anxious to get their place in the spotlight once I'd opened the floodgates.

So, navigating through wild and dangerous streets, my mind wandered.

Not to my friend who could very well be dead. I couldn't think of that. Self-preservation.

And there would be nothing of me left to preserve if my girl was dead.

Not that there was much right now.

"We've just landed in sunny Los Angeles. If this is your final destination, welcome home." The pleasant voice on the intercom possessed none of the irritation it had when she'd been telling me that she would no longer serve me alcohol.

"I think you've had enough, ma'am."

I scowled at her and her superior glance to my disheveled hair and dusty white tank. "I'm still sober," I protested, without an inch of a slur. "That means I haven't had near enough."

She raised one perfectly manicured brow. "You've had twelve tequilas, ma'am. We are lawfully obliged to cut you off."

I rolled my eyes. "One mustn't break the twelve-tequila law," I snapped. "They'll most likely put you in jail where the only person to do your eyebrows would be a dyke who benched more than The Rock."

Suffice to say I did not get my thirteenth tequila.

Because of *the law.*

The law. The big fat barrier, reinforced with steel, electrified and topped with barbed wire. The thing that sat between everything I wanted.

Well, the two things I wanted.

Luke and tequila number thirteen.

Right now, though, I wanted more than anything for my best friend to be okay.

The two flights had been the longest ten hours of my life. I wanted to scream for how helpless I was, thousands of feet in the air, unable to do anything.

And that was on me.

"Excuse me, coming through," I shouted, almost bowling over an elderly lady with a hatbox. I didn't have the time to feel bad. "Sir, if you'd kindly get the fuck out of my way," I requested pleasantly to the man who'd decided to turn getting his bag from the overhead locker into a process as complicated as splitting the atom.

Both he and my friend the flight attendant scowled at me. Most of the passengers smiled at me. I was just saying what everyone else stuck behind this idiot was thinking.

As I pushed past him, I smiled at Mrs. Perfect Brows. "You have a fulfilling life enforcing the law 30,000 feet up," I said to her.

I didn't get her response because I was out of the plane and sprinting to get to whoever was waiting for me on the other side.

In my worry about Lucy, I forgot that I had a wrath-filled brother waiting for me. I was reminded of that once I entered the arrivals section and saw him, standing wide-legged with his arms crossed, two feet of space all the way around him, despite the fact that LAX was packed. His fury, not to mention his leather cut, created a force field that people purposefully avoided.

His furious gaze landed on me and I ignored it, running up to him.

"How is she?" I demanded, expecting him to start walking toward the exit so we could get to Lucy.

Instead, he stayed rooted to the spot, not moving, face a mask of masculine alpha fury. I was used to it. It was almost a default with me.

Something inside me softened at seeing that again. My badass, cranky, and loyal-to-the-bone brother. In the flesh. It was the longest I'd been away from him. From everyone.

"She's still unconscious but through the worst," he finally grunted, saying every word through clenched teeth.

My entire body, which had been wound up tighter than Mrs. Eyebrows' chignon, sagged at the news. "So she's going to be okay?" It was more a prayer than a question.

He nodded once, curtly and stiffly.

I sagged some more, exhaling the breath I'd been holding for hours. Then I snatched the tree trunk he had for an arm in an attempt to pull him toward the exit. The action was the exact same thing as yanking at a tree trunk. It didn't move.

"Cade!" I whined. "Forget about being mad at me for like two-point-five seconds and let's go. You can yell at me in the car."

He didn't move. Nor did he speak. He just stared at me in that way that had all his enemies quivering in their boots, before they pissed their pants.

It didn't work on four people: his wife Gwen, his two infant children, who literally laughed in the face of his wrath, and me.

"Cade, you—"

I was going to protest some more when he moved. He didn't shout or curse or tell me what an irresponsible idiot I was. Instead he hugged me. Hard. I was pretty sure I heard some bones in my back crack with the force of it.

I relaxed into it, wrapping my arms against his iron body, clutching at the leather that was the backdrop of my childhood. I took a deep inhale, motor oil, smoke and nostalgia creeping into my nostrils.

Home.

It wasn't a place to me.

It was people. A lot of them. One of my favorites, clutching me to him as if he sensed I needed a vacation from all the horrors chasing me and all those I carried with me. I was safe from all of them for the duration of that hug.

Cade pulled back and looked down at me with a stare that, to the outside observer, would look empty and full of menace. Though the outside observer would take into account all of his tattoos, his sheer height and size, and the rough stubble on his sharp chin, plus his motorcycle cut, and add all that into the equation. But I knew better than all that. I knew that was the mask he wore when he was feeling a little too much and didn't want to let the world see it.

"I was so fuckin' worried about you," he growled, kissing my forehead.

"No need. I'm always okay," I said with false cheer designed to calm his worries.

He stared at me, the way only someone who shared your blood could. "No, kid, you always make sure you *act* okay. It's not the same thing." His eyes searched me some more. "Fuck," he whispered under his breath. "You've added more."

"More what?" I whispered back.

"More fuckin' darkness to eyes I wanted to make sure never had a shred of shadow in them," he replied.

I was surprised, at what he said and the tone of anger in regret in his voice. "I'm not designed to exist without shadows. It's in my blood," I said, cupping his cheek.

He furrowed his brow. "Fuckin' trouble's in your blood," he muttered.

I was relieved. I didn't need heavy when I was already carting the world around on my shoulders.

"Now can we please go see my soul sister?" I whined.

He looked me up and down, face blank once more. "Yeah, once we get you showered." He paused. "On second thought, maybe if you don't, she'll smell you and wake right up," he said dryly.

I smacked his arm, bruising my knuckles in the process. "Personal grooming wasn't really on the agenda when I got the call, buttface."

We started walking toward the entrance, his brow raised at me in warning.

I rolled my eyes. "The super-badass routine doesn't work on me, remember? I don't care if your patch says 'President,' you'll always be my buttface brother," I teased.

He shook his head. "And you'll always be my Roe," he replied. "Which means I'll always be the one to put the bullet in the temple of the people who put the shadows in your eyes. Sooner or later."

His words weren't teasing like mine.

They were a promise.

I hoped to God that he didn't find out it wasn't rapists or murderers or general scum of the earth who put those shadows there.

It was Luke.

Because if he found that out, he would follow through on the promise.

Law be damned.

Then again, there were a lot of things that Cade would never find out about Luke.

What he'd done for the club.

What I'd done that Luke had turned a blind eye to.

CHAPTER SIX

ROSIE

AGE TWENTY-FIVE

I learned a lot from the men I grew up around. How to throw a punch. How to hack into a computer. How to pick locks, hotwire a car, load and shoot a gun. The basic bread and butter of outlaw life.

I also knew how to blow things up.

Not so much the bread and butter, but a handy skill.

Handy when the same gang that raped, tortured, and murdered my best friend then kidnapped, beat and almost killed my brother's girlfriend. The woman I was certain would become my sister and the mother of my nieces and nephew.

When she was taken, the club lapsed back into that dark and colorless version of hell that haunted us. The one we thought we'd left behind in the past but the one that had been waiting, biding its time to strike again, when we didn't expect it. And we didn't. Cade didn't.

I didn't recognize my brother in the hours that Gwen was missing. He wasn't the man who'd taught me how to ride two different kinds of bikes, who let me crawl into his bed for two months after we lost our father. Who screamed at my mother when she came back into our life after that loss, telling me my father had failed making me into a 'woman.'

He wasn't that unseen kind, caring, and selfless version of my brother.

Nor was he the man who'd crushed a man's jaw when he'd heard him talking shit about me at a club party. Or the man who'd ordered a hit on the guy who took my virginity. Or even the man who had told me my death, or at the very least my exile, would come from a romance with the enemy,

He wasn't that cold, calculating murderer who the outlaw and inlaw world feared and respected.

He was something different entirely.

Something that scared me almost as much as what was happening to Gwen in those hours that he was like that.

It terrified me, the thought that he might permanently be like that if we didn't find Gwen in the way she'd been hours before: laughing, beautiful, happy. He'd be Bull. And that man's loss was felt in all of our souls. I didn't know how the club would survive something like that again. It would crush them.

So when we found her, badly beaten but still herself, we dodged a bullet. A big fucking one.

Cade had called Luke in the second she was missing.

That meant a lot of things for me. A lot of things I couldn't focus on. I focused on what it meant for the club. It meant that any retaliation couldn't come from them.

The law would be watching them closely. The law, on the other hand, would not be watching me at all. And it hurt for other reasons, but it was great for my current ones.

I sat and watched the last of the bikes pull into the Spiders' clubhouse. The one I'd snuck into earlier and planted my home-made bomb in. I'd shooed out some women, most of whom were beaten, and all of whom were defeated. I promised them that I'd take care of them, get them away from this life for the price of their silence.

They all agreed.

It was only the guilty who were in there when my bomb exploded, killing each and every one of them.

I drove back to the club numbly, without any particular emotional response to being responsible for mass murder. Did it still count as murder when the men were scum?

I guessed it did.

Still, my conscience was clear.

My first destination when I pulled in was the bar. I didn't really feel like I needed to escape my decision, but Jose Cuervo was as good of company as any.

"Proud of you."

I glanced up at the gravelly voice, its owner the man who was the closest thing to a father I had left.

I poured him a glass. "What? For drinking this straight instead of swirling it in 'liquid sugar and bullshit'?"

He laughed. "Well, that too." He drained his glass and poured himself another. "The explosion at the Spiders' compound. No survivors."

I drained my own drink. "Well, looks like Lucifer's gonna have himself some houseguests," I muttered.

"Wasn't any of my boys," Steg continued.

"I think not, with the police watching you like hawks," I said, feigning disinterest.

Steg's wrinkled and tattooed hand closed over mine. "Was my girl." His other hand went to my chin, moving my gaze from the chipped wood of the bar to his steely gaze. "You don't wear a patch, babe. Even if you did, as president, I'd have a shit show tryin' to control you."

I grinned. "Of course."

ANNE MALCOM

"But today you were more of a Son than anyone wearing a patch. Know no one's gonna know. No one can know. Place we need you is right here, keeping our family together, not behind bars. So no one will know what you put on your soul tonight, what you did for us. I will. And your daddy will too. He'll be proud, baby. Prouder than me, and that's a tough fuckin' feat." He paused, and I took that moment to inwardly smile at my adopted father telling me my dead father was looking down—or up, depending on your view—at me, proud of mass murder.

And Steg wasn't wrong.

"Takin' lives, it's a funny thing. At the time, when the blood is hot and the temper is hotter, it don't seem like much. Fuck, it don't seem like enough. But we cool down. We're not meant to run that hot. It's when we cool down that it gets to us. Even if we were doing the right thing." He paused again. "Our version of the right, at least. Even the worst of souls answers to themselves for taking another. And you, my girl, are not even close to being the worst. Better than most. As better as I think one can get. So you don't think it'll get to you, but it will. I'm here when it does. For now, let's get fucked up."

I smiled shakily. "Best offer I've had all night."

I opened the door and debated closing it again for two reasons. One, the sunlight was extremely offensive to my soul and my pounding head. Two, Luke was standing at my door.

In uniform.

Looking too fucking hot for his own good.

And mine.

Because I reasoned that I looked like one of those witches who ate people's hearts in order to preserve my youth. And I hadn't had my protein in a while.

I didn't close the door. Because I was a masochist like that.

"Do you take to knocking on doors at dawn for fun, or has there been some sort of zombie incident you're telling everyone about?" I groaned, blocking the sun with the back of my hand.

"It's noon," Luke said.

"Like I said, dawn," I countered.

Luke didn't crack a smile. "Can I come in?"

I dropped my hand. Blinked.

Luke had never asked to come into my house. Come to think of it, I wasn't even sure Luke had knocked on my door.

But there he was.

And a cop, in uniform, asking to come inside the house with a grim expression meant bad things. Especially if the cop was Luke.

"Oh my God, is someone... has someone... has there been an accident?" I spluttered, my heart thundering as much as my head.

Luke's face changed, gentled some. "Shit, no, Rosie. Everyone is okay."

I sagged. "Okay."

I was so overcome with relief that I actually stepped aside and let him walk in, passing by so close I could smell his aftershave and feel the warmth of his body enrich the air.

I held my breath and closed the door behind him.

He was already sitting on my vintage sofa when I made it to the living room. I knew he wouldn't exactly fit in my environment, but I didn't think he'd stick out so much. Neatly pressed uniform, smoothed hair, clean-shaven. Fucking beautiful. Against my chaos.

If I ever needed a photo of just how ridiculous my feelings were, I just needed to remember this. I sat gingerly on the armchair across from him, expecting him to engage in some kind of small talk.

"Spiders' compound blew up last night," he said, without pleasantries.

I did my best not to let the lack of... anything in his voice get to me. Nor the sick feeling curling in my stomach about this being the topic of conversation and me being the fucking criminal, the murderer.

"I'd say I'm sorry, but I'm not," I said. "They've deserved something along the lines of a fiery death since Laurie died."

It hurt, every cell in my body, saying that out loud. It was a year ago but it felt like a minute. I tried not to remember the way Luke held me that night. The way he saved me. Because if I did, then it was all over.

Like it wasn't already.

Luke didn't betray anything, didn't make me think that my words had any kind of effect. "Scene is pretty much burning bone and rubble," he said, voice flat. "Not much evidence to be found."

"Bummer for you, dude," I snapped, trying to keep my voice casual and cold like his.

Luke didn't react, didn't even blink. "I said *not much*. Didn't say none."

His grim, detached face caught me then, chilling me when paired with those words. "Well, isn't that great? You might just find justice for the rapists and murderers yet," I said, sarcasm concealing the fear in my tone.

Luke didn't reply, just reached into his pocket and dangled a piece of chain from his thumb and forefinger.

I stilled, and then, stupidly, my hands instinctively went to my bare neck.

The necklace, in sloping script, read *Rosie.*

I had literally left my motherfucking name at the crime scene.

The thought filled me with cold dread, the image of life in a cold and dank prison cell. A life trapped.

But then something else filled me.

Gloveless, Luke was presenting evidence. Evidence he'd not bagged and tagged, as was procedure. Evidence he'd pocketed. Luke had, quite literally, taken my motherfucking name from the crime scene.

A crime in itself.

A big fucking crime.

He was grim-faced and silent as he handed it to me. Woodenly, I took it.

I fingered the metal in my hands, cold and way too light for the weight it represented. The silence lasted long. Too long. Uncomfortable, the still air grated against my skin, drilling into my bone with the truth of not what I'd done, but of what Luke had done for me.

"Luke," I managed to choke out, not sure what I was going to say afterward.

He held up his hand, face still blank, empty. "Don't say anything, Rosie." He stood. I immediately stood as well. He ran his hand through his hair. "Just don't fucking say anything, Rosie."

Then he turned and went to leave.

I watched his back.

"I had to," I whispered, my voice barely audible.

But he heard me, because he stopped. "I know," he replied, voice soft. "And that's the fucking tragedy of it all."

And then he was gone.

PRESENT DAY

"You cut your hair," Cade observed.

I flinched at the noise. I'd been staring out the window at the streets whizzing past, my mind, for once, empty.

"Yeah," I said.

Cade had taken me back to a hotel and let me shower. He even had clothes for me. Well, the me he'd known before.

He didn't say anything as I gave him a nod of thanks before retreating into the bathroom to slip back into the persona I'd left behind.

Someone, most likely Gwen, had packed a bag of cosmetics —I

didn't think Cade would have the forethought or knowledge to pack primer, concealer, and bronzer, let alone my entire makeup collection. I presumed she put together the outfit too.

The tee was meant to be a shirt, and she'd packed leather shorts to go with it, but it tumbled down my thighs, long enough to be a dress. I went with it. I'd changed. I couldn't slip back into my old skin like nothing happened. I had to somehow repurpose it. Work with it. Starting with the dress was easy; it was the other stuff that wasn't.

I slathered on makeup to hide my lack of sleep, the sallowness to my skin. But makeup could only do so much. Plus, I didn't give a shit about it all.

My girl was in the hospital. Unconscious or not, she needed me there.

Cade hadn't said a thing when I emerged, just directed me out the door and back into the truck. The hair comment was the first thing he said. Which was surprising, since I thought I would've been met with demands of where I'd been and a lot of yelling.

His stare was physical, even though I kept looking out the window.

"Your hair isn't the only thing you've changed," he murmured, a lot more beneath the words.

"No," I agreed again.

I waited for it. The wave of anger that Cade was so well-known for. That the wayward and unpredictable Rosie was so well-known to be receiving of.

Nothing came.

There was pressure at my hand. I looked down at the sloping script 'Isabella' at the top of my brother's large hand, jumping out from all the other ink there. He gave me a firm squeeze, silent support, silent acknowledgment of the fact that I wouldn't talk right then.

I couldn't.

I squeezed back.

"Whatever version of you you've become, I'm just happy to have my sister back," he said quietly, once his hand left mine.

I didn't reply.

Did he really have his sister back?

<hr />

The room smelled of death. They'd tried to cover it up with all sorts of cleaning products, so strong it stung my nostrils, but you couldn't cover up death. Not to the people who were used to the fragrance.

It froze me. Right in the doorway.

I never froze. Not in the face of gunshots, blood or violence. Or even death. All of that was the backdrop of our childhood.

Well, not never. Even never had its exceptions.

Once, I had.

Frozen completely and utterly. In a moment not unlike this, me, standing in a hospital room, watching a desperate man bend over a small, prone form in a hospital bed. The air stale and rancid with despair.

Death wrapped around me like a coat. Too hot, uncomfortable and scratching every inch of my skin.

It wasn't my death.

It wasn't even Lucy's.

It was Laurie's.

SIX YEARS EARLIER

I watched the grim reaper twitch, moving rapidly up and down. It would have been comical really. But standing here in this doorway, watching that grim reaper on Bull's cut move with the force of his sobs, I didn't think anything would be funny again.

Every part of me was glued to the door, unable to move into the room, unable to run out. I knew if I walked in there, I'd have to face it. The loss. The grief. The wretched and ugly reality lying in that bed, the remains of my beautiful and remarkable friend.

If I went back into the crowded and somber waiting room, maybe I could trick myself for a little longer. Convince myself that this was all some sick dream, and I'd wake up hungover on the sofa at the clubhouse to see Laurie and Bull walk in, hand in hand, smiling, the soft glow of true love enveloping them. I'd watch them, certain that something so pure, so perfect, was bulletproof.

That fantasy was ripped away from me with brutal quickness as the room and the death inside it beckoned me.

Something that pure, that beautiful, it was the opposite of bulletproof. Like a flower growing out of a crack in the sidewalk, it was beautiful, remarkable even. But it wasn't supposed to be there, and eventually someone stepped on it.

Crushed it.

I continued to watch the grim reaper's journey.

Bull's mammoth form hid most of her. Laurie. It always had. He was like a massive jigsaw piece, and she was the tiny one that slotted in just so.

The only one who would.

And now she didn't fit.

Because she wasn't there.

Her body was. Broken and battered and ruined.

But her beautiful spirit was nowhere to be found. I would know. A room wouldn't feel this horrible and cold if Laurie's light was still there. The only sound, beyond the deafening roar of death and the silent scream of Bull's sorrow, was a mechanical beeping informing the room that Laurie's heart was still beating.

Just because a heart was beating didn't mean someone was still alive.

They'd had her for twenty-four hours.

I tasted bile.

Laurie—the real Laurie, not what was being measured by that machine—died twenty-three hours and fifty-nine minutes before.

She was never coming back.

Agony ripped through my body as the thought took root in my broken heart. I was only standing underneath the weight of the pain because I didn't move. I was perfectly poised between life and death. In my spot, Laurie wasn't quite alive, but she wasn't quite gone either.

Gentle hands at my waist shocked me from my silent suffering. My eyes met the gray gaze of my brother.

I flinched when I looked into those eyes and saw nothing. Every inch of Cade was stone, like a walking robot. Despite what people might think, there was never a time when Cade was emotionless. He had made an art of making it look that way, but I'd known him my whole life and knew better.

There was always something working. And he was as kind as he was tough. That kindness shone through only on rare occasions with people he adored.

Me, for example.

Laurie, for another.

Cade, like everyone else in the club, treated her differently than even me. She was like a sheep that had wandered into the lion's den. Instead of harming her, those lions made it their mission not just to protect her, but to ensure the sheep never knew the brutality of the jungle.

Cade had been different with her. Had a connection. He'd loved her like the softer, more innocent sister he never had.

And he'd lost her.

I glanced to the moving reaper.

Cade was losing his brother too.

"Rosie, you shouldn't be in here," he said flatly.

I sucked in a ragged breath. "Where else should I be?" I whispered.

I didn't know why I whispered; neither of the other two

people in the room could hear us, both of them gone in different ways.

The girl formally known as my best friend had to be in the place reserved for all the best souls. The man sitting beside her broken body had forfeited his soul to the worst of all places.

Cade merely looked at me, that same empty expression hollowing out his features. "I don't know, kid," he whispered back. "I don't know."

He just stood there, unable to offer me the support he'd given me over the entirety of my life, unable to protect me.

He couldn't protect me from the death in this room any more than he could protect me from the smoke from a fire.

For the first time in his life, Cade was helpless.

And heartbroken.

I reached out to squeeze his hand.

It was stone underneath my fingers.

He stared at me for a long moment.

"You should go. You don't need to see this."

It wasn't a command. It wasn't anything. Just a last-ditch attempt to save me from something.

He didn't even wait for me to comply, just leaned in and touched his icy lips to my head, then strode toward the bed like there wasn't something yanking at him, holding him in place. He waded through it, all the death and turmoil, until he stood at the center of it, hand on Bull's shoulder.

"Brother," he said.

There was something in his voice then. I got it now. Whatever strength he had left in him, he was saving for Bull, trying to use it as a life raft to stop him from drowning.

Bull didn't move. He just continued to drown.

"Don't fuckin' touch me right now, Cade."

I flinched again.

Bull was never exactly expressive, but the voice that came out of him wasn't just empty.

It was hardly human.

It was like death itself was forming the words, with no personality, no individuality behind them.

Cade's form was stiff. He heard it too. But he didn't shy away from it. "This isn't your fault," he tried.

"The fuck it isn't," Bull snarled.

At least it was Bull. At least he wasn't really gone, that disembodied and terrifying voice not replacing the low boom of the man I considered blood. But then, hearing the raw and exposed pain in his tone was even worse than hearing nothing at all.

"This shit"—he jerked his head toward the bed in a violent movement—"is all on me."

A tear rolled down my cheek. His tone was full of certainty. Of sentencing. He had already thrown himself into the pit, taking on a blame that wasn't his, owning up to a crime that he didn't commit.

I nearly moved then, nearly braved the death and broken image of my best friend to comfort him, chase away the devil that licked at his soul.

"Bull," Cade said, full of the fight that I was desperately trying to rouse in myself. The fight to save one member of our family so we didn't have to dig two graves.

Bull's head moved in a blur. I could see his profile, witness half of the grief etched in his face. It wasn't even him. I barely recognized the man glaring at my brother.

"They fuckin' *raped* her!" he bellowed.

I clapped my hand over my mouth to stifle the guttural moan of pain that stabbed me with his words.

Horror echoed through my skull.

"Repeatedly," Bull continued, not finished torturing himself, or me. "She's scared of *mice*," he said on a low whisper, the words cutting with their broken edges. "Laurie's fuckin' terrified of tiny things."

A single tear trailed down my cheek. He was right. She

couldn't stand bees. But she'd never kill one. Never hurt a living thing. She cried once when she accidently hit a rabbit driving home, calling herself a murderer.

That beautiful girl considered that murder.

And this was her fate?

How could the world be so cruel?

"She's afraid of mice," Bull repeated. "How do you think she felt when they were doing *that* to her?"

I choked on his words. On the images. Of the broken and bruised and burned parts of my best friend that I glimpsed lying in that hospital bed. Every glance was a knife, tearing away at my soul, carving away at my interior flesh.

"Yeah, that's on me," Bull said. "Girl who lived her life in sunshine, losing it in the blackest, ugliest depths of hell."

My grief swallowed me as the hurt, the utter defeat in Bull's voice ricocheted through the room.

The silence that followed meant that we could hear it.

Or couldn't hear it.

The mechanical beeping stopped, signaling that even Laurie's heart couldn't take it anymore.

And that was it. I was no longer standing between life and death anymore.

Death was all around me.

I wanted to cry.

Scream.

Break down.

But most of all, I wanted revenge.

───

Flashing lights in my rearview mirror illuminated the inky blackness I'd been driving through.

"Fuck," I cursed.

I considered putting my foot down. It felt heavy, ready to press down on the gas and speed away from the law. From everything.

Grief and anger may have warped my thoughts, but it didn't take them away completely.

I slowed, pulling off the road and onto the shoulder. I had been so close, just outside of Amber's limits, which meant I was going to be out of the watchful eye of anyone patrolling the place.

I had been thinking of the club, not the law.

I didn't even attempt to hide the gun laying heavily on the passenger seat. I had a permit. I was also a Fletcher. No cop would fuck with me.

Not any day.

Not today of all days.

I stared forward, winding down my window as dirt crunched beneath the feet of the approaching officer.

I didn't let myself think it was him.

Didn't let myself hope.

I prayed it wasn't.

God had been looking the other way for the past twenty-five hours, so he didn't hear my prayer. A light illuminated my car and I squinted, accustomed to the darkness surrounding me, in both my exterior and interior worlds.

"Jesus, Rosie," Luke snapped.

I glared up at him and saw his furious eyes were focused on the gun in my passenger seat.

"Get out of the car," he ordered.

I clenched my hands on the steering wheel. "I haven't broken any laws, wasn't speeding. I'm not sure why you need me to do that, *Officer*." I was horrified to notice that my voice was disembodied, mimicking that empty and emotionless tone that Bull had employed before he tore half the hospital room to the ground.

I flinched.

Before Laurie died.

My hands tightened to the point of pain. Or what I imagined

might've been pain if I wasn't focusing on the hot agony pulsing from my heart, pumping poison to every inch of me.

"Rosie, get out of the fucking car!" Luke bellowed.

The sound echoed over the deserted road, seeming to travel up to the heavens with its ferocity.

But the heavens were currently closed for business.

Hell, on the other hand, was open and here on earth.

I'd never, not in my entire life, heard Luke yell like that. Heard him inject so much fury into a sentence. It scared me enough to get out of the car. As soon as I did, Luke slammed the door shut so I was backed right up against the vehicle.

He boxed me in, eyes glowing like a wild animal's under the illumination of his patrol car's headlights.

"Tell me you're not going to get yourself killed too," he whispered.

I didn't flinch at the mention of it. The shadow following me around, like a stalker, lying in wait, watching me, waiting for me to acknowledge him.

"Where I'm going is none of your concern," I said, my voice still not my own.

The flat of his palm slammed down on the roof of my car in a fury I'd never seen.

From anyone.

Maybe because fury, even uncontrolled fury, wasn't surprising when it came from someone like Cade.

Like Bull.

But from Luke, who normally locked down such emotions, who was all about calm and order, it seemed to shake the very foundations of the earth beneath us.

"I beg to fucking differ. You going out to your death is a great fucking concern," he yelled.

He did it again. Mentioned the D word.

I had to acknowledge it now. Its ears had perked up, it had leaned forward, rancid breath at the back of my neck.

"It's not my death I'm going out to meet," I whispered, like if I said it low enough, maybe it wouldn't hear me.

Luke stared at me, eyes still glowing in the light like a lion's, but the fury retreating to its cage. "Rosie, you know I can't let you do that."

"You have to," I choked. "You have to let me do it because there's nothing else I can do! I'm bleeding. My family is bleeding. Everything is Fucked Up. I have to fix it."

The hand that brutally slammed down on the roof of my car gently caressed my cheek. I didn't even have it in me to feel anything at the contact. All of my feelings about Luke before that day seemed so far away, locked in another room of my mind.

"Baby, you can't fix it," he whispered, hurt rippling through his words.

"But I have to!" I screamed, rebelling against the still, the quiet. It could get me there. Death. I tried to escape him, tried to get back into my car. Luke's caress became a restraint, stopping me from moving. "I have to!" I screamed again, pounding at his chest. "You need to let me go. I need to fix it. I need to...."

Despite my frantic attempts, it caught me. And I collapsed under the weight of it. Right into Luke's chest, my hot cheek resting against the cool metal of his badge.

He stroked the top of my head, clutching me to him, rubbing my back.

"I've got you," he murmured.

And he did. For who knew how long, he held me, right there on the side of the road, let me sob into his chest, weathered the first wave of my grief with me.

Stopped me from seeking out the men who had killed my friend.

Saved me from the same fate.

Because I would've died that night. Some intuitive part of me knew it when I'd started driving. But I was blind. Maybe I didn't care.

95

Maybe I wanted to. In that horrible time between immediate and unexpected horror and lucidity at accepting that you have to continue to live despite it, I was touched with almost suicidal insanity.

Whatever it was, Luke saved me.

No one ever knew.

That night, Luke stopped the club from digging a second grave.

Ensured my broken heart was his forever.

And no one would ever know.

PRESENT DAY

This time, the doorway was different.

I didn't have the luxury of falling back on anyone. Especially not Luke. He was done saving me.

I made sure of that.

But this time I had seen more. Death was a begrudging friend rather than a terrifying monster, snatching away everything I loved.

I was stronger now.

Or maybe there was less of me to break.

So I sucked in a breath and moved my feet forward, into the room that stank of death and pain.

It was familiar.

Keltan was leaned over the bed, murmuring quietly. Everything in me exhaled. He was murmuring not to himself, not to the world for taking something away.

But to someone else.

Lucy.

Her husky tones murmured back.

So I wasn't getting another part of me chipped off today.

Thank fuck.

"I don't care what kind of sweet nothings you're murmuring,"

I near-yelled, puncturing their private moment. I stomped into the room with my usual bravado, wearing my previous persona like a costume that someone else had stretched out. "This is my best friend, who almost died." My breath hitched on that part, a mental stutter of the reality of it all. Though I managed to recover before anyone noticed. "I'm getting my own sweet nothings."

I reached the bed, eyes flickering to Keltan, who was smirking at me. But like me, he was wearing a mask of his own. Stretching it over his face so the woman in that hospital bed didn't see the horrible scar that the grip of death had left on him.

I focused on Lucy and congratulated myself for not visibly flinching. The bed almost swallowed her, sucking her into its fatal embrace.

Almost.

She'd always been pale, my best friend. But now her skin wasn't that milky white tone that even Snow White couldn't mimic. No, it was a sickly gray, almost translucent. Somehow, her hair managed to look like it was fresh out of a shampoo ad, midnight locks tumbling down her head, doing even more to emphasize the pallor of her skin.

Her eyes were too big, sunken in, filled with something that I hated having to see in them. Something like what Keltan was trying to hide, but worse.

I swallowed.

"Bitch, I go away for a hot minute and you get stabbed," I snapped, going for jaunty blasé but failing as a tremor hit my voice.

I was horrified to see my hand was shaking as I snatched Lucy's free palm, lying weakly atop the polyester of the hospital sheets.

Something more than the shadow of Hades flickered in her beautiful face. Something welcome. "Hot minute?" she snapped. "Try almost a year."

I flinched inwardly again, seeing beyond the anger in her voice to the hurt that lingered beneath it.

I had been doing it for her.

No, who was I kidding? I'd been doing it for myself. I was selfish, running from my problems, deserted everyone who cared about me without a word.

I wouldn't be surprised if Lucy punched me.

Though she'd probably have to get Keltan to do it, since she was otherwise engaged with recovering from a stab wound.

I flinched inwardly again.

My best friend had been *stabbed*.

And I wasn't there.

"I needed a hiatus," I said truthfully. *Nice euphemism for cowardice.*

"From what?" she demanded.

I blinked at her in her hospital bed. Then it wasn't her—it was Laurie. Her corpse all shriveled up, decaying, empty eyes staring at me in horrifying focus. Another blink and it was Skid, half his head gone, blood all over my white dress. Then it was me, pulling the trigger, ending a life. More blood.

Then it was *him*. Pulling another trigger. Ending not just one person's life but two. His own included.

I yanked myself out of my waking nightmare, hoping my panic didn't show on my face. "Death," I said, unable to utter anything else.

She scoured my face, seeming to see through everything I was masking it with. Best friends, after all, knew when a dress, guy or expression didn't fit you.

"Looks like death brought you back," she said finally, her eyes flickering to the heart monitor. "Or almost death."

I looked at the monitor too. And for a terrifying second, the sound stopped, the emptiness signaling the finality of death. Thankfully, it was just another hallucination—or flashback? A sign I was really going crazy? Properly *One Flew Over the Cuckoo's Nest* crazy?

I was sane enough to regard my friend, tears filling my eyes at the realization of just how much I'd missed an integral part of me, how I'd almost lost another one. "No way would you die and leave me in this world without you," I choked. "I'd kill you if you did that."

She gave me a wonky grin. "Renewed motivation to stay breathing."

I glanced from Lucy to the stoic man at her side, who'd been silent during the whole exchange. He didn't look pissed that I'd hijacked his moment, nor impatient for me to leave. He seemed content enough to sit there in silence, grasping Lucy's hand and listening to her. Watching her. With an intensity that told me he was terrified that if he let go, if he stopped watching, she'd float away.

Something jerked in the vicinity of my heart.

Another one bites the dust.

It wasn't jealousy. It filled me with joy, watching the people I loved grasp onto love that didn't seem real unless you witnessed it in person. But I was becoming an outcast in an ever-growing club, I was happy to live in my desolate wasteland if it meant my family were happy. But I couldn't help but wish for my own version of it.

I shook myself. "No, I think you've got enough right there." I jerked my head to Keltan with a smile.

It was a real one.

Lucy had been dancing around this hunky Kiwi for years. Even when I was drowning in my own heartbreak, I saw that twinkle in his eyes the second they met. Watched them tumble in and out of their own heartbreak. Watched my beautiful friend mask her pain, doing it almost as well as I did.

Now she didn't have to. She'd stopped running from it. She could be still and happy.

She squeezed my hand. "I've got more than enough," she whispered.

My eyes threatened to leak once more, the force of my absence hitting me. I was only just realizing how little I'd been living, breathing in this past year without the people who made me somewhat whole. A single tear trailed down my cheek and I snatched my hand from Lucy's grasp to angrily swipe it away.

I couldn't believe this was when I lost it and cried. After this entire year of horror, this was the moment.

I couldn't let it linger or else I'd never stop. I'd break completely.

"God, what I am, a girl or something?" I said. "Too sappy. Plus, there's an entire motorcycle club, your mom and dad, your sister, and other hot guys I don't recognize but approve of in a big way all waiting for you," I continued. I'd breezed past most of my worried family, sneaking away before I could face their wrath, or worse, their love and concern. "I better go out and do the whole 'she's alive' thing," I finished, mimicking Dr. Frankenstein and trying to lighten the heaviness surrounding me.

I fastened my mask firmly back on, made sure my costume wasn't going to fall off again.

It couldn't.

Lucy narrowed her eyes, like she'd seen my slip, seen the fucking colossal mess underneath it all.

"Just to be clear, you're only going to the waiting room. No going," she demanded.

I mentally pinched myself at the fear in her voice, the expectation of me disappearing again.

I beamed falsely. "Of course. I've already taken up your old room. Polly is living in some loft that I'm almost certain is a front for a cult," I told her cheerfully.

She didn't blink. Polly was the ultimate wild child. Different than me, and dangerous too. I was a little worried about my adopted sister. But there wasn't much you could do with the wild ones. I knew that better than anyone.

"You're moving here?" Lucy focused on that little gem.

I'd made the decision on a whim, like I did most of my decisions. But LA was always supposed to be where Lucy and I would go to live out our dreams. Ultimate bachelorettes with a great apartment and fabulous jobs and few worries.

But like most dreams, it hadn't quite turned out that way. Lucy got hers, the one she didn't even know she wanted.

Mine weren't important.

"Well, not here exactly, because hospitals creep me out, no matter how hot the nurses are. *Grays's Anatomy* was serious false advertising. But yeah, watch out, City of Angels. The Devil has arrived." I winked, speaking the truth but disguising it with humor.

If only my best friend knew what I'd turned into. Even the men in the club would blanche. So I had to bury it all. Dig a grave and put this new version of myself in it. Try to resurrect the girl from before.

"Okay, so you're not leaving," she repeated, like she almost didn't believe me.

I hated that too. Trust between girlfriends was almost as sacred as those naked photos you only showed them. I broke that.

"Nope. Not too far, at least. I'll be back, I promise. See you never," I said, trying to stick to old Rosie's script.

Lucy's face warmed to a smile I didn't deserve. "Love you always."

I gave her a smile and Keltan a wink before turning and purposefully walking out the door, as if I didn't have a care in the world.

As if I wasn't close to collapsing.

I couldn't.

I still had a part to play to the entire crowd of people in the waiting room.

I wanted to see them all, despite the bitter taste in my mouth at seeing the stranger I turned into when I dove back into my previous life.

Running was the easy part. It was coming back that was the bitch. Nothing went away while you were hiding; everything stayed exactly preserved, like a fossilized demon of all your mistakes.

I just had to stop being such a coward.

It was a family reunion, not a firing squad.

So why did it feel so much like the latter?

Just before I made it to the waiting room, a hulking form rounded the corner and I froze.

There he was. The fossil I had craved just as much as I'd dreaded uncovering.

Luke.

CHAPTER SEVEN

I t would be nice if life was like the movies. Not only would I always look fabulous, regardless of whatever dirty situation I'd come out of, but everything would turn out for the guy and the girl in the end. After a long and painful separation, they'd finally reunite, run into each other's arms and forget all the differences, the suffering that kept them apart.

But that shit only happened in the movies.

Reunions like that weren't glamorous, or passionate, or romantic. They were stiff, awkward and hurt more than a bullet through the chest.

Which I would've taken my chances with, me being in a hospital and all that. They could work with physical wounds.

Emotional ones were a shit show.

His presence hit me. Physically. Took the air right out of my lungs. And not in a good way.

"Rosie." He didn't say the word as much as breathed it. But not delicate and quiet. It was like he'd yanked it up from some visceral part of him, the five letters of my name cutting at his throat as they passed through it.

I couldn't even manage the four letters of his at that point. I couldn't manage any four-letter words. I knew what I did would have consequences. With all the stupid shit I did, I knew.

Mostly I didn't care about the consequences. Or thought they were worth it.

But these consequences, staring me in the face in the form of a broken man I used to know, almost brought me to my knees. Which was saying something since I'd just stood at the bedside of my best friend who nearly died and managed to keep my shit together.

This man always knew how to get me undone, without even knowing he was doing it.

"Luke," I said, my voice scratchy and low.

One glance at him and I knew he'd changed, but what he did the seconds after I spoke showed me just how much.

He grabbed my shoulders roughly, so slim darts of pain shot up from where his hands pressed into my skin. I didn't cry out, despite it hurting and being surprised. I had good practice at keeping quiet when in pain. Who knew that what I'd learned from Venezuelan human traffickers would come in handy with the gentle and kind cop I used to know?

He slammed me roughly against the wall, boxing me in with his body.

"Where. The. Fuck. Have. You. Been?" he clipped, each word as physical as his previous grip on my shoulders.

I stared into his blue eyes. The ones that used to be liquid and soft, inviting like a calm ocean in July. These weren't those. I was looking at hard granite, the stuff that could crush you, that was colder than the wildest ocean in the middle of December.

There was a lot more different about him too. The way he got my attention physically, violently. Yeah, that was new. Even now, when he wasn't even touching me, his hands resting on the wall beside my head, there was a pulse radiating around him. Similar to the one that hummed from Gage when I got close enough, which was rare.

It was rare because most people didn't radiate on a level beyond normal. It was the level of murderers, men who walked through the valley of the shadow of death without anything anyone to protect them from evil. They faced it alone. And part of them still resided there.

I'd put Luke there. Me.

He used to wear his dirty-blond hair longer, mussed, boyish almost. It was clipped close to his face now, making the angles of his face harsher, sharper. Stubble darkened his jaw and ran down the cords of his neck that were pulsing with his obvious fury.

He wasn't wearing a uniform, the absence of a shiny metal shield accusing me with its nonattendance. Instead, he was in all black, as if it was a poetic statement about his transition. Muscles that were subtly defined before now strained at his skin.

I swallowed roughly. "Around." I was going for flippant, but it turned juvenile, pathetic.

"You're fuckin' *shitting* me," he seethed. "You disappear, not a trace, not a fuckin' word to anyone, no one knowing if you're dead or fucking alive, and the best you can say is *around?*" He ended on a shout, his previous open palm turning into a fist before he slammed it against the wall above me.

I flinched, not at the violence but at who it was coming from.

"It's not your business," I said.

His eyes glittered with a danger I didn't recognize. Or maybe I did, but I didn't want to see it residing in him. "Oh, it's my business. You're my fuckin' business. We both know that."

He glanced around. He'd garnered a couple of concerned stares from nurses. A glimmer of something familiar flickered on his face, letting me exhale a little. Maybe he wasn't truly gone.

He stepped back, sighing and running his hand through the hair that used to be there. Another shadow of before. "This isn't the place. But we're going to talk. *You're* going to talk," he rectified.

I stepped back from my spot in the corner. Nobody, not

even the man I'd loved since I was five years old, put Rosie in the corner. I pasted on my most sarcastic 'fuck you' smile. "I can't wait," I shot back with all the courage I could muster.

I was going to turn on my heel and let him watch me walk away, but he beat me to it, giving me one hard glare before turning on his boot and leaving without a backward glance.

I gaped after him.

Maybe I was wrong. Maybe he was truly gone and only shadows remained.

I couldn't chase shadows.

But I would.

Because I wouldn't be Rosie if I wasn't chasing the next big Fuck-Up.

LUKE

He was sure that hospital, with its taunting smell of sterile death and unhurried pain, did something to her. He knew it. Because it did something to him, teased a memory from six years before upward, when he was watching Rosie from the shadows of the hallway of the hospital, standing half in Laurie's doorway, halfway between two worlds.

One was her regular wild world that had horror and bloodshed peppered in, but somehow manageable, expected bloodshed. Something that came with the territory. Something that she never should've had to deal with, in a perfect world. But the world was far from perfect, and therefore she did deal. She did it fucking well. She decorated around the blood and death and violence and somehow made it glow, made it beautiful. To herself and surely as fuck to him.

Not that he could ever let that opinion show.

Especially not now.

Not when another world opened up like a hole in the ground,

not only exposing Hell but sucking everyone in. Everyone who didn't deserve to be there.

Laurie was the first. Rosie had been fighting the inevitable. She'd have to go in there, seeing Laurie, everything that had happened to that poor beautiful and innocent girl.

Luke had dealt with gore in his line of work. Even a small-town cop had to, at some point, but his small town more so thanks to the resident motorcycle gang. Regardless of the fact that they hid the majority of their bodies in shallow graves. He'd still peeled men off the road after motorcycle accidents, seen what remained of a human head after a bullet tore through the skull, turning the brains inside out.

He was as used to death and violence as a person could be.

But seeing what had happened to Laurie, the sheer cold and needless brutality inflicted on her, had threatened to empty his stomach. If there had been anything more but coffee in it, maybe it might've stained his shoes. But he'd been up for almost twenty-four hours looking for her, hoping for the best, but knowing the worst was inevitable.

He'd thought he'd been prepared. He'd thought he'd separated himself from the girl he'd grown up with, who'd taken in birds with broken wings and read to the people at the town hospice.

He'd been sorely fucking mistaken.

Cruelty was always hard to witness. To clean up after. It made it really fucking hard to keep faith in humanity when you could taste what humans did to each other.

His faith was hanging on by a fucking thread after that shit. And that thread was standing upright, dry-eyed in a doorway, watching the life seep out of one of her best friends.

So he'd had to leave, before she broke down. Because if she did, if he saw the strongest person he knew—including the men who considered themselves above everything—broke down, then he'd have no fucking faith left.

It was cowardice, pure and simple. Leaving her there when

he'd known that she'd had to face the Devil himself. But he'd had no fucking choice when the Devil was family.

SIX YEARS EARLIER

Delivering news of the death of a loved one to the surviving family was hands down the worst part of the job. Death was fucking hard too, but the person, the corpse he observed after the fact, was no longer a person. No longer in pain or suffering. They were at whatever passed for peace. Whether it be some kind of afterlife or total fucking darkness—which was what Luke suspected was the case—they didn't have to worry about the ills of the world, but the world sure as shit worried about them.

The people left behind had the death to cope with, to fight with. Not the one it happened to.

Luke couldn't decide if watching strangers suffer was worse than those he knew. Not that he delivered news to many strangers, not in a town this small. Being strangers with someone was a luxury small-town cops were rarely afforded.

He found himself wishing he was telling strangers that their only child was brutally tortured, raped, and murdered instead of the two people who'd raised a beautiful, polite and kind daughter. They'd raised her that way because they were polite, kind, and all-around good people. Peter, her father, had come to Luke informally after Bull and Laurie had gotten together.

Not for Luke to arrest Bull for taking up with his barely legal daughter.

No, to tell Luke that it was okay.

"Now I know you have a certain opinion on those Templar boys," Peter had said after Luke had invited him in for a beer. Peter had visited him at home because he was that kind of guy. He was good friends with Luke's own father and would always rather greet both Luke and his father as the pals he considered them to be rather than the law enforcement officers they were.

"Men, sir," he'd cut in quietly and respectfully. "They're not teenagers playing rough and harmlessly with bikes. They're men who get into trouble. Plenty of harmful trouble." He didn't want to sound like he was lecturing the man who'd ruffled his head at ten years old after he'd hit a home run at the baseball game his father hadn't been at because of trouble with the Sons.

Peter took a swig of his beer, regarding the bottle thoughtfully as he did so. "This is a good brew. Light, sweet," he said instead of answering Luke immediately.

Luke was impatient in the silence that followed but forced himself to wait until Peter said what he was going to say, to show him that respect.

His eyes met Luke's. "I know your opinion of these boys." He paused. "These men. And I'm not here to challenge that or say it isn't founded. I have many concerns of my own, don't you worry about that. A father's natural state is concern, especially when they have a daughter. Especially when they have one like Laurie. We've always known since the start that she was different. Special in a way, like she got one less layer of skin than everyone else, the one that protected people from the world but that also obscures them from seeing the true beauty of that world. Now, instead of trying to force her to grow that cynical skin, educate her on the ugliness of this place, my Christine and I have tried to preserve that view. Make sure nothing happens to obscure it. And it just so happens that Laurie seems to attract people who want the same for her."

Peter gave him a pointed look. "Know you're one of those people, my friend. So I know it'll be hard to hear this, and even harder to listen to what I ask, but I know you'll respect me and Laurie enough to listen. Your first instinct is to go to that man, give him threats, ultimatums, anything to reconsider his gaze on my daughter. I will say that thought did cross my mind too. But then I focused on his gaze, the way he looked at her. Then I recognized it. He's another one of those people. Maybe not like you—"

"Nothing like me," Luke interrupted, unable to help himself.

Instead of looking angry at Luke's words, Peter just nodded. "We don't have to all be alike to see something that needs protecting and go about our job at protecting it. Way I see it, this is a different kind of protection than me or even you could offer. This is from the man who's not only seen the true ugliness of the world but is willing to brave it to protect my daughter from it. You say and think what you will, but you know those men protect their kin, their women especially, with their lives. And as a father, knowing your daughter's in the hands of someone who would do that, well it helps with the concern." He drained his beer. "Never anything or anyone who's gonna take it away, but it quells it some."

He stood, and Luke stood too, placing his own beer on the coffee table in front of him.

Peter held out his hand. "I'm not asking you to agree here, just asking you to understand, let Laurie get another form of protection. Can't hurt, can it?"

Looking back, Luke wished he'd done fucking anything other than take Peter's hand in his and say, "No, guess not."

But wishing didn't do shit.

So there he was, across from the same man, years later, telling him the news that not only had Bull been unable to protect her from the world's true ugliness, but that he was the reason for her having to not only see it but have it eat her alive. They'd been hopeful when he'd first told them she was missing, because they were hopeful people.

He'd never thought he'd be wishing to be peeling a wrecked corpse off the side of the road.

He did now.

Peter didn't swear, yell, go for the gun that Luke knew he kept in a lockbox in his garage. Instead, he kissed his quietly sobbing wife on the head, pausing a moment to close his eyes and stay there, maybe dance with the notion that none of this was real. Then he let her go and focused his clear, dry gaze on Luke, who was having a hard time keeping his gaze anything but.

"The boy, how is he?" he asked.

Luke didn't answer straightaway because he wasn't quite sure if he was hearing him right. He couldn't be hearing him right.

"The boy?" he repeated, voice rougher than he'd like.

Peter nodded. "Bull."

Luke clenched his fists where they were lying atop his knees. Peter, the man who'd just learned that he'd never walk his daughter down the aisle, never be a grandfather, never see her smile again, was asking if the man responsible for this was *okay?*

At first, Luke didn't trust himself to speak, so the silence between Peter's words and his response was yawning and awkward. The only sound was Christine's muffled sobs.

When Luke trusted himself enough to meet the grieving man's eyes and not show an ounce of his own fury, he did so. It was fucking difficult, but he did so. "Yes, sir," he said, his voice gratingly flat. "He has his men around him. His family."

It cost Luke a lot to say that. But the price of comforting a good man who'd just lost his daughter was never going to be too high for Luke.

Peter nodded again, face entirely too lucid and yet too far away at the same time. He stood.

So did Luke.

He held out his hand.

Luke took it.

Peter looked him straight in the eye. "Thank you, son."

It cost Luke every fucking thing to look back at him and say, "You're welcome, sir."

The man was thanking him. *Him.* Who'd failed in his most basic job of protecting the innocent, prosecuting the club before this could happen.

Just as much blame rested on Luke's shoulders as it did Bull's.

———

Luke barely remembered driving to the Sons of Templar

compound. He vaguely recollected wondering about the sheer lack of bikes or signs of life as he pulled in. He hadn't pondered on that for too long.

But he was completely lucid as he pulled out his gun and rested the barrel on the back of Cade's head, who was sitting in front of the bar, one bottle of whisky in front of him.

He didn't flinch.

Nor did he even turn.

"Expected you might come," he said calmly, and clearly, despite the bottle being almost entirely empty. "Didn't think you'd be using your weapon. My money was on the handcuffs."

Luke's grip tightened on his gun. "Don't have anything to arrest you for. In the eyes of the law, you're *innocent.*" He spat the word at him.

Cade turned, clearly not minding that when he did so, the barrel of the gun now rested comfortably between his eyes. He met Luke's gaze with icy determination, a snatch of sorrow dancing in those cruel eyes, something that he didn't try to disguise.

"And in your eyes, we're not," Cade said.

Luke tried not to let the sheer depth of Cade's obvious suffering get to them. "My eyes, God's eyes," he gritted out.

Cade raised his brow. "After everything. After...." He was unable to continue for a moment, taking a long and unhurried swig from the whisky. "After what happened to Laurie, you think there's a man up in the sky protecting the innocent, punishing the guilty?"

Luke's hand danced on the trigger. "No, I don't think there is. Which is where I come in."

Cade gazed at him thoughtfully. "You gonna shoot me, then?" he asked calmly. "Thought that would go against your ironclad morals."

"Nothing's ironclad after what I saw today. After telling Peter and Christine that their little girl was never coming home."

Cade flinched. Actually flinched.

Luke's grip on the trigger softened.

Cade took another swallow. "Do it, then," he invited. "Shoot me. I sure as fuck deserve it. We sure as fuck deserve it. We never would've laid a fucking hand on that girl. Each and every single one of us would've fucking died to prevent her from getting a goddamn hangnail. Wasn't our hands, but that doesn't mean the blame doesn't lie firmly with us."

Luke's resolve flickered. He hadn't consciously made the decision to come here. Nor had he intended on murdering a man in cold blood. Whether that man was a murderer or not, he didn't think he'd have been able to do that. Then again, a human being was able to do anything and everything under the right circumstances, more so under the wrong ones.

He toyed with it. The idea of pulling the trigger, calling in that he'd come here to take a statement and that Fletcher had pulled his piece, self-defense. He wouldn't be the first cop to do it. Despite the fact that Cade wasn't even carrying. His gun was, for some reason, right at the other end of the bar.

Later, he wouldn't like to admit just how close he'd come in that moment. How easy it would've been. How selfish such an act would've been. He also wouldn't like to admit that one thing, one person stopped him.

The girl with wild hair and an equally wild heart. Though it may have been wild, that didn't mean it wasn't big, vulnerable, and already bleeding.

If Luke pulled that trigger, he'd be responsible for breaking that beautiful wild thing.

And he might've been able to live with murder, but he sure as fuck wouldn't have been able to live with that.

So he lowered his gun.

Cade looked at him with surprise. And relief. Or maybe disappointment. Luke wasn't sure which. He didn't want to think too much on that either, because that would've meant that Cade was much more than the simple outlaw that Luke had pegged him as.

"No, that would be a disservice to Laurie's memory," he said. "That girl would've chosen that exact same fate if it meant no blood would've been spilled but her own. I want you to live with that knowledge. And the rest of that fucking horrific shit. You can barely deal with the knowledge of that, but imagine how Laurie felt *living* that." Cade flinched again but Luke ignored it. "That's more of a punishment than a bullet could ever be. Bullet for you is mercy, and you deserve none of that. Maybe this will make you see what your club is doin'. Killing. Not just people who chose this life, but people who were forced into it by their hearts." Luke regarded him with contempt. "Maybe. But I expect not. I expect you'll need a lot more blood. Not your own, of course. Maybe your family's, maybe your sister's, to make you see fucking sense. And then, like now, will be too fucking late."

With Luke tasting the bile of even entertaining the idea of Rosie sharing a similar fate as Laurie, he lowered his gun and left.

He didn't start shaking until he left the lot. He might've even broken down completely if he hadn't seen Rosie's car speeding past the lot and toward the outskirts of town.

The small glimpse of her face in the fading light told him she wasn't heading for the outskirts of town.

She was heading for Hell.

And no way would he let her near there.

Not alone, at least.

ROSIE

PRESENT DAY

I went to a bar. Straight from the hospital.

I knew it wasn't the best coping mechanism, but I didn't feel like shopping. My best friend was recovering from almost dying so I couldn't exactly unload on her, and my family would likely excommunicate me if I went to them with the truth. Not the lies I hid behind after I'd survived my encounter with Luke.

The waiting room was full of everyone I loved, which meant they all descended on me.

Lucky snatched me into a fierce hug. "We've been worried sick," he said into my hair, then pulled me back to inspect me. "Well, Cade's been worried sick. I've just been pissed that you didn't bring me and Becky along for the fun. We're a boring old married couple now." He pouted.

I rolled my eyes and looked to his beautiful wife. My beautiful friend. Somehow smiling and whole after she was shattered. She'd put herself back together, made friends with her demons.

I wish I could've done that.

"You blew up our car two days ago," she said dryly.

Lucky huffed. "Because I was *bored*. And no one even blinked. Like we have one car bomb and suddenly, poof! It's not even a big deal anymore."

She grinned, her face lighting up as she did so, cupping Lucky's cheek. "I know, babe. It's not fair."

My heart smiled. Or tried to.

"I'm sorry I didn't make it to the wedding," I said.

Becky focused on me, yanking me into a hug. "You should be fucking sorry," she hissed. "I had the cashmere mafia planning my wedding. Not that I don't love those babes, but they wanted me to spend five grand. On *flowers*."

I laughed as she let me go. "I'm sorry I wasn't there to rescue you," I said sincerely, sadness creeping into my tone.

She regarded me shrewdly. Not only did Bex not buy into bullshit, but she saw right through it all. Once you'd made it through the other side of Hell, you recognized the people only halfway there.

"I think you need a break from the rescuing," she whispered, reaching out to squeeze my hand. "Sometimes even the kick-ass biker babe needs rescuing too." She said it so low, even her eavesdropping husband couldn't hear.

We shared a moment, both too long and too short before the rest of the family interrupted.

Steg yanked me into his chest, and I inhaled the smell of the man who had turned out to be my father when I lost mine.

He held me back, regarding me with shrewd, wrinkled eyes. He didn't say anything for the longest time. I knew he was like Bex. He saw it too. But he wouldn't say anything. He may have loved me like a daughter, but he wouldn't rescue me. Knew he couldn't. He was one of the ones who'd taught me how to rescue myself.

"'Spect there's a story behind those eyes. Guessin' it isn't pretty," he observed.

I blinked at him. "Is it ever?" I whispered.

He stroked my cheek. "No, baby. But you always will be. Despite the ugly that surrounds you. Best remember that."

Then he let me go, not one to linger on the emotional shit. I silently thanked him for that.

He let his wife, the only mother I ever knew, descend upon me.

Unlike a mother, she didn't cry or yank me into her arms, declaring how worried she'd been.

She put her hands on her hips, narrowing her blackened eyes at me.

"You took your time to turn up," she said sharply.

"Had a long trip," I replied.

"I don't know how. Hell isn't that far from LA," she deadpanned.

I got it now, those lonely people you saw withering at the end of the bar, staring into a glass as if something could be found in there.

That was me, staring into my own, realizing I'd never felt more alone. And because I felt alone, empty, I had to fill it up with something.

I pushed the glass away. "Another."

He complied.

And although I'd traveled from the hellish destination where I'd taken my demons for vacation, in that dark and dirty LA bar, it was like I was back there. I could've been anywhere.

But I was nowhere.

Maybe that was the idea.

CHAPTER EIGHT

ROSIE

AGE TWENTY-FIVE

"You're gonna need to stop doin' that," Evie ordered. "You're annoying the piss outta me."

I glanced at her and saw her narrowed eyes were focused on my knee. I had been jiggling it up and down furiously since we'd been sat here by a grim-faced orderly after we'd been 'bothering' the nurses too much.

I didn't do well with sitting still. Being helpless.

Didn't do well with sitting in a hospital fighting for both joy and agony.

Joy that my little niece was born healthy and beautiful and that my sister-in-law was okay.

Agony because in order for my niece to be born and my brother to still have the love of his life breathing and whole, the man who was the closest thing I had left to a father had to get shot.

In the chest.

I'd dealt with a lot of shootings in my time with the club. More than I cared to admit. Some were stupid accidents by idiotic prospects. Most were results from fights with rival clubs.

Some of them required me to stitch up flesh wounds.

Others required our off-the-books doctor to come and perform minor surgery.

Then there were these ones. The life-or-death ones that required hospitals.

Hospitals meant cops.

Which was reason for my churning stomach, but not for my jiggle.

Hospitals, more often than not, meant death.

But I stopped. Because of Evie's narrow eye. Evie's dry, narrow eye. She hadn't shed a tear, hadn't cracked her hard façade. She'd sworn at a lot of doctors, though.

Then she'd just sat there, still, her hands clasped on top of her knees, displaying the huge rock standing amongst the array of silver on every finger.

Steg got it for her for their twenty-fifth wedding anniversary.

"I can't do this," I whispered. The first time I'd done it. Given up. Sank down from the weight on my shoulders instead of continuing to put one foot in front of the other—in heels, no less.

She regarded me shrewdly, with none of the emotion I expected on her face. None I could see, anyway. None anyone could see. I expected that was the point.

"Yes you can," she said in her no-bullshit, no-sugarcoating, gravelly voice. "You can because you have to."

"What if he doesn't make it?" I choked out.

She didn't look at me. "He will."

"But what if he doesn't."

Her gaze cut to me, sharp and venomous. "He will," she snapped. Her hand squeezed mine at the same time as she addressed me harshly.

ANNE MALCOM

I got it. She said he would because there was no other option for her. He would because he had to.

I squeezed her hand back.

"He will," I whispered.

Surgery took a long time. Too long for me to sit stationary next to Evie. Ranger and Lizzie took over, both giving me firm embraces and soft looks.

I took to wandering around the sterile halls.

I hated hospitals.

You could smell the death, lurking around the corners, waiting to snatch someone up.

And you also ran into police officers with no chance of escape.

His form jolted the second he laid eyes on me, still at the other end of the long hall.

My eyes darted at either side of me, and I almost laughed out loud at the door that signified my salvation.

Chapel.

I didn't hesitate to slip inside, hoping that Luke's cop business would be more important to him than chasing me.

No, I didn't hope that. I hoped for the opposite.

I knew better.

So I sat on a pew in the small room, staring at Jesus.

The door behind me opened and closed, the harsh footfalls of boots on hardwood signifying his arrival.

I jerked with surprise when he sat next to me. Right next to me.

I didn't look at him, my eyes still focused on Jesus.

"You runnin' from me, Rosie?" Luke asked softly.

"No," I lied. "I came here to...."

"Pray?" he finished for me in a disbelieving tone.

I darted my gaze to him. "I could be. You don't know."

He rose his brow. "Know you're smart. Too smart to believe in this shit."

I gaped at him. "You don't believe?"

He shook his head. "Fuck no."

"But... you go to church every Sunday." I didn't realize I'd disclosed that stalker detail until it was too late.

Luke didn't acknowledge it. "Dad's the sheriff. I'm the dutiful son." He shrugged. "It's habit."

I stared at him, then laughed.

"What?"

"It's just I think that's the only time Luke Crawford has done something as rebellious as not believe in God."

He quirked his mouth.

My chuckle died away. "You seriously don't believe?" I asked soberly.

"Seriously. And you do? After everything you've seen? Went through? You think there's someone cruel enough to let you go through that?"

I jerked at the softness of his voice, the tenderness in it. "Maybe not exactly him." I nodded to the man on the cross. "But something. I've got to believe there's something more to this. That there's some kind of method in the madness."

"You're looking for a method in the madness? You live for madness."

I hid my response to his perception of me. "On the surface, maybe. But there's only so much chaos even I can welcome. I need to know that there's something more so I can live in the chaos, you know? I don't know if I could keep on keeping on if I thought there was nothing. If we're all just here on a chunk of rock by chance."

Luke tilted his head. "I don't think it's chance."

I trapped myself in his stare. "I know it's not. And I need miracles, need to believe in them. I got shown one today, when I heard my niece was born with ten fingers and ten toes and beautiful green eyes," I whispered. "And I'm holding out for another one."

Luke squeezed my hand.

I was so surprised at the touch, and how my whole body relaxed into it. How the simple gesture made me feel safe.

"Didn't believe in miracles," he murmured. "Not till I saw one right in front of me. Not until I was lookin' at the miracle right now. So I'm thinkin' you've still got a few." He paused, like he hadn't just sucker-punched me in the chest. "He's gonna be okay, Rosie."

"Yeah," I whispered.

And then we sat there, holding hands and staring at the guy who was staring woodenly back at as. I found support and strength in that chapel. Enough to get me through the worst of it and then some. Until Steg woke up cursing at nurses and demanding a cigarette.

I didn't find salvation. No, because I loved Luke then. More than ever. That conversation, that small touch, the sitting there for hours wordlessly, that was enough to hold onto. To pretend that something on his side existed too.

A sliver of hope that the man I loved irrevocably might just love me too.

That wasn't salvation.

That was damnation.

* * *

LUKE

PRESENT DAY

Luke followed her.

He knew he fucking shouldn't. But what else was he meant to

122

do? Where else was he supposed to go? When she disappeared, dropped off the face of the earth, it was like his center of gravity drifted away along with her. So he was plunged into free fall. She ripped the paper fucking background of his life away and left him to deal with the emptiness.

He was fucking furious with her for that.

He was even more furious with himself.

For letting her leave. For being such a dumb fuck for half his life.

He knew what everyone thought about him. His job had been to know things. Maybe it still was now. But his job was to know things and not tell anyone but the person who was signing his paycheck, not using those things to lock people away. Using them as ammunition against those who broke the law.

A small-town cop knew a lot of things. All part of the job description.

He knew that Evan Goodall brewed moonshine in the dense part of his ten-acre property. He knew that Laura Maye had a couple of pot plants growing in her sprawling and wild garden. He knew that one of his deputies moonlighted for a security company, despite it being against the law.

He knew those things.

But he also knew that Evan Goodall was a quiet man who owned a bookstore, and that brewing that strawberry-flavored hooch was the only thing he'd ever done that was against the law. He'd never even gotten a speeding ticket.

He knew that Laura Maye might've smoked some of that pot herself, but mostly she baked it into brownies and took it around to those in hospice whose insurance didn't cover enough pain relief.

He knew that his deputy was struggling to pay his daughter's medical bills since she'd been diagnosed with leukemia.

So though he knew that most of the town considered him a

hard-assed cop who took the law to the letter, he didn't mind what they didn't know.

They also thought they knew that he had such an intense hatred for the Sons of Templar MC that said hatred spread like a rotten root to everyone connected.

Or that maybe it didn't mean hatred for those like Lucy and Ashley, but it was a warm indifference. With them, and with Rosie. The woman everyone thought he was kind to but didn't notice as anything more than the kind girl whose brother epitomized everything Luke was trying to eradicate.

What they didn't know was what Luke really saw when he looked into her hazel eyes.

What they didn't know was how fucking hard Luke had worked to feign that warm indifference to that beautiful wild girl since the moment he'd seen a little five-year-old in all black and combat boots throw a pretend punch to her father, with crazy curls and a beautiful smile.

They didn't know how much that day on the wharf had broken his heart, but also somehow made it uncomfortably large in his chest while he witnessed a seven-year-old girl quietly and bravely grieving the loss of the only parent she'd ever known, dry-eyed, watching the waves and clutching his hand so tightly his fingers were bruised for days.

How he'd labored not to yank her into his arms and kiss her, despite her youth, when he'd seen her threaten to blow up bullies, her protection for those weaker than her fiercer than a lion.

How he'd actually been gripping his gun with the intention to use it when he'd seen some gangly asshole with his hands and mouth all over Rosie in the back of a car.

How that night that he had to inform Laurie's parents that their only child was murdered and brutalized in a way even he'd never known humankind was capable of, how that night he had fire running through his veins. How he'd been close to going to do… something. To exact revenge and not justice.

And then he'd seen Rosie's car speeding past the compound where he'd nearly killed her brother and he'd followed it. That night, all he'd wanted to do was make sure his arms were her home for the rest of her life. How he'd forsake the shield at his chest to become one for her so he'd never have to see that broken women shattered by the ugliness of the world.

He'd done none of those things that had been more natural than slipping on his uniform each day. And because he didn't do those things, it became harder and harder to slip on that uniform that had once fit so perfectly.

It became harder to face himself in the mirror as he pursued women who weren't her, who weren't for him, who made him ashamed beyond belief.

It became harder to chase the image of her away from the forefront of his mind.

And then, when everything had finally blown up, after all those years, she was gone. And then the image of her in his mind was the only thing he could chase.

Grasp on to memories that had seemed to fill his entire mind before. But with her absent, they scarcely filled a corner of the wasteland that was his mind.

He needed to fill that up.

To chase her.

And he intended to do that.

To the ends of the earth, if need be.

"Should I snap this or post it on Instagram?" The nasally voice punctured through Luke's thoughts like an air horn after a night out drinking. He'd had a night of drinking. Just not out. He'd sat outside that bar, staring at the shithole that the love of his life was drowning her sorrows inside of, torturing himself with memories, cursing himself for being a coward and not walking in and taking her, claiming her. Imagined how he'd do it, the way she'd taste, her sweet body writhing under his. Fantasized about her in his car like some kind of sicko.

It wasn't even the sex stuff that got his dick hard. The thought of lying with her, imprinting her scent onto his pillows, onto his body. Seeing her smile, watching her fucking laugh.

That empty look of hers in the hospital haunted him. Taunted him. Showed him what a fucking failure he was. He wasn't good enough. Didn't find her in time. Something beat him to it, whatever it was that sucked the life out of those once vibrant eyes.

She was still beautiful—more so, if that was even possible—but it was a cutting, harsh sort of beauty that was difficult to look at. Hurt to look at. Because he knew to get that fucking beautiful, she had to see horrors, real ones. Not these fucking bullshit ones that the airhead he was working for called disasters. Bad photo angles. A snub at some awards show. People talking shit about her online. Ones that idiots like this movie star couldn't even act out in some stupid film, let alone experience.

That's what made Rosie that much more beautiful. That pain. Because you knew she was strong enough, deep enough to withstand it. Something powerful and ugly enough to change the very foundations of her, yet she still lit up a room like no superstar ever could.

He'd seen that and he'd been so angry. More than he already had been since that day. He'd been carrying his anger around like a dead weight, his cross to bear for the mistakes, the sins of his past. It was unfamiliar and ugly. Ugly because wearing that anger was becoming too comfortable. He was growing used to it.

He was pissed at her for running. Disappearing. Leaving him with the fucking skeletons she'd let out of both of their closets, to bury them alone and then to function without her. Furious.

He was most angry at himself, for spending his life absorbed in so much hate that he couldn't see a fucking scrap of truth.

So he'd stewed in that anger in his car, outside that shitty bar, until he couldn't breathe around it. Until he scared even himself with the magnitude of it. Then he'd driven both him and his anger home and drowned it in Jack.

Hence the headache. And the hangover.

The headache being the movie star.

"I think I'll just do SnapChat. Makes me more accessible—hey! What are you doing? I told you, no one is allowed to drink Pepsi in this house. I have a phobia."

Yes, the bitch had a fucking *Pepsi phobia*. Among other things. Like no one was allowed to wear white. It was *her color*. Everyone who entered her house had to wear stupid little booties on top of their shoes so they didn't track dirt into her house.

Never mind the fucking carpet-pissing dogs that ran around shitting everywhere. Not that she noticed. There was a designated person for picking up the shit. Yes, this person literally picked up shit for a living.

And he took it from this vile creature. But not the booties. He'd been firm on that.

"My job is to protect you. I'm not gonna be able to do that when I'm wearin' fuckin' booties," he'd spat out. This earned him a sharp glance from the manager who hired him.

The starlet blinked at him, obviously unused to having someone not obey her every whim. Her botoxed forehead had twitched and he thought she might yell. Fire him. He'd hoped for it. This assignment was bullshit, despite the fact that it paid three times more than his salary as a sheriff. He would rather shovel shit for money, as long as it wasn't for this bitch. But he wouldn't quit. He wouldn't. He'd done that enough.

But she didn't fire him, merely nodded and instructed him to keep his boots clean. "I do admire a man who takes protecting me so seriously," she'd purred, her vulture eyes inspecting him.

He'd restrained a glare. "It's my job, ma'am," he said flatly, hoping to communicate his immense disgust in the proposition she was making with her eyes.

She hadn't seen it, or had ignored it. Because after that, she'd relentlessly and horrifically come onto him at any moment she could.

Even if she wasn't a raging bitch, Luke never would've gone there. In fact, if it was just that, he probably would have. Women who stood for everything *she* didn't were the only kind he took to bed. Some kind of warped respect for the woman he couldn't have. The woman he loved. So he only let himself take the most horrible women to bed. As his punishment. Reminding him that he had a good, wonderful woman within reach and he'd fucked it up. Majorly.

But it wasn't just the fact that she was horrible. She was like a Monet. Maybe pretty from a distance, airbrushed and covered in makeup, but up close she was a mess. Her skin was sallow and almost yellowing, the effects of all the cocaine she did on a daily basis, Luke guessed. Every bone in her body stretched over her skin, protruding like a starving child. She would never eat. She couldn't. She'd order all sorts of shit at some restaurant and just push the food around, then have it taken away. Her fridge was stocked with everything imaginable, most of it untouched and thrown away after a week. It was disgusting, her waste. Luke knew of the people struggling to put one meal on the table and here she was throwing two weeks' worth in the trash, too dense to even donate it.

Everything about her was hollow. And ugly.

She tapped away on her phone, the fake claws on her fingers clicking on the screen.

He wasn't supposed to be in there, watching her tragic life play out. He sure as fuck didn't want to be in there. He was supposed to be stationed outside, on the perimeter. Despite the fact that in the two months he'd had this gig, he had never even sniffed a threat, she'd apparently contacted Greenstone because of her serious concerns for her safety.

Luke was beginning to think that she thrived off the attention, and also that she'd heard the stories of the men who worked for Greenstone. They were quickly becoming one of the most sought after agencies in the city, with Keltan having to employ more men. Which was how Luke tumbled into the gig. He'd first come to LA after handing in his badge to employ Keltan to help him find Rosie. He'd tried himself, with the resources at his disposal. That was why he delayed handing in his gun and badge, not because of reluctance to leave the only job he'd ever known, the only job he thought he'd ever have. No, he'd stayed so he could misuse his power to find her.

Something his self-righteous past self would've rebelled against. But he had already crossed that line he'd set in the sand the day he put on his uniform.

Once he'd crossed it, there was no going back.

He didn't *want* to go back.

Which was why he'd left. Searching for her. He hadn't planned on staying; his plan was just to get a lead, chase her. He'd stayed because he realized that she wasn't like any other women. She wasn't running because she wanted to be chased. To be rescued.

He just had to wait for her to come back so she could rescue him from the hell he'd been renting in her absence.

"Luke, so sorry to keep you waiting," the nasally voice interrupted his thoughts.

He would never get lost in them on a job usually. But this wasn't normal circumstances. And this job was a fucking circus.

"I just had to finish some important tasks," she finished, setting her phone down.

Luke barely restrained a snort. This woman wouldn't know important—or hard work, for that matter—if it bit her on her bony ass.

"No problem, ma'am," he replied, crossing his arms and watching her approach blankly.

She clearly thought she was sashaying, the bottom of her robe trailing behind her, purposefully untied just enough to show her chest. Though there wasn't much to show but bones rising up from the skin.

"Must you call me ma'am?" she whined. "It makes me feel positively *ancient.*" She stopped in front of him. Too close. Luke's jaw hardened as her perfume choked him. "Plus, it's so formal. I like to be informal with employees. Treat them like friends." She eyed him with a clear intention in her eyes.

One that made Luke feel vaguely sick. Beyond the fact that what she'd said was a flat lie. She treated her staff like slaves, screaming at them routinely and firing at least one person a week.

"I prefer to keep friends and business separate, ma'am," Luke said firmly. "Now what is it you called me here to talk about? I need to get back to work."

She flinched a little at his tone, and he didn't give a shit. Normally he gave women respect and actively tried not to hurt them. This was an exception.

She straightened her shoulders and tightened her robe sash. Luke's eyes stayed upward, uninterested.

"I have an event tonight. Black tie," she said. "I need you to come with me."

No question. Luke bristled.

"And you only just ask this now?" he gritted out.

She regarded her nails. "I only just decided I wanted to go. And of course, it will be full of overzealous fans. I need you there. It's your job, after all, no?"

Luke clenched his jaw. "Yes, ma'am."

***

"We can't fire a client, Luke," Keltan said, the fucker grinning at him from behind the desk. "Especially not one who pays as much as that empty-headed Barbie doll."

Luke clenched the beer in his hands. "She wants me to go to a gala with her tonight," he gritted out.

Keltan choked out a chuckle, swallowing it with his own beer when he caught Luke's glare. "No shit?"

"I look like I'm joking?" Luke didn't joke these days. Or smile much.

Now that Rosie was back, he had even fewer reasons to smile. Having her in the same city as him with that empty and haunted look behind her eyes was almost worse than not knowing where the fuck she was.

No.

Nothing was worth than that.

Keltan's smile disappeared, and despite his current predicament, Luke kicked himself for being responsible for that. Keltan hadn't had many reasons to smile for the last few days.

In fact, the last few days had given him reason not to smile for the rest of his life.

Luke shuddered inwardly at the memory of his friend's face when he'd been at the hospital after watching the love of his life almost bleed out in his arms. Watched the life seep out of him as he entertained the possibility of existing in the world without her.

Existing. Not living.

Luke knew, at least in part, what that was like.

He'd been existing for a year.

Without her.

Fuck, if he wanted to be honest with himself, he'd been existing for thirty-five fucking years.

Without her.

He'd been lying to himself for that long. Then when he was prepared for the truth, no matter how ugly it was—because even ugly would turn beautiful with her where she belonged, with him—when he finally got that, it was just in time to lose her.

Not that he'd ever really had her.

There wasn't much worse than only half living your life and not realizing what you were missing out on, but barely living at all and realizing why was way fucking worse.

Which was why he'd handed in his badge.

He'd expected a lot from his father. Disappointment. Anger. What he didn't expect was pride.

"Well, it's about time."

Luke almost choked on the whisky he'd poured himself upon entering his father's den.

"What?"

"You've lived life on the straight and narrow, son. Enforced the law to the letter. By the book. Saw it all in black and white like a good cop does." *He paused, clipping the end of his cigar. It tumbled away onto the carpet, making its escape. His father's nimble hands snatched at it with a deft speed that betrayed his almost seventy years. As did the sharp look he gave his son. "You tell your mother about this, I'll take my badge back just to send you to lockup," he promised.*

Luke smiled. He wanted to chuckle, but he didn't feel like it right at that moment. Hadn't wanted to in a long time. He wondered if he'd remember how.

His father leaned back in his weathered and peeling La-Z-Boy, sucking at the end of the unlit cigar.

"All those things," he continued on his tangent, picking up right where he'd left off like nothing had happened. "Yeah, they make the perfect cop. Problem is you can be a perfect cop, but in order to be that, you've got to be an imperfect man. You can't be a perfect man. It's in our nature. We're all works in progress." He took the cigar from his mouth, twirling it in his fingers, regarding it. "Heck, maybe one day I'll learn to stop enjoying the things that may one day kill me."

He shrugged, reaching for the gold Zippo Luke had gotten him for his sixtieth, lighting the cigar and taking a long inhale.

"Maybe I won't." He blew out a plume of smoke that smelled like nostalgia to Luke. "Got to die somehow. I'd much rather it be because of something that gave me small amounts of joy for most of my life." His eyes went to Luke. "What I'm trying to say, son, is life ain't meant to be lived on the straight and narrow, by the book. I'm proud as hell of the man I've raised. The cop I've trained. Thing is the perfect cop isn't what I

want my son to be. 'Cause he ain't gonna be the man who finds joy where he can, even though he knows exactly where to find it. Exactly where to find her. *That man won't do that because that cop won't let him. 'Cause that joy is lying in a place that ain't black or white. Nor is the life that comes with it."*

Instead of feeling better with his father's sage wisdom and perception floating in his mind, Luke felt like he'd chewed barbed wire.

How fucking stupid had he been?

He didn't hesitate.

As soon as he'd left his father's house, he'd left.

Left Amber, and the life that had seemed so fucking important for his entire life. The purpose he'd clung to, ruining the gang that he thought were evil. Maybe he'd been so intent on destroying them not because of their crimes, not even because of their responsibility in Laurie's death.

But because of Rosie.

Because of that little five-year-old girl with wild hair and combat boots. The one who he believed didn't have a chance to be innocent when she was surrounded by guilt. That little girl who'd turned into a wonderful woman, the woman he wished had more.

And he'd been so fucking blind because he didn't see that she had more. She was more. That gang he'd been so intent on villainizing weren't even the worst.

He was.

He would've thought it would've been hard to end a lifelong vendetta, to leave behind all the hard work, hate, and sleepless nights.

It was the easiest thing he'd ever done.

He hadn't known where he was going until he ended up sitting in front of Keltan Brooke at the Greenstone Security offices six months back.

"I need you to find her," he said, *barely seconds after they'd sat down.*

The man's face was impassive, certainly not surprised. Then, in the face of Luke's terse words, bordering on aggressive, he'd smiled.

It wasn't cruel, or intended to laugh Luke out the door. It was something different than that.

"It's 'bout time, mate."

Luke jolted. "Come again?"

Keltan leaned forward, clasping his hands together, his smile trickling away. "I've been waitin' for you to pull your finger out of your arse and start this war. I'm already smack-dab in the middle of mine."

Luke blinked. "War?"

Keltan nodded, reaching underneath his desk and coming out with two cold beers. He handed one to Luke, who took it more out of reflex than anything else.

"Love, mate," Keltan said, sipping from his beer. "It's a bitch of a fight, isn't it?" His eyes moved with something that Luke only recognized because he'd seen it in the mirror.

He knew Keltan and Lucy had been in some kind of dance for months. Knew she ran away, right into the city where he'd set up a security company. And that look told him that Keltan had finally caught her.

Lucky bastard.

Then again, he didn't look like he'd triumphed in that war of his.

"Yes," Keltan mused to himself. "Thought mine was a bastard, a long fuckin' wait. But you've got me beat. You were fighting long before I entered the fray." He eyed him. "I'm thinkin' you'll be fighting long after I've lost."

Luke failed to hide his surprise at the brisk Kiwi's sage words. They hadn't interacted much, but when Luke had encountered him, he'd had a grudging respect for the man. Another outsider falling for someone inside the club. Someone who didn't understand it, who didn't want his woman involved.

"Lost?" Luke repeated. "You think you're going to lose her?"

Keltan chuckled. "Nah, mate. I'm never gonna lose her. No fuckin' way. Which means, of course, I have to lose the war."

Luke tilted his head, not sure if that was the most profound thing he'd ever heard or the stupidest.

"Already lookin' for her," Keltan continued, not giving Luke enough

*time to come to a conclusion. He frowned. "Got my best guys on it.
Nothin' yet. Your girl, she's good." His tone was a mingling of impressed
and sympathetic. "So for now, I can't give you her, but I can give you a
job. How's that?"*

And somehow, Luke had said yes.

*Those months were full of frustration and dead ends and battles.
Against himself. Trying to figure out who the fuck he was outside of
Amber, outside of his uniform.*

Without her.

That was easy.

He was nothing without her.

And there he was, in the same seat where he'd begun his
search. And he hadn't found her. She'd found herself. And he still
didn't have her.

Keltan had been right. This war wasn't gonna be short.

"How about we sort that when we get back?" Keltan said,
standing.

"Where are we going?"

Keltan grinned, the lingering demons of Lucy's almost death
tainting it. Luke guessed he'd never smile properly, not for the
rest of his life, with that memory.

"My wedding, of course."

CHAPTER NINE

ROSIE

"I can't believe you're getting married in a hospital bed. After being stabbed. In *polyester*." I screwed up my nose. "I don't know which is worse."

"Neither do I," Lucy admitted. "And I was the one who was stabbed." She laughed and the motion jerked my hand, which was applying eye shadow to her closed lid.

"No moving," I snapped, hitting her shoulder. "I'm trying to work my magic."

Lucy went still but scowled at me with closed eyes. "You just hit me," she gasped. "I've been stabbed."

"You're fine," I shot back. Because her eyes were closed, she couldn't see the utter disconnect between my joking tone and my horror-stricken face.

I was only joking because it was one façade I could clutch onto with my newly applied acrylic nails. The other option was complete mental breakdown.

That was not happening.

This was my girl's wedding day. Even if the wedding was taking place in a hospital room that reeked of cleaning products.

Despite my magical skills with a makeup brush, it was hard to mask the thin pallor of death still clinging to my friend's beautiful face. It was sticking, etched in there like a scar you could only see if you looked really close, or if you had one similar.

Or if you'd inflicted one similar.

I was doing all three.

The only thing that could chase that darkness away from her was the happiness that pulsed around her, the warm glow fighting the cold grip of death. It was working.

It would work.

One had to only look into Lucy's violet eyes to see that. To taste the air when she and Keltan were together.

Which was, since I'd been back, every moment. I tried to alternately give them time together while greedily claim my friend back before she was lost to me forever.

We'd still had the unbreakable connection we'd forged as children, but she was moving into a different club, not the motorcycle club we'd welcomed her into.

"You must love him," I whispered, "if you're forgoing Vera for Hospital Gown, off the rack."

She smiled. "Yeah, Rosie, I love him. Very much."

I swallowed a lump in my throat. "I'm sorry I wasn't there. That I haven't been here for you," I choked. "I know from experience that the courtships in our family never go without one, or a thousand and one, hitches."

Lucy reached out and squeezed my hand. "You're here now."

I sucked away my tears. "Yeah."

Lucy's beautiful eyes narrowed. "You want to talk about it?"

I stiffened, leaning back and fiddling with putting away my makeup so I didn't have to meet Lucy's eyes. "About where I've been?"

She shook her head. "No, babe. That's a conversation for

another day. When it's not so fresh, and when talking about it can be done with a safe distance of time and memories," she said. "No, not about where you ran to. But about *why* you ran. It wasn't the same as the other times, was it?"

I froze, my hands on a makeup palette but somehow not.

My hands were covered in blood, one year old and yet it was somehow still sticky and warm. The past had preserved it perfectly for me.

ONE YEAR EARLIER

My dating life had been decidedly sordid. As a stupid, heart-broken and reckless teenager, I decided if I couldn't have the man I wanted, the man I needed, I'd have every other man I possibly could.

That didn't mean I jumped into bed with every man who was half-decent to look at and had three legs. I wasn't *that* bad. Also, a lot of the fuck-worthy men in my vicinity wore leather cuts and answered to either my adopted father or my brother.

Both of those men would've happily had me virginal until marriage, or preferably death.

But I was a biker princess. They made me that way. I hadn't been virginal since I walked into the clubhouse and saw Lucky fucking some chick on the sofa.

I was maybe seven.

Lucky got in *a lot* of shit for that, especially since he was barely patched in. Even bikers didn't like seven-year-old princesses getting firsthand knowledge of what 'doggy style' was.

Despite my barriers, my family, I dated. A lot.

I liked variety in my wardrobe, and I also liked it in men. I got bored easily too. Not many made it past a couple of weeks. Or a couple of dates. And I made sure to hunt for my next distraction in neighboring towns or cities when I felt like a road trip. Which was a lot.

There were a few good guys. I dropped them quick. I needed good guys like I needed a punch in my face. I was trying to get over the good guy. Which meant I needed to make sure whoever I got under was as different from Luke as possible.

There were a lot of average guys. Also a lot of wannabe bad boys. Then a few really nasty ones, which I somehow managed to stay with longer than the rest.

It wasn't because of low self-esteem or daddy issues. It was because they gave me some sort of sick excitement. Or maybe I liked the bitterness of a toxic relationship, craved it on some level.

Of course, no one, not even Lucy or Ashley, knew about the real nasty ones. Especially not the club. They would immediately intervene, and things would get decidedly messy. Because I went for nasty guys, they were tangled up in equally nasty things.

I could handle myself with every single one of them.

Until Kevin.

Absurdly boring and harmless name for an absurdly unpredictable and dangerous man.

I didn't particularly like him, but he was better at distracting than the rest, and he fed that ugly evil part of me.

So I kept seeing him.

Despite the red flags.

Despite the protectiveness and jealousy that was driven by anger.

Despite the fact that the sex began to scare even me.

It took a lot to scare me.

But I was also at the peak of my fucked-up state of mind. Luke was dating too. I think it would've been better if it was a revolving door of girls, but it wasn't. It was some empty-headed bimbo with fake tits and faker Choos.

He was staying with someone like that, letting her into his life, in that spot I coveted, instead of me.

So I stayed with Kevin, fed into that ugly hunger that turned ravenous after seeing Luke with someone who was only better than me because she wasn't connected to a motorcycle club.

Then he hit me.

I can't even remember why. I spoke back to him, most likely.

I do remember lying there, on the ground, where the force of his blow had put me. I held my cheek in surprise rather than pain. Don't get me wrong, it hurt, a fuck of a lot, but I could handle pain. The humiliation that I'd stayed with someone who thought it was okay to beat a woman who wasn't as silent as a mouse, *that* was what I couldn't handle. No matter how fucked up I was, I shouldn't have landed myself there.

And I was sure many millions of women had thought that exact same thing in my exact position before.

I was shocked too. I'd seen violence. Lived a life of it. My best friends had been subjected to some of the most brutal and ugly acts that could be dealt at the hands of men. Most of them had not only managed to survive it but thrive after it.

One of my most treasured girls didn't survive. I thought witnessing that, seeing the people I loved most in the world being broken like that, was worse than anything I could experience.

And it was.

But that didn't mean I didn't freeze from the surprise of experiencing this violence firsthand from a man for the first time in my life.

Kevin utilized that, my shock, kicking me in the ribs. I grunted as the force of the kick expelled a painful gasp from my lungs and rolled me toward the coffee table.

"See, you're a hot piece, babe. The hottest. And I care about you, I really do. But you just have to piss me off. Why do you do that?" he asked, as if I was the one hurting him. As if it was my fault.

I barely listened to him. I blinked through the pain that wasn't as bad as it could've been since he was barefoot. My eyes focused on my purse, which, thanks to the kick, was now within reach.

I wasn't frozen anymore. I didn't hesitate to dart my hand forward, into the opening, and clutch the gun that was always in there.

I turned onto my back with some pain the moment he reached my side, standing above me. The barrel of the gun blocked out his handsome face.

"You don't touch me again unless you want it to be the last thing you do," I said, my voice even.

It was his time to freeze. And he did it long enough for me to scramble clumsily to my feet.

By the time I'd done that, still pointing my gun at him, his face changed from dumb shock to a dumb snarl. A cocky confidence fed by women who didn't have enough strength to stand up to him.

I was doing this for them, and, of course, myself.

"You're not going to shoot me."

He barely got the words out before I replaced them with a gunshot.

His screams were embarrassingly loud for someone who prided himself on being the big bad drug dealer who beat women.

"You fucking bitch! You fucking shot me!" he bellowed from the floor, which he'd collapsed onto as soon as the bullet went through his lower leg.

I raised my brow. "I don't do empty threats, *babe*," I said, then snatched my purse from the ground, keeping my gaze on Kevin while I did. "You know, I think we should break up."

"I'm going to fucking—"

"Tut tut. I wouldn't go about making promises you can't keep." I narrowed my eyes. "And trust me, you can't keep any promises of revenge that you're going to throw at me like that weak punch." I rubbed my cheek. "I'm not like the other girls. In all the best ways. And all the worst. That means I will fucking kill you if you come near me again. I'll make sure I chop your dick off first. Oh, and I'll be having someone keep an eye on you. And your next girlfriend. If she has as much as a hangnail, I'll come back. And I'll give you a lot more than a hangnail."

I eyed him, clutching his leg and glaring at me. He was angry. Furious. This was probably the first time a woman had ever got the best of him.

I really hoped it wouldn't be the last.

I also hoped that he wasn't stupid enough to mess with me again.

I should've known better than to hope.

It took a while for everything to line up just perfectly for my life to be ruined. I'd pretty much forgotten about Kevin by the time all the drama with Bex came to a head. Which was comical, since it was him, not the drama with Bex, that ruined it all.

It was a strange thing when all the seemingly isolated clouds in your life joined together, creating the perfect storm that even George Clooney wouldn't dare sail through.

It shouldn't happen, such a storm. Even in my dramatic and barely believable life, such events, like the one of that fateful day, should not have stitched together like at the hand of Frankenstein itself, creating a monster I'd provided all the parts for.

Like most of the shouldn'ts' in my life, it got turned into a "surely will." Imagine that in a Southern accent too, just for kicks.

It was just another Sons of Templar courtship. The most recent of the five, and this time, finally, Lucky got his girl. But shadows as black as midnight yanked at the both of them, taking two members of my family on the darkest journey the club had seen since Laurie.

Just another day in that courtship meant a car bomb.

Specifically the car Lucy and I had been about to get into until Bex saved our lives. The message was to her and the club. By the person trying to destroy it all.

They failed, just like everyone beforehand had.

But it was close.

Emergency trip to my brow lady kind of close.

But everyone was fine, save Lucy's broken wrist.

But an explosion in the Sons of Templar compound didn't go unnoticed by local law enforcement.

Specifically would not go unnoticed by Luke.

I knew that, which was why I had been trying my level best to escape the aforementioned compound before Luke arrived.

Yes, I was running and hiding, though not from the reasons that I also got blown up.

From the man who would've liked to protect me from all that.

From my family.

Who would've done that by destroying it.

But my overprotective family—more precisely, my overprotective brother—wasn't about to let me escape without being under observation.

So while the men fought amongst themselves, trying to control a situation that was already chaotic, the sound of shrill sirens cut through the air.

"We're gonna have cops crawling the place right about now," Brock said, hard eyes on the windows showing the smoking remains of my car.

Every part of me froze.

"Yeah, well, let them come," Cade growled from in front of me, where he was currently standing as if to make sure he hadn't overlooked a missing limb. "We've got nothin' to hide, and as much as I loathe Crawford's little visits, maybe we can make the boys in blue work for our taxes and fuck around while we find out who did this."

I unfroze at the mention of Luke's name, and at the utter hatred in my brother's voice.

I darted up from the chair they'd banished me to. A woman couldn't possibly be expected to stand after she survived an explosion. As if being vertical would be the thing that ended me, not the explosives.

"I've got to go," I said, my voice bordering on hysterical. Hopefully everyone would think it was due to an explosion that almost killed me, not the police officer who was much more dangerous.

Bex eyed me shrewdly.

Cade foiled my escape attempt, his eyes hard. "Are you fuckin' *insane?*" he demanded. "No, wait, I already know the answer to that question. But you were almost just fuckin' blown up, kid. You're not goin' anywhere." His voice rippled with fury, as did his eyes, only I could see the concern lingering beneath the granite gaze. And a flicker of fear.

That one day we'd stop getting off lightly with scratches and ruined jeans and broken bones.

That we'd lose one.

Another one.

My eyes quickly touched on Bex, the demons dancing on her face, even now that she had a man who adored her and the horrors of her past behind her.

Though our horrible past was never really behind us. For Bex, it was in the memories and waking nightmares she struggled with every damn day.

For me, my own horrible, beautiful nightmare was about to strut through that door. Bex couldn't run from her nightmares, because they were incorporeal. I could at least scamper away from the physical portion of mine.

"I'm fine," I lied, eyes on the windows, watching the patrol cars screech in. My escape would be impossible soon. "My eyebrows bore the brunt of it," I continued, struggling in Cade's arms. "Nothing a spa day can't fix. Now I've really got to go. I think I left my straightener on."

My struggles were becoming more and more frantic, more and more feral, like a wild cat trying to escape the embrace of someone trying to domesticate it.

I could not be domesticated.

Which was part of the problem.

Another big part of the problem was the two different sides of the law that Luke and I called home.

"I'm a police officer. Let me the fuck in."

Speak of the Devil's slightly more well-behaved brother and he shall appear.

Luke's cursing and tight, bordering-on-uncontrolled tone surprised me. He wore his professionalism like a mask, indifference for me scathing in its almost authenticity when he was around the club.

Though I couldn't say anything else would take away the sting over the fact that whenever he was around the club, he was trying to take them down.

Despite all that, my eyes went to Luke, latching onto his baby blues even though I knew I couldn't really do anything. Couldn't really be anything to him.

Fury rippled off Cade as he followed my eyes toward Luke, who was stomping toward me.

He let go of me immediately to shove himself between Luke and me.

He didn't need to create a physical barrier; the ideological one worked well enough.

"The flaming and smoking remains of the bomb that almost killed my sister are outside, Deputy," Cade said, almost spitting the words at him, though his tone was somehow flat. "I assume that's where you should be *doing your job.*"

Cade's tone, his entire demeanor, betrayed something.

I flinched. *Could he know?*

No. He's Cade just being Cade.

I couldn't rip my eyes away from Luke's glacial stare, every inch of hatred spearing me in the heart with its intensity.

Though it didn't stay on Cade for long. He didn't seem interested in a macho-man stare-off. Instead, every inch of the glacier

melted, hate disappearing, leaving something much more complicated in its wake as his eyes once more focused on me.

"I'm right where I need to be, Fletcher."

I blinked. Uncomfortable silence bathed the room as everyone
watched Luke's blatant statement of something he'd made his
business to keep secret.

He didn't even seem like he noticed or cared about what he'd
exposed with those words as his eyes catalogued my entire body,
zeroing in on even the smallest of scratches and my charred
clothing.

"Are you okay?" he little more than whispered.

My heart began to beat all the way in my throat, making me
unable to form words. The only thing I could do was nod weakly.

His soft gaze didn't stay on me for a second longer, he finally
commenced the macho-man stare-off Cade had been hanging out
for. "I see the story of you going *legit* was a total pack of lies," Luke
hissed, unbridled anger poisoning his voice.

I didn't know why I expected anything more, that just because
he gave me a handful of words and a lingering gaze, that would
repair decades of hatred. I shouldn't have expected it. I should've
known better. It didn't mean it didn't hurt any less.

"What did you do now to put your own flesh and blood in
danger? That's low, even for you."

The air shimmered with masculine fury as my eyes brimmed
with tears I would never let fall. My mask was in place.

"Careful, Deputy," my brother murmured. "You're getting very
fuckin' close to sayin' somethin' you might regret."

Luke's hand subconsciously went to his belt. "You threatening
me?"

"Yeah," Cade replied immediately. "If you keep talkin' shit 'bout
my family, my club, lookin' at my sister in a way that isn't professional, you bet your ass I am."

I flinched. Cade had seen it.

The entire club was focused on the exchange. I wondered if

there was a possibility for me to slink away while the testosterone clouded the air.

Luke's gaze focused on me.

No such luck, then. "She's comin' with me."

The response to Luke's declaration was instantaneous. Brock and Dwayne stepped forward, blocking Luke's path to me with a wall of muscle. Showing that the bars to my cage were not iron, but men who benched a lot of it.

"No she's fuckin' not," Cade said evenly.

Luke didn't back down. "She needs a hospital. So does Bex."

I sucked in a breath. Luke was really going for gold today. I prayed my family was serious about the 'legit' thing. Then maybe they wouldn't murder the man I loved.

It could've gone bad. I tasted it in the air. Luke was using his state-given authority to try and take women who the club considered their God-given women. It may have been archaic—actually, it definitely fucking was—but it was the way. The men spoke and acted for the women.

Or until they fell in love with the right ones who were attached to their voices and unafraid to use them.

"I don't do hospitals, Captain America. They mess with my complexion," Bex said easily, as if she wasn't choking on male fury. "Plus, the nurses here are way hotter." She grinned wickedly in Lucky's direction, who, uncharacteristically, wasn't grinning. Much of his relationship with Bex took away his easygoing nature and infectious laugh. But sometimes in the midst of the worst horror imaginable, if you came out on the other side with the right person, that horror was better than any empty happiness before it.

Luke's eyes went everywhere at once, his professional mask returning as he understood what was—or more aptly, wasn't—going to happen. "None of you go anywhere," he ordered. "I'm gonna want statements from fuckin' all of you."

He gave me one hard glance before he turned on his heel and

left, taking one of the small and few remaining pieces of my heart along with him.

I froze in place, watching his uniform retreat out the door.

Freezing didn't do well in the face of fury. Especially my brother's fury. He gripped my shoulders and dragged me away while conversation somehow returned to normal.

As normal as it could get after an explosion.

"What the fuck was that, Rosie?" Cade demanded in a harsh whisper.

"What was what?"

The pads of his fingers dug into my shoulders, betraying his frustration. "Playing the innocent act stopped working when you came out of the fucking womb," he hissed. "What have you got going on with Crawford?"

I flinched. "Nothing."

He glared at me, searching for both the truth and lie in my eyes. There was a little of both.

"He's dangerous," he said. "To the club. To you."

I lifted my chin. "I'm well aware of that."

He narrowed his eyes. "And I'm well aware that you chase danger for fuckin' cardio."

I yanked out of his grasp. "I'm not fifteen anymore, Cade. You can't give me lectures and hope they stick. But yeah, I get bored, I cause a little trouble. It never touches the club. I can handle my own shit. And there's nothing to handle with Luke. You made sure to tell me that my entire life, essentially telling me I wouldn't have one if I considered him as anything more than the scum you do." My gaze didn't falter. "And that one stuck, Cade. Lectures don't stick with me, but death threats certainly do. Especially when they come from my own brother."

Cade flinched, like I'd struck him. "Roe—"

"No, Cade," I hissed. "Don't worry, you don't have to say anything else. I'm a lot of things, but I'm not suicidal."

And then, before I could betray anything else, I turned on my heel and left.

So he didn't think I was running, I did it farther into the club. But I knew every inch of the place where I'd grown up, especially all escape routes.

Which was exactly what I did.

Escaped.

But then again, I lived in a cage, so there was only so far I could go until someone found me.

And it was the person I wanted to find me more than anything. I also hoped he never would, because it would eventually mean he lost himself.

———

I didn't go home because that would've been the first place they looked. I didn't go to a bar because that would be the second.

Not that they needed to. I'd texted Cade to tell him I hadn't been murdered or kidnapped or joined the circus. Then I'd turned my phone off, because despite that text, I knew Cade would've had Wire trace my phone.

This outlaw life of freedom sometimes had more bars than the cages of society boasted.

I was resigned to that when boots hit the dock I was swinging my boots off.

It was only a matter of time before someone found me. My heart stopped because I knew who the someone was. I knew it before he sat down beside me, before his profile danced at the edges of my vision and his clean smell mingled with the salty ocean air.

He was the only one who knew about this place.

Our place, as I'd come to think of it.

It was a delusion, sure. But everyone needed a delusion or two to get them through reality.

ANNE MALCOM

"I don't need a lecture on rights and wrongs and evil and good right now, Luke," I said, keeping my eyes on the ocean, even though every part of me yearned to drink him in.

There was a long pause, and the air around my hand changed as Luke rested his own on the wood of the dock, right next to mine, then coiled his pinky with mine.

One small touch, barely anything, but for us, it was more than everything.

I expected him to pull away. He didn't. He just kept it there and I held my breath.

"I'm not here for that, Rosie," he said finally. "I'm here for you."

I whipped my head sideways. He was still watching the ocean. The words winded me for a split second, but then I hardened. "Here to arrest me? Question me?" I asked coldly.

That time my words made him shift his gaze. I restrained a flinch at seeing the hurt in it. I knew that wasn't why he was there. We both knew it.

"I'm here for you, Rosie," he repeated.

I swallowed roughly. "You can't be, Luke," I whispered.

His eyes hardened. "Where else can I be, Rosie? With the memories of the flaming remains of the fucking bomb that almost erased you from this earth?" he demanded. "With the fucking replay of what would've been if everything had been a little later, if you'd been just a little closer? I've done too much of that, staying away and chasing at the demons that remind me just how acquainted you are with death. I can't fuckin' do that anymore, Rosie. I can't do any of it."

I froze. "Any of what?"

My heart soared and sank at the same time.

He turned fully to face me, yanked my entire hand into his strong and dry palm. His gaze didn't waver.

"You know what," he murmured, so quietly the waves almost stole his words away.

But they didn't. I snatched them out of the air and held them tight.

Inside was the only place I would let myself hold on to them, to the feelings of Luke's hand entwined in mine. That gaze directed at me. I steeled myself, garnered my strength, then snatched my hand back and pushed myself up.

Luke did the same, frowning.

I ignored this. "And how do you think it would work?"

"What do you mean?"

I rolled my eyes. "Come on, Luke. Don't pretend to be dense. You went to college, got that degree in criminology. I'm sure that means you can decode what a criminal says," I spat at him, hating the words as they came out of my mouth and the ugly tone that structured them.

"Jesus, Rosie," he snapped, rubbing his palm over his clean-shaven jaw in frustration. "Stop fuckin' fighting it. Me."

I put my hand on my hip. "Clue in, Luke, fighting you, fighting this, it's the only option."

His eyes darkened and he stepped forward. I stepped back, to the edge of the dock. If he came closer, my only retreat would be the ocean. At that moment, I'd take my chances in the water.

He didn't move forward.

"There's another option," he gritted out.

I stared at him. "No there isn't," I said firmly.

"There is."

"You enforce the law, I break it. That's it, if we want to make it simple," I snapped.

"We're not simple, babe."

I blinked at him. Blinked away the tears that threatened to shatter my tough-girl façade. "We have to be, Luke. There's no other way for us."

His face was etched into determination, like he'd decided in that moment that there was going to be an us. That despite the previous decades, nothing was going to stop him.

ANNE MALCOM

"I'll make a way," he promised.

I did it again, grasped onto those words, bathed in the moment for a heartbeat and then continued fighting. Despite what Luke said, despite his decision about the way things were going to be, the truth was it wasn't his decision.

I stared at him, forcing myself to school my features, to clench my fists at my sides.

"You know what my worst fear is?" I asked. "It's not spiders, being burned alive, clowns or anything else painful or horrifying that can happen to me. My worst fear is what happens to the people who make up me. My family. My worst fear is losing them. And it's ironic then, you see, that I fall in love with the man who wants to do that. To take everything from me. The man who somehow both embodies my worst fears and my unuttered dreams at the same time. So I can't live it out. Whatever we have. Because in that moment of selfishness that I would take, it would be the end of everything."

"Rosie—" he choked out.

I held my hand up, disgusted to see it was shaking. "No," I whispered. "You can't decide that everything else doesn't matter. It does. Including the one pivotal truth," I said. "You have so much hate for the club, Luke."

His brow furrowed. "My feelings about the club have nothing to do with you."

I laughed. It was ugly and cold, and I hated the sound coming out of me. "No, that's the thing. They have *everything* to do with me. Everything I am or ever will be is because of my family. They are the world to me. And they're what I've built my world around. So by hating the very thing that put me together, that keeps me together, you hate me. There is no one without the other. And as long as that hate exists, there is no you and me." I paused. "Not that there ever was."

Then I turned on my heel and left.

He didn't follow me.

The anchor of truth was fastened around his ankle, so I doubted it was even physically possible for him to follow me.

That didn't mean I didn't pray for it.

"What are you doing here, Luke?" I asked, trying my best to block his path. It only kind of worked—he stopped his purposeful stride toward the clubhouse, sunglasses directing themselves at me. His hand still rested on his gun, and he held his jaw hard.

It was just shy of a month after that day on the dock, after the explosion that blew everything between us right open.

We hadn't spoken. Until now.

"Rosie, get out of my way," he clipped.

I cocked my hip and narrowed my eyes. "No. Not until you tell me why you're waltzing onto private property. You don't have a warrant."

He pushed his shades onto the top of his blond head, the mussed strands catching, though he didn't notice.

I tried my best not to let the focus of those blue eyes affect me, but like always, the only thing I accomplished was to hide the way they affected me outwardly. Inwardly, I was knots.

Whichever asshole painted love as this amazing and wonderful thing must've be on acid.

A lot of it.

Love was not amazing. Or wonderful. It was painful, horrible and did its best to kill everything independent inside you so all of your feelings were dependent on one person.

One man.

The one in the uniform who was trying to destroy your family.

And the one who was so intent on destroying your family that he barely even acknowledged your existence.

At least Romeo and Juliet had the whole mutual love thing going on before they killed themselves.

153

"I don't need a warrant," he said. "Got a tip."

I raised my brow. "A tip?" Disbelief saturated my tone.

He nodded once. "From a concerned citizen."

I put my hand on my hip. "A *concerned citizen?* Give me a fucking break, Luke." I paused, anger seeping out of me as quickly as it had inflated me. "When are you going to stop this? Can't you just let them be? Can't you just...." I caught myself before saying what I had been going to say. Which would've not only labeled me weak and pathetic, but a traitor to my family.

Can't you just notice me? Like really notice? Take a second to realize that I'm more than Rosie, the little sister of the man you hate, and remember that I'm the Rosie you've shared those stolen moments with. The ones you do your best to forget as soon as they've happened.

Something changed in his expression, a softening at the edges, a shimmering depth in those eyes that had been so full of ice before. Giving me a glimpse of it, what my mind had asked for but what I was sure I hadn't said out loud.

"Can't I just what?" he said, little more than a whisper, stepping toward me so I inhaled clean linen and peppermint.

Luke scent.

He even smelled different.

But then, as moments that shouldn't be usually are, it was broken. Exactly the way moments were broken in my life.

With a dead body.

Okay, maybe not *most* moments in a normal person's life, but it had been established just how far from normal I was.

"Can't you just—" My words were cut off when my eyes wandered, too cowardly to meet Luke's eyes. "Oh my God," I choked out, my voice half-broken, half of it trying to remember to keep my shit together.

Luke was immediately on guard at my exclamation. He knew I didn't have an affinity to calling out things dramatically, and I guessed my face was painted in a look of horror.

"What?" he demanded, hand on the butt of his gun.

I didn't answer, just skirted around him, sprinting toward the motorcycle boots just barely visible behind the car parked in the lot. And the thin, almost invisible but unmistakable stream of liquid trickling past the boots.

Blood. It had to be a lot of it for it to travel that far.

Obviously why Luke hadn't noticed on his approach; his angle meant he didn't see them, and then he'd been distracted by me.

The few seconds it took to make it to the body were the longest of my life. Those motorcycle boots were the unofficial uniform of the Sons of Templar. Everyone wore them, some with variations. The only person I could rule out was Gage, since he had those cowboy spikes on the back of his. I would say only for decoration but I'd be lying.

In those few seconds, I listed all the people those boots could belong to, each choice more horrifying than the last. Every single choice was a bullet to my heart, the thought of losing someone else in our family unthinkable.

I skidded to a stop, going to my knees in the puddle of blood beside the man who had long left this world. There was no saving him. Not with half of his head gone.

My white dress pooled around me, getting stained in blood.

That's why I don't wear white, I thought with detachment. Bloodstains.

My shaking hand went to what was left of his forehead.

"Oh, Skid," I whispered, a single tear trailing down my cheek. Skid was a kid. A prospect only a few weeks shy of getting his cut. He was quiet but as loyal as they came. He'd been taking care of my friend and Lucky's woman, Bex, for as long as she'd been in trouble with drug dealers and an abusive ex-boyfriend. After she was kidnapped, raped, and beaten by those very men. He was never far from her side, and to this day, meant to be on her protection duty.

My heart dropped about the second Luke's bellowed, "Rosie!" preceded him coming to Skid's other side, gun out.

155

I glanced up at his blank face, regarding the dead body and then me.

I gently closed Skid's opened eyes. "He's dead," I said quietly, pushing up from my spot, wiping the blood from my hands on my already-ruined dress.

The smell of blood and death danced in the air with Luke's clean scent, polluting it. It was an ugly poetic example of just how vast our differences were.

"Rosie, I need you to get in my patrol car, lock yourself in and call for backup," he instructed, his voice cold, eyes scanning the empty parking lot for signs of a threat.

I wanted to laugh and tell him just how similar to Cade he looked doing that. But he wouldn't appreciate that, so I settled for saying something he'd appreciate even less.

"Yeah, like fuck I'm locking myself safely away and calling more cops in here," I scoffed. "This is my *family*. I'm not hiding, and I'm not sitting down while someone else, someone who hates them, is going in there"—I jerked my head toward the building —"firstly to see if there's something you can to do finally bust them, and only secondly see if you can save whoever else is hurt."

He glared at me, the look somehow mingling with a tenderness that I couldn't understand. "Rosie, I don't hate them. Not now. Not with... everything. But I'm going to protect you, and I'm not letting—"

He was cut off by a sound I was all too familiar with.

A gunshot.

I didn't hesitate. I went running into the building where the shot came from.

The thump of police-issue boots and the cursing behind me told me that Luke followed.

CHAPTER TEN

I went in prepared for the worst, my blood both ice and fire. Ready to face both grief and revenge. Because someone committed the ultimate crime of spilling the blood of our family and doing it inside our gates.

We may have gone legit, but that didn't mean that action didn't have one consequence.

Death.

We'd had blood spilled in our family ever since we lost Laurie. And I'd had poison in my veins from that. From losing one of my best friends. And having to face it consistently throughout the past five years. I was used to fighting, to death. But I promised myself that I wouldn't let it be any more of my family.

I let out a breath when I burst in to see both Lucky and Bex intact. My eyes went to the bullet wound at Lucky's shoulder. Well, mostly intact. Just a flesh wound. He'd live.

He was circling a man who was bleeding from between his legs. A small grin tickled the corner of my lips, betting that the man had Bex to thank for that. She was bleeding from her head, focused on both Lucky and the man crumpled on the ground. He was familiar.

"You're going to die. But not yet. Not even in the near future," Lucky said.

Luke arrived behind me, breathing evenly. He didn't declare his presence, obviously scanning for threats and seeing none, then pausing to collect evidence.

"But it'll happen. I've got a brother who's so very anxious to meet you," Lucky continued.

And that was it, the moment I recognized the man. Devon. The son of the man who'd kidnapped Amy years before. Who had almost killed both Bex and me with a car bomb.

As those thoughts filtered through my mind while witnessing a man I considered a brother holding a gun to someone bleeding out from a dick wound, I thought about how fucking dramatic our life was.

And it could only go up from there. Or down, depending on your perspective.

"Step away from him and put down the gun, Lucky," Luke said, his voice even and hard.

So he'd decided to make his move.

Lucky's response to Luke's command was to swing the gun from the prone man to the doorway where we stood. It stayed raised as his eyes went to Luke, though he immediately lowered it when he realized he was pointing it at me too.

I met Bex's eyes, giving her a wonky sort of smile as if to say, 'just another Tuesday in paradise.'

Lucky wasn't perturbed at Luke's presence. "Can't do that, Luke," he said, voice casual. "This swine"—he delivered a swift kick to Devon's midsection, resulting in little more than a pained moan—"is the reason Skid is dead. The reason Becky almost fuckin' *died.*"

I was putting all the pieces together. He was the reason Becky got kidnapped, why I walked in on her hacking at her hair in front of the mirror because she couldn't even stand her reflection after she was raped. The reason why, for months, she was little more than a haunted shell of a person, forced to live inside the house of horrors that was her head.

I knew what I needed to do, the only thing that could be done with Luke there that would both save my family and deliver the revenge that needed to be dealt. I reached into my purse, looking for the gun that was always there, along with my favorite lipstick —Mac, Ruby Woo, if you were wondering.

Lucky focused on me, still addressing Luke, whose gun was still raised. "Why Rosie was almost blown into a thousand pieces." The way he said it, giving Luke a pointed reminder of how close this man came to killing me, told me Lucky saw a lot more than he let on. "So I suggest you leave, pretend you didn't see a thing," he instructed Luke.

Though I knew the situation was serious, I wanted to choke out a laugh. Asking Luke to forsake his badge and his morals by helping the club he despised to commit murder was like expecting Cade to cooperate with a police investigation.

Luke's gaze and entire body hardened. "My father may do that shit, but not me. I can't turn a blind eye to this." I felt his pause, his struggle, when, for less than a second, his gaze flickered to me. He was putting the pieces together too. Hesitation. That hesitation gave me the hope I'd been waiting for all my life, that little piece to go with my collection of moments that told me maybe there was something inside him that felt what I felt.

I stopped believing in hope before I stopped believing in Santa Claus. That didn't mean it didn't puncture me when his shoulders stiffened and the gun continued to point in Lucky's direction. "Don't make me shoot you."

Like me, Luke didn't do empty threats. I knew he didn't want to shoot Lucky. If pressed, like maybe if someone was removing some fingernails, he might admit he actually *liked* Lucky. It was impossible not to. Though he looked like a cold-blooded murderer, and certainly was one, he had an infectious smile and the sense of humor of a twelve-year-old.

He was soft, under all that hard. With the biggest heart you'd ever see.

Which was why he was able to break every barrier Bex put up after she was attacked. Why he went through his own personal Hell after rescuing her too late. Why he waited months for her to even speak to him. Did everything in his power to heal her, give her whatever tainted happiness was left for her.

And she got that. My broken friend was put back together mostly thanks to her own strength, but also thanks to the kind of man who killed every single person responsible for hurting her.

She was his world. And he was hers.

Which was why she glared at Luke, looking ready to scratch his eyes out, gun or no gun. "Dude, in case you hadn't noticed, he's already been fucking shot," she snapped, not betraying any outward trauma of being in the middle of yet another abduction. She was a diamond, she didn't break easily. Or at all.

I wasn't about to let Luke chip at that. I reached up to tug his shoulder, in a gesture to get his attention rather than actually physically stop him. I braced against the reaction I got from touching him.

"Luke, don't do this. You know what he did. You know he deserves this. Just leave. Let us handle this." My voice was small, as close to begging as I'd ever get.

Luke didn't pause, didn't react outwardly, if not for a twitch in his blue eyes. Not enough, though. "I can't do that, Rosie," he said, his voice still flat, simmering with doubt and unease. "I don't want to, but I'll shoot him if I have to."

His voice may have been simmering with unease, but that didn't mean he wasn't telling the truth. Whatever small changes were working within Luke weren't going to destroy something that underpinned his entire character, his ultimate and unyielding view of the law.

My stomach was ash as I nodded, seeing that chasm between

us once more, as if it had never been wider. "Yeah, I know," I murmured, my hurt and heartbreak seeping into my voice.

I couldn't let that moment be the one when I let this shit get me down. So I didn't. I moved. Right in between Luke and Lucky, in front of the gun, shielding Lucky, shielding the club. I paused to give Luke a pointed look as his aim wavered. "But you won't shoot me," I said, that time with more strength and resolve.

I didn't pause to regard what was in his eyes, the betrayal. I wouldn't. I couldn't. I had a job to do. One mustn't think too much about the job of killing when it needed to be done. I learned that after, because I didn't think hardly at all when I crossed the room, pulled my handgun out of my purse and discharged a single shot. One that found its home in Devon's skull, ending it once and for all. Delivering the justice the club needed, while at the same time protecting them from the strong arm of the law.

A thick roar erupted in my ears after I did it. Killed a man. Despite my upbringing, I'd never done that before—well, at least not as intimately. I wasn't sheltered. I'd seen a lot. Almost all there was to see.

But killing was, until recently, a man's job. Feminism may have gotten us equal pay and the vote, but in the Sons of Templar, murder was still exclusively a male-dominated industry.

The girls and I were shaking that up a bit.

I didn't want them to; in fact, I wanted anything but to see myself through Luke's eyes. Regardless of want, my gaze locked with his. Bile crept up my throat, not at the act of killing itself but seeing my reflection on Luke's face.

"Holy fuck," Lucky muttered, pride in his voice as he broke the deafening silence.

"You got that right," Bex agreed, in a 'you go, girl' kind of tone.

I fought hard to keep my composure, not to break down as I put the final nail not in Devon's coffin but in the one of that secret Luke and Rosie fantasy that had been dying a very slow death.

"You going to arrest me?" I asked flatly, already knowing the answer, though it broke my heart.

Luke didn't speak, or couldn't, I didn't know which. He shook his head. And then, as if a weight pushed it down, he lowered his gun in a gesture of defeat. His eyes stayed on mine, communicating everything and nothing at the same time.

Then he turned his back on me and walked out.

I saved the club.

And broke my own heart in the process.

Bravo, Rosie.

But wasn't that what love was?

Destroying yourself for the sake of others?

My hands were shaking as I struggled to put the key in my lock.

The hands that pulled the trigger on a gun. Ending a man's life.

Splattering his brains all over the floor.

I killed someone.

The sentence came from inside my head, spoken by a strange disembodied voice that didn't seem at all familiar. Spoken by the person, the monster, I'd created in that split second.

I'd seen plenty of dead bodies. Kept company with plenty of murderers, otherwise known as my family. Death himself was like that horrible uncle who gave you the heebie-jeebies but turned up unexpectedly, never telling you how long he was staying before he left so you could relax, forgetting he existed until he returned again.

Now he was there, breathing down my neck as I fumbled with my keys, putting a shadow on the day that I was sure had been cloudless before.

Before I'd killed a man.

But the worst thing was that wasn't why my hands were trembling, why my mouth was dry, stomach full of bile.

The killing itself was horrible, but not that horrible. Not something that would follow me around forever. Maybe it was because something was broken in me. Whether it was a product of my upbringing or just nature, it didn't matter. The killing didn't. Not really.

It was because Luke watched as I did it. Watched me transition, finally, into the embodiment of everything he so despised.

Before that, I was sure he thought of me as a participant of the life he loathed. An unwilling one who had nature and biology to thank for my place in the club, and was therefore somehow removed from it all. Somehow cleaner.

Ending that bastard's life saved the club. It also killed, messily and violently, any small, miniscule chance Luke and I had.

Not that the chance was ever going to mature into reality.

I had never been clean. It just took Luke that long to realize it.

I sucked in a gulp of tainted air as I finally stumbled through my front door, slamming it behind me and sinking against it, worried my knees might not support my weight.

But I shouldn't have worried about them supporting anything since the painful impact of a fist hitting my cheek set me off them so I tumbled to the floor.

I blinked up at the blurry ceiling, confused, and struggled against the blackness that threatened to turn into unconsciousness from the force of the blow.

Then I wasn't looking at the ceiling anymore. Two figures towered over me, sneering down at me.

"You thought you'd scared me off, did you?"

A boot connected with my ribs, and I choked out a gasp at the ricocheting pain through my abdomen.

"You think I'd be scared off? By a *woman*?"

I blinked through the pain, swallowing the cry that ached to get out from my throat.

It wasn't two men.

Just one asshole.

One I'd seriously misjudged.

"You need to leave if you want to live," I croaked.

I eyed my purse, which had fallen directly in my entranceway, about three feet from where I was lying. I was in a lot of pain, reasonably sure I had a broken rib, but I could make it to there.

And more importantly to the gun, lying slightly out of my open purse.

The one I'd already used to shoot someone that day. What was another dirtbag?

Just as I was about to dart toward it, another brutal kick landed in my midsection.

That time, even though I didn't want to, I did cry out. And now I wasn't reasonably sure I had a broken rib. I was certain I had several.

Kevin had taken to wearing steel-capped boots.

I must've blacked out, though it wasn't black I saw but blinding white-hot pain, because when my vision cleared, Kevin was standing above me, holding my gun and grinning.

"See?" He waved it before settling the barrel on me. "I've learned."

I coughed, the jerking motion sending pokers of agony from my ribs to my toes. "Do you want a medal, asshole?" I croaked.

A storm settled over his face. He bent down, and I could see the madness and violence mingling in his eyes. "You don't get to say shit," he hissed, spittle flying from his mouth and settling on my cheek. "I'm the one in control here. Not you. I'm the one who's got the gun. Who will fucking kill you if you don't do everything I say."

I stared into the abyss of his eyeballs, frozen. Because I saw the truth there. He did fully intend on killing me.

I was tied to the bed.

In my underwear.

I didn't remember my clothes being taken off.

I couldn't decide whether that was a good or bad thing.

The pain was the bad thing. It sucked. A lot. He'd decided that being in control meant he pretty much got to beat the shit out of me.

He'd pistol-whipped me finally, and I'd lost consciousness. Which he'd taken advantage of. My entire body ached. My ribs screamed. One of my eyes was swollen shut.

On a good note, I hadn't been raped.

Yet.

I was thinking that being handcuffed to the bed in my underwear meant it wouldn't stay that way for long.

I was not getting raped. I would die first.

I had to get out of there.

He wasn't in my bedroom, but I wasn't stupid enough to think he was gone.

The thump of a bass from my sound system in the living room told me he was still in the house. Somewhere. My instincts told me that too.

Men like that were unpredictable. Men who valued women little more than slaves and thought beating them was acceptable. Bullies. Just like the ones in high school. If you stood up to a bully, most of the time they moved onto weaker prey. They were cowards at the end of the day.

But there was a small percentage of those bullies who wouldn't move on. Who refused to be bested, to become the weak one. So they bided their time, made it their mission to make you pay. So much so that it consumed their minds and they would do whatever it took to get their victory. With little thought to consequences.

Kevin obviously thought his victory was raping me, degrading me, showing me that he was in control, and then killing me. The consequences of that were a slow and painful death if my family ever found out.

So I guessed the killing me portion would go toward making sure I couldn't point the finger at him, since none of my family knew about him. I had given him the ingredients to get away with murder. They wouldn't be looking into my life if I turned up brutalized and dead.

They'd be looking into their own.

Into their history.

To a time when this had happened before. To my beautiful friend.

And that time it had been on the club. They'd assume that would be the case this time. And they'd be so blinded by hate that they'd most likely start a war. And there would be blood. On both sides.

Like before.

I would not let that happen.

I would not let any blood be spilled because of me. Not my family's. Not my own.

Luckily, being a biker princess meant my bedroom may have been home to kick-ass furnishings, almost the entirety of Sephora's makeup department, and some well-cared-for secondhand designer footwear, but it also held an arsenal that rivaled that of a small-town police station.

Though most of it wasn't within reach since both of my hands were handcuffed above my head on my wrought-iron headboard. I craned my head upward, ignoring my battered body's painful protest.

"Man, he used my own handcuffs? What a dick," I whispered to myself.

I knew I only had a limited amount of time before Kevin came back from whatever he was doing, so I didn't screw around. There was a gun taped underneath my bed on my left side, but I was handcuffed slightly to the right and I wouldn't reach it.

The knife underneath my mattress on the right it was.

I shimmied awkwardly, my hands not giving much in the handcuffs. Mostly because I was an idiot and didn't get the soft erotic kind. No, I had to go authentic.

Yes, I was aware that I needed a therapist to dissect that.

My body screamed at me as I moved, my ribs so painful I almost vomited.

I didn't, of course. I was a Fletcher.

By birth, I was a Templar.

More importantly, I was Rosie.

I bit my lip as I tried to work my hands downward enough to reach my mattress. The swirl of my headboard that I'd thought so fucking artful was what hindered me, stopping at least six inches short of where I needed to be.

Frustrated tears streamed down my face.

"Fuck!" I hissed.

"Not trying to get away, are we, babe?" Kevin asked pleasantly.

My eyes snapped to him. He was in his underwear—boxer briefs. Scattered tattoos decorated his muscled body, the one I'd used to excuse all of his hideous behavior. Before he'd started hitting me, of course; no amount of muscles in the world could excuse that.

I focused on the gun dangling from his left hand as he walked toward me.

Sauntered.

Like he was trying to seduce me.

I had to get the gun from him if I had any hope of surviving.

"Get away?" I parroted as he approached the other side of the bed. "Of course I'm trying to get away, dipshit. The thought of you raping me would have me gnaw my own fucking hand off if I could reach it," I hissed through my teeth.

I knew it wasn't smart. Being docile, vulnerable, and weak would've been his preferred version of me. It definitely would've stopped him from backhanding me so hard that my head snapped back painfully against the iron of my headboard.

But I wasn't docile. And I certainly wasn't weak. And no way was I ever going to act like anyone's preferred version of me. Especially not my would-be rapist and murderer.

As I recovered from the hit, he positioned himself on top of me, pressing against all my bruises so his face was inches from mine.

"You're a fucking stupid bitch, you know that?" he rasped, his voice stinking of Jack.

My fucking Jack.

"You think because your brother is the president of some motorcycle club that you're untouchable? You think you can act how you want? Talk to me like that without fucking consequences?"

The hand not holding the gun to my temple traveled down to squeeze my nipple roughly and painfully.

It wasn't the pain that had me blinking back tears, it was the degradation of it all. The helplessness. He was victimizing me.

"You're about to see consequences," he whispered, his mouth at my neck. His hand continued downward, leaving trails of pain and disgust in its wake until he reached my panties.

He didn't hesitate, ripping at them, his hands rough and painful as he groped me.

As they went inside.

Violated me.

It took every single ounce of my strength not to let my tears fall. Not to squeeze my eyes shut. Not to beg.

Instead, I met his stare, unblinking, unyielding, challenging.

"You're going to die," I croaked, my throat raw, my mind itching to escape the present, the horror of what he was doing. What he was going to do.

I'd witnessed it.

The women in my life going through stuff like this.

Laurie went through this.

Bex went through this.

Laurie died.

Bex survived.

I'd always been so angry at Laurie's fate. Cursed every deity out there.

Now, as I was experiencing only the horrific appetizer of what she was exposed to, I was wondering who was luckier, Bex or Laurie.

Because as Kevin continued to violate me, my body was not my own anymore. The one sacred thing that was ours in this world was being trashed and tarnished. Not just my physical body but my mental one.

I wanted to be like those strong women survivors you read about, who talked about their body being taken but not their soul.

I'd always thought I'd be one of those women.

Always considered myself strong.

That was until the second his fingers went inside. Clutching at my soul and shredding it. Dirtying it. Showing me just how fucking vulnerable it was.

"You're nothing," he hissed in my ear, pressing down on me.

He moved and his hand wasn't inside anymore. It was yanking at my panties, and I knew his intention.

"Fuck you," I whispered.

Then I lifted my hips with a rush of adrenaline that gave me enough strength to buck him upward and backward, obviously not expecting the sudden fight.

I didn't hesitate to kick at him, the heel of my bare foot hitting the bottom of his chin, the resulting crunch of bone sending waves of satisfaction shooting through my body.

Whether it was intentional or whether the shock and pain caused him to squeeze, Kevin fired the gun at the same time he grunted a wet, pained sound and tumbled off the side of the bed.

Luckily for me, the way his hand was positioned meant that

the bullet went upward, into my ceiling, instead of horizontal, into my forehead.

I hoped that gunshot was enough to get the cavalry coming.

I was friendly with my neighbors, older couples and a young family. Not people who I'd want to endanger themselves by intervening. But they were also born and bred here, which meant they knew who to call.

No, not Ghostbusters.

Or the cops.

My heart clenched at that thought.

Luke.

In that little part of my brain that I pretended I couldn't hear, I'd been thinking about him. Replaying all of our moments. Regretting being such a fucking coward. Thinking about choosing a man who would rape and kill me because I was trying to escape the man who would die for me.

That was not to be thought about.

Survival was top of the list at that juncture.

Kevin scrambled up, blood pouring from his mouth.

"Yu-ooh bitch," he spluttered, blood and bits of his tongue he'd bitten off flying onto my white comforter.

He took a shaky step forward at the same time he lifted the gun. His eyes glinted with something that had me thinking my survival was not looking good right now.

"Yoo-u're dead. You're fucking—"

The gunshot cut him off.

Just not the one I was expecting. Not the one that splattered my own brains across my comforter.

Just his.

I blinked against the blood and brain matter covering me, against the ringing in my ears.

A figure rushed toward me, muffled shouts of concern addressed at me.

I expected the figure who'd just murdered a man to save me to be wearing a Sons of Templar cut.

I did not expect it to be wearing a uniform.

I did not expect it to be Luke.

But that little part of me, that part that I had no choice but to listen to, she was more relieved than anything else in the world.

He'd just killed someone for me.

He'd just ruined his fucking life for me.

He wasn't clean anymore.

We'd be tainted together.

There might've been a small chance for us now that we were both sinners.

So why didn't it feel better?

LUKE

The gunshot had paused everything and also sped it all up. Not the one that came from his gun but the one before that. That had come from Rosie's.

As she'd killed a man right in front of him.

As she'd killed a man for her family.

Put a mark on her soul for them because, in her mind, she had no other choice.

He hated her a little in that moment, for chipping off another piece of herself, amassing more demons for her to fight against, sacrificing part of her peace so her family could have justice.

Revenge.

He hated her a little, but he'd never loved her more.

And that made him hate himself.

Because he didn't feel disgust watching her murder someone. At her doing it because she knew he wouldn't arrest her.

That was Rosie.

She would never sit around and wait for someone to solve things for her. Save people for her.

She'd save everyone. Even if it killed her. Wouldn't blink.

She was the strongest person in that club. She *was* that club.

He'd known it all along, of course. Just hadn't admitted it to himself. Hadn't let himself. Had some warped fucking idea that he'd save her from it.

His version of saving her was her version of him fucking destroying her.

He saw that now. In her eyes after she'd killed that man. He was a despicable human. Luke knew that. Rosie would never end someone's life if they had even a shred of humanity lingering in their soul.

That didn't make it right.

Not Luke's version of right, at least.

But Rosie's was different.

Didn't mean it was wrong either.

He saw it all, all his fucking mistakes in that lingering moment that paused after that gunshot. Then it sped up. And he found himself in his cruiser, driving away.

Like his father had that day.

For different reasons, perhaps.

But he got it now. Why his father did it.

And fuck if he wasn't furious at himself for punishing his father too.

He'd driven around. Not to the station, though he fucking itched to walk in there, hand in his gun and badge and be done with it all. Those hours were a blur of running through the years, inspecting how majorly he'd fucked up while believing he was doing the right thing.

Believing that trying to end the Sons of Templar was somehow a noble cause.

And maybe it had been. At the start, when they were running guns, when there were dead bodies littering the battle lines of their war. When Laurie was murdered.

When he'd had to sit in front of two innocent people and tell them they're even more innocent only fucking child had been brutalized and then murdered. Because of no other crime but loving the wrong person.

But even then, his cause, his noble fucking cause, had poisoned into a vendetta.

And when the club started going legit, when they started learning from their mistakes, when they started to try and live their version of a normal life, that's when he should've stopped.

Should've shrugged off his hate, buried his hypocritical self-righteousness and inspected his own mistakes. Tried to learn from them.

But he didn't.

Somehow along the way, he'd become worse than the men he'd considered criminals.

"Fuck!" he roared, slamming his hands on his steering wheel.

He'd been driving around like a coward for all these hours because he didn't know where to go.

He still hadn't learned from his fucking mistakes.

It was like that day when he was a kid all over again, his dad driving the cruiser away, abandoning the girl.

But this time he had control. This time he didn't have to abandon the girl.

He couldn't save her, because she didn't need saved. But he could fight for her. And fucking save himself.

He hurried across town to her house, though he didn't exactly know why. He'd waited thirty years for this; what was a few more minutes?

But when you'd waited thirty years, a few minutes was everything.

Life and death, as it turned out.

He folded out of his cruiser, not quickly, but not casual either.

173

His gait was purposeful, bordering on impatient. He knew then that it would likely be one of the last times he climbed out of that cruiser.

His only regret was that he hadn't done this sooner.

All thoughts of firsts and lasts went out the proverbial window when he was halfway up Rosie's path.

When a gunshot filled the air.

A muted gunshot.

Coming from inside Rosie's house.

He didn't think, didn't hesitate, just reacted. His piece was off his hip in moments. He kicked Rosie's door down, not thinking, not caring about the fact that he could get plugged with bullets crashing in.

He didn't. Which meant it was coming from farther back in her house.

Her bedroom.

He hadn't hesitated when he'd heard the shot, but he did freeze for a moment once he got into the doorway of Rosie's bedroom.

When he glimpsed Rosie cuffed to the bed. Bruised. Battered. Almost naked.

Even his heart froze witnessing that.

Then it didn't.

Then he found the justice that he'd been serving wrong his whole life.

He found justice in revenge. In murder.

It wasn't as hard as he thought it'd be. It wasn't hard at all. In fact, breathing was a trifle fucking harder as he stomped over the dead body to the bed.

The bed where a broken Rosie lay.

She blinked at him—one eye only, the other swollen shut.

It took everything Luke had not to turn around and empty his clip into the half-headless body behind him. Rage, white hot, burned through his body, at a rate he had never before experienced.

"Luke?" a small voice croaked.

It was that small, quiet voice coming from the loudest and bravest women he knew that had him check that fury running through his veins.

It had him mask his flinch at seeing her ripped panties halfway down her thighs.

He tasted ash.

"Shhh, baby, you're safe now," he murmured, putting everything he had into gentling his voice.

In an action that was the hardest thing to do in his whole fucking life, he gently pulled up Rosie's ripped panties, his body vibrating as he did so. He didn't let himself think of that right now. He had more important things to worry about.

The most important thing.

Rosie.

First he shrugged off his jacket and covered her, cataloguing every inch of her bruises, feeling the blows in his own body.

Then he used his universal key to unlock her.

He caught her arms as they collapsed, rubbing her red and raw wrists as if he were rubbing the wings of a dove.

"He's dead," Rosie said, her voice disembodied. Empty.

Luke broke at that point, pulling Rosie into his arms, gathering her up.

"He's dead," he whispered.

And then she clutched his shirt and sobbed.

And Luke vowed to make sure for the rest of his life that she would never have a reason to sob like that again. That nothing would break her again. That he'd shield her from everything and anything.

ROSIE

Luke got rid of the body.

Cleaned up the blood.

Cleaned up my mess.

Cleaned me up.

That was after he lost the battle taking me to a hospital.

But he won another one.

A big one.

The fight that my broken and Fucked-Up soul tried to wage in the wake of the shooting. After he'd killed for me, came to my bedside, demanded I be taken to a hospital.

After that, he'd sighed, glared, swore, but respected my wishes.

He stroked my hair, so soft and tender that it somehow hurt more than any of the hate-filled blows.

"I'll fix you up," he lied, like such a thing was possible. "Your first aid kit in the bathroom?"

Most people weren't prepared enough to have comprehensive first aid kits. That was only in the movies. But then again, most people weren't me.

So that meant I had implements to treat everything up to a bullet wound in my bathroom.

I nodded.

He leaned forward and kissed my head. I closed my eyes to hide the tears that welled up at the gesture.

Then I watched him stand, eye me for the longest moment, turn, step over the dead body beside my bed and walk toward my bathroom.

The way he did that, stepped over that body without a glance, while wearing his uniform, something about that hit me. Sent me plummeting back to reality.

"You should go," I blurted, awkwardly and painfully getting up.

Luke didn't hesitate in turning and glaring at me. "No. You're not doin' this shit," he growled.

I frowned. "What shit, Luke? I'm doing you a favor. I'm not going to make you do this, break more laws for me tonight. I can't." I choked out the last two words. "I've got people, family more accustomed to dumping dead bodies where people like the law can't find them. That's their life, for better or for worse. They're used to bloodstains. I'm not letting you become used to them too. Not for me."

He stepped forward purposefully, stopping at the edge of the pool of blood originating from Kevin's head. "Clue in, Rosie. I'm plannin' on doing everything for you. Anything," he declared. "I've got a lot of time to make up for. A lot of mistakes to make up for."

I fought against the impact those words had, almost pushing me off my feet. But I had to fight.

Not for me.

For him.

"See, I think you've got some image of me, some little fucking made-up version of Rosie in your mind. The sweet girl who lost the genetic lottery and was raised by wolves. The little princess who you've now noticed needs saving and have taken the job of doing so." I pointed my gun to the body on the floor. "In case you haven't noticed, princesses don't murder men right in front of the police officer they just happen to...." I caught myself before I said *they just happen to love.* Then I continued, like the stutter in my speech and the hole in my shield hadn't been revealed. "In case you haven't noticed, I'm a wolf too. And I'm not ashamed of that. I've never been ashamed of who I am. Until you look at me like that. And despite how much I love my family, how I've learned to love myself, this little evil, fucked-up part of me hates all of that. Everything that makes me *me*, because that's exactly what stops you wanting me. And that fills me with so much self-loathing I can't even breathe around it. Around you."

His face contorted in pain at my words. Real pain, like I'd taken the broken edges of myself, made them tangible and sliced through his chest with them.

"Rosie. I—"

I held up my hand, both to silence him and to physically stop his advance. I needed the distance between us right then, nothing else holding me together but the empty ear that pressed against me with our separation.

"No," I snapped. "I'm not done." And I wasn't. I was on a roll. It happened now and then when I was really excited or really pissed off. Or, as I was quickly discovering, when I was really fucking heartbroken.

"This Rosie, you've made her by taking the real me, warts and all, and smashing me into little pieces. And you've scooped up the things you like about me, the things that are convenient about me, glued them all together and made a little mosaic of me. The broken pieces that are unused are the things that are inconvenient to you. Things that don't work for you. My little transgressions, both by purpose of identity and accident of biology." I sucked in a painful breath. "You see, those things that you've left out of your little mosaic, left to be swept up and discarded? Those are the integral things that make me *me*. And despite what I want from you, despite the fact that I want—" I stuttered on the word I almost said. *Everything. I wanted everything.* I straightened my shoulders. "Despite the fact that I want something different than the situation we find ourselves in, I won't break myself in order to make that happen. I won't let you break me to do that either."

It was a lie, that last part. He'd already broken me. At five years old, I was split in two with the love for exactly who I was and that ugly and secret yearning to be anybody else as long as it was someone Luke could *see*.

Luke waited a long time after I'd spoken the last word. Presumably for me to decide I wanted to say something else. Not that I could; I'd yanked out every single word from its hiding place in those soft parts of me and flung them at him like bullets.

The chamber was empty.

I watched him and came to the conclusion that he wasn't just waiting. He was inspecting my words like he might the statement of a criminal, testing them for inauthenticity, to see if he could find the lie.

"You think I want to break you?" he said finally, voice clear and even, eyes granite.

I fought to mimic the blank look on his face. "No, I don't think you want to."

He continued to stare, mulling over my harsh words with lack of elaboration. "You may be right, Rosie," he murmured, the coolness gone from his voice as vulnerability snaked in. "Despite me wanting to rip off my own arm before I let hurt come to you, before I hurt you myself. You're right and you're wrong. It's not the things that are... inconvenient"—he frowned using my word, as if it tasted bitter—"about you that I want to discard. It's the things about myself. Those things I want to rip out but can't, because they're like fucking barnacles clinging to the inside of me. I can't fucking get them off."

He stared at me, his gaze juxtaposing the desperation in his voice. "But I'm not the only one who wants to leave broken pieces at my feet. You're making your own mosaic too, babe, no matter which way you look at it. You're focusing on all the things that are part of you keeping us apart. But you've made your own version of me, out of the broken pieces you've chipped off. The ones that are too shiny, too much of a mirror to show you a little piece of reality. The reality that you've been using excuses and your love of your family to forsake your happiness."

I stared at him. For a long time. Under normal circumstances, it would've been a long time; when I was dirtied, inside and out, beaten, and smelling the pungent aroma of death that circled around the room, originating from the body on the floor, it was a lifetime.

Maybe more than one of them.

Maybe it was all the lifetimes I could've had, that *we* could've had if we'd made different decisions, if we were different people.

But no matter how many times I changed my hair color or my wardrobe, I was always going to be the same person.

So was Luke.

And our decisions, like his to pull that trigger minutes before, they were as lasting as a scar. They were there in the flesh of our past, were obscuring the growth of something new for the future. Obscuring it altogether.

"My happiness?" I repeated. "And what would you know about that?"

Luke watched me, his face struggling with different emotions. By the way he held his chin, I knew he was frustrated, even beyond that, at the fact that we were standing there having that conversation while I was hurt. We were having that conversation before he could help me.

He couldn't.

His face also showed something else. Tenderness, but something intense as well, a full glimpse at what he'd only hinted at through the years.

His feelings for me.

Perhaps his love for me.

The thing I'd wanted him to show my entire life. To acknowledge. You always think you want your dreams and fantasies to come true, but then when they enter the realm of reality, they're tainted, blackened, and tarred by that reality.

It didn't matter. I realized that. We could both want each other, but we couldn't have each other.

He stepped forward, though he couldn't completely, considering there was a dead body between us and all.

He frowned down at it for a beat, then stepped over it, without even blinking, so he could frame my battered and bloodied face in his hands.

"I'll admit that I don't know much about your happiness," he rasped. "About being the reason for it. For making it. But I'm gonna learn, babe. I want to learn. I've wanted to learn my whole fuckin' life, Rosie. I was just too fucked up."

"I'm fucked up too," I whispered.

He eyed me. "So let's be fucked up together." It was an invita-

tion, that look, those words, the fact that he'd stepped over the
body he'd created to get to me instead of stepping away from it to
call it in.

It was that pivotal moment.

And I knew what I needed to do.

But I wasn't strong enough to do it then. I was going to treat
my broken and battered self to a taste of the fantasy.

"Okay," I whispered.

He patched up all of my outward bruises, his face hard, eyes
soft. His hands moving over me so lightly it was like they almost
didn't touch me at all. At the same time, his touch felt heavy,
grounding, like without it I'd float away.

And I'd let him.

Do all of that.

Take care of me.

I didn't rattle on about how I could do it, about feminism,
about how strong I was, about my lineage and ability to handle
such situations.

Because if I said any of those things, I would've lied.

I was done lying to Luke.

So I let him take care of me.

He didn't say a word while he did so, maybe sensing that I
couldn't speak, that all of my energy was going toward trying to
patch up my insides as well as my outsides. He didn't demand
answers as to how it happened, why. Didn't order me to call it in.
In fact, he very purposefully ripped off his badge and set it on my
nightstand.

It was a gesture.

A big one.

Huge.

One I couldn't do anything with, couldn't even process.

That didn't mean I didn't stare at that shiny piece of metal
lying against the lipsticks and body creams on my nightstand.

That didn't mean I didn't feel it stare back at me.

"Rosie?"

I jerked my head up.

Luke stood at the edge of my bed, white shirt stained with blood, hands stained with blood.

Soul stained with blood, a voice I didn't recognize told me. *Because of you.*

I looked behind him. To where the dead body used to lay. To where a puddle of blood had stained my rug, seeped onto my polished hardwood floors.

The body was gone.

Same with the rug.

And the blood.

I wondered where he put him. Why he didn't call it in. How much time had passed.

I didn't ask any of those questions.

I met his eyes. "Have you ever killed someone before?" I asked, my voice flat.

He flinched, though I wasn't sure if it was at my question or at the unfamiliar tenor of my voice. There was a long silence as he stared at me. Very long.

"No," he said finally.

I hid my flinch.

"Neither had I," I whispered. "Well, technically I have, I guess. But today was the first time up close and personal." I laughed without humor. It was ugly and empty and I hated it. "Guess I popped both our cherries today."

Luke's stiff body moved, as if he couldn't hold himself away anymore. He knelt at the bed. Then, not taking his eyes off me, he slowly moved his hands, making a point of showing me his intention, giving me the chance to stop him.

I didn't.

He gently cupped my face. "I've got a lot of regrets in my life, Rosie," he said. "A lot. Fair few of them involve the beautiful woman I'm lookin' at right now."

I flinched. And I didn't hide it that time.

His brow narrowed. "Don't you come to your own wrong conclusions hearin' that," he ordered. "None of them are because of you," he said firmly. "They're 'cause of me. 'Cause of the wrong things I did, the right things I failed to do. 'Cause of my fuckin' archaic views of what constituted right and wrong. Of all the things I regret in this life, pulling that trigger will never be one. Never." He pulled my head slightly toward him. "You're not gonna try and put it on you, tell yourself the fault lies with you for what I did. Because that's bullshit. There are some good things I've done in my life, and I hate to say there's not enough that involve you. I intend on changin' that. But if there's one truly good thing I did, it was murder that piece of shit. My conscience is clear on that count."

I blinked at him. And then stared at him for a long time. There was a lot to process in that monologue. A lot of things I could've said. A lot of things I wanted to say.

"The blood," I said instead, looking between us.

"What?" Luke followed my gaze, as if he'd forgotten we were both covered in it.

Him more so.

I tried not to dwell on that.

"Shit, yeah, okay." He stared at me. "You gonna be able to get up, Rosie?"

I didn't answer, ignoring the pain as I sat up, swinging my legs to touch the floor that stank of ammonia.

The room was crackling with the strength of his anger, his frustration. I glanced to his fist, which was eye level. It was clenched so hard the smooth tanned skin was whitening under the power with which he was restraining himself. From helping me up.

He wanted to. More than wanted to. I guessed every inch of him needed to. It was his job, after all, protecting those people who couldn't help themselves.

But I could help myself. I had to.

He'd already lost enough protecting me.

"Rosie," he choked out as I pushed to my feet, grimacing against the pain.

"I'm okay," I whispered, focusing on the floor. Putting one foot in front of the other.

The second I stumbled, I was no longer on my feet. I was in his arms.

I didn't even try and protest. I couldn't. Shame washed over me. Not at needing help, but at the warmth that spread through me from Luke's tenderness. That sick little person inside my head telling me that this was what was needed to happen to get *us* to happen.

I needed to blacken his soul so he had no choice but to come down to the gutter with me.

He brushed my sticky hair from my face as he walked us into my bathroom. "You don't have to be," he murmured.

I jerked my head up to meet his gaze. "Have to what?"

He set me down next to the tub, keeping one hand on my hip to steady me, reaching over to start the shower with the other. He straightened, cupping my face carefully, avoiding the worst of the bruises. "Be okay," he said. "Pretend you're okay. Be strong. I already know how strong you are, baby. Spent my life learnin' just how strong, so you don't need to convince me of anything. Don't need to protect me from it either. Know you live in a world where strength is part of the job description, but there's no need for that with me, Rosie. You don't have to do anything, be anything." His hard jaw clenched even more. "'Specially after today. You don't need to be fuckin' okay." His grip tightened, as if he momentarily forgot he needed to be handling me with care. "*I'm* not fuckin' okay. That shit"—he jerked his head to my bedroom—"is gonna be burned on my brain for the rest of my life. So I'm gonna have to spend it reminding myself that it didn't take you from this world. From me."

I blinked at him. My body hurt. Like a motherfucker. My soul was ripped, bleeding too. But those words ruined it.

Everything. Me.

They were everything I wanted to hear. Everything I hoped for.

But too late.

He didn't wait for me to speak, seemed to realize I couldn't.

Luke stepped back.

"I'll let you clean up," he rasped.

"No," I pleaded.

His eyes jerked upward.

"I need... I want.... I want you to clean up too. To clean me. And I can clean you."

I said it like it was possible. Like all I needed was soap and water to wash away the filth he'd attached to his soul. Because of me.

Luke's eyes stayed on me, his body jerking as he understood my meaning.

I expected a protest. For him to be the good guy. Tell me I was too vulnerable, that such a thing would be taking advantage.

For him to point out that great fucking elephant in the room. The one that had always been in the room. The one that stopped him, every day, every moment, from ever doing anything that would've had us right here. Together.

"Okay," he murmured.

I flinched.

I'd expected him to be the good guy. But he wasn't anymore. I'd made him into something else.

I hated myself for being so happy about it.

"Rosie?"

He cupped my cheek that was both hard and soft at the same time.

I blinked up at him. "Yeah?" I whispered.

Again, I expected him to ask me if I was sure, if I was okay. Again, the good guy Luke remained elusive.

"Take off my clothes," he commanded, eyes shimmering.

I didn't hesitate to comply. Maybe because I was scared that I'd only knocked out the good guy and he'd wake up at any moment. The sick, ugly part of me hoped he'd never wake up again the moment my shaking fingers exposed the column of his neck.

The other part of me, the part that had loved Luke for who he was, was sickened at the thought of what I'd done. What I'd made him do.

But that Rosie had been in charge for twenty years. She was tired. Weak. Vulnerable.

So the evil part of me continued to undo the buttons of his shirt.

He hissed out a breath when my nails raked at his washboard abs, scoring the taut skin.

I stared at it, his exposed torso, as his shirt fluttered to the ground. Luke's smell, his aura, engulfed me, both sweet and sour at the same time.

Both a dream and a nightmare being lived out in real time.

I was here, with Luke. Alone. He was half-naked. He *wanted* to be here.

"Now you," he growled.

I didn't even have time to properly listen, let alone answer, before his hands went to the shirt that swamped me.

The steam from the shower swirled around me, beads of moisture erupting on my exposed skin as the tee mingled with Luke's shirt on the ground.

He let out a harsh sound from between his teeth as his eyes went to my half-naked body.

Despite the heat in the room, I felt a chill, my nipples hardening from that and the raw, carnal look on Luke's face.

"You're beautiful, Rosie," he said. That time, his gaze wasn't on my breasts—which I'd always considered my best feature—but my eyes.

The way he said it, declared it, somehow told me that statement had nothing to do with my great rack. That it somehow had to do with whatever tarnished and broken soul I had left.

He kept his eyes on me as he lightly grasped my hands and brought them to his belt, undoing it using my fingers as puppets.

Flush warmed my cheeks as an uncertainty I didn't recognize blew through me when I started to unbutton his jeans.

I wasn't modest.

Far from it.

Physical nakedness was something I was completely and utterly comfortable with, something I didn't blink an eye at.

But peeling off his clothes wasn't just exposing his magnificent physical body. It was peeling off the clothes we wore over top of our souls every day. Exposing both of ourselves emotionally.

Stripping myself bare.

That, I was about to blink an eye at.

I wasn't physically modest, but I was sure as fuck emotionally modest.

And I was terrified.

Somehow the most terrified I'd been in this whole twenty-four hours.

Because maybe violence and death and pain were all familiar. Somehow comfortable. But showing myself, utterly and completely, to the man I'd been trying to hide my truth from, that was one of the scariest things I'd done in my life.

I itched to flinch away. To cover myself and my soul.

But I kept looking into Luke's eyes. Saw what he was giving me.

And I kept going.

Until he was completely and utterly naked right in front of me.

I stared at every inch of his chiseled and lean physique. The one I dreamed about and envisaged every time I had another man inside me.

And it was even better than imagination.

Because it was real.

"You're beautiful," I rasped, looking into his ocean eyes, communicating the same thing as he had to me. I didn't just mean the V pointing to his amazing erect penis. Or the powerful thighs. Or the sculpted biceps.

No, it was that thing inside him. The soul that wasn't all good, like I'd thought it was. The flecks of black that rippled through it somehow made it more than pure innocence and goodness could.

He reached out to trail across my collarbone and then downward, tracing down the side of my body until he reached my panties on my hip.

"Been dreaming of doin' that for as long as I care to remember," he whispered.

I swallowed the sandpaper of desire at my throat from not just his touch but from his admission.

That I wasn't the only one battling this, thinking about this for years.

The desire that threatened to overwhelm me was polluted the second his finger hooked into the edge of my panties, intending to bring them down.

My hand was a blur as it moved to circle his wrist in a violent grip.

Even though I was strong, that movement in itself wouldn't have stopped Luke. But the gesture did.

His hand stopped moving and his eyes locked on mine.

Filth settled over me as I remembered the last man who forced his way in there. The knowledge that my most private place wasn't my own. I wasn't my own gatekeeper anymore. I didn't have control over who went inside my body.

I nearly collapsed under the weight of the memory. Of that realization.

There had never been a wider chasm of how dirty I was and how clean Luke was. Because I was now. Because of the choices I'd made in a man, in a life, I'd dirtied myself, inside and out.

Luke went granite as I spiraled and started to shake.

I waited for anger, fury, as I could taste it in the air. And even though I was used to anger and fury, I was terrified of the onslaught. I'd never survive it. I'd shatter in a thousand pieces if I had to face that.

So I braced to be shattered, and then he pulled me gently into his arms. Like he knew how close I was to breaking. Like he would never let that happen.

And I let him. I burrowed into the safety of his embrace.

"He didn't r-rape me," I stuttered, my voice weak and foreign.

Luke's body was marble beneath me.

"Just so you know. He didn't rape me," I repeated, either to Luke or to myself, I wasn't quite sure. "He didn't quite... get there."

Then my body, like my voice, started to shake.

He kissed my hair. "You're okay, Rosie. I promise. You're okay." He stroked my back, his touch light. Then, carefully, he pulled me back just enough so our eyes met. "I know what he did made you feel like you're not clean. Gave way to some fucked-up reasoning that it's somehow your fault. I'm here to tell you, to promise you, that none of that shit is true," he said. "I'm here to remind you that you're beautiful and clean on the inside. Always have been. Always will be."

He let go of me with one hand to open the shower door.

"I'm gonna get you clean on the outside first," he said, walking me into the shower with my panties on.

The hot spray burst onto my chilled skin, shocking it numb for a second until Luke stood under the bulk of it, pulling me into his arms.

We stood like that for a while. I didn't know how long.

Then he cleaned me.

On the outside, at least.

And that was the only place he could.

Because no matter how certain he'd sounded before, I wasn't clean on the inside. Not after what happened. Not before, either. And before the story of us was concluded, I'd be tarnished more than ever.

CHAPTER ELEVEN

I awoke feeling like shit. Not an unusual occurrence since I liked to party hard, and partying hard meant hangovers.

And I also had experience of being punched, being in a car accident, and almost being blown up—and I knew waking up the day after was not fun.

But that morning was like all of those experiences packaged into one. Everything hurt. My eyeballs hurt. My ribs screamed. My cheek was on fire, the skin stretched uncomfortably tight over the bone, pulling at my face.

But that wasn't the worst of it. It was the wounds inside that worked to push against my lungs, chain me to the bed with the force of my pain.

My shame.

Kevin's fingers were inside me once more, shredding me, dirtying me, defiling me.

I clenched my teeth against the tears that wanted to fall, the scream yearning to escape from my throat.

I didn't for a lot of reasons, a big one being the smell of coffee and the sound of life coming from the direction of my kitchen. My kitchen rarely had sounds of life coming from it, unless it was the blender making margaritas. And since Bex moved out, there was never sounds of life coming anywhere that wasn't from me.

Luke was here.

It wasn't the cliché rushing of the events of the night before that came with waking. I knew what happened the second I opened my eyes. I didn't have a luxurious second of ignorance. My gaze wandered to the space where my rug used to be.

Luke hadn't left.

Luke was in my kitchen, presumably making coffee. By the sounds of the clanging of metal, breakfast too.

He was doing that because he was a good guy. And that was what good guys did for the women who they'd held in their arms the entire night, not letting go, giving them silent strength. Giving them silence.

My eyes went to the pinkish stain once more. Then, with pain, I craned my neck to my bedside table.

His badge was still lying there. I had a terrible premonition, looking at it, that it wouldn't be going back on him again.

Because of that stain.

Because of me.

He wasn't blaming me. He hadn't left. Escaped. He'd made a choice to pull the trigger. To dump the body. To take off the badge. To stay the night. To make me breakfast.

It was the choice I'd wanted, been waiting on for years.

But it was a forced choice.

I'd killed a man. In front of him. Forcing that choice.

Then I'd forced it even more by making him kill someone too.

My violent life caused this.

I yanked back my covers, intending on just as violently getting out of bed, forcing myself to stomp into the kitchen and end this beautiful thing born out of violence before I could make it ugly.

But the pain hindered that.

So I was forced to gently and gingerly get myself up, tiptoe to my robe, every step, every movement a jolt to muscles and bones that resented me for it.

The time it took me to get to the kitchen was also time for the smell of bacon to drift through my house. I followed it to see Luke's corded and muscled back, bare, in front of my stove.

I froze, all intentions forgotten with the picture of Luke shirtless in my kitchen. The back of his hair was still mussed from bed. The one he'd woken up with me in.

For a second, I entertained the idea that I could have this. That I'd wake up without all these injuries and pain, step over carpet that wasn't stained with blood, find Luke in the kitchen and not have to expel him from it. From my life. I could live it with him inside it. That we could somehow fit.

But when you loved someone, truly loved someone, you'd never shave away parts of who they were, cut them up. Which was what I'd have to do if I was to make Luke fit in my kitchen, my life. Cut him to be able to somehow slot into my life. Take away things that made him *him*.

I couldn't do that.

I wouldn't do that.

Because he was an alpha male, and a cop to boot, he sensed my presence.

"Rosie!" Within seconds he was in front of me, hands resting lightly on my hips as if he expected me to topple over. "You're not meant to be out of bed." He frowned at me, anger glittering as his eyes went over my face. Featherlight, his touch followed the pattern of what I guessed was an epic shiner. "If I could kill him all over again, I'd make it much slower," he gritted out, the fury and violence in his voice utterly foreign.

I flinched at that, the readiness to once again unleash something that wasn't meant to be inside him.

Because he was Luke, the good guy—kind of—he immediately pulled his hand back, fear that he was hurting me filling his eyes.

"Sit down, Rosie. Where does it hurt?"

He gently placed me in a chair and I let him.

He pushed the hair from my face, his own expression granite. "You need a hospital."

I frowned. "I don't."

He glared at me. "I hate that that's a fucking lie, but that doesn't mean you're going to go to one, does it?"

I gave him a smile. It was faker than the Chanel bags sold out of trunks in the Valley.

He frowned deeper. "Remember what I said last night, Rosie. You don't have to be okay here. You don't have to be strong for people. You don't need to shield your feelings from people who you're scared of hurting or burdening more. I'm not here because you need to protect me from shit. I'm here for the opposite reason. I'm here to be your fuckin' shield."

The intensity of the words stole all my oxygen, stole even my heartbeats. There was a second where it all hung on the edge and I almost did it. Let go of everything, let it overtake me, let Luke do that for me. Showed him the Rosie no one had ever seen me be.

Almost.

"Your bacon's burning," I said instead.

His face flickered with a lot of things, but then he turned, because his bacon was indeed burning.

He didn't rush toward the burning bacon. No, Luke didn't do such things. He purposefully turned his head back to me as he sauntered toward the smoking pan.

"This isn't over," he promised.

I waited until he had his back to me to reply, whispering, "It has to be."

I waited until after we ate, maybe because I was a total fucking masochist. Or because I just wanted one memory to hold onto.

Eating the breakfast that a shirtless Luke made me. Chewing on bacon with him across from me.

I could sink into a fleeting fantasy that we were that simple, breakfast and snatched glances.

Granted, he was watching me like a hawk, his eyes haunted as my bruises stared at him harder than my eyes did.

But it was all I could have.

So we ate.

He washed up.

I stayed sitting, watching him.

He sat back down. "You haven't called Cade," he said, observation more than a question.

I shook my head.

"You're not going to." Another observation.

Another head shake. "I'm not dragging them into this."

He regarded me. "They'll be upset, to say the least, if they find out about this. If they find out you didn't tell them," he said.

I narrowed my eyes. "Since when do you care about my family being upset?" I snapped.

"Since I realized they're an extension of you," he said quietly. "So them being upset is hurting you."

"You *just* realized that? It's not been a secret," I said, my voice harsh. "Especially not in the years that you tried to destroy everything I know and love."

His face was blank. "Yeah, and that's something I'm going to have to pay for. Rest of my life."

"What is this?" I whispered, not understanding where these forever promises were coming from.

His face was no longer blank. It was so full of something I thought I'd dreamed up. It hurt to look at. "You know what this is, Rosie. What we're meant to be. What we should've been all along."

I let those words swim in my soul for a little before I hardened myself. "It can't be. We can't be," I said, wishing my voice was firmer, more resolute.

His jaw hardened. "Yes, we fuckin' can. We tried it that way, that other way, for all these years. That way, that's what we *can't* be. Not anymore."

"What? So you bury a body for me and that counts as going steady?" I snapped.

He grinned. "You could say that."

I let the grin bounce off the shield I'd constructed in those moments, the one I had to construct or else I'd melt, thinking pretend promises and grins were all we needed to make things right. "It's not that fucking simple, Luke. I pushed you into this choice. You're here because I fucking *trapped* you. Stopped you from being who you are."

"That's bullshit," he growled.

I tilted my head. "Is it really? Because I don't know what the truth is anymore. All these years, you were so blinded by hate that you didn't see...." I caught myself before saying *'you didn't see I loved you.'* "Me," I finished lamely instead.

He pushed out of his chair, kneeling beside me so his hands were clutching either side of my neck. I thought he was going to speak some more. Say those beautiful words that hurt so much.

He didn't.

Instead he did something much worse.

He kissed me.

Years of running around each other, of lies and pretending and other people who meant less than nothing. That's what that kiss was.

And so much more than that. So much more painful than anything he could've said. Because it was magnificent. Perfect. Taunting me with what I couldn't have.

"Yeah, I was blind," he said huskily, pulling back. "Don't think the phrase is 'hate is blind,' though." His thumb moved over my bottom lip. "I see you, babe. I saw you. In black motorcycle boots at five years old. Beautiful and unique, even then. I watched you blossom into an incredible beauty, the most spectacular individual. But in the middle of something I could only see as violent and bloody and dangerous. Something that endangered my spectacular individual." He paused, watching me, drinking me in. "And I hated that," he continued. "Hated my visceral reaction to that. Because the idiot boy inside me thought that gave me purpose. To be the hero. And to be a hero, I had to create a villain. And I did that. Just didn't realize it would turn out to be me in the end."

I blinked rapidly, trying to recover from the life-shattering words. The life-shattering kiss. Trying to gather all the broken pieces of me together so I could make my escape.

"And that's just it, Luke," I whispered. "You're not meant to be the villain. *We're* not meant to be anything, period. I'm not living my life blaming myself for turning you into that. I can't." I shoved my chair back, ignoring the hurt in my body and my soul as I did so. "I don't know what this is now, this change of heart." I waved my hands between us. "But it won't last. You'll stop seeing me as the victim the second my bruises fade, and then you'll see me for what I am, or what you'll come to think I am. Just like my family. Which is something I'm proud of. And you'll make me ashamed of that."

I sucked in a breath, waiting for him to say something, to tell me I was wrong, anything.

The words didn't come.

"La douleur exquise," I whispered, almost to myself, in the moments that came afterward. "The heart-wrenching pain of loving someone completely unattainable." My eyes met Luke's.

And then I walked out of my own house, barefoot and bruised.

Hotwired my own car and drove around for hours.

I was hurting, hungry and exhausted when I got home.

To an empty house.

Though it wasn't empty. The emotional muscle memory of the past twenty-four hours pulsated from the walls.

So I packed a bag.

And left.

197

And ran.

Again.

LUKE

He let her leave.

It would haunt him for two hundred and forty-four days.

That knowledge.

Knowing that while he stood paralyzed by her words, shocked at the pain in them, he'd missed the pause. That moment, that lingering moment every woman gave the man she loved before she left him. Truly left him.

That chance.

That pause in the middle of the storm to give him a chance to grasp on to them, to her, fight for what they had before it was all too late.

Now it was.

Hindsight being 20/20, that pause lasted a lifetime, the memory of it taunting him with his failure.

He tapped at a thick file sitting on his desk in front of him. The one he'd been staring at, unopened, since the moment he got there at 7:00 a.m.

There was something beside that file.

His resignation letter.

He'd hand it in, but he'd given himself a few months leeway to train a replacement. Really, it was to utilize whatever meager resources he had to find Rosie. Hopefully it wouldn't take a few months.

He'd written the letter at 7:15 a.m.

Then he'd stared at them both, not really seeing them. No, instead he was staring at the memories that were both trapping him and out of his grasp at the same time.

"La douleur exquise. The heart-wrenching pain of loving someone completely unattainable."

At the time, he'd missed the moment, the pause. Barely saw it pass him by because he'd been blindsided by her words. The passion in them. The fucking pain and heartbreak.

All of that, he'd caused.

He would've utilized that fucking pause, fought until his last breath for them. That was, of course, if he hadn't been so blind.

It would haunt him, that last moment. Because it cost him a year. A year that had a thousand lost lifetimes crammed into it.

Not that he could know that while sitting in an office that felt cold and foreign, tapping at a file that contained his life's work.

He glanced down at it.

Opened it.

A black-and-white image of Lucky and Bex coming out of a warehouse. There were dark stains of blood on both of them. The next photo showed who the blood belonged to.

The man he'd later learned had abused Bex as a child.

He clenched his fist.

Turned another page.

Brock and Bull leaving the flaming remains of a mansion in New Mexico. The mansion where Amy had been held captive and tortured for a week. The home of one of the most ruthless and notorious criminals in the world.

He turned another page.

A sworn statement from the inmate who had stabbed Jimmy O'Fallhan, saying that Cade Fletcher had ordered the hit.

The same Jimmy O'Fallhan known for raping and murdering women. Brutally. The same Jimmy O'Fallhan who had nearly raped and murdered Gwen. Brutally.

He sucked in a rough breath, slamming the folder shut and pushing back in his chair.

The folder he'd been collecting since the second he got on the force. Waiting. Biding his time for an airtight case. It had been airtight for years now, but something had stopped him from doing anything with it.

The very thought of it felt wrong.

Because of the someone he'd be destroying, completely and utterly, if he did anything with that file.

Rosie.

But not just her.

The lives of all those broken and brutalized women who had been put back together gently and with care by members of one of the most ruthless outlaw motorcycle gangs in the country.

Luke rubbed at his jaw.

He'd be setting flames not to a handful of families, but to whatever chance remained for his future.

For his happiness.

With her.

That thought had him acting without hesitation. The file was flaming in the garbage before he even blinked.

He watched his years of work burn away in seconds.

He'd never felt like he was doing the right thing that whole time. Not really. He'd convinced himself that he was. Made himself think that so he could sleep at night. But this was the only time in all those years that he knew he was doing the right thing.

He wasn't happy as he watched his misguided and fucked-up form of righteousness burn up in flames. He couldn't be happy knowing that Rosie was somewhere hurting, nursing both physical and emotional wounds alone.

No way he could be happy with that knowledge.

But something settled inside him as the smoke dissipated and the flames started to disappear, revealing only ashes.

Something like satisfaction.

Maybe relief.

The door to his office swung open, rattling on its hinges.

"What the fuck have you done to her?" Cade bellowed, fists clenched at his sides as he stormed into the room, murderous eyes glancing around to make sure Rosie wasn't hiding behind the file cabinet. Satisfied she wasn't, the grim and hot fury of Cade's glare settled somewhere it was quite familiar with—Luke.

One of Luke's deputies scurried in behind him, hand on the butt of her gun, face flushed with uncertainty. "I'm sorry, Luke, but he didn't stop," she said, eyes darting to Cade like she expected him to shoot up the place at any moment.

Luke stood. "It's okay, Lara," he said calmly, eyes on Cade.

She swallowed, hand still at her gun. "Are you sure?"

Luke nodded tightly. "You can shut the door on your way out."

The quiet click of the door behind Lara seemed to echo in the loaded silence that she left behind. Though it didn't stay silent for long.

Cade stalked the remaining distance to Luke's desk, slamming his palms down on it, knocking off case files and framed pictures.

He didn't even blink at them.

Likely he would've if it'd been the Sons of Templar case file tossed open. If that case file wasn't now ashes that he'd never recognize being the end of his entire family, his entire life.

Not that Luke would ever educate him, or anyone, on that. He wasn't that much of an asshole. He was also ashamed of himself, not for making that file in the first place—he was a stupid kid who thought he had something to prove at the beginning. No, after, when he began to know better. Began to realize just how deep his feelings for Rosie ran. How deep they'd always ran. When he knew that using that file would hurt her beyond comprehension.

So it wasn't all selflessness that had him swearing to himself that he'd never utter a word about that file. It was the opposite, actually.

Cade's murderous face demanded his attention even more ferociously than his demons did.

"You have ten seconds, Crawford," Cade bit out, "to tell me what the fuck you did to her and where the fuck she is. After that ten seconds, if I'm not satisfied, and I suspect I won't be, I'm going to start smashin' shit." His fists clenched. "And I'm going to start with your face."

This wasn't an empty threat, Luke knew. Normally, with the club going legit and Cade having his family to worry about, even Cade wouldn't assault the sheriff in the middle of a police station for anything but the most extreme of circumstances.

His sister, his love for her, and the thought of something threatening her, were considered by Cade as the most extreme of circumstances. Luke didn't doubt that Cade would put a bullet in his brain right here and now if it meant that Rosie wasn't hurt for another day in her life.

Which was why, among many other reasons, Luke didn't say shit about the fact that Cade was threatening a police officer.

"I don't know where she is," Luke said instead.

Cade's façade flickered for a moment at his response, but he recovered quickly. "Like fuck," he spat. "Got witnesses that place your fuckin' cruiser right outside her house all fuckin' night two days ago," Cade seethed. "Two days ago, when she disappeared without a fuckin' trace."

Luke sat forward in his chair, suddenly choked with fear. "You mean she didn't say anything to anyone? Just left?" he demanded. He'd been haunted for the past two nights, sleepless. The only reason he hadn't torn apart the country looking for her was because he assumed she'd left of her own free will. As much as Luke hated it, she could take care of herself, better than most men could take care of her.

Especially him, or the man he'd been in the past.

But Luke knew how much she treasured her family, knew she'd never put them through the pain and worry that they'd be feeling to just disappear without a trace. She was far too fucking selfless for that. She'd cut her own hand off to spare anyone in that club a second of pain.

Cade didn't reply immediately, only stared at him.

Luke's own anger, fueled by fear and worry, erupted at that moment, and he pushed out of his chair so hard it clattered to the floor. "Tell me!" he roared. "Did you or did you fuckin' not hear from her that she was goin' somewhere?"

The fury in his voice almost scared Luke. It didn't scare Cade —the man lived in the face of fury every day—though it did surprise him. Luke could see that.

Cade didn't answer immediately. Luke knew it was a power play, and fuck if it didn't make every square inch of his skin crawl letting the asshole have it.

"Yeah, she called me, left a message. Texted Gwen."

Luke sagged. Visibly. Every ugly thought about her coming to more harm than she already did had rendered him immobile, the blame for anything happening to her settling firmly on his shoulders for letting her go.

"You better start fuckin' talkin', Crawford," Cade demanded, still watching him closely. "You sure as shit know somethin' about this, and I'll beat it out of you if I have to."

This was Luke's time to stare him down. "I don't doubt you will," he said. "Though you might wanna wait until I hand this in before you do, so you're not assaulting a cop." Luke nodded to the letter on his desk.

Cade's head snapped down. "What the fuck you talkin' about?"

Luke stayed impassive. "You know what I'm talking about. So you can beat me, shoot me, whatever, but I'm not sayin' shit about Rosie, because it's not my shit to say. I know you're tryin' to protect her. Know you've been doing that your entire life, in your own way. That's the only reason I'm talking to you calm-like. But you've gotta realize something that I've come to realize. Protecting Rosie is caging her. I'm sure that's the last thing you'd want to do with that woman, but it's the truth anyway. She can't be protected, because the greatest danger that she's ever gonna face is herself. I'd do anything to change that shit, but I know it won't." Luke eyed Cade, who was openly gaping at him. "That doesn't mean I'm not going to look for her, and I'm sure that doesn't mean you won't either, 'specially with all this comin' from me. But maybe it might make you think twice about chasin' her if you find her. Yanking her back to a cage."

Luke took out his gun and laid it on the table.

Cade watched, still gaping.

"I've got some chasin' to do, and I don't wanna have the law on my side when I do. Took a long time to realize that's my cage. Gotta chase freedom now."

And with that, he walked out the door. He half expected Cade to snatch him by the back of his collar and beat the shit out of him. He might've even deserved it.

But he didn't.

So Luke walked, unobstructed, toward freedom. Finding it, though, possessing it, that would take him through Hell and back.

Not that Luke minded. Not when Rosie was the destination.

CHAPTER TWELVE

ROSIE

PRESENT DAY

Up until the past few years, I hadn't been to many weddings. Scratch that, I'd been to one.

Ranger and Lizzie's. And I was young then.

I barely remembered the actual nuptials. No, I spent most of my time perving on the various attractive men from various chapters who'd come in for the celebration of love.

Or more accurately, the party and the booze.

Though I wasn't even legal, I did my level best to get myself wasted and laid.

I only got one of those.

Guess which.

You'd think getting laid in the middle of a biker party would've been as easy as getting wasted in the middle of the biker party.

That was not the case.

So instead of focusing on the magical taste to the air that only happened at weddings, I glared at my brother, sucked down beers and sulked.

I was a teenager, after all.

But all—kind of—grown up, I'd gotten to see that magic. Let it warm my heart that some of the best people in my life got to experience it.

Cade and Gwen.

Amy and Brock.

Macy and Hansen.

Mia and Bull.

Asher and Lily.

Bex and Lucky.

Killian and Lexie.

All of them, they got it. That wonderful magic.

And now I got to taste it, so strong it drowned out all the hospital smells, even chased away death for a short time.

"I do," Lucy whispered from her spot propped up in bed, eyes twinkling. I'd never seen anyone look more beautiful. Audrey was right, happy girls were the prettiest.

"I fuckin' do," Keltan growled before the priest could even get the words out.

Then, after a pursing of his lips, either to restrain a grin or in disapproval, he pronounced them man and wife. I would've thought that with Keltan's intensity, he would've snatched Lucy off the bed and kissed the shit out of her. I'd seen it before.

But he didn't. He paused for what might've been either the longest moment in the world or the shortest one. Staring at Lucy like he was trying to imprint her every cell into his memory. Then he slowly, purposefully, leaned down, taking her face in his hands, and he kissed her.

It was sweet. Beautiful.

And so very private.

So I subtly stepped back, letting them have their moment.

They deserved it.

Heath was grinning as he did the same, though he wasn't grinning at them. He was grinning at Polly.

She was scowling.

There was totally a story there.

Especially when she blew her distracted sister a kiss, winked at me, scowled at Heath once more and stomped out of the room. Heath stopped grinning and followed her, without acknowledging anyone.

I would've thought more on that if they'd been the only ones in the room.

My eyes went to him like a magnet. As soon as I locked with his, I knew he'd been staring at me the whole time. Though I'd known that the whole time. Which was why I'd made an extremely concerted effort to look anywhere but him.

Though my whole body repelled that idea. I needed to see him. Drink him up. Catalogue every change that had occurred in the year we hadn't seen each other. Both marvel and despair at it.

But I couldn't.

Because happy girls were the prettiest.

Heartbroken girls were not.

They were something sad and horrible and broken.

Lucy was not having sad and horrible and broken. Not on her wedding day that somehow still reeked of love and joy despite the lingering shadow of death.

It'd hurt.

It'd killed.

But I did it.

There was only so long I could do it for.

"Woo, congrats, you're hitched!" I said in a faux cheerful voice, my eyes ripping away from Luke to see the lovebirds had detached.

Barely.

Their foreheads were touching and they weren't even speaking. Just staring into each other's eyes. It somehow didn't make me want to puke. It made my heart swell in happiness for my friend that she got it, the 'it' that everyone wanted, pursued, even the ones who said they didn't. Especially the ones who said they didn't.

Me, for example.

So no, the moment did not make me want to puke with the saturated beauty and love of it all.

It did make me want to cry my fucking eyes out. Scream at Cupid for being such a prick to me that I'd love someone I'd never get to do that with.

I did neither of those things.

"Though the venue blows, and the lack of champagne is a bummer, it was a beautiful wedding," I continued, still smiling bright. "I'm going to... go and just... go," I said, unable to find an actual excuse.

Lucy frowned, but it didn't really work. Someone who was that happy couldn't physically frown. "You don't have to," she replied, glancing sideways at Luke, who I knew was still staring at me.

"No, babe, I totally do. It's kind of the point to kick everyone out after the I dos so you can, you know, do the nasty." I glimpsed at the priest. "Sorry, Padre."

He smiled. "You're quite all right."

I winked at him, then gave Lucy and Keltan a smile. A real one. "I'm so very happy for you two," I whispered.

Then I left.

I had to.

I expected to hear his footsteps chasing me down the hallway.

Dreaded it.

Hoped for it.

The footsteps never came.

ONE MONTH LATER

"I'm in love."

I sipped my wine, not even raising a brow at Polly's dramatic proclamation. "Again?" I deadpanned.

She scowled as she sipped at her own wine, eyes dreamy. "This time he's the one, Rosie. I know it. It's different."

I nodded. "I'm sure it is." I did my best to sound genuine, but it was hard.

Polly, bless her heart, fell in love as often as I fell into trouble.

She was the ultimate romantic. Believed in the fairy tale. Which was funny, since both her sister and I had always been adamant that the fairy tale was a load of shit. The only thing true about all those tales was in *Cinderella*—the right shoes can change a girl's life.

The wrong man can ruin it. Fuck, the right one will destroy it.

Polly had *a lot* of wrong men, yet somehow her life stayed intact. Well, her life was a hurricane, but it remained that way. As did her beautiful smile, unblemished by the bitch known as reality.

It should've annoyed me. On anyone else, it surely would have. But with Polly, it was different. I wanted to protect her delusion, not set her straight. I feared the day when she learned the hard way.

When some asshole showed her that.

Then I'd show him the sole of my size 9 Jimmy Choos.

"I know I've said this a few times before," she said, draining her glass and pushing herself up.

I restrained my snort.

"But I think that every time before was leading up to this, you know?" she asked.

I nodded. I had no fucking clue what she was talking about.

But then my mind went to that moment with Heath last month, the intensity that saturated the room, not drowning out what was coming from Lucy and Keltan but operating on a different plane. Lucy hadn't noticed because even though she had a stab wound and was wearing a hospital gown while getting hitched, she was on the love and rainbows and happiness plane.

You couldn't taste the heartbreak and difficulty unless you were suffering from something similar.

It was safe to say I was.

So I noticed.

And I'd brought it up with Polly when she finally did get home late that night and I'd been on the sofa, watching *Say Yes to the Dress* and drinking martinis. In sweatpants, but also in full makeup because that stupid hopeful shred of me that hadn't been killed—don't ask me how—by the years before had thought that maybe Luke would turn up on his slightly tarnished white horse and save the proverbial day.

He did not.

Men on white horses, tarnished or not, didn't exist.

Or maybe he had and I had killed him, and his horse too.

So she'd come in, face unreadable.Which was a change, considering Polly always wore her feelings on her beautiful face and her heart on her sleeve.

Both of those were hidden.

She'd been uncharacteristically quiet, and when I'd suggested that perhaps Heath was the reason, she uncharacteristically snapped at me.

I'd been so shocked at that, I'd let her stomp out of the room and slam the door before I knew what happened. It was her temporary room, since she spent most of her time at a loft apartment she shared with a handful of other free spirits I was vaguely worried about being in a cult. But she seemed okay, not planning on drinking any Kool-Aid.

She'd apologized the next morning, but nothing more was said about Heath.

So now, as she downed her wine and was declaring love and

something being different, with the Heath thought in mind, I maybe believed her. Because whatever it was between them was different. The kind of different her very own sister had. But then again, right then, she looked too happy for that kind of different. Because the real, life-changing, heart-wrenching kind of love didn't make you happy. Not at the start, at least. It made you miserable. Even well after the start, I was still fucking miserable. So I was confused.

Not that I dared speak Heath's name again. I just waited for Polly to educate me.

She put her glass in the sink, then checked herself in the mirror before snatching her purse up from the table below it. She turned, her face beautiful not just from bone structure, excellent hair and an expert hand at makeup, but from happiness. However transient that may be. She was glowing.

"He makes me feel different. Like he sucks up all the air when I'm around him and I can't breathe. I need him to breathe."

I frowned. I didn't like some motherfucker doing that, yanking a beautiful and kind girl into his orbit and bespelling her. And Heath, the way he looked at Polly, that told me he'd suck all the air out of his own body, forsake oxygen just to make sure Polly breathed easy.

"What's his name?"

She beamed. "Craig."

I frowned. No one should be beaming about a man named *Craig*. I itched to ask about the Heath situation, but previous experience told me I'd see it all soon enough. I really prayed my little hopeless romantic didn't have car bombs or stabbings in her courtship.

We'd had enough drama.

For me to say that, it was legit.

"When do I get to meet him?" I asked, wondering when Lucy and I got to set his car on fire.

Polly smeared some gloss on her lips. "Oh, soon," she said vaguely. "I'm just not ready to share."

I pursed my lips. That meant she knew that we wouldn't approve.

Not that we'd ever approved.

Her phone vibrated. She glanced down. "That's my Uber," she said.

I frowned again. "He doesn't pick you up?"

"He lives all the way in the Valley, so it makes no sense," she replied, leaning down to kiss my cheek. "I'll be staying there tonight, all going well."

And like the hurricane she was, she was gone.

I chewed my lip. Then I got my phone. "Wire, I need info on a guy Polly's dating," I said without hello.

"Another one? Jesus," Wire muttered.

This wasn't the first, or even the fourth time that I'd gotten Wire to check on Polly's boyfriends.

"It's Polly," I said in answer.

He sighed. "True. And I was getting a little bored. Was thinking of changing the nuclear codes just for fun."

I laughed, but I didn't doubt that's what he would've done. Wire was crazy. Not a Lucky type of crazy. Nor a murderous borderline sociopath Gage type of crazy either.

He was a computer guy. That didn't mean he didn't know how to handle himself in the 'real' world. He only looked skinny because he was surrounded by men who resembled Chris Hemsworth's more cut brothers. He was lean and kickboxed every day.

I knew that because whenever I was home, I trained with him. I had him to thank for a lot of my takedowns in Venezuela.

"His name's Craig."

There was a pause.

"Last name?"

"I don't exactly have one."

Another pause and sigh. "So you want me to look up a guy Polly's dating who shares a name with approximately two hundred thousand men in the United States?"

I grinned. "Yeah, well I didn't want to make it easy for you. If you can't do it—"

"I can fucking do it," he snapped. The tap of keys rattled behind the phone. "Just need some time."

"Here's hoping by the time you've got the information, Polly's moved on to someone who actually picks her up for dates instead of making her Uber," I muttered.

"Motherfucker did *what?*" Wire seethed. Another thing about being a Son. You respected women. There was a definite right way to treat them. And many, many definite wrong ways too.

They didn't tolerate any of them.

"Yeah," I agreed.

I had a bad feeling about this one. Something I couldn't put my finger on, but the feeling was familiar, like before all the shit went down with all of the other women in my life. There was a taste to the air, something about the way Polly's face looked.

Or maybe I was just being paranoid.

Though I had reason to be.

Maybe our life had reached its quota of disasters and rocky waters. Maybe it was time for some smooth sailing, finally.

Or maybe we hadn't even seen rocky.

"On another note, you did good," Wire said, jerking me out of my melancholy and grave premonitions.

"Oh I know. In life generally I do excel," I replied. "Though what specifically are you referring to?"

Wire chuckled. "Your little disappearing act. You almost got me too. Didn't even know about that third passport. And the diverting flight through Mexico. I taught you well, grasshopper. Too well. Almost."

I gaped in the phone. Wire hadn't just taught me how to kickbox, he'd also passed on some of his more basic hacking and counterfeiting skills too.

"I thought Cade said you couldn't find me."

"That's what I told Cade," Wire replied. "I hacked into the FBI before I started high school, do you really think I wouldn't be able to find a rogue Rosie in Venezuela? I found you, kept tabs on you, made sure you didn't do anything too stupid, like start the third world war, and then I left you to it." He paused. "Figured you needed it. You don't get much of that. Time. Peace."

I laughed. "If you were keeping tabs on me in Venezuela, you know the time I spent there couldn't quite be described as peaceful."

"It's all relative, chica. Chaos can be peace when wild is the way of life."

I stuttered at this profound thought coming from the man with a serious Vitamin D deficiency and an addiction to Red Bull.

"Okay, I've got to go search through the Craigs. Try not to keep me too busy, okay?"

And without waiting for a goodbye, he hung up the phone.

Wire was pretty social considering he spent eighteen hours a day with only a computer screen for company, but that didn't mean he was well versed in all social niceties. I liked that.

But I still didn't like the reigning silence that followed the abrupt end of the call. Since the moment my plane landed, I hadn't had silence. I had the hospital, all my ghosts screaming at me, I had my family in the waiting room. The family who, by chance had only just left after their second visit since I'd been back, with Cade promising he'd lock me up until I grew up if I got into any more trouble.

"You know I'm not ever growing up," I'd said sweetly.

"That's why I'll throw away the key," he'd grunted back, before yanking me into his hard and yet soft embrace, kissing my head. "Love you, kid. Don't disappear again."

I didn't plan on it.

But the second it all stopped, and I had a moment alone to realize it, I wanted to. I wanted to run to the edges of the earth. The only thing that stopped me was that I knew the silence would follow.

There was another one too, but I was trying to convince myself that he wasn't.

Because I hadn't heard from him in weeks.

I'd dreamed of him pounding down my door, us having a screaming match followed by the craziest sex that had almost two decades' worth of foreplay.

Dreams weren't free. Not when they didn't come true. They almost cost me everything.

Worse than that, I'd been scouring the gossip pages, as was my morning ritual now that I was back in civilization, and I'd seen it.

Luke's hand on the small of a very small back. Almost brushing a very perfectly proportioned and toned ass, encased in couture.

On a red carpet.

Oh, did I not mention that she was one of the most famous actresses on the planet. I used to like her. Now I wanted to make a voodoo doll in her likeness and snap off her perfect blonde strands one by one.

I hated that. I'd always been one to support my fellow women, never blame them for the actions of a man.

With a few exceptions.

Ginger being one.

But that was necessary. That bitch had a hand in Gwen almost losing her baby, in my brother missing out on months of watching his daughter grow in her belly. Had to suffer while he knew Gwen was at home grieving the loss of her brother without him.

I bled during those months, watching the pain contort my brother into something almost unrecognizable. He went so close to that abyss that welcomed all brokenhearted men and women, when their love was taken from them. The one that Bull, before

Mia, had resided in. A part of him was still there. I think a part of him would always be there.

Because I loved my brother, and loved my sister almost as much, I didn't pull any punches with Ginger.

I'd let quite a few of them loose, in fact. With a promise to put a bullet through her skull if she came near my family again.

It wasn't empty. I would've done it.

That memory, like most of mine, were connected with Luke, coiled up in my life, in the club's life like barnacles on a rock. Most of them tried as they might to rid themselves of it, but it wasn't going anywhere. Me? Even then, I would do anything for it to stay, no matter how much pain it caused.

I'd been icing my hand and salving my soul with a martini when the knock came.

I assumed it'd be Evie to drag me to the club to try and cheer Cade up. Again. Or Lucy to drag me to a bar. Ashley to suggest a girls' night in. Maybe Lizzie to ask if I could babysit. All of those were common occurrences. Not that I would ever have it any other way.

But for the first time, someone foreign to my doorstep stood there. Someone I'd never expect. Someone I never knew how much I wanted to be there.

Last time he'd been there, it was as an officer of the law, ready to accuse me but not arrest me.

I didn't say anything, I was that shocked. He wasn't in uniform. Most of our encounters had him donning the clothes that blatantly high-lighted our distance.

The white tee that clung perfectly to his sculpted torso and faded Levi's jolted me for a second. Because he could've just been a man knocking on a woman's door.

Simplicity.

But my life was never meant for simplicity.

Luke's eyes fastened on my bruised knuckles, his brow narrowing.

"You want to tell me what happened there?" he asked.

I swallowed my hurt at the tone. The cop tone.

This was not just a man coming to visit a woman.

This was a police officer coming to interview a criminal.

Again.

"Who wants to know?" I retorted acidly.

"I do," he almost growled.

I narrowed my own brow. "You, Deputy? Or you, Luke?" I pretended to pause. "Oh, wait. They're one and the same. I bumped it, Officer. Didn't realize that was a crime."

Luke's eyes turned liquid for a moment during my words, betraying something behind his façade. Not for long enough, though.

"Jesus, Rosie. You hurt your fuckin' hand. I just wanted to know you're okay."

I pretended the visceral tone didn't affect me. "I'm peachy, Luke. I'm always okay."

It was a lie. One of many I told when Luke was around. I told most of them to myself.

Like the one I was telling myself right then that his moving a little closer so I could feel his breath on mine didn't do anything to my heartbeat or my panties.

"You don't have to be," he whispered.

"Have to be what?" My normal tone was harsh against the soft air he'd created.

"Okay." He searched my face and his gaze was somehow like a physical embrace, like we'd tumbled down some rabbit hole where Luke could whisper to me like that, where he could look at me like that. "You don't always have to be okay, Rosie."

I stared into his eyes, the welcoming water in them, urging me to show myself to them. Emotionally skinny-dip in them.

I almost did.

Even leaned forward slightly so our torsos brushed.

But then, even I wasn't about to get into that much trouble.

I snapped my body back, so quickly I got emotional whiplash. "Whether I am or am not okay is not why you're here," I stated.

He stared at me with those liquid eyes once more before they solidi-

fied. "Saw Ginger this morning," he said, his voice firmly back to professionally detached.

Though that was what I'd pretended I wanted, it hurt.

I didn't let it show, of course.

"I hope you got yourself a course of antibiotics," I said.

He chose to ignore that. "She was pretty banged up." He looked pointedly at my hand, which I didn't try to hide.

"Being a meddling and evil whore is a dangerous job," I replied dryly. "You're at risk of having all sorts of accidents."

He pursed his lips.

"I'm guessing she didn't make a statement?" I continued.

I knew she didn't. She wouldn't. No matter how much she wanted to, no matter how much she wanted revenge, she wasn't that stupid.

"No," he gritted out between his teeth.

I tilted my head. "Then I don't exactly know why you're here, if it's not to arrest or accuse me. Not blatantly, at least. You've got no proof, no statement, so no need for handcuffs. I know you won't like to use them in the way I like, so I repeat my earlier pondering, why are you here?"

Luke's body was rigid, eyes glittering. He stepped forward and I itched to retreat, but I was too stubborn for that, so I let him come close, let his scent envelop me, his fury caress me.

"You know I'd never fuckin' arrest you, Rosie," he rasped. "You know."

He pressed the weight of his last visit heavily on the air, without saying anything.

I breathed heavily, gazing at him through hooded eyes. "Do I, Luke? I would think it'd be a prize, arresting one of the big bad outlaws."

"You're not one of them," he clipped.

I glared. "Yes I am. That's exactly what I am. You just can't reconcile that in your head. What do you want me to be, Luke?"

He stayed silent, eyeing me, not answering.

"Yeah," I whispered, then stepped back, not caring about it being a sign of weakness at that point. "You're so convinced that I couldn't belong to something you think is so evil just because it's not normal. It's *spectacular. Not always good, not always bad, never fitting into labels like that."*

My eyes found his cruiser, parked at the curb. I wondered how many people would see that, how long it would take to get back to the club. My gaze went to the perfectly manicured lawns beyond it.

"Look at it." I thrust my hand outward.

"At what?" Luke's eyes didn't move from me, seeming like he wouldn't move that gaze if the world was burning around us.

Or maybe that was just another little fantasy.

"This fucking lifestyle you're trying to preserve," I said. "This hamster wheel that begins with preschool, elementary, high school, college. Then a shitty entry-level job. Find a woman, one who maybe started out okay, but then due to constant demands, leaving the seat up, kids who ruin her vagina, a husband who ruins her identity, she gets shitty too. And then both of those people grow to hate each other, resent their kids, and hate themselves most of all. And they work at it, all of it, until they die." I wrenched my gaze away from the yards back to Luke's eyes. "And they're all wearing masks. All so fucking unhappy. That's what you're trying to enforce. A life like that. You're trying to destroy people who refuse to get on the hamster wheel, who refuse to settle for shitty and decide to look for spectacular instead. You're trying to ruin that because it fucks with your status quo. It's anarchy, and you live for order. You enforce order, so you have to destroy the spectacular. If I have anything to do with it, you won't. Because that's destroying me too, whether you choose to believe it or not. I'm anarchy too. You're order. Let's see who wins. I'm thinking it'll be neither, but I'll be okay with that."

"Rosie...," Luke said, his voice almost a whisper, all professional façade crumbling away with my words.

I didn't react. "Get back in your cruiser, Deputy. To your order. You won't find that here."

He looked at me for the longest moment, too long. Too short too.

Then he turned on his heel and left.

Emerging from the memory, I sat there staring at the rapidly

ANNE MALCOM

disappearing images of Luke and me, of the variety of interactions that had both broken and swelled my heart, if that was even possible.

I sipped my wine, hating that I was so fucking stubborn. Why didn't I find him? He was in the same city, for fuck's sake. It would be a lot better than sitting on my own, drinking a glass of wine and feeling sorry for myself like Bridget fucking Jones.

But then I thought of the image with that starlet. Of his life he was trying to rebuild that didn't have broken girls with wild hearts and chaotic lives blowing everything up with the drama that came with her.

That was her.

That was me.

So I sat there, drinking my wine, pining after a guy I couldn't have, like a million other women.

So fucking cliché.

220

CHAPTER THIRTEEN

ONE MONTH LATER

Settling into civilian life—well, *my* version of civilian life—was hard.

Hard for a variety of reasons. Killing people and risking your life on a daily basis became my norm for six months. Not just that, it somehow felt natural amongst the unnatural feeling of heartbreak and loneliness.

It jolted me, waking up somewhere I didn't have a chance of being shot at, raped or murdered.

It wasn't even that.

It was because when life and death was my nine-to-five, it made it easier not to let myself be consumed by my heart. Not impossible, because he was always there, even in the midst of the worst of it, but not so demanding in the forefront of my mind.

Because I'd replaced the blood I'd made him spill with the blood that I spilled. Waking up in a warm bed, in my own apartment, in my own country was not just a level of monotony but another level of Hell.

Because I'd stopped running. I had the memory of his skin on mine. His touch. His taste. How perfect he fit me. How utterly safe I felt in his arms. And it took everything I had just to function without showing what a fucking wreck I was.

Nights were the hardest. Daylight made it easy to see all the reasons why it wouldn't work.

Why it couldn't work.

A handful of weeks since I'd been back, since I'd been both praying that I didn't run into Luke and wishing he'd arrive at my door, I got my wish.

And it went exactly as you'd fucking expect. A complete Fuck-Up.

Lucy told me to meet her at the Greenstone Security offices for lunch.

I didn't like it, tempting fate by going somewhere he walked the halls. Where he worked now.

I didn't know if she did it because she was trying to push something I'd refused to even mention for a month, or because Keltan kept pretty tight tabs on her since she'd been released from hospital.

Maybe it was a little of both.

I walked into the offices absolutely fucking terrified.

Of course I looked absolutely fucking fabulous. I still hadn't put on the weight I'd lost since I'd been gone, but I was getting there.

That also meant I got to go shopping.

I was wearing brand new Jimmy Choos, studded, sky-high and completely badass. My jeans molded to every part of my body and were so tight I couldn't eat breakfast. I had a simple white tank on top, no bra, which was totally visible from the chill in the air, and my short curls were split into pigtails. Tendrils escaped and framed my face, which I'd chosen to put little makeup on except bright pink lipstick.

He wasn't in the foyer when I walked in, which was good. The receptionist informed me that Lucy was waiting in Keltan's office.

"Down the hall to the right." She smiled.

I tried to do the same and pretend that the hallway didn't look exactly like the one from The Shining.

I almost got there unscathed, but I wasn't designed to walk around life unscathed.

Luke came out of a door to my left, almost bowling me over.

His entire form stiffened as he took me in, his eyes roving over my body.

They stopped for a considerable amount of time at my chest. My nipples hardened visibly with the stare, and he hissed out breath between his teeth. Then his eyes dragged themselves upward, finding mine.

"You changed your hair," he murmured, his voice rough.

I swallowed against his voice, touching my pigtails self-consciously.

"I like it," he said.

"I didn't know you were going to be here," I whispered.

His dark eyes narrowed, losing all softness of before as he stepped forward. I backed up as he did so. "I bet," he hissed. "Which is why you're here, right? Still running, Rosie?"

I hit the wall. Nowhere to run at that moment. "No, I'm not running anymore."

"Yes, you fuckin' are," he growled.

Then he kissed me.

No warning, nothing. He was just there, his lips on mine, devouring all the words I was going to yell in protest, devouring every sense of strength I had left.

His hands found my breast, tweaking my nipple painfully and exquisitely. I pressed myself into him, running my nails over the tee on his back.

His hand was in my jeans before I knew what was going on. Then, just as he was about to reach the magic spot, the point of no return, I yanked my head back and circled his wrist with my hand.

"Luke," I choked out, breathless. "We're in a hallway."

His blue eyes seemed black. "Don't give a fuck, Rosie. I'm finally tasting your mouth and it's sweeter than I ever imagined. I can only imagine what your pussy tastes like. I don't want to fuckin' imagine."

My aforementioned pussy clenched with the sex dripping from his words, from the feeling of his hardness against my thigh. I could barely think straight.

But I had to.

"No, Luke, we can't."

"Don't you fucking dare," he hissed, yanking his hand back and caging me against the wall. "Don't spout that shit, now of all times. I've been patient, let you come back. I've been trying to let you come to this yourself because I know you're too fuckin' stubborn to let me force you into it." His mouth was inches from mine. "And fuck, do I want to force you into it right now."

I almost did it, almost leaned forward, captured his lips with mine and let him fuck me against a wall in broad daylight in a public place. The public place thing wasn't what bothered me.

"What, it's on your bucket list to fuck a murderer?" I spat, acid in my voice, hating myself for it.

He flinched back as if I'd struck him, and I hated myself even more. "What the fuck, Rosie?" he gritted out. "How the fuck could you even say that?"

"Because that's what I am," I hissed. "I blew up dozens of other murderers just like me for vengeance. I shot a man in the head right in front of you. And you knew about it, but you couldn't do anything because of this twisted painful thing between us. Because of the truth of what we are. What I am." I paused, breathing heavily. "And isn't that what you think I am? A mass fucking murderer?" I yelled. "I knew you thought that the day you came to my house with my necklace. The way you looked at me told me that, so why the fuck didn't you arrest me? Make your career instead of ruin it?" I spat the question I'd been burying for years, among others.

"I don't think that! Fuck, I was fucking proud of you," he yelled back. "I couldn't fucking say it out loud then, and I couldn't fucking say it to myself because my thought was never going to be to arrest you. My first thought was, and always will be, to protect you."

I simmered down, my anger deflating as quickly as it appeared, melancholy replacing it. "And protecting me ruined your life, Luke," I whispered. "Don't think I can forget that. That I can move past it. That we can. You know we can't."

His own anger remained. "I'll admit that I don't know a lot of shit, Rosie. Don't know why the universe saw fit to give us so much suffering and fucking pain for wanting each other. Don't know why, with a soul as light and good as yours, there's been so much dark to damage it. I don't know any of that shit. But one thing I do know is that we fucking can move past it. Know it in my fucking bones, and you know it too."

I stared at him. He was right. We could. But it would mean dragging him down even further. I wouldn't do it.

"No, I don't," I lied. "You're always going to be Luke, the cop, and I'm always going to be Rosie, the criminal. It's that simple."

"We're not fucking simple," he growled. "And I'll always be Luke, the man, and you'll always be Rosie, my woman. That shit ain't changing. But I'm not stupid enough to stand here and argue with you about it. You're determined to hurt yourself because you think you're doing the right thing." He eyed me. "Maybe it is the right thing. But I'm not about right anymore. Never want to be again if that mean's I'll never sink into that sweet pussy." He moved forward, so every inch of his body was a hair's breadth from mine. "And I will be. Just so you know, this isn't me walking away. This is you pushing me away. Not for good, but for right now."

Then he turned around and left. I watched the empty air for a long time.

Then I calmly walked to the last door on the right, opened it.

Lucy smiled at me, sitting on Keltan's knee.

I smiled back, pretending I wasn't bleeding inside. "Lunch?"

So yeah, light and its unforgiving glow showed me in stark detail why I needed to stay the fuck away. But then night came, the darkness snatching away all those reasons and whatever strength and resolve I'd built when the sun came up.

One night, I found myself lying awake, unable to sleep, unable to hold onto a thought that didn't involve Luke.

I needed a life without him. And I sure as shit needed a mind without him too. It didn't help that I was determined to make up for all the time I'd missed with my family, with my best friend, so I tried to see her as often as possible, help keep her insane while she fully healed.

That meant I ran into Luke. Not often, but even a second in his presence, under his cold gaze, was enough to fuck with me. Destroy me.

I was done with that shit. Heartbreak.

We normalize heartbreak in our society. Mostly because of how painfully normal it is. So when we hear a song, read a book, watch a movie, all crammed with the dramatic truth of it, maybe it reminds us that we're not alone. That there's more out there, and our heartbreak isn't the end of the world.

It's a nice thought.

But it's utter bullshit.

We are, and always will be, alone with our own pain.

And heartbreak may not make this chunk of rock in space stop spinning, but it is the end of someone's world. Despite how well we keep up appearances.

And I was walking, talking, laughing Rosie, covering up the pain, just like the rest of them. I thought I was doing good, great even, at hiding it all until Polly's wedding.

Yes, *wedding.*

She'd dated Craig for three weeks, then married the fucker.

We'd tried to gently change her mind, but she was like me: stubborn and would never let anyone change her heart. Which was funny, since she was jumping right in with her heart, and I was yanking mine right out.

We hadn't been able to find anything on the fucker, which meant we had to watch our beautiful, romantic, and innocent girl marry an idiot named Craig and pretend we were happy.

I was already pretending.

Or so I thought.

"So," Keltan said, standing beside me on the rooftop where the

wedding was being held, watching Polly and Craig dance. "How is it being home, back to reality?"

I gave him a sideways glance. "Wouldn't exactly call our life reality," I answered.

He grinned, sipping his beer. "You are not wrong, not wrong at all. You ladies get more action than I did in the desert in the middle of a war."

I sipped my own. "Yeah, well, that's just how we play it. We don't like boring."

"You're not at risk of that," he said.

We were silent for a second, watching Polly dance, watching a smiling Lucy talk to her father.

"He's a mess," Keltan said quietly.

My head whipped to him.

"Luke," he continued. "Has been since the day he sat down in my office, askin' me to look for you. Was before that too, I'd say. He's pretty darn good at hidin' it. Didn't know him before so I'm not an expert, but the man I've worked with for well over a year, he's not whole, babe. I know it 'cause that was me too." His eyes crept over to Lucy, unhidden love and devotion sparkling in them. "Thank fuck I am now. Couldn't imagine a lifetime of it. That's not a life at all." He turned his gaze back to me. "You're not whole either. You're trying real fucking hard. I'm not even going to be arrogant enough to suggest I know the shit between you. It's gotta be big, I'm guessin', for two good people to think they're doing the right thing, making themselves unhappy. Bet it's not fucking simple. But just in case you were thinking that he was livin' whole and happy and that's what was stopping you, he's not." He sipped his beer. "It's my piece and it's not my place to say it, but I don't give a fuck. You're Lucy's family, which means you're mine too. And I don't like my family hurting. Don't like my mates hurtin' either. So my place or not, I'm gonna do what I can to rectify that shit. Ultimately up to you. But just remember, he's survivin', not livin'. Just like you."

Then he kissed my head, not expecting me to answer, and went over to my soul sister.

And I stared after him, his words swirling in my head.

That was last night. And I should've done something to listen to those words. Because they hurt. Every single one of them.

But I didn't. Because I was a coward.

Instead I went out and did what I'd been doing in the darkness for the past month. I'd started the old job again. New location, no team, same objective.

Looking for lowlifes.

Teaching them lessons.

Maybe not my smartest idea, since the laws in LA regarding grievous bodily harm were somewhat stricter than in Venezuela. And I didn't have someone on the force to bail me out anymore. Though, in the dregs of society, wherever you were, life was always the same price. Dirt cheap.

So that's what I was doing that night, running away again from decisions, when darkness made my decision for me.

I'd been doing it for a month. Using my connections in the underworld to find out who the real assholes were. Not the ones who had to bend a few rules and break a few arms to get their heads above water, but the ones who ruined lives and trampled on dreams for sport.

"You know, you really give outlaws like me a bad name," I said conversationally to the man I had my favorite gun pointed at. That was, of course, after I'd relieved him of his own weapons. Couldn't be a full-time drug dealer and part-time rapist and not have somewhat of an arsenal.

"Fuck you, bitch. You're *dead*," he spat. "Do you have any idea who I am?"

I tilted my head at the man with a steroid-enhanced body, prison tattoos and too much jewelry for anyone with a Y chromosome.

"Yes, that's why I'm here, Jerome," I said, circling him. "I know *exactly* who you are. I know you cut your dope with kitchen cleaners to make it go further and rip off people already down on their fucking luck. I also know that a seventeen-year-old boy overdosed on your little cocktail just last week. Mother of three the week before. Police didn't find her for three days." I shot his foot and he let out a yelp of pain, collapsing onto the floor. "Her kids were surviving off moldy bread and curdled milk," I continued over his screams.

"You fucking bitch!" he yelled. "You *shot me.*"

I stopped circling him and aimed for his other foot, in my line because he'd stilled and was tending to the bleeding one. The gunshot was nostalgia, my childhood lullaby.

"Oops, look, I did it again," I said while he screamed. "That was for the kids." I bent down, yanking his head back by clutching his greasy hair.

Tears and snot ran down his face.

"Please," he cried.

"Begging? Already?" I tutted. "A man like you should be much stronger than that. But then again, you like to be the one hurting women, not the other way around. Like Chloe Thompson, walking home from a double shift at the hospital. Missed the bus, so she risked the walk because I guess she was dog tired and wanted to get home to bed instead of waiting twenty minutes for another one." I yanked my knife from my boot. "Now, a woman in any neighborhood should be able to walk home after caring for sick people all day. She should be able to go straight there, no trouble, since she gave the world no trouble herself and did nothing to deserve it." I paused. "In a perfect world, at least."

I ran the tip of my knife down his neck, drawing blood as I did so. "This is not a perfect world. So she didn't make it home. Some wannabe gangbanger tough guy comes across her. Knocks her out, drags her to an alley and rapes her." I pushed the knife deeper and he cried inconsolably. "Brutally," I hissed. "Now she's in the hospital, being nursed by people just like her. But now they're not like her, are they? You made sure of that. You made sure she'd take your despicable actions and place them on her soul. The one that holds not an ounce of blame for this shit. But she'll carry it. She'll fight demons never meant for her. Maybe she'll win. Maybe she won't. Maybe her life is ruined because of one fucking night. Just because there're assholes like you in the world who can ruin a woman's night, her life, when she was just trying to get home."

I had risen to somewhat of a screech by the end, and my knife had found its home. Right between Jerome's legs.

The wet sound of blood gurgling around steel should've made me sick. It probably meant something about my own soul that it didn't.

I pushed the dead weight of his body back as I retrieved my knife. I shoved it back in my boot and looked down, satisfied with the blood pooling at my feet.

"Maybe you'll survive this," I said. "Maybe you won't." I stepped over him toward the door. "And it's all because a woman missed her bus one night and decided to walk home. Because of you. Remember that, asshole."

And then I was gone.

I shoved my leather gloves in my pocket. I didn't really need them. If he did survive, he wasn't likely going to report the attack to the cops because it would mean them investigating his house, the scene. His house that doubled as a meth lab.

And if he died, the police would eventually find and investigate the scene. But it was corrupted enough with all the comings and goings that they would find dozens of suspects. I wouldn't be on the list, considering I didn't know him from Adam and didn't run with those types of crowds.

Plus, my prints didn't even exist in the system. Wire took care of that.

It was hard and very fucking risky, but he did it for me. He couldn't do it for everyone because the chances of getting caught and traced were higher. Plus, almost everyone had a record a mile long. Kind of hard to delete that shit from the system.

I had no record.

Not because I didn't commit any crimes, but because I'd never been arrested.

Because of Luke.

I walked out the door, not at all perturbed by the gunshot that rang out in the night, or the stares of the group of youths across the street.

Even with this shit clogging my mind, I still thought of him.

It was because I was thinking of him that I was caught off guard as I cut through the alley where my car was parked. I may have had zero to none chances of getting caught, but that didn't mean I was about to tempt fate by parking my car right outside the scene.

Cutting through the alley, I didn't think of the lingering stares of the boys as I passed, nor the roughness of the neighborhood or the potential for Jerome's boys to find him and then go looking for me.

Each and every one of those things could result in death or at the very least grievous bodily harm for me.

I didn't think of them.

I thought of Luke.

And I still thought of him as someone snatched my shoulders roughly and slammed me against the wall of the alley. The grip my attacker had on my shoulders was viselike and made it unable for me to grab my gun. I tried to kick out my legs, but his entire body pinned me.

"Are you fucking insane?" a deep and murderous voice hissed.

My gaze snapped upward, only then focusing on my attacker's face.

Luke's face.

"Of course I am," I snapped, only relaxing slightly. My heart was still thundering, despite the fact that I wasn't in any danger. Bodily, at least. "What does that have to do with you attacking me in a fucking alley?"

His glare was unyielding, angry, and foreign. It scared me for a moment, like looking into the face that you thought you knew so well, the man you'd etched into your soul, and finding a stranger.

"Are you serious, Rosie?" he growled. "You just waltzed around one of the most dangerous and crime-ridden areas of LA, into the house of one of the most deranged characters in this neighborhood, assaulted, tortured and maybe fucking killed him, and you're the one who's wondering why you're getting attacked in an alley?" he hissed.

His grip, which was before firm but harmless, was bordering on painful as his anger crept upward. Again, the stranger reappeared, and I wondered if the stranger was Luke now.

"Have you been following me?" I accused.

"Not exactly," another accented and familiar voice cut in.

My head snapped sideways to see Keltan's attractive face emerge from the shadows.

Luke's grip slackened and I stepped away from him. "What are you talking about?" I demanded, pointing all my energy at Keltan.

He leaned on the wall, casually. The man was so laid-back all the fucking time it was a miracle he stayed upright. Or pretended to be. In the times I'd hung out with him and Lucy, which was as often as possible, that mask slipped and you saw the man underneath. The man bracing for the next fucking horror.

He didn't look like he was bracing now; he looked like he was having fun. "Well, I may not be a native, haven't been here long, but I'm good at makin' friends." He winked. "Think it's the accent. You Yanks find us Kiwis exotic, of all things. Mad, but it works for me." He shrugged his impressive shoulders. "My friends have been filling me in on this new woman on the block, causing trouble for the scum of the underworld. Naturally, I thought of you. And I wasn't exactly tickled pink to find out I was right once I put Duke on you. Wasn't surprised, though. He was impressed, by the way. Taking down three armed men? Even some of my guys couldn't do that without at least a shiner to show for it."

"Yeah, well girls do it better," I snapped. "And it sounds like your employees must be lacking." I gave a pointed look to Luke, even though he was anything but lacking.

He was the opposite. All-consuming of the space he was inhabiting. He was in all black, so he almost melted into the inky darkness around him, but the lines of his body seemed to jump from the night air, hinting at his muscles beneath.

Luke glared back at me.

"Perhaps," Keltan said.

"So is this an intervention, or do you want me to take a workshop or something?" I asked, feigning impatience. "Because trust me, you couldn't afford me. And you definitely couldn't handle me." I directed that one at Luke too.

"We can fuckin' handle you," Luke seethed.

I tilted my head. "Give it a try, then," I invited. "Is that why you're here, to 'handle' the female?"

"No," Keltan said. "We're here—"

"We're here to ask you what the fuck you're doing?" Luke interrupted. "You think you're some kind of Robin Hood? Or do you think it's up to you to punish the guilty?"

I didn't blanche at his anger, his fury. "No, but I think it's up to someone to avenge the innocent, and I'm as good a woman as any."

Luke's glare endured. "You're a *woman*. Out here on your own. That's no place for—"

"Be very careful about what comes out of your mouth next, Luke. About what you say I can and can't do because of my tits. And my genetic predilection for being more awesome than anyone with a Y chromosome."

"You're not doin' this shit anymore," he said instead.

I raised my eyebrow at the same time I tapped my gun against my thigh. "Really?" I asked placidly. Calmly. In a tone that most men who valued their lives would recognize.

Luke's face told me he didn't currently value his life. Or at least he didn't take me very seriously as a threat to it.

He wasn't the first man to make that mistake.

He wouldn't be the last, either.

"Really," he gritted out.

The following moments could've gone a lot differently had it not been for Keltan, a man who did recognize my tone. Mostly because he was a lot smarter and because he was married to a woman who likely taught him about said tone.

"Okay," he said, fluidly stepping between us. "Let's not do anything we'll regret."

I smiled. "Oh, I won't regret it."

Luke's anger pulsated through the open air and he stayed silent, his version of disagreement.

I'd never met anyone more stubborn than him, apart from myself.

"Oh, I beg to differ, darlin'," Keltan said casually, his laid-back demeanor cutting through the tension rippling between Luke and me. "Now, how about you put the gun away and we'll chat."

I focused on Keltan and did not put my gun away. "Now, if your chat is going to entail you trying, in your endearing little accent, to tell me not to do something, I'll tell you that being married to my best friend and having a cute accent isn't going to change my answer to that question. It'll just reduce the curse words and death threats."

Keltan, instead of taking my threat as a promise, smiled. Instead of finding it supremely irritating, it was somehow reassuring, not patronizing as it most likely would've been coming from men who underestimated me—i.e. Luke.

"No, I'd never dream of doing such a thing. Unlike Luke, I actually value my nuts. I wanna have kids one day," he said, glancing to Luke, who was still glaring.

I idly wondered what the record was for the longest continuous glare. Luke was surely close to beating it.

"I'm going to offer you a job," Keltan continued.

I blinked and said, "Seriously?" at the same time Luke said, "What the fuck?" Actually, he yelled it.

Keltan, interestingly, didn't look at the man who'd yelled at him. He acted like he'd never even heard him.

Neat skill.

"Surprising, I'm sure, but I'm serious. I'm more serious about talking about this in a slightly more savory environment and with a beer in my hand. Fancy going to our place? I'm sure Lucy would love to see you and hear about your secret identity as Batman."

I grinned. "Although black is timeless and chic, my secret identity would obviously be Superman. I look kick-ass in blue, plus flying is *so* much cooler than driving an obnoxious car. Wouldn't mind the butler, though."

Keltan grinned.

Luke stepped forward, in front of me and right in Keltan's grill. "You can't be fucking serious right now. I called you here to help me stop this bullshit, not encourage it," he seethed.

Keltan kept his easy expression. "Now I'm sure you know Rosie better than to think anyone, especially us, can stop her from doing anything," he said. "Stopping her was never gonna work. I'm offering a mutually beneficial solution."

"It's not very fucking beneficial," he clipped.

"In time, you'll agree with me. For now, let's get off the street before the fuzz comes." Keltan looked to Luke. "Guessin' you're not ridin' with me?"

Luke shook his head once and Keltan grinned, turning to leave in the opposite direction of my car.

"Oh, the police are already here," I snapped to Keltan's statement, despite him walking out of earshot.

It wasn't for his benefit anyway.

Luke snatched my arm. "I'm not a cop anymore. You're well aware of that."

I thought I did well at hiding the pain his words held. "Once a cop, always a cop. It's those pesky morals. They don't disappear as easy as a badge does."

His eyes glowed in the moonlight. "You'd be surprised what doesn't disappear and what goes away completely," he murmured, half dragging me to the car. "Like me imagining the taste of your pussy on my tongue. Or the way it's gonna clench against my cock when you come. That kind of shit isn't gonna leave me ever." He pinned me against my car, my entire body pulsating with his words, the way they roused the memory so stark that I could feel his lips everywhere, despite his mouth being inches away.

"I'll be turning those imaginings into reality, make no doubt about that," he rasped. "But first, you're getting in the fucking car," he demanded.

CHAPTER FOURTEEN

M y downstairs area was pulsating as I sat in the car, my panties wet from just the pure sex in Luke's tone. As he got in beside me, I wanted to jump him right there, forget the rest of the other shit, my anger, our fucking heartbreak.

I just wanted him.

I was close, very fucking close to doing just that when he spoke.

"This isn't your job, Rosie."

I started the car, screeching away from the curb, seething in the lost moment, being deprived of sexual release.

"Well, whose job is it?" I snapped, hands tight against the steering wheel. "It's not yours anymore. And even when it was, who was it deciding what constitutes right and wrong and how wrong is punished? And more aptly, how to get off fucking easy? Huh? Fat guys in expensive suits with bad hair and worse tans are sitting in their comfortable seats in their big white houses, controlling things. Controlling the law. How it's enforced. Controlling what we think about the fucking world. What's good and bad. I've seen bad. Experienced it. Felt it. I feel like I know better than those fat guys what constitutes punishment, so I disagree with you there. It is my job, much more than it ever was yours."

"That's what you've been doing?" he asked, clenching his hands against his knees, obviously in male frustration since I hadn't let him drive my car. "Skulking around some of the most dangerous streets in America, asking for fucking trouble?"

"Well not just that. I also had a *Stranger Things* marathon. That show is the shit," I replied. "Plus, I don't go looking for trouble. I am trouble."

"Yeah, I fucking knew that. Just didn't think you were stupid."

I glared at him. "And why am I stupid, Luke? Because I don't know my place in the kitchen, in the nursery, minding the babies? Because I don't let myself be weak just because I'm a chick? I think that's reasonably damn smart. But I see from a man's perspective, one who thinks the man's job is to shield, protect, it could be perceived as stupid. Never mind that whole perspective being fucking stupid, not to mention utterly dated," I shot back.

"Fuck, Rosie, this isn't about whether I doubt your strength, or because you're a woman. It's because you're *my* woman. Anyone, me included, going out there alone is putting their life in the hands of something that isn't them. Of people who consider life to be worth less than their next fix, the patch they wear, the crime boss they answer to," he seethed. "So no, this has not a fucking thing to do with the fact that you're a woman. This has everything to do with the fact that you're you. You're precious. You're fucking irreplaceable. So yeah, no matter how dated you think my notion is, when a man finds something irreplaceable and he has it in his hands, he does anything and everything to protect it." He paused, anger filtering away like a deflated balloon. "I thought you would've realized that by now. After everything."

There was something in his voice that had a similar effect on my own anger. It was a kind of hurt, a manly and brisk one, but hurt just the same.

I thought. Backward. Through everything, through every interaction, every sacrifice, every stolen moment.

He did it.

Everything.

For me.

To protect me.

And he might've succeeded.

But even he couldn't protect me from myself.

"Luke," I whispered.

But we were pulling up to a familiar apartment building. I hadn't even realized we were this close and I was driving. Driving under the influence. There wasn't a breath test for that one, though.

I was under the influence of Luke.

Of love. Otherwise known as fucking insanity.

"Okay, so let's talk about this job," I said, right after I'd sat down and Lucy had handed me a cocktail. She settled next to her husband, who immediately yanked her to his side, as close as she could possibly go.

I glanced to the purposeful space between Luke and me, ignored the strange and intense pain that came with that tiny space, and focused on Lucy.

"Job?" she repeated.

I nodded. "Your dutiful husband has offered me a job. Though I'm guessing it's to placate me and I'll likely be expected to sit behind a desk, look pretty, and do the bidding of various alpha males."

Keltan stroked Lucy's arm. "I look like I came down in the last shower?"

I shrugged. "Looks can be deceiving."

"I wouldn't offer you a job doing that shit, firstly because I know you'd refuse, and second, I suspect you'd suck at it," he said, grinning.

"You're not wrong," I agreed. My employment career was almost as sordid as my relationship one. I barely stayed anywhere long enough to get to know my manager's last name. Helping run Gwen and Amy's store was my longest-running venture.

Legal, at least.

The Sons of Templar men may have promised to stay above the law. I made no such promises.

So that meant I was rarely idle and rarely hurting for money. I also liked shoes, expensive ones, and I had nosy relatives, so I needed the appearance of a job. Not that Wire didn't already know about my various ventures—fuck, he was involved in half of them. Which was the reason why Cade didn't know. Wire knew if my brother found out that he'd helped not just run a site on the deep web that worked like an outlaw version of eBay and Facebook merged into one, but helped create it, Cade would likely skin him alive.

But we weren't under *much* risk of getting caught.

There was always risk. That's where the fun was.

"What the fuck is this job, then?" Luke demanded.

I rolled my eyes.

Lucy smiled into her cocktail glass.

"Same job as you have… almost," Keltan said.

I smiled. I liked the 'almost' part. He made it sound like the 'almost' was the badass part.

"We've become popular since we opened."

"Four guesses why," I muttered. "Biceps, abs, ass, face, in that order," I continued.

Keltan grinned. "Whose?"

"Take your pick. That's the point."

Luke let out a low growl at that.

We all ignored it.

"Well, I'd like to think it's because we're fucking good at our jobs," Keltan said.

I shrugged. "That too."

"The demand is going beyond regular security shit. Which makes sense, since my guys have experience way beyond security. We've been getting a few bail skips. Family members of victims whose attackers have been let off on a technicality, frustrated with the police. These are off the record, of course, though the bail skips are legit."

"Yep, I was right. Almost meant awesome." I smiled at Luke, resisting the urge to poke out my tongue.

"Depending on your view, yeah, awesome," Keltan agreed. "It's not quite the same as seeking out crime lords on the street and pistol-whipping them, stabbing them so they can't reproduce, but it's along the same lines," he continued. "And you'll get paid." He looked to a seething Luke. "And she'll be a fuck of a lot safer. Monitored. You can ride out with her." He paused. "If she lets you."

"That's not happening," I countered at the same time Luke said, "Of course I fucking would."

I sipped my cocktail with a frown. Almost didn't just mean awesome. It meant babysitting.

"You've been lucky so far," Keltan said, "not to be caught by the authorities. Despite the fact that you're doing society a favor, the laws don't like favors done by civilians. Especially when they highlight what a fucking farce law enforcement is. Can't hurt to have people making sure you're not arrested. Or killed."

He was talking to both me and Luke.

"Am I missing something?" Lucy cut in, her eyes narrowed on me. "What the ever-loving fuck have you been doing that could get you killed?"

I shrugged. "Existing."

She scowled. "And you didn't even invite me."

Keltan lost his easy demeanor pretty fucking quickly. "And she never fuckin' will," he growled.

Lucy poked her tongue out at him, and he yanked her into his embrace, as if to make sure she was real, as if the mere thought of her in danger changed the past so she didn't survive that day on the sidewalk.

I glanced at Luke, who was intent on me with a similar look Keltan had.

Fear.

Pain.

"Okay," I said immediately, hating to be causing that.

Luke blinked in surprise.

Keltan pulled back. "Really?"

I nodded. "It'll be a step in the right direction to you equalizing your workforce. Feminism happened, you know."

He smirked. "I'm aware."

"And I'll have to demand equal pay. Oprah says so. You have to listen to her."

"Of course," he agreed.

"And I make my own hours," I continued.

Keltan smirked. "Wouldn't dream of telling a Fletcher where to be and when."

I smiled back. "Smart man."

Luke leaned forward, likely with something to say. Likely with a lot of things to say.

Keltan's eyes went to him. "How about we take a cigar?" he asked, kissing his wife and standing.

Luke frowned at me. "I don't smoke fuckin' cigars."

"Bro, it's gentleman speak for 'let's let the woman talk and let's let me talk you off the ledge.'"

I resisted the urge to giggle.

Luke was far from giggling.

"You're not to leave this fuckin' house without me," he declared.

"Wouldn't dream of it," I replied sweetly. Despite my sarcasm, I wouldn't, actually. I was tired of fighting. Against I didn't even know what anymore.

I was plain tired.

I just wanted Luke.

So I would stop with this shit.

He stared at me long and hard before he got up and followed Keltan.

Lucy didn't waste any time crossing the space between us to sit right next to me, much closer than Luke.

"Bitch, you've been holding out on me," she snapped. "Spill. Now."

"Well, I was bored, so I decided to call a few LA friends, ask them who the dirtbags were, teach them some lessons," I began.

She waved her hand dismissively. "Not *that*," she said. "That's just another day in your life. I'm not surprised. What I need is the goss on you and Luke. Now. No more evading, no more lying. Something's going on. Something has been going on. For *years*. I respected your silence, didn't like it, but I got it. Guessed you'd tell me when you were ready. But I almost *died* without knowing. You're obliged to tell me."

I raised my brow to conceal the stab of ice that mention of her almost death dipped into my heart. "You know you're only allowed to use that card once," I said. "Sure this is the time? Don't want to wait until we fall in love with the same pair of shoes?"

Lucy gave me a look. "I'm sure."

I thought it'd be hard to talk about something I'd kept so close to my heart all these years. That I wouldn't be able to explain it properly, that there wouldn't be enough words.

Two cocktails and a lot of tears—all Lucy's—later, there were enough words. Too many maybe.

It was a weird thing keeping secrets from the women who were meant to know all of your secrets. It was an uncomfortable feeling, like a pebble stuck in your shoe. Unnatural. Hard to walk normally on.

Telling her was releasing that pebble from my soul.

"So now we're... I don't even know what. We can never really *be*, because I don't want my family to kill him. Because I'm too scared of having to choose between the two things I love most in this world." I sucked down the last of my drink. "Wow, I didn't mean to dump all that on you, I'm sorry."

Lucy glared in the face of my apology. "How many times, in the decades since we've known each other, have you whined to me about a guy, asked for my advice, bathed in happiness and heartbreak at the same time?" she asked.

I screwed up my nose. "Is this a trick question?"

"Yeah, that's right, none," she said, nodding. "So don't rob me of one of my most important friend duties of talking you through a relationship. Being a shoulder. I might not give the best advice, and you don't even have to listen to my advice, but I need you to let it out, Rosie. You've had enough of the silence, of being stubbornly determined that you're going to do this alone, feel this alone, when you don't have to. It's written in our rulebook. We don't let our girlfriends go through this alone." She squeezed my hand. "You're not alone."

A single tear escaped. "I know," I whispered. "And maybe that's harder than being alone. I don't know. I'm so fucked up right now. Even more than usual."

The men chose that moment to walk back in, but Keltan and Lucy's living room was large and open plan, which meant they were out of earshot, loitering by the kitchen, as if they sensed the lady powwow wasn't over.

That didn't stop my eyes from locking with Luke's, finding home there.

Lucy smiled. "Despite popular opinion, babe, love doesn't make you feel good all the time. Fuck, it doesn't make you feel good most of the time. You're handing another person your heart,

SHIELD

you soul, your sanity." She paused and raised her brow at me. "Not that you've got much left to give, but you're giving that all to one person to look after. To treasure. And there's pain that comes with that. And fear, constant fear. It doesn't feel good to hand yourself off to someone else. It makes you more vulnerable. You just need to find that right person who treasures you enough to forsake themselves to take care of what you gave them, even on your worst days. Even when they don't particularly like you, they should treasure you." She paused, glancing up to her husband. "They're rare, those men. Not everyone gets them. Definitely not enough women who deserve them. So don't do the ones who are never going to have that a disservice by throwing it away because of fear. Because that love isn't recyclable. He isn't going to use it on another woman, just like you would never go through all the pain and suffering you've gone through for anyone but Luke. You're it for each other. I know it. And you sure as shit know it, so quit screwing around."

I blinked at her. "Wow," I said. "You've gotten really deep since I've been gone." I looked her up and down. "And bossy."

She grinned. "Staring death in the face will do that to you." She looked back to her husband again, her gaze like a magnet, never wavering from the thing that tethered it for too long. Keltan was already looking at her. "Staring life in the face will do that to you too." With great effort, she moved her eyes back to me. "And you've looked at both of those things. Don't go looking for the former anymore. We've had enough."

I looked back to Luke, then back on our history. To all the separations and hurt and drama that came with love for my family. I was making it so much fucking harder than I needed to. Of course, I couldn't realize that myself. Luke couldn't even make me realize that. There were some jobs in life that only girlfriends, true soul mates, could do just right.

I didn't know what to say. Mostly because there was nothing *to* say. I was getting educated.

And I didn't have time to say anything.

"Rosie," Luke called.

I snapped my head up.

He was crossing the distance to us, and he'd called my name obviously because he knew we were talking girl stuff and he wanted to warn me that he was coming into earshot. It was an old Luke gesture, coming from this stoic-faced, black-clad, ripped impostor.

"We're going," he declared, standing beside me and holding out his hand in invitation.

I looked at the hand, then to Lucy. She gave me a 'what the fuck are you looking at me for?' kind of look.

My eyes crept upward to the new Luke.

His face was still etched in granite, jaw covered by stubble, but his eyes had turned liquid.

Lucy's words bounced around in my head.

I took his hand.

The drive back to my place was quiet. But not silent, despite the fact that neither of us said a word.

We didn't need to. The tension in the air fizzled around and snapped at our consciousness in a way words couldn't.

Luke was driving.

I hadn't said a thing as he'd taken the keys from me, gently running his thumb over the top of my hand as he did so. As soon as he'd gotten onto the street, his hand had found my thigh and stayed there the whole time.

I didn't move it.

He parked in the lot of my apartment building and neither of us moved, even though he'd turned off the car.

Then we did move.

I wasn't sure which of us did it first. Maybe it was me.

But our lips and tongues and teeth were clashing together moments after we sat silent across from one other.

He was everywhere with that kiss. His hands tore through my hair, roughly and painfully, a continuation of that day at the offices. But this time it was private, just him and me, nothing else.

And I dove in, let that drown me. Until I really thought of him and me. The bodies, the pain, the fucking demons.

That night at my place. Kevin. His hands on me rough, like Luke's. It didn't matter that Luke's rough was different, that it wasn't from hate but from love. The two were so close, inches apart, that my brain didn't know the difference. My heart might have, but that wasn't in control right then.

I ripped my head back, meeting Luke's dark stare.

"I can't," I choked out, fumbling with the door and almost falling out of it.

Then I ran. Not figuratively like before but really ran, sprinting away from Luke, from my own demons, from everything.

I flattened my back against the door to my apartment, breathing heavily.

I was safe. Alone.

But that felt more dangerous than ever.

LUKE

Luke sucked in a breath.

Then another one.

He tried to calm himself. Swallow his anger.

"Fuck!" he roared, slamming his hands down on the steering wheel so hard the impact and vague pain reverberated up his arms.

It wasn't new.

Pain.

It was his default those days. Pain at watching Keltan and Lucy

247

and their easy happiness. Knowing that it would never be them, him and Rosie.

But then again, it wasn't easy for Keltan at the start either.

Maybe that was the truth.

It wasn't easy for anybody.

But they had periods of ease.

Fuck, he and Rosie hadn't even had a fucking second.

He wished it was, that when she came back they could've come together, the absence clearing out every single ounce of pain that came before.

Every night, every fucking night since she'd been back, he'd had to drink himself into a near stupor just so he didn't drive over there and claim her, like every part of him itched to. But he couldn't. It wouldn't work that way for them. He knew that. They weren't like that.

They'd never be like that.

And it might've been painful. Almost unbearable, but he wouldn't have it any other way.

These months, they'd been worse than having her out of the country. Because then he got to pretend that's why they weren't working it out. Now he couldn't pretend. They couldn't pretend.

He wasn't surprised when Keltan told him what Rosie had been up to, but that didn't mean he was impressed.

Especially when he found out Keltan had had Duke tailing her before he even sat Luke down.

"Okay, mate, before I say this, I want your word that you won't break any furniture," Keltan said, *sitting down across from him.*

Luke braced. "Fuck, is it Rosie? Is she—"

"No, bro, she's not been kidnapped, blown up or shot at," Keltan said *immediately.*

Luke sagged.

Keltan grinned. "Well, at least not lately," he added.

Luke glared. It was his default these days. Go to work, glare at whatever idiot he was working for. He'd walked out on his empty-

headed client the second she came onto him. *Messily and fucking pathetically.*

Keltan hadn't blamed him, and he'd done exactly what he said he couldn't. He fired the client.

There was blowback, but it barely affected business; if anything, it made them busier. Which, for Luke, was good. When he was idle, that's when it was worse. So he took as many jobs as he could.

"But still, I need your word."

Luke eyed his friend. He'd never really had friends before. There were the guys from the force, but it wasn't real friendship. They had beers, talked about sports, whatever woman they'd fucked—them, not Luke, because he never talked about shit—nothing real. Nothing deeper. Maybe that was because Luke had known that he wasn't where he belonged, with fucks who thought enforcing the law made them the adult equivalent of high school football stars. Meant they could use it to get women into bed and wield their power over others. Not that many of them went across the line, but they danced close to it.

He was looking for something bigger than that. And like Rosie said that day, something spectacular. Beyond normal. Outside the law.

He'd belonged there all along, but he'd just convinced himself that enforcing it was where he should've been.

"Fine," Luke said.

"I've had Duke tailing Rosie," he began.

Luke clenched his fists. "What the fuck?" he hissed.

"Remember the promise," Keltan said. "I really like that chair." He nodded to the one Luke was sitting in. "I've been hearing shit about someone causing trouble for the scum of LA. A woman."

"For fuck's sake, Rosie," Luke cursed.

Keltan nodded. "Yeah, I kind of immediately thought of your little spitfire. Hence Duke tailing her."

"Why the fuck didn't you tell me?"

"I'm telling you now," Keltan said. "Now that I'm certain. You've got to play this carefully, brother."

Luke glared. "What the fuck is she doing?" he demanded instead.

"Nothing out of character. Causing trouble for people who deserve it."

"Fuck," Luke cursed again. "You know where she's gonna be tonight?"

"Not likely, but I'm thinking we should relieve Duke from his duty,"
Keltan said.

"I'll go," Luke volunteered. "You don't need to worry about this shit."

*"Oh, I disagree. When you go lumbering in there with the same anger
and protectiveness that I'd have if the situation were reversed, she might
just shoot you. Women are testy like that. You're a good worker, better
friend, so I'll come, make sure you don't get shot. Deal?"*

*Luke wanted to tell Keltan he was wrong, that this was his woman
and he'd handle it and he'd be level-headed and Rosie wouldn't
shoot him.*

*Thing was, he wasn't sure about any of those things, apart from
Rosie being his woman.*

But it was a fuck of a lot more complicated than that.

"Deal," he said.

Before, he knew it wasn't the right time to walk up to her door
and claim her.

But it wasn't before anymore.

So he pushed out of Rosie's car, slamming the door shut, and
headed for her apartment.

To claim his woman.

Fucking finally.

CHAPTER FIFTEEN

ROSIE

I was still standing with my back against the door when it started banging.

I jumped, turning to look at the offending wood.

It's him, a little romantic voice inside me said. *It's him not putting up with any of your shit and finally getting you two where you need to be. Together.*

No it wasn't. I'd done enough. Pushed him away enough. Even I was sick of myself.

I expected it to be Polly, telling me about the epic breakup of the marriage. Or Gage, telling me he wanted to go blow things up. He'd learned a few things from me on that score.

Or my downstairs neighbor who I'd become fast friends with wanting to have a *Supernatural* marathon.

I expected all of those people.

I didn't expect Luke.

But there he was, in all his glory, his kiss still echoing on my lips.

I expected words.

He was the good guy. When the good guy turned up on your doorstep, there were words. Proclamations. Declarations. Apologies. Accusations. Tears. Whispers.

But he wasn't the good guy. Not anymore. And I was reminded in the most exquisite way.

"What are you—"

I didn't finish my sentence because the words had nowhere to go but Luke's mouth, which was plastered on my own. He didn't hesitate in plunging his tongue inside, kissing me mercilessly, pushing me inside the apartment with so much force a vase shattered on the floor.

I barely heard it.

And the slam of him kicking the door shut.

The roar of my heartbeat almost drowned everything out.

Luke's hands were not chaste, they were not hesitant, not tender, worrying about the demons they summoned with such a passionate touch. Not like before. Not like last time.

The last time was the striking of the match.

This was the unleashing of the entire fucking inferno.

I knew, as he ripped my tee off me, sucking at my nipple through the lace of my bra, that there would be nothing remaining of me amongst the ashes when this ended. And it would end. Infernos burned hot and quickly.

His hand went straight into my panties, landing on the perfect spot without needing to search.

I cried out in surprise and pleasure. He bit at my lip, drawing blood.

And then his fingers were inside me.

And I didn't care what little would be left at the end.

Endings didn't matter when you were at the midst of the most beautiful of beginnings. Or maybe this was just another in a long line of endings.

I didn't give a fuck.

Not when Luke had me naked in front of him, his eyes

burning with carnal desire. His gaze devoured me, saying every-thing he thought about my naked body without uttering a word, as if we knew words would ruin this, bring about reality, sever the connection.

Then he knelt like he was worshipping me, the most tender of gestures juxtaposed by the raw and brutal look in his eyes. He stayed like that for a moment, and then his mouth was on me, *right there.*

I screamed. I couldn't help it. Maybe it was because he hit the perfect spot with the perfect amount of pressure and tongue. Maybe it was because I hadn't realized I hadn't had good, carnal, and brutal sex in... forever.

Or most likely it was because it was Luke.

It was *Luke* kneeling at my feet. It was *Luke's* mouth on my most intimate part of me, *Luke's* kiss that mingled with the taste of blood in my mouth.

I clenched his hair as he stoked my fire, unleashing the climax that turned my knees to jelly. His hands immediately came to my hips, steadying me, holding me up as my shudders washed over me.

Every aftershock was jarring, hitting all my fragile nerve endings. The loss of Luke's mouth and the rush of humid air on my bare skin sent shivers vibrating through me.

His mouth immediately covered mine, which was expelling breath so rapidly I vaguely wondered whether I'd pass out.

I really hoped I didn't pass out.

His taste mingled with my own served to build up the desire that I'd thought he'd just sated. My hunger for him was not quelled after that. Not after this long.

We had years to make up for.

He growled as my fingers ripped at his tee, detaching from my lips for the second it took to yank it off his body. The second he was separated from the material, he yanked our naked torsos together, the electrifying combination of his skin against mine something beyond perfect. I scratched at the flesh of his back, moaning at the same time he hissed out a breath when I broke the skin. His eyes were almost black, telling me he liked it like that.

Which almost made me stutter. This glimpse of the new Luke, the bad Luke, who was going to take me hard and rough and drew my blood and liked it—no, *loved* it when I drew his.

But then he yanked my hand to the hardness straining from his jeans and all my feelings of guilt disappeared, swallowed by the power of my desire. I was desperate, feral almost, as I yanked at his belt buckle, a small sting in my forefinger telling me I'd broken a nail getting it loose. Not that it mattered. Not when I was freeing him in all his glory.

I caressed him for a moment, freeing him from jeans but leaving them on. He grunted as my hands ran over the smooth and hard flesh. And then they weren't anymore, one of his hands circling my wrist, yanking it away from him. The other made short work of his jeans and then somehow—maybe I collapsed, maybe he pushed me down—we were on the floor. And then he was inside me.

Both of us stilled on that first thrust, all the ferocity of before disappearing. He just stayed there, inside me, both physically and emotionally, stare locked on mine. The moment that passed was not one fueled by aggressive and almost-crazed desire. This lucidity was almost painful in its exquisiteness, in the way we passed a million words in that one glance, acknowledging how long this had been in coming, about how perfect it was.

About how this should never have happened. About how imperfect it was.

And I wanted to throw away all those other moments I'd snatched from between us so I could make room for this one. Steal it out of the present and store it to become my ultimate treasure.

But I didn't have time.

Because his lips were on mine.

And then he moved.

And then there was no room for coherent thought.

There was room for nothing but our bodies and our passion, and for once, simplicity.

But all good things come to an end. And the worst ones too. I just couldn't figure out which one this was.

I came to my senses quickly. Well, after five orgasms. But after a handful of hours with a man who could give five orgasms, one could describe that as quick. Because most women, most *sane* women, would hold onto that, not let it go after a mere few hours. No, a sane woman would put a fucking ring on that shit.

It had been well established that I wasn't sane.

Therefore, the first words spoken from my mouth after some of the most beautiful hours of my entire life showed me and the world—the world being Luke—how fucking off the reservation I was.

"This was a mistake."

Luke's hand, which had been lazily drawing circles on the underside of my breast, froze. His head, which had been very intently inspecting the underside of my breast, moved too.

His expression was unreadable as his glacial stare locked with mine. "Say again?"

I pushed him off me. Or at least tried to. Luke was on top of me, much stronger and therefore in control. He did not let me push him off me. The old Luke would have. No matter how much it pissed him off, my small gesture would've been taken as an order to his morals to get off the woman he was using his strength against.

This was not the old Luke.

"Get off me," I ordered.

His stare remained cold. "No fucking way."

"Luke."

"Rosie."

I glared at him. He glared right back at me.

"You're really going to keep me here for the rest of my life, Luke?" I snapped.

He didn't move. "No, just for however long it takes to talk, or fuck, some sense into you."

The extremely sensitive part between my legs jumped at the pure sex in his tone. Who was I kidding—all of me jumped at the pure sex in his tone.

But I couldn't waver.

I knew I couldn't.

"Newsflash, Luke. People have been trying my whole life to talk some sense into me. Hasn't worked," I replied. "Different people have also tried to fuck some sense into me too. That didn't work either." That was a low blow, and I almost regretted it the moment it came out of my mouth. Almost. I was fighting for my life here. And, more importantly, his. I'd ruined it enough. That motivation was enough to have me fighting dirty.

He flinched at my words, jaw turning to stone. His hand moved to circle my neck, not loosely, but only dancing with the point of pain. I could still breathe, but he was making his point.

And it was turning me on even more.

"I'm not most people," he growled. His hand squeezed. "*We're* not most people." His eyes searched mine. "And I'm not tryin' to change you, Rosie. I've fucked up enough thinking that's something that I needed to do. Somethin' you needed. I ain't fuckin' up again. The only shred of sense I'm going to make you see regards you and me. Everything else in your life, in you, can stay as beautifully and chaotically senseless as it is." His hand moved, stroking the column of my neck that he'd just been squeezing, and his fingertips moved upward to trail along the sides of my face. "That's what made me fall in love with you. All that exquisite senselessness."

I froze. Even my heart stopped beating. Every inch of me was suspended in time, in the moment following those words. The ones I'd thought maybe could've been true when I'd had too much pink wine and watched too many Julia Roberts movies. The ones I taunted myself with, with their impossibility of coming out of Luke's mouth.

Sure, whatever we'd had, whatever Fuck-Up that was us that hinted at feelings—I wasn't that much of an idiot. I knew he felt something crazy and intense for me in order to explain everything over the years. But I hadn't dared to let myself actually believe it was the ultimate crazy and intense thing.

Love.

"What did you just say?" I choked out.

He held my eyes, continuing to stroke my face. "You know what I said, Rosie. You know what it is between us. We've been tangled up in each other for two decades, coiled into the core parts of each other. I can't get you out. Sometimes, I've wanted to. Not for me, but for you. Because I was convinced that all there was for us was pain. And I didn't want more pain for you. Nothing more than life had already dealt you. But now I'm convinced of another thing. We have more than pain. And I sure as fuck don't want you out of me. Not in this lifetime or the next."

I blinked at him. At his words. The freedom with which he said them. Though, by the sounds of it, they'd been caged for twenty years, so maybe freedom wasn't the right word.

I didn't feel free right then. I'd imagined I would. When what had been unspoken between us all this time was finally uttered. I thought it'd be some kind of release of all of this pressure. It wasn't. It somehow created more of it, tightened the chains around me so I could hardly breathe.

Fear almost paralyzed me.

The only thing worse than loving someone you couldn't have was having someone you were scared to love. Scared because of what you knew it would do.

ANNE MALCOM

Destroy everything.

"I know you love me too," Luke demanded my attention. "Get yourself the fuck out of your head. Stop trying to create reasons why this isn't going to work. We've had enough of them. We can do this, babe. After this long, we *have* to do this."

"No," I whispered. "We can't. After this long, after everything, it's too much. There's too much pain." I sucked in a harsh breath. "Loving you has been pain, ever since the start. Since I was five years old. Don't you get that?"

His eyes danced with regret. "Yeah, babe, I get that. I've been livin' that pain too. The only thing worse than that is living another fuckin' second of what I had to get through this year. And the years before it."

That was it. The words that I was thinking, but with more shape and definition and sense. That's what we were—pain, together and apart. But all we'd known was apart, and that was the worst kind of pain. So why was I fighting for more of that? I'd tried my entire adult life to get rid of him from under my skin.

I'd failed.

The pain didn't lessen over time, as so many fucking inspirational idiots liked to preach. It was worse. Every year, every moment I wasn't with Luke, it was worse. My life was bursting with chaos, with love, with life, with death. It was happy. But it wasn't full.

And I'd been stopping myself.

For what?

A reel of everything in the past played on a rewind. The dead bodies Luke created and buried for me. The ones I created, stamped on his soul and conscience.

"We were bad," I whispered. To my horror, my voice was shaking like the rest of me. I never even trembled when facing rapists, human traffickers, drug lords. But there I was in front of the man I loved, and I was terrified.

"Yeah," he rasped back, never letting my eyes go. It was only

258

fair, I guessed, since he'd never let my heart go either. "But I'm no good anymore. I'm ready for bad now. I've been ready my whole life, just pretending to be good, trying to fit into a life that never quite fit. It took me a long time to realize that. So we've got a lot of making up to do. Half a lifetime, to be exact."

"It's not going to be that easy," I said, instead of doing what I wanted and sinking into him and letting us take care of each other. "There's still so much shit. So much fight."

He stroked my face. "You're so eager for it, the battle. It's your default," he murmured, his thumb tracing the outline of my lips. It was strange and beautiful, the ease with which he was touching me, like he'd been doing it forever, not four hours. "You're fighting right now."

I swallowed my butterflies, inhaling his scent and letting it seep into my pores. "Fighting? I'm simply breathing," I lied.

He regarded me, his gaze long and measured. "You're not simply breathing. You're fighting. With every breath you take."

I sighed. Weary of the conversation, of the situation. Of everything. I got it now, that phrase 'world-weary.'

"Isn't that the same thing?" I asked.

His stare was unwavering. "In your world, I guess so. But it shouldn't be," he said.

"My world is the only world I've got," I shot back.

He regarded me. "It's all I've got too."

I swallowed, taking him in, trying to reconcile this Luke with the one who'd been there when I left. "You've changed," I observed. He'd gotten *harder*. Not just in the muscle department, though he'd changed a lot there too.

But *him*.

He'd been soft—not in the muscle department—kind, good before.

Now?

He was starting to resemble the men I'd grown up with. The men I called family.

Criminals.

That's what he was now, I guessed. It was what he'd been since I'd made him that. Made him rip off that badge, take off that uniform that was everything to him. That defined him.

Of all the people I'd killed, causing that little death inside Luke would be the thing that would haunt me to the grave.

His eyes didn't waver. "So have you."

My replay reel went to Venezuela. "Yeah," I agreed.

He moved so he was on top of me. "We've got a lot of talkin' to do, babe. Lot of fightin', I'm sure. Lot of shit. Complicated. For now, I feel like keeping it simple. Me fucking you. How does that sound?"

His fingers were inside me before I could say anything else, but I didn't need to give him permission. He'd had my permission since forever.

"Sounds perfect," I breathed.

CHAPTER SIXTEEN

"I'm gonna ask you some questions, and I want the truth."
We were in the kitchen. It was either very early or very late. We'd ordered Chinese and I was storing it in the fridge, where I'd intend to eat it for leftovers but it'd just sit, spoiling for a week until the smell made me throw it out.

Simple, amazing, breathtaking, life-shattering simple was over.

Not that I wanted it. I just didn't think I could handle one more orgasm.

And it was time for complicated, it seemed.

I eyed him. "No you don't."

"Rosie," he warned.

I sighed dramatically. "Be careful what you wish for."

"That's a yes?"

I raised my eyebrows impatiently in response.

"Where were you? This year."

Okay, starting with an easy one. "Venezuela. Mostly."

He narrowed his eyes. "And how is it that you were *mostly* in Venezuela and there's no record of you leaving the country?"

I narrowed my own eyes. "You've been sneaking into some databases you shouldn't be. I'm impressed."

He scowled. "I've got friends. Answer the question."

I shrugged. "Used a fake passport."

His left eye twitching was the only visual form of his surprise. "You have a fake passport?"

"I have three." If he wanted honest, I'd give him the dirty, ugly truth. Then I'd look at the Luke-shaped hole in my door once he'd heard it all.

"Three?" he repeated.

I nodded.

"And Cade knows?"

Surprising question, but I went with it. "He knows about one, hence the need for the other two."

"How did you get them?" It seemed to be asked more out of curiosity than need.

I grinned. "You're not the only one with friends."

He didn't grin back. "What were you doing in Venezuela?"

"Escaping, mostly. Tanning. Drinking. For a start, at least. Stumbled onto something and I started to tan a lot less. Drink some more."

He caught it, the chilling of my tone, the darkening of my eyes. His hands clenched into fists. "What did you stumble onto?"

I took a breath. "A human trafficking ring."

He stared at me. For a long time. "Only you would 'stumble' onto a human trafficking ring while tanning and drinking."

"Well, I was in Venezuela. Stumbling onto trouble was inevitable."

"I don't think that counts. You could stumble into trouble on a Mormon compound."

I scowled. "Hey, that priest started it," I protested.

He narrowed his brow. "Continue."

I rolled my eyes. "Well, I couldn't very well do *nothing*—"

"Nothing is exactly what you should've done, Rosie. You can't do anything about something as huge and institutionalized except get yourself killed," he said sharply.

It was time for a scowl of my own. "Really, Luke? This is what's coming from *you*, of all people? I see human beings being abused in the worst ways imaginable and I'm to just walk away? That's righteous Luke Crawford's advice."

"I've changed."

"I've noticed."

His eyes went hard, something flickering behind them. Hurt, maybe. Vulnerability.

"You have too," he said, little more than a whisper. And that time it wasn't the same as he'd said it before. I knew his mind was in my bedroom, one year back. I hadn't visited that memory since it happened. I couldn't.

I swallowed. "Yeah."

He ran his hand through his hair. "Rosie, how could you be that stupid? Risking your life, no one knowing where you were. No one to save you—"

"I don't need saving," I interrupted, voice harsher than I intended.

Luke eyed me. "You didn't need to come home in a body bag," he countered. "You have family. People who love you. What the fuck do you think they would've done if you hadn't come back at all? If you'd just dropped off the face of the earth, tossed in some shallow grave? How the fuck were they... how the fuck would *I* be able to go on with a big fuckin' chasm in my life?"

I flinched. "You never gave me the space to take up any of your life, remember?" That time I did intend to sound harsh.

He moved forward, cupping my face. "No, Rosie. I gave you all the fucking space. That wasn't the problem. I didn't tell you that. That was my fucking mistake, and I'm gonna learn from it," he promised, and I couldn't help but think the promise was more to himself than to me. "I'm gonna learn from it and I'm gonna make sure you know just how much space you take up in my life. How without you in it, there's nothing."

I blinked at him. "How can we go from all we've ever known to this? How are nevers suddenly being turned into forevers?" I whispered.

He searched my eyes. "You know why, Rosie."

I shook my head. "No, it can't have been from before...." I couldn't say it. That's how weak I really was. I couldn't even utter the description of the day that changed everything. I swallowed. "I loved you the wrong way, before," I whispered instead.

His hands flexed, and his eye twitched. "There's no wrong way to love someone."

I blinked at him. "Yes there is. There's blood, murder, pain, lies. To everyone we know, we care about. Lies to ourselves. To each other."

"No, babe. I'll admit it, that I lied to myself, but never to you. Even when I tried with my words. You knew better. I fuckin' know you did."

I pursed my lips. "Maybe."

"Definitely," he corrected.

"I can't go from zero to a hundred, Luke." I went for a different route. The truth. Or maybe it was another lie. I couldn't tell the difference anymore.

"Yes you can," he argued. "Your life is zero to a hundred."

I stared at him. "And my life has been a consistent series of Fuck-Ups."

He frowned. "Don't do that. Don't belittle everything you've done, everything you've become. It's the furthest thing from a fuck-up I've ever seen."

I chewed my lip. "It's all about perception, Luke. You might see it differently, but it doesn't matter. What does that I don't want this, us, if we really do this, to be another Fuck-Up."

"It won't be. We won't be," he promised.

I swallowed, deciding to say something else, to him, to myself, instead of answering properly. "Ever since I can remember, I was a nomad," I whispered. "Not in the sense that I didn't have a home. The Sons of Templar have been and always will be my home, of a sort. But spiritually, I'm a nomad. Since birth, maybe. Definitely since my dad died and I was put in a world where I was in without a patch. Where I would always belong but also didn't. Then I met you, and my spirit found a home. Or it wanted one. But it couldn't reside there or in me, so that's what this, my whole life, has been about after that. Trying to find a home in someone else and trying to find a home in myself." I stepped forward so my body pressed into Luke, so my body found its home. "I've never, not once in my life, felt like I was exactly, precisely where I needed to be. Where I belonged. Not completely. Because I was fighting. Because I knew it was right here that I needed to be." I stroked Luke's chest. "And I knew I could never be here. Thought I couldn't, at least. It's weird, isn't it?"

He stroked my head. "What, precisely?"

"Peace," I whispered. "I've never felt it. It's like a pair of shoes that fit exactly perfectly but you're suspicious because no pair of shoes is that perfect."

Luke chuckled. "I'm the pair of shoes in this analogy?"

I smirked. "*We're* the pair of shoes. A pair."

He leaned down and kissed my head. "I knew there wasn't a lot of things in life I could give you, not when I've taken years from you because I was running from this for all the wrong reasons—"

"We both were."

He took that with a hard chin. I knew he wanted to disagree, but he kept going. "Whatever it was. If there was one gift I could give my beautifully wild, wonderfully chaotic woman, it would be peace." He gave me a look that held the whole universe. "Even if it's fleeting, because I know my wild woman can't entertain peace for too long and stay sane. I can be happy, content, knowing I've given you that."

I fought the tears, the happy ones, welling in my eyes. "It's not fleeting," I choked out. "It's you. It's us. We are each other's peace, aren't we?"

He lightly kissed my lips. "Yeah, and we're each other's chaos."

ANNE MALCOM

"But it works."

"Oh, it more than works."

I traced the side of his head with my hand. "Can we just keep this slow? Just for us?"

He searched my face. "Don't want slow," he muttered. "Also want to shout from the rooftops that you're mine." He sighed. "But I get what you want, why you want it, and fuck if I'll say no."

I grinned. "It bodes well for me, that does."

He shook his head. "And not for me."

Luke closed the door quietly, his hands finding the back of my neck, landing on the exact spot that had been throbbing from tension and rubbing at it.

I sank back into his touch, the warmth of his front igniting the back of my body.

"I don't suppose you'd consider not taking the job and stopping the vigilante stuff, even if I asked real nice?" he murmured, lips on my ear.

I shivered. "Not a chance," I whispered, failing to find any anger at his request. "One or the other. You pick, buddy."

He kept rubbing for a long while.

It was evening, the next day. Right after our first day at work. There were no stakeouts or foot chases through the streets; as I was disappointed to find out, it was more paperwork and meetings. And meeting the team.

I totally got why Greenstone was the most popular security company in LA. You threw a rock in those offices and it would hit a hot guy.

Not that you wanted to throw a rock at these guys. They all radiated menace.

The hot kind.

"Well, let me be the first to say that I'm very happy Keltan has

266

finally been listening to my lectures on equality in the workplace," Matt—one of Keltan's kiwi buddies from the army, I'd found out later—said, grinning at me wickedly. "I'm *all* about women's rights. And I can't wait to see your moves." He winked.

I thought Luke's head might've exploded at that.

He was begrudgingly sticking to our secrecy pact.

That meant professional in the workplace.

Well, he'd fucked me on his desk about five minutes after that meeting. Oh, and then he'd buried his head between my legs and gave me two orgasms in the weight room a couple of hours after that. So it wasn't *strictly* professional, but it was as close as I'd get.

"I don't want you to get hurt," Luke said, back at my apartment. There had been no question that that's where he was spending the night. "That is the last thing in the fucking world that I want." He paused, sucking in a breath and looking away. Even though he was focused on my sofa, I knew he was somehow still looking at me. Just not the me standing in front of him. A past me, perhaps. Or maybe the version of me he'd made in his head. The version he could completely nurture, love. The ideal Rosie. Maybe he was looking and her and wishing he could swap us out.

"I want to protect you," he finished, cutting off my dangerous interior game of *which Rosie does Luke actually want.*

I laughed, more to shake off the chill that came with those thoughts of the ideal Rosie. "Protect me?" I repeated. "From getting hurt?" I glanced down to his hip. "Well, then there's only one thing to do if that's what you want. Put a bullet in my temple." He flinched, visibly and harshly at my cold words. I ignored it. "Death is the only thing that's certain to protect humans from the horror of life. Death isn't the bad and scary thing everyone makes it out to be. In fact, for those in the business of dying, I suspect it's a welcome reprieve from the pain of living. After the fact, of course. Death is only bad for those left behind."

My mind, as it always did in conversations such as this, flickered to Laurie. Even though years had passed, fresh agony ripped through my midsection with the memory of my friend being gone. I sucked in oxygen through the pain. "Pain is a recreational hazard in the job of life, Luke," I said. "You'll only be able to protect me from it if you're willing to end my life."

The words hung in the air bitterly, their truth polluting everything. Not that it was untainted. It had never been clean and fresh. Even when it began at five years old, the time in life where everyone was supposed to experience pure naivety, it was blackened, dirty. Gray. I was born into a gray world.

Luke had been holding a hard jaw while I spoke, it setting like marble the more I said.

"I know you were makin' a point," he gritted out, stalking toward me. "But don't you dare make it with mention of your death at my fuckin' hands. Ever. Again." He was in front of me now, fury rippling behind him like some kind of cape.

He didn't wait for me to reply. Didn't seem like he wanted me to speak at all. "You've seen a lot of shit, Rosie. Ugly shit. The kind that slithers into the core of you, coils up and routinely clutches onto you, hurting you. Sometimes when you expect it to, other times when you're unprepared, happy." His gaze glittered, the words making my own blurry. "I know I can't protect you from the thing that hurts you the most: yourself." His hands framed my face. "But I'm gonna try so hard to distract from that, to give you so much sweet to hold onto that it drowns out the bitter." His breath was hot and minty on my face. "And when I can't do that, I'll make sure you've got someone to share your pain with. But in no fucking way, figurative or literal, am I going to let any part of you die. Is that understood?"

I nodded. "Understood."

He picked me up and I didn't hesitate to wrap my legs around him, my sensitive core pressed to his hard length.

"Now I'm going to remind us both just how fucking alive we are," he growled.

And he did.

Twice.

"Have you told anyone, babe?" Luke asked the ceiling.

"What? That you quite possibly just broke my vagina? Dude, it just happened. Gimme a second to tweet it to my fans," I said, also to the ceiling.

It was two weeks after the big... whatever Luke fucking me on the floor and spewing out all our truth was.

He'd been over often.

In other words, every night.

Luke's arms tightened around me. He did that often too. Squeezed me like he wasn't quite sure I was real and needed to make sure I wouldn't fade away into smoke. I knew it because I did that too.

"No, babe," he said softly. "About what happened to you that day. That night. The one before you left."

His words were soft. Their impact was not.

Dirt settled over my skin as the memory rushed into every cell of my body. I wanted to escape. Cover my nakedness so my skin didn't touch Luke's. I tried. Luke had clearly anticipated that. He didn't let me go.

I chewed my lip. I really wanted to say something flippant and dismissive. Something strong. But I couldn't. I was naked now, in every sense of the word. I didn't have the energy to lie to Luke. I was using it all to lie to myself.

He waited, for me to get my shit together, to find something inside me to push the words out. "No, no I haven't," I choked out, barely above a whisper.

I expected him to reply immediately. To chastise me for bottling things up, not asking for help, all the clichés. He didn't. He just let us lie there, tangled in each other, staring at the ceiling, staring at the past.

"Let's say if Lucy, or Ashley or Polly went through something like that on their own," he murmured. "How would you feel for them if they didn't have the support you know they'd need?"

The question somehow wasn't accusing or confrontational.

It hit the right spot, though.

He didn't wait for me to answer. "I'm never going to completely understand what you went through, babe. I only know what *I* went through witnessing the aftermath. And that was the worst hell I've ever experienced. Knowing you went through something worse?" He shuddered. "I wish there was something to do to take that shit away. But there isn't. Know there isn't. I'm gonna love you. Be here. Let you deal with this in whatever way you can. I'm not forcing you to talk to me. I'm never going to force you to be a certain way around me. I do want you to think about talking to your girls, babe. Doesn't have to be about us, though I would like that to be on the future cocktail agenda."

He kissed my head. "I know your girls are your soul mates. Biggest compliment I'll get, apart from knowin' you love me, is you sharing us with them. When you're ready. But this isn't about me. This is about the girl who lives for her sisters, her family. Who makes herself up from those people. I know you're not whole, keepin' these big chunks of yourself from them. Want you whole, babe. Want to be the man who makes you that way, but I'm not stupid. I know that one person can't make another whole. Not with you, at least. Your heart's too big for that. I'll settle for a corner. A large one."

Tears streamed down my face and I couldn't control them. I hadn't cried, really cried, since that day they found Bex.

I was at the wharf.

It was the only place I could think of... after. After I'd seen Bex brought into the club.

Or more aptly, Bex's body.

She was breathing.

But it was still her body.

Something important had been taken. You could tell by looking at the emptiness in her eyes. Her body was beaten, broken. Her spirit was all but ruined.

As was Lucky's. The man who lit up the lives of so many people, reminded us all not to take life so seriously, was gone.

How could you stay inside your own optimism when the person you loved was raped? Beaten? Tortured? Taken from you. Despite being able to retrieve her, she was gone.

It was too soon to tell if she was coming back.

And I couldn't handle it all. I was weak. But I couldn't let my weakness show. I wouldn't.

So I came to the place where I could be weak with only the ocean to witness it, to wash it away, like it had never happened.

Like always, he was there. When I was at my lowest, he was there to shield me from it. From the worst of it all. From the worst of myself.

He didn't touch me at first.

Didn't speak.

Just stood beside me, watching the wild ocean.

I wondered if he was wishing it would wash away all of the pain my family had to endure. That Bex had to endure.

Probably not.

He was practical. Practical men knew the frivolity of wishing.

It came out of nowhere. The wave. Not out there in the ocean, but in there, in me.

My feet just stopped holding me.

He caught me. Easily swept me into his embrace, like he'd been expecting it. And he held me while I clutched at his shirt and sobbed, broke down. He held me, kissed my head, murmuring everything and nothing at the same time.

And somehow, by doing that, he stopped my whole world from falling apart. So then I could help Bex put hers back together.

It occurred to me that every single time I really cried, really let myself go, I was in Luke's arms.

I moved almost on instinct so I was on top of him, straddling him, framing his face with my hands. The whiskers of his stubble rubbed against my open palms.

"You have a corner," I whispered through my tears. "You occupy the prime real estate, Luke. You have since I was five years old."

And with that open honesty, I kissed him, the flavor of my tears mixing with the flavor of us.

Because the memories made me feel him inside me, and every instinct I had was to crawl away and let that dirt turn to rot, I went against them. My hand fastened against Luke's, pushing it down, right to my perfect spot.

We both hissed out rough breaths as he rubbed me. Then, as if he knew what I wanted, what I needed, his fingers went inside.

He may have not been clean anymore, but he worked at washing the dirt away.

CHAPTER SEVENTEEN

I may have been intent on keeping Luke and me under wraps, and I was usually pretty good at the whole undercover thing.

I just didn't take into account how much I'd need Luke naked and inside me.

And the fact that almost all of my family had keys to my apartment.

And they didn't knock.

"Luke," I breathed, scratching at his back, my nails breaking the skin, creating new wounds to replace the barely healing ones from earlier in the week.

Luke's hand bit into my hip, likely imprinting fresh bruises to join the fading ones.

It turned out that we enjoyed hurting each other.

Not that this was new information.

"Don't you come yet," he commanded roughly. "You come when I say."

He was also bossy in bed. Really fucking bossy. I loved it.

I was about to disobey him when the front door opened.

"Surprise! I pried myself away from Cade's spawn to come shopping—oh my God. Shit, I'm so sorry!"

Luke and I were on the sofa. My apartment opened onto my living room.

Both of our heads snapped toward where Gwen was standing, hand over her eyes, keys dangling from her fingers.

"I'm just going to go away to Chanel. I'll be hours. *Hours*," she repeated. She then turned and paused, hands still over her eyes. "I just want to say that this makes me very happy. Well, not me totally barging in on you doing the nasty, but *you and Luke* doing the nasty. It's, like, fucking awesome," she yelled.

I cringed.

Luke grinned.

Then the door shut.

"Did Gwen just walk in on us in the middle of having sex?" I whispered.

Luke's grin widened. "Yes, she did."

I expected him to pull out, discuss this turn of events. He did not, he moved his hips in deeper and I gasped. "In the middle," he rasped. "Which means I've got *a lot* more fucking to do."

And then discussing the turn of events didn't seem important.

At all.

———

There was a knock at the door. "Is it safe to come in?" Gwen yelled.

It was three hours later.

She really had good thoughts about Luke's stamina.

She wasn't wrong.

One-point-five of those hours was filled with delicious sex.

Another one of them was filled with us arguing. Screaming, actually.

"I can't believe Gwen walked in on us," I said, pacing the room, my silk robe trailing behind me.

Luke was sitting on the sofa, jeans on, commando, top button undone. It was really fucking distracting.

"She's had better timing," he said, smirking.

I stopped pacing to glare at him. "Is that all you have to say?" I snapped. "She has both the biggest heart and biggest mouth in Amber, maybe the world. She'll be on the phone to Amy right now. And Amy's mouth is even bigger, somehow. She'll tell Brock. And those men gossip like old Italian woman." I put my palm to my head. "Cade will know by now," I groaned.

Luke pushed off the sofa, and my eyes devoured his chiseled abs, the V of his stomach and the peppering of hair peeking from his jeans.

He grabbed my neck and my gaze went to his eyes. "They were gonna have to know. Somehow. Eventually. I know you wanted it secret, but I plan on forever, and forever with you is forever with your family. And there's no secrets in your family. It was better to get it sorted sooner."

I glared. "*Better?*" I repeated. "Really? Do you think since now you don't have a badge and secret folder on the club—which I'm sure you didn't think I knew about but I know you, so I know it exists, or existed—that they'll welcome you?" I paused, stepping out of his embrace. "No, they won't. You'll still be the cop to them. Always."

The softness left his eyes. "I don't give a fuck if they think that," he clipped. "As long as to you, I'll always be your man. Not the cop. But that's not the case, is it? I'll always be the cop to you too, won't I?"

I stuttered at the hurt in his voice, despite the fact that it was rising with anger. "I'll always be the woman who stopped you from being that, won't I? From being what you were meant to be. And Gwen, my sister, the one who just walked in. She's the one you should've been with. Who you *wanted* to be with."

Luke froze. Actually froze, like my words had rendered him immobile. He didn't seem to breathe for a long second.

"You didn't just fucking say that," he hissed.

I crossed my arms, wishing I hadn't said it, but I did, so I had to own it. "It's the truth."

"It is fucking not!" he roared. He kicked at the coffee table and it wobbled slightly, then toppled to the ground. "I know you're scared and hurt, and this is fucking so magnificent that it's terrifying, but that's no fucking excuse for you to spew that absolute bullshit." He glared at me.

I didn't blanche at the glare. I used anger as a vehicle for my most vulnerable thoughts. "You wanted her when she first came. Even with what we'd been through before," I accused.

"No I fucking didn't!" he yelled. "I wanted you so fucking bad, and it hurt every inch of me that I couldn't have you, that I never would. I could barely even look at you, Rosie." He began pacing the room. "I could barely fucking look at myself. So I started to do shit to try and make you hate me. Because I'd never stop loving you. It would be painful but at least fucking bearable if you hated me. If I knew you weren't bathing in the misery I would be submerged in." He paused. "So yeah, I turned myself into that man. Let my anger and hatred for our situation fuel that shit. You need to know, that night at the opening was one of the fuckin' hardest things I've ever had to do. Second to watching you collapse into my arms in the shower a year ago. So no, I've never really wanted anyone but you. I've pretended to. I got really fucking good at that, and I almost fooled myself. But *never* was it the truth. You should know that. You're meant to know that, know me better than that."

He yanked on his boots.

"And you're fucking one to talk," he said, straightening. "You did everything but parade your men in front of me."

My hurt from his words mingled with anger. "And what was I supposed to do, Luke?" I yelled. "Stay chaste and innocent on the slim fucking chance the high and mighty cop might choose to slum it with the *criminal?* I was pretending too, Luke. And I fucking *sucked* at it. You, on the other hand, no doubt had calls from the Academy for your fucking stellar performance."

He stared at me while he pulled on his tee.

"I'm not stayin' here while we spew this shit at each other. One of us will say somethin' we regret." He paused. "I'm done doing shit I regret in regard to you. You'll always be Rosie to me. Just fucking Rosie. *My* fucking Rosie. And it's that simple for me. But it's not that simple for you, is it?"

"No!" I yelled. "Of course it's not that fucking simple. Us, we were never fucking simple. Stop expecting me to be someone who's going to relax into this and forget the world around us exists. Forget the past exists. I'm torn in fucking two, Luke, and I don't know what to do, who to be."

"You, Rosie. Just be you." He said it softly, but it impacted as if he'd yelled it.

And then he walked out.

"Yes!" I yelled back to Gwen, the events of the hour before still echoing in my mind. I reached for another glass so I could pour her some wine. I'd already had two. And now that she wasn't breastfeeding, she had a lot of making up to do.

I had a lot of making up to do with my sister. It had been a year. A year of her being a mom, being a wife, being a crazy fucking bitch. I'd missed out on a lot. I missed her.

I should've hated her.

Gwen.

Not at first. At first, she was the beautiful, exotic woman with pain behind her eyes but a kind smile that swept my brother away from himself. Who yanked him into something that wasn't the quest for revenge he'd started the day our father died.

To set him on some sort of track for living instead of just fighting.

The day of my barbeque, when he only had eyes for her, when

he dragged her off like a caveman in a show of his version of affection that was almost unheard of, I didn't hate her. No, I loved her. Because even though he didn't smile—in fact, he scowled more than usual—I knew my brother was venturing toward happy.

Because of her.

And he deserved whatever version of happy that our version of life could provide him.

And by the looks of the ghosts and demons behind Gwen's pretty face, she deserved it too.

But life, or love, was rarely that simple.

Or casualty free.

It just so happened that I was the casualty of my brother's bloody and drama-filled road to an unexpected fairy-tale ending.

The one where he knocked up Gwen, lost her when she left after her brother died and she found him in bed with another woman, and then he went halfway across the world to get her back. And he brought her back here, where she belonged. At the club. With him.

She ended up shooting and killing the man who shot Steg— while nine months pregnant. And then she gave birth to my niece in the clubhouse with my brother delivering the baby. Oh, and her kidnapping came before that.

So not the traditional happy ever after.

Though, considering every man's road to love, marriage, and the babies in the baby carriage, it kind of was the Sons of Templar version. It wasn't a courtship without at least one kidnapping, an explosion or a drive-by shooting.

You'd think I'd be kidding, but I wasn't.

Though, those weren't my stories, despite the fact that I managed to get tied into every single one.

Me and Luke.

But because of the drama-filled romances that demanded

every inch of the club's attention, our relatively uneventful dramas went unnoticed.

Which was the way it needed to be.

The way it had to be if I wanted to keep my family.

So back to my point, where it all began. For Gwen and Cade, at least.

They wouldn't say it, or at least Gwen wouldn't—my stoic brother turned to a marshmallow around his wife and children and would shout from the rooftops that it was love at first sight. That didn't mean that it was a *relationship* at first sight.

Gwen's demons were dark, even for Cade. Or maybe they resembled Cade's so much and that was why she fought it. Why she gave Luke the prime opportunity to distract himself with a woman who didn't represent everything he despised.

A clean woman.

And that's why I should've hated her.

My mind went back to that moment, before she and Cade were concrete. When I realized how brittle Luke and I were, despite everything that had already happened between us.

It was a week or so after Gwen came into town, four years ago now. At the store where I would end up spending some of the best times of my life. It just so happened one of the worst occurred at the opening party. At the opening when Luke only had eyes for her. Or no, it was worse than that. His eyes had touched mine the moment he set foot in the store. But they didn't stay on me. The pointed movement of his gaze, of his attention to Gwen, hurt more than if he didn't see me at all. But because I was Rosie, carefree on top of all of those monsters I was so good at hiding, I did the only thing I could think of.

Drank myself into oblivion.

But I didn't shift the blame of that hurt to Gwen. It would've been easier. That's why so many women threw around words like "skank," "slut," "bitch." Because it was easier to blame a skank for taking away your man than it was to realize that man wasn't really yours in the first place.

So I didn't do that, didn't poke my head in the sand and blame an innocent woman who I hoped would become my sister one day.

Instead, I accepted a job in her store, swallowing all my pain and banishing it from sight.

And I did what I shouldn't have done.

I hoped.

Firstly, my hope wasn't for me. It was for my troubled brother, who didn't look it but was extremely vulnerable. I hoped that he would finally find some kind of happiness that made him live, not just survive. That he'd have someone to fight for instead of someone to fight against.

And then there was my own selfish hope. That I'd somehow imagined the dismissal, the intensity of Luke's gaze toward Gwen.

But hope was for idiots.

That day in her store when Luke came in, eyes and coffee only for her, invitation of an uncomplicated and drama-less life open.

I didn't hate her.

I couldn't.

I did hate myself a little in the moment they walked out the door, Luke's hand on the small of her back. I hated that I wasn't clean and uncomplicated and that I represented everything Luke despised.

There weren't very many times in my life when I wanted to be something other than who I was.

That was one of them.

I hated Luke a little in that moment too. For making me crave another skin, another identity, for showing me what a fucking farce I was. What a fucking fraud.

But that was it. Love and hate were entwined; one could not exist without the other. And sometimes they existed at the same time. Within the same person.

Gwen burst in, almost weighed down with various Chanel bags. Her eyes went to the couch first, grinning wickedly.

"I half expected you to still be going at it," she said, waltzing into the room, eyeing it as if she was expecting a naked Luke to be hanging off a sex swing. "You have a lot of making up to do, after all."

I poked my tongue out at her. That was better than crying. Or telling her that we might've been over before we began. And I felt profound fucking guilt at using the smiling beauty as a weapon in a fight with Luke.

That was low. Even for me.

She grinned wider, dumping all of her bags on my dining room table.

"These are all because of you, just so you know," she said, nodding to the bags.

I raised my brow and handed her the glass of wine. "I'm pretty sure you had a love affair with the double C before you met me."

She took the wine. "True, but I'm a mum now. I have a love affair with my children and my husband. You made me cheat on them with Chanel. And seriously deplete their college funds." She regarded the bags, chewing her lip.

I laughed. "You'll always cheat on Cade with Chanel."

She nodded. "True." Her attention went to me, eyes narrowing like an eagle's. "Now spill," she demanded. "Everything. And then you better apologize to your favorite sister-in-law for not calling her the *second* this happened. If I like the sordid details and apology enough, I might just give you your birthday gift early." She nodded to the bags.

"My birthday is in ten months," I protested, not sure why I was arguing against a free Chanel bag.

She sobered a little. "Well, a late one, then. I missed the last one."

I opened my mouth to give her yet another apology.

She held up her hand. "I get it, babe. Trust me, I do. Your

brother did, even if he'd never admit it. You've been almost front and center with every drama we've had. Every wound, every blow, it hits you too. I should've seen it earlier." She squeezed my hand. "I'm sorry."

She was apologizing to me for me running away and leaving my family in the lurch? Yeah, I could've never hated her.

"It's not up to you to say sorry," I whispered.

"It's a girlfriend's duty to see things in her sister that she doesn't see in herself. So yeah, I do owe you an apology. But I also demand details. You and Luke, how long has this been going on?"

I grinned. "Oh, about twenty years."

"Tell me something I don't know. But I mean the porno-worthy sex on the couch kind of stuff."

I raised my brow. "You knew?"

"About the porno couch stuff? Not until I was presented with it. Luke's got a great ass, by the way. And your rack is perfect." She winked.

I rolled my eyes.

"About the stuff before?" she said. "Yeah, I knew."

I frowned. "Was it that obvious?"

She smiled. "It's a girlfriend's duty to see things in her sister that she doesn't see in herself, remember?"

I swallowed, remembering a conversation with Laurie in high school so long ago. My heart ached for a moment, and I let it. I'd learned that, when it came to grief that came with loss, it was pointless to fight it. That was one thing that even the strongest person couldn't fight against. You had to let yourself feel the pain or else it would eat you alive.

"You're not going to say anything to Cade, are you?" I asked.

She frowned. "Of course I'd never snitch. Even to my husband." She drained her wine, walking to the counter to fill her glass once more. Mine was still full. She turned to me while pouring. "But why is this a secret? It's something you need to be shouting from the rooftops. Or at the very least something to share with the people you love. Let them exhale, finally knowing that you've got the happiness you deserve."

I sipped my wine. "It's not that simple, Gwen. You know that. You know the club. You know my brother. He hates Luke. He'd hate me too for bringing him into the family."

Gwen scowled. "Your brother adores you. You could blow up his Harley right in front of him and he'd compliment you on your bomb-making skills. Nothing, especially your happiness, would make him hate you."

I took another sip. "It's not that easy to erase the history of hate."

She continued to frown. "It is. You're just making it hard. What are you clinging to, Rosie? Honestly? If it's the club, you know they'd bleed for you. Die for you. So you think that them getting over some stupid macho feud in order for you to be happy is going to be the end of the world? Maybe when things were different, before my time and these men hadn't been exposed to love and happiness and how it's so much better than a life of blood and bullets. And if you're worried about your brother, I'll take care of him."

"No, it's not that. Or it's not that anymore. But it's him. I've ruined him, Gwen. He was on the straight and narrow. He was good, and I pushed him off his path. He killed for me. He went against every single one of his morals for me. How am I meant to live with that?"

Gwen pursed her lips. "Firstly, he might've been walking on the straight and narrow, but have you ever heard of happiness being found on the straight and narrow? No. He was walking that line and maybe, without you, he would've stayed on that line. But thank God he didn't. That would've been a long and lonely road. Unfulfilled. I knew it the second he looked at you. Or, more aptly, actively tried not to look at you." She sipped her wine. "And here's another thing. Not that either man would ever admit this, but Luke and Cade are similar. Almost identical. Albeit on different sides of the law, but alpha knows alpha. And they don't make decisions that they don't want to make. They don't want to forsake that control for anything or anyone except the one. They're serious about that. Luke wouldn't have taken off that badge for anyone unless he *knew*. Trust me, he knows. He took a long time to get there, not because of how he felt about you but how he felt about himself. Maybe that's why he was so conflicted about all of this, because he actually respected all the men he thought he was so determined to lock up."

I gaped at her, then fiddled with my hands, remembering Luke's words. "There's something else too," I whispered.

She grinned. "Of course there is."

She stopped grinning when I started talking.

By the time I was finished, she was crying.

Then she hugged me, tightly, her tears mingling with my own.

I expected her to yell at me for not telling her sooner, declare war on an already long-dead dirtbag. Tell me I needed to join some support group.

She did none of that when she pulled back with red and makeup-streaked eyes. "You are good. And clean. And strong. What happened should *never* make you feel opposite, Rosie," she said firmly. "You didn't tarnish Luke, and especially not yourself. I don't need to talk to him to know you saved him. And, more importantly, yourself. I know you can do that without anyone's help, but how about you let me lend you my shoulder? Whenever you need it. I'm always here to remind you when things get hard." She squeezed my hand. "And so will Luke, babe. I know you think you sentenced him to damnation just because he doesn't drive around in a car with flashing lights, but you gave him something different. I saw it in his eyes, well beyond the crazy sex maniac look." She winked. "I saw salvation. You're always going to be different, Rosie. Extraordinary. So that means salvation might look a little different, darker in hue, but that doesn't change the meaning. You better remember that, or I'll kick your ass."

I sucked in a ragged breath. "I love you."

She smiled. "And I love you right back. So does Cade. And the club. Forever. No matter what. So just be happy. Just be you."

I sipped my wine. "I'll try."

It was dark by the time I heard a key in my lock. Gwen left after only one more glass of wine, telling me she had a drive to make.

I felt significantly lighter once she was gone.

But then I started to get heavy with worry when Luke didn't answer his phone, didn't come back. I started to convince myself that I'd majorly fucked up this time.

The second his large form came through the door, I exhaled, properly. Then I ran, right into his arms. He hadn't expected it, so he went back on one leg, but that didn't stop him from catching me.

I didn't say anything, just clutched him, just inhaled clean air. Not just Luke, the both of us. Clean.

I eventually let him put me down, but he didn't let me go. He clutched me tightly, eyes stuck on mine.

"I'm sorry," I whispered. "I said shit I didn't mean and it was ugly, and I'm sorry. But you're right, I don't know how to be me. Not really." I paused. "Life's just a big party, you know? A costume party. Most people don't realize that. They take it so fucking seriously. The little cages they live in. The lines they've got to stay between. I'm not a different person every day because I have deep-rooted psychological issues." I toyed with Luke's shirt. "Okay, maybe that's part of it, but mostly I'm a different person because *I can be*. It's that simple. People don't realize it. The little pleasures. Wearing head-to-toe sparkles one day and then black lipstick the next. That's what life is, the little pleasures. Not the big moments. They take too much energy, too much planning, too much fucking artifice. All those big moments are to show the world you're happy. The little ones are just to *be happy*. Not for the world, for you. So yeah, I take pleasure in the fact that I don't know what person I'll be in the morning. In the fact that I don't have to know. Because my life would be a pretty fucking bleary place if I didn't."

He leaned forward, face unreadable. "You're trying to convince me about something that made me fall in love with you," he said. "I love that I'm going to be as surprised as you are when you decide who you'll be every day. I don't give a fuck that you don't know what person you'll be in the morning. I fucking love that. As long as that person is someone who wakes up next to me, I'm good, babe. That's my little pleasure."

"You can't keep saying things like that, not after saying nothing at all for years," I whispered.

"Even when I didn't speak, I've never said nothing at all," he murmured. "You know that. You owe it to us, to yourself, to do this, Rosie."

"Yeah, I do," I agreed.

"Something good did come of this afternoon," he rasped, moving his hands up to cup my breasts softly.

I sucked in a breath. "And what's that?" I said, voice heavy.

"We get to experience makeup sex," he growled.

"Why do we have to keep this a secret?" Luke asked sometime later, after possibly the most fucking amazing makeup sex known to man. "Especially now that Gwen knows."

I drew circles on his bare chest, my tattooed hand contrasting against the naked skin. "Can you think of any other way, Luke? Think of us reading the paper in the morning, getting brunch with our friends and family? Being that couple? No. We don't fit that way."

He moved me so our eyes met. "Listen to you, Rosie, talking

about fitting, molding. Wasn't it you who once told me it was the greatest farce of them all, trying to squeeze into some role? I'm not asking for that. I never fuckin' would. I'm askin' to sleep with you, a full night. Wake up with you. Not have snatched fuckin' moments with you, I need it *all* with you."

I narrowed my eyes. "What about the club, Luke? I'm a package deal. As much as I sometimes wish Templar, along with Trouble, wasn't my middle name, it is, and always will be. You can't reconcile your hatred. Being with me, out in the open, in the daylight, means them too. That's my world. It's not yours." It was what we kept coming back to, what Luke had never really, properly addressed. It was all well and good stepping over it in the romance of the moment, but it was quite another thing living with it.

He cupped my face. "You're my world, so I'll come into it. I don't have hatred for what makes you you."

I pushed up on my elbow and raised my brow. "So you'll come home, to Amber, this weekend, and come to a party? At the club. As Luke, my boyfriend, not Luke, the sheriff?"

He pulled me into his arms. "I was never Luke, the sheriff. I was always Luke, Rosie's man. Even before I knew it. Definitely before you knew it."

I swallowed. "Is that your alpha and dramatic way of saying you'll come?" I still wasn't used to it, those hearts and flowers declarations. They didn't feel real. They couldn't feel real. Then again, all the shit, the horrible shit we'd been through up until now, was real, so why couldn't some of the good stuff be real too?

He chuckled and kissed my nose. "Yeah, babe."

I sank into his embrace for a moment and his lips found the top of my head. He inhaled, and I leaned back. "Did you just sniff my head?"

He smiled. "Sure did."

"That's weird, dude."

He continued to smile. "I've had twenty years of wondering

287

what every inch of you smelled like, tasted like. Had to restrain myself from finding out because I didn't think you could be mine, not biblically at least. Now that you are mine, finally, there's nothing to stop me from doing any of that. So I will, as often as possible," he murmured.

Fuck. There it was. More hearts and flowers. It was almost as hard to deal with as the shit that came before. For different reasons.

"You do realize that someone will almost certainly brandish at least one weapon at you, on principle," I said, skipping acknowledgement of his words once more.

He didn't seem to worry about me not fulfilling my feminine duty to whisper sweet nothings back to him. "Bring it on, babe."

All my excuses and warnings used up, I sank back into his embrace, defeated. Or victorious. I wasn't sure which.

CHAPTER EIGHTEEN

Despite all my bravado in the fight that led to Luke and me being in a car a few minutes out of Amber, I was nervous.

Among other things.

The car was heading directly for my home. Not my house, but the Sons of Templar compound. My house didn't feel like my house anymore. It surely wasn't my home.

I'd brought it with the proceeds of some of my extracurricular activities. To solve any of the questions I would've gotten from buying said house with money that no one—apart from Wire—knew I had, I took the offer for the loan of a down payment from Steg. And from Cade. And then paid them back with each other's money.

I wagered they'd never find out because men didn't talk about that kind of stuff at the best of times, and at that point, Cade and Steg were very far from the best of times.

It was now mortgage free and had a tenant by the name of Gage living there.

Which stopped it from being my house, because I didn't even

want to entertain what twisted shit he'd gotten up to. He'd put me to shame.

But we weren't going there.

It was weird, taking your boyfriend home to meet the family. Much weirder when your family was a motorcycle gang who would shoot anyone they decided wasn't good enough. It was off the reservation when your boyfriend had not only met but arrested at some point or another almost everyone in that entire family. Had spent a previous life trying to take them down.

But this wasn't that life anymore.

He wasn't coming to raid the compound, look for evidence.

He was coming as my boyfriend.

My heart was thundering so hard I wondered if it might jump right out of my throat. I had never been this scared on a single mission in Venezuela.

That might've been because of the visit—the unexpected one—I'd had from Cade a few days prior. I thought it was a good idea to call ahead and tell him Luke was coming so I didn't spring it on him and my brother didn't shoot him on reflex.

After I'd told them, there was silence on the other side of the line. "Hello? You didn't die, did you?"

"I'll be there in two hours," he growled, then hung up.

I didn't think my older brother would actually drive that far just to yell at me.

I should've known better.

He and Gwen turned up a little over two hours later. I reasoned the delay was because he didn't want Gwen coming. But she was there. Because he was a marshmallow.

Not right then, though.

"Him?" he roared. "Really, Rosie?" He began to pace the room. "I know you like to push the boundaries, consider yourself a rebel amongst rebels, but this is fucking...." He ran his hands through his hair.

"Love," Gwen interjected quietly, eyes on me and then her husband. "This is love, Cade."

I'd adored my sister-in-law since the moment I met her, but right then, I could've kissed her feet. For her gentle gaze and strong vote of support. For going up against Cade. For me.

He glared at his wife, but there was no iron behind it. "It's fucking not," he hissed. "It's Rosie being Rosie."

Gwen rolled her eyes. "Seriously, dude?"

"Don't call me dude," he snapped, real anger directed at his wife. "I'm your man."

Another eye roll. "Yes, you're my man," she agreed, eyes twinkling. "But you're also acting like a dude." She said the word so it sounded like an insult. "You're not blind, Cade Fletcher," she continued, her voice softer. "I know you like to think that you only see black, white, and red. That you don't see the emotional underpinning of this world we live in. The love." She gave him a look. "But I know better. You taught me better. You saw inside me what I didn't even know existed. That maybe I didn't want to know. So you're not going to bullshit me and say you don't see it in your own blood. This is Rosie being Rosie. Acting for Rosie. Not for you, not for the club, not for the countless women who owe their happiness and sanity, at least in part, to her. She is finally following her heart. You know the one that beats for the club? The one that all your grumbling men treasure above all else yet take for granted? The one that you're trying to blindly protect but instead are breaking by being the pigheaded macho man holding onto ancient grudges that don't mean shit if your sister's happiness and future are a casualty of it?"

He blinked at his wife. His glare was still in place, but it wasn't directed at her. His eyes changed, the entire structure of his body changed, under the weight of his wife's words. I thought he might still yell. Swear. Throw something.

He didn't do any of that. Instead he stared at his wife.

"Fuck, I love you, baby," he murmured.

Gwen grinned. "I love you more."

So he'd left drunk on Gwen, forgetting to even give Luke a death threat.

There were no guarantees, though.

Luke's hand fastened over mine, stilling them when I hadn't even realized they were moving.

He rubbed his thumb over my palm. "You're fidgeting," he observed.

He was driving again, his truck this time. And I didn't mind because that meant I'd gotten to take healthy swigs of the margarita I'd put into a sippy cup before we left.

I glared at him. "Yes, that's what people do when they're nervous."

He smiled at me, and damn if my glare didn't just melt away. It wasn't as if I'd never seen Luke smile before, but I hadn't seen him *really* smile. Showing me he was happy, unobtrusively. And that I was the reason. Unobtrusively.

It quelled my nerves, that smile. Only a little though, because I was picturing a bullet, or at the very least a fist going through it as soon as we arrived.

Luke's hand moved to engulf mine and bring it to his lips so he could lay a kiss on my palm.

"It's going to be okay," he said.

I huffed but didn't take my hands from his. "That's what people always say right before everything goes to shit."

He chuckled. "Shit with you isn't shit, babe."

I gaped. "You're not nervous? Worried about the state of your body when you leave versus when you arrived? Because I am. I *like* the state of your body. The muscles and stuff, obviously, but the whole breathing and walking and talking thing too."

"I would've thought you might be happy if I was mute for a bit," Luke teased. "I always seem to piss you off with the talking."

I roll my eyes. "It would piss me off more if you *didn't* do it."

"Babe, we've got this, okay? You always think of the worst because you've always had to. Because too often, you've had the worst," he said, face turning serious. "But that's done with. No more worst, not before it goes through me. And your family will have to put a bullet somewhere to change that. But they won't, because they love you. I'll take a punch, babe. I've had worse."

I sighed and hoped he didn't get worse.

It was like Cade sensed that someone was coming to challenge his masculinity, because he was waiting in the parking lot, shades on, arms crossed when we parked.

"Oh, Jesus," I muttered. "He's decided to go *Leon: The Professional*."

Luke smiled and got out of the car.

I was too busy stewing to be quick enough to get out at the same time, which gave Luke the opportunity to get my door, which he groaned about not being able to do. Some of the good guy remained, the best parts.

"Ready?" I asked as he grasped my hand and walked toward Cade.

"Since you were five years old," he murmured.

I glared at him. Of course he'd say something that sweet right as we stopped in front of my brother, the man who looked like he might actually shoot Luke.

"Rosie, go inside," Cade barked.

I turned my glare to him, who was directing his murderous stare at Luke, who, surprisingly, was mild-faced.

"Hello to you too, big brother," I snapped.

He whipped his shades to me. "Rosie, I need to talk to your...."

"Boyfriend?" I finished for him.

Cade scowled and nodded once.

I squeezed Luke's hand. "You're not throwing your macho shit ordering me around and beating Luke up." I moved forward, in front of Luke, shielding him from any blow that Cade might decide to land. "You'll have to go through me first."

Cade pushed his shades to the top of his head in frustration. "Really, Rosie? The dramatics necessary?"

I gaped. "Seriously? I'm not the one who was standing in the middle of the parking lot like Snake Plissken."

There was gentle pressure at my hips as Luke turned me. "Babe, it's okay," he murmured.

"No it's not. You don't have to play this game. It's a dumb dick-swinging contest. I have it on very good authority that you don't need to do that." I was disappointed that I didn't get to see Cade's glare at the comment, but the fury was hot on my back.

Luke kissed my head, smiling and shaking his own. "I appreciate you lookin' out for me, babe, but this needs to happen. I can take care of myself. And no matter what, I'm in there, right behind you, okay?" he promised, nodding to the clubhouse.

I paused, frowning. "I don't like this," I grumbled, turning to scowl at Cade. "And you hurt him, I will shoot you," I promised. My gun was in my purse.

Cade didn't answer.

"Thought tensions might be high," Luke said, putting his hand in his pocket and opening his palm to reveal a handful of bullets. "Took them out to make sure you don't do something you'd regret."

I would've had a lot to say about that had I not seen the corner of Cade's mouth twitch. In Cade World, that was considered a smile.

I pointed between the two men who I loved immensely in different ways. "Play nice," I ordered.

Luke grinned. "Always."

Cade, again, didn't answer.

I gave Luke one more lingering glance before I walked into the clubhouse.

I'd always felt easy, relaxed, walking in there.

But without Luke at my side, it didn't feel right.

I prayed that he was true to his promise, that no matter what, he'd be right behind me.

294

LUKE

He braced. Hard. For the hit—fuck, for the bullet. He was certain the former was coming; the latter was an educated guess. You didn't just walk into the compound you'd been trying to burn to the ground for years, stand in front of the man you'd hated for your entire life, the man whose life you were trying to ruin, tell him you loved his baby sister and get a pat on the back. No. Even in a normal situation you wouldn't get that. And this was so far from a normal situation he would laugh if he wasn't so fucking nervous.

Not about the inevitable punch or the semi-inevitable bullet.

He'd experienced a lot of the former and a fair few of the latter in his years wearing the badge. He was used to them. He sure as fuck wasn't afraid of them.

He was afraid of any life without Rosie. Fucked up, but he was finding it hard to remember that he had any life before her. It sounded ridiculous, like he was a character in some Nicholas Sparks book for even thinking it, but it was the truth. It was all murky, the before, like a half-remembered dream.

At least it was when he was with her.

Now that he was staring in the face of the man who could alter the course of his life, his past, that dream, was promising an ugly and stark reality of a future without her if this didn't go well.

Rosie's family were everything to her. Some women built their worth on things, on looks, money, the men they could bed, the fucking image they put on their social media. Not Rosie. Her worth, her life, her happiness were packaged into that clubhouse, gated off and secured with barbed wire. She'd let him in, but the man in front of him could kick him out.

He'd never thought he'd want to so badly be in there.

They stared at each other for a long time. The length of a lifetime he'd be promised if this went to shit. Cade had this way of staring at a man like he had all the time in the world to cut his guts out and show them to him. Just for fun. It didn't scare Luke. At least not before.

"You love her?" Cade grunted finally, breaking the uneasy silence.

Luke was momentarily surprised it was words that broke the silence instead of the unmistakable sound of a fist on flesh or a bullet discharging, but he recovered quickly.

"Yeah," he replied.

Cade gave him that stare once more, testing the truth in that single word.

Luke supposed he had a lot of practice in staring at a man and looking for a lie in his eyes. Probably more than Luke did, though he'd never admit that out loud.

Cade nodded once. "Okay. Let's have a beer."

Luke gaped at him. Openly gaped. He could feel the loss of his poker face and didn't have it in him to regain it.

"You're shitting me," he spluttered. "That's it?"

Cade nodded again. "That's it."

Luke ran his hand through his hair. "You're not spiking my beer with arsenic?"

Cade made a grunt that sounded suspiciously like a chuckle. "Poison's a woman's weapon. Not my sister's, of course. Hers is a G42. Subtlety is not her strong suit. Runs in the family."

"But it can't be that simple," Luke said, a smile of his own threatening the corner of his mouth.

"Not many things in life are that simple," Cade said. "It's fuckin' tiring dealing with them. Why the fuck try to make the simple things complicated too? Lost patience for that shit the second I saw life without my wife. My kids." His eyes went dark. "So you love my sister. She's happy, really happy this time, so that means she loves you. Do I wish she was with someone who didn't spend the majority of his career trying to bring down my club? Perhaps. But then again, maybe not. Not my choice. Know by experience it's not yours, or even hers either.

We don't get to control that shit. We're just lucky enough to live it."

Luke stared at Cade. The man who, up until recently, he'd thought of as a criminal, as a cold-blooded killer. Who he'd never heard that many words from... ever.

"Don't get me wrong. You hurt her, I'll cut off your dick and feed it to you," Cade continued conversationally. "After she's done with you, of course." He eyed him shrewdly. "Don't expect I'll be needing to do that, though. I repeat the question. Do you love her?"

Like before, without hesitation, Luke answered, "Yes."

Cade shrugged. "Then it's that simple."

He turned on his heel, walking toward the entrance of the clubhouse that Luke had never been an invited guest of before in his entire life. If there ever was going to be an invitation, Cade's shrug and small monologue followed by his exit that didn't include a death threat or the brandishing of a weapon was it.

Luke stared at the patch on the back of Cade's cut, the grim reaper taunting him: 'The Sons of Templar MC.'

All his life, he was convinced that piece of leather, all who wore it, and everything it represented were nothing short of the Devil. He tried to think of what specifically gave him that impression, that bloodthirsty need to see the entire club and its members dismantled and cuffed.

Laurie's death? No, it was before that. But that certainly fed into his obsession.

He could stand there and ponder the origins of that hate. Or he could choose to leave it right there in the dirt, the last scrap of what remained of his previous life. His badge was long gone, and sometimes he missed the weight of it, but then he thought about that weight on his heart. The buck fifty of it, the chocolate curls that tumbled over it. Rosie's favorite place, and his favorite place for her—besides on his dick.

The decision wasn't so hard then.

Cade was right. It really was that simple.

He followed the grim reaper.

ROSIE

The moments you expected in life to be climatic and chaotic usually weren't that way. When you built something up to be either terrible or utterly awesome, most of the time you were disappointed or relieved.

Not that I ever really *expected* chaos or climatic. I lived in it. Normal would've been more unexpected.

But I did expect Luke, out of uniform, next to my brother, walking into the clubhouse during a party to have somewhat of an effect.

Especially when his eyes immediately found me, then his feet, then finally his arms.

There was a pause in all the noise, in all the chaos, so small I might've imagined it. Then it was gone, the music was loud, the men were louder, and drinks were flowing.

I didn't notice any of that, too busy cataloguing Luke for injuries.

He laughed. "I'm not bleedin' or bruised, babe," he said, rubbing my arms.

I frowned. "I'm not convinced. I'll have to give you a very thorough physical. Later."

My stomach dipped even as I said the words, my skin prickling as Luke's eyes darkened.

"Your brother didn't shoot me on sight, Rosie," he growled. "Don't push your luck by making me take you to an empty hall and fuck your brains out." His lips brushed my ear and my panties dampened. "Though, I'd risk getting shot to be fucking you hard and fast against a wall."

I swallowed roughly, glancing around the room. "Stop, Luke," I whispered. "Because you keep talking like that, I might let you.

And I don't want you to get shot."

His hand brushed over my ass. "Later," he murmured, just as Lucky sauntered up, grinning, his arm around Bex.

"Well fucking well," he said as greeting. "The white sheep of the family returns, and she brought a friend." His eyes went to Luke. "More than friend. So it's good I didn't shoot you, isn't it, buddy?" He was grinning, none of his previous distaste for Luke showing. It was as if he hadn't been in this very clubhouse a year ago, about to be shot and arrested by Luke.

Lucky didn't hold grudges.

I grinned, and so did Luke. "Yeah, I'd have to say I'm fuckin' glad too," Luke replied easily.

Seemed he didn't hold grudges either.

The conversation was interrupted by Brock and Amy—or, more accurately, Amy.

"You little fucking bitch!" she yelled, yanking me out of Luke's arm with a wink and into her cloud of Chanel No.5. She squeezed hard, then let me go. "I fucking knew this was going to happen," she said confidently. "But I'm kind of disappointed. You didn't blow anything up or get shot or anything during the courtship." She frowned. "I expected more from you."

I laughed. "The night's still young."

Brock yanked his wife back into his embrace. "For fuck's sake, Sparky, don't jinx shit like that," he growled, kissing her head with a tenderness that didn't match his gruff tone. "Perhaps we've had enough of that drama, thought of that?"

He squeezed her tight, as if he was scared her drama involving the father of the man I shot last year was going to rise from the grave and almost kill Amy a second time.

Though even flesh-eating zombies would have a hard—try impossible—time snatching Amy away again.

She rolled her eyes. "There's no such thing as too much drama, right, Bex?"

Bex grinned, toying with Lucky's wedding ring. "Oh, I don't

know. I'd say car bombs and shootings are quite enough drama." Her eyes went faraway for a second, the year anniversary of that drama fast approaching. The day I shot someone. The day we lost Scott. It hit her hard, that loss. Cracked the pieces she'd only just put back together.

Lucky sensed it, as the men seemed to do, understanding their women's distress. He tilted her head up and kissed her on the nose. "Love you, baby," he murmured, loud enough for everyone to hear and not giving a fuck about it either.

She smiled. "Love you."

"Can you not engage in full-on s-e-x right now? I have an impressionable young child approaching," Mia yelled, Rocko grinning beside her. His little hand was grasping his father's large, tattooed pinky. His father was a giant compared to him.

Bull was holding his wife's other hand.

Bex grinned wickedly. "As if we'd start having sex right here."

Mia grinned back. "You did it last week."

Lucky shrugged. "I put a sock on the door."

Mia laughed. "No you didn't." Then her eyes went to me, glowing. She snatched me from Amy, yanking me into her arms. "I'm so glad about this." She gestured between Luke and me, then looked at her beautiful brute of a husband. "Zane is too, but it mucks with his street cred to squeal about the love fluttering in the air. He did it at home though." She winked.

Bull merely shook his head, grinning.

Such a facial expression was commonplace for most people, but for Bull, it was pivotal. Because not so long ago, he didn't smile, didn't laugh, didn't live. His body was walking around in this world, but his soul was somewhere else. Somewhere horrible where the day of Laurie's death was on repeat.

But Mia brought him back.

Even if she wasn't completely awesome, and completely insane with a hugely famous rock-star daughter, I'd love her for that alone.

I caught Lily's eye from where she was sitting on the sofa. She was cradling her tiny newborn, Emily, in her arms. Asher had his arms around her, his other hand cradling his daughter's head.

I blew her a kiss.

Luke claimed me, back to his front.

And I fit. Perfectly.

Funnily enough, so did he.

"Cade is talking to Luke and not shooting him. I'm impressed," Lizzie said, sitting down after giving up on chasing her children around to try and stop them getting into trouble.

They were with Rocko, so trouble was inevitable.

I sipped my beer, watching Cade's mouth move, saying something to Luke that didn't resemble a death threat.

"Yeah, I'm as surprised as you," I told her. I looked around at all the people who made me who I was, then to Luke. "Do you think they hate me?" I whispered, letting out my last insecurity to one of my oldest friends, one of the club's first old ladies, apart from Evie.

Lizzie's beautiful face screwed up. "You've been fighting for all of these people your entire life," she said, gaze going around the bustling outdoor area, touching fondly on her husband and her daughter for a moment. "Fighting tooth and nail." She focused her attention back on me. "Taking every inch of pain away whenever you could, absorbing it yourself. You're the central nervous system of this club, babe." She looked around again, finding Gwen, squealing with laughter as her husband yanked her backward into his embrace. "You were there for Gwen when she arrived in this town, despite her catching the eye of the man you loved."

I couldn't hide my flinch at Lizzie's observation, her offhand comment betraying her knowledge of a secret I'd guarded with ferocity my whole life. She said it like it was nothing. Not that it didn't mean something, but that my very emotion toward Luke wasn't some kind of betrayal.

She didn't stop to let me mull on it.

"You accepted her into your family. Took care of her when this life threatened everything she'd built. Took care of your brother when she left a gaping hole in his heart when she left. Welcomed your niece with a love that spread through the whole town when she came back, all the while standing with Steg and Evie throughout his recovery." She moved her gaze to Amy, who was staring so hard at her husband cradling my adorable nephew, Kingston, in his large arms that she spilled her entire cocktail onto the yellowing grass and didn't even notice. "You gave Amy everything she needed when she was going through the grief of losing the man she loved and the guilt of loving Brock more than that. Fuck, you even almost died with her driving to get *booze*."

I rose my brow. "Booze is important, even though Amy has forgotten that." She'd now discarded her empty glass and was going to sink into her husband's embrace. He kissed her red hair first, then her mouth, like he wasn't holding a two-year-old kid. Then again, I was sure Kingston had already seen his parents' PDA.

Lizzie smiled. She didn't stay on them for long; instead she found Mia, chasing around Rocko, who seemed to have some form of weapon in his chubby toddler hands. I smiled myself. That kid was going to be crazier than both Lucky and Gage combined when he grew up. Shit, he was crazier than them *now*.

He let out a little scream of joy when his normally stoic father scooped him up with smiling eyes, kissing his son's head and shaking his own at the same time when he saw what was in his small hands. Mia put her hands on her hips, scowling at her husband with a glare filled with love.

"You helped a single mom understand that the man she loved was broken almost beyond repair, and you helped her figure out how to fix him," Lizzie said softly. Her eyes glimmered. "Even though seeing him with someone else who wasn't your best friend hurt every part of you. You were finally saying goodbye, realizing she was finally gone." Her words were thick with emotion, true to the core, as if she'd plucked my grief from my mind.

Laurie was part of her life too. A big part. Which meant even now, years later, we both felt the wind whistling through that empty piece of us.

I leaned over to squeeze her hand. She smiled, the expression full of melancholy, then squeezed back. She sucked in a painful gulp of air, then moved her gaze once more. It found Lily, sitting slightly removed from the chaos, pushing a stroller with that absent rhythm a mother has, almost without thinking. Her eyes were far away, focusing on the horizon. Then they weren't. Then they focused on her husband, lighting with love and happiness so genuine and beautiful it was almost hard to look at. He returned the gaze tenfold. Seeing them apart, you would never guess the shy, beautiful woman would fit with the large, muscled biker. He reached her, gently removing her hand from the stroller, though not before checking inside with that same love glowing in his eye, visible even from across the party. It'd be visible from the moon. Satisfied his daughter was safely slumbering, he yanked his wife into his body, kissing her fully and not at all chastely on the mouth.

And there it was. They fit.

I was still staring when a voice punctured the quiet beauty of the moment.

"Gabriel, you asshole! Put me the fuck down," a voice demanded.

Lizzie and I focused our attention on the source of the yell, both of us already grinning. We couldn't see Bex's midnight cropped hair, just the top of her ass cheek that rested on top of Lucky's cut as he carted her inside over his shoulder.

He caught my eye and winked at the exact same moment he landed a firm slap on Bex's ass.

That resulted in another string of curses. Lucky's grin widened. As did mine.

"You took in a beautiful and immensely broken girl," Lizzie whispered. "Took her into your home, took care of her when she couldn't take care of herself. Protected her the best you could from her own demons, even if it meant living with your own." She paused. "You pulled the trigger on a man who deserved to die, even though you didn't deserve the nightmares that came from taking his life."

Her words, her tone, were as gentle as the touch of a feather, but the memories they carried weighed on me like a stone.

"You did that, even if it meant putting a bullet wound in your own happily ever after. Without a second of hesitation."

Lizzie's hands squeezed mine, and I blinked away the grim reaper that beckoned me as a comrade. A friend.

I focused on her midnight-blue eyes as they crossed the party once more, meeting Ranger's as he wrestled with a toddler to try and clean ice cream off his face.

"Little help, babe," he bellowed across the party.

Lizzie grinned. "You're a big bad biker. I think you can handle it," she teased.

"I'll handle you," he growled, eyes glowing with erotic promise.

Lizzie's cheeks reddened as she giggled like a schoolgirl, even almost a decade into her marriage. She was still madly in love with her husband. Like a teenager. And even though he was wrestling a toddler much like a man might wrangle with an alligator, his gaze never left her for long, as if he was afraid if he didn't glance at her enough, she might slip away. The way a man might look at the stars to make sure he didn't get lost forever in dark and lonely woods.

"You rescued a marriage that had lost its way," she said, almost too low to hear. "You did something that made sure two people weren't walking around bleeding without a half of themselves for the rest of their lives. You made sure I still had this wonderful life that I let others pollute and taint."

I blinked away the tears at the corner of my eyes. Not many people knew about the darkest days of Lizzie's and Ranger's lives. They were two of the cornerstones of this club. Never in the spotlight, but always there. Throughout all the drama and death, they remained constant support. Like Steg and Evie, or Goldie and Kurt, they were the couple that made you not give up on the magic.

For a moment, the magic gave up on them. They had to fight harder for anyone else in this club for a love that blew Romeo and Juliet out of the water.

No one knew.

Because that wasn't my story to tell.

"You've fought for us all. And each and every one of us knows you'd fight to the bitter, or hopefully happy, end," Lizzie continued. "But you need to start fighting for yourself. The one person you've neglected all these years. You have been God knows where doing God knows what. I don't want to know because I'm not like you. I'm not strong enough to handle what one of the most precious people in my life has struggled through. I don't need to know because it's written all over your face. It's changed you. And I know you went through that because you were helping someone. Know you would've plunged into horror that would even make Gage blush if it meant you were helping someone. Fighting for someone. But you're home now. You've done it. Saved everyone who needed saving. Now it's time to do it for yourself. Save yourself, babe."

I looked at her, my eyes blurry once more, barely able to hold in the emotion she'd roused within me. "I can't do that," I choked, hating the weakness in my voice. "Admitting I need saving is admitting I'm...."

"Human?" Lizzie finished for me. "I'll tell you a secret. We all are. Even these idiotic macho men who think they can crush cars

305

during bicep curls," she joked, eyes moving to her macho-man husband for a second. "It's okay to be human, you know. It's painful, immensely so, but the rewards are worth it. But it's not easy. Not like the movies. True love doesn't fall into place. It isn't as easy as breathing. It's a struggle. Takes work. Every day. You've got to fight for it, but it's only the most beautiful of things that are worth fighting for."

I sucked in a ragged breath, my eyes finding Luke. His had been on me for what looked like a long time.

"Fuck yeah it is," I whispered.

Lizzie was hauled away by her husband not long after her heart-to-heart. But not before he kissed my cheek and smiled at me, his wrinkled eyes sparkling. "Happy for you, girl. You deserve this."

Then he left. No long speeches, no drama, just saying what he meant in as few words as possible.

That was Ranger.

The space beside me wasn't empty for long. My eyes were focused on Luke chatting with Brock in what actually looked like a pleasant conversation, so I hadn't realized Evie had sat down until she spoke.

"Sure know how to shake things up, babe," she commented, her eyes following mine.

I grinned. "Don't I always?"

She lit a smoke. "True, but you shake things up in what people think are some of the most dangerous ways, but until now, they were the safest."

I frowned at her. "What do you mean?"

Evie was still focused on Luke. "You've spent a lifetime being strong, babe." She drew in her cigarette. "Not just for you, but a whole club full of men who are only really as strong as the women they love and the women who love them." She blew the smoke out. "You saw that shit, what it did. So you kept being strong and made sure you didn't wear the particular brand of love that made you weak. That dangerous kind." She eyed me shrewdly. "Don't doubt your courage, girl. You've got more of it than any man in here." Her gaze went around the party, focusing on Steg for just a moment, her hard eyes softening at the corners. "But the bravest thing you'll ever do in your life is let someone love you, and love them back." Her eyes went to me, squeezing my hand in a rare gesture of tenderness. "Don't turn into a coward now when it means the most."

I looked at her, at the woman who was more of a mother than my own mother ever could've been. "I won't," I promised.

"Ah, impressed you stayed away for this long," Evie remarked, eyes no longer on me.

I focused on Luke, who'd obviously made his way over to us during Evie's version of a heart-to-heart.

He grinned, sitting beside me. "Stayed away for long enough already, ma'am. Not looking to do it much in the future."

She nodded, face mild. "You call me ma'am again, we'll have problems."

I swallowed a giggle.

Luke's eyes twinkled. "So noted."

Evie got up, brushing ash off her jeans. She focused on Luke, that mild look still on her face. "Her will and courage are stronger than that of anyone I've ever met. Unbreakable, like a fucking diamond. Her heart, though, it's as fragile as glass. You'd do well to remember that, if you're fond of breathing." It wasn't a threat exactly, but there was a violent undertone.

Luke nodded again, and then Evie was gone, in the direction of Steg.

Luke's arm went around me and I immediately sank into him. He kissed my head.

"You're not considering running away yet?" I asked, half joking.

He pulled back, eyes serious. "Never fucking running away from you, babe. And I won't let you do it either."

"I won't," I promised. "I don't think I physically could."

He kissed me hard on the mouth. "That's the way it should be."

It seemed that the day I'd thought everyone in my family would disown me—the day I brought Luke home—was the day that everyone told me what an idiot I was.

But in a more delicate way.

Not one single person had shown any hostility toward Luke or me.

But there was one noticeable person who hadn't said anything.

He was sitting at the bar, on his own; Evie had taken Belle and Kingston home so Gwen and Cade could have a night together.

"You gonna be okay here if I go talk to Steg?" I asked Luke.

He squeezed me, then let me go, eyes following mine as I stood. "'Course, babe."

We were on the sofa inside, shooting the shit with Bex, Lucky, and Gage.

Gage clapped his large hand on Luke's back. "Sure, he'll be fine. I'll take care of him," he promised.

I gave him a look, then turned to Lucky. "You do not let him do any fucked-up shit to my boyfriend," I ordered.

Lucky shrugged. "Hey, he might like it."

I shook my head and went to sit beside Steg. He silently poured me a drink. I sipped it, letting the silence simmer, waiting for him to say something. He didn't.

"You're not disappointed in me?" I asked hesitantly.

I had to ask, but fuck, I didn't want the answer. This man was rough, dangerous, cold and sometimes downright cruel. But never to me. Never. He taught me everything he knew about being an outlaw, and I taught him how to be a father. It wasn't his choice or his calling, but he took to it, went all in, doing the absolute best he could.

And I loved him. Felt safe with him. Protected.

So he did his job.

He looked to me. "Disappointed?" he parroted. Then he looked to Luke, who had somehow gotten Gage laughing. "Fuck no, girl. Not even surprised."

I blinked.

"You're a rebel in a world of rebel. Rule breaker in a world where there are no rules. It's only logical that you'd search for somethin' to be the ultimate rebellion. 'Spect that might've been part of it, at least at the start maybe." He regarded me. "More likely you saw a good man thinking he had to go down a path that's famed to be paved with good intentions. Different road to the one some of the brothers have walked, but same destination, though. And like you've done with many of those brothers, this one included, you took him off that path. You being you, you probably convinced yourself that was a bad thing. *You* were a bad thing. 'Cause that's you. Thinking with your heart, forsaking it for others. But he's here and there's light in your eyes, so I'm guessin' he convinced you that you're far from a bad thing. And he looks at you like you tether him to this earth. Plus, you got the biggest unbribeable lawmaker off our asses." He chuckled. "Disappointed? No, my girl, I am not. I'm happy. Finally happy my family is there."

"Where?" I asked in a small voice.

"*There.* The place where they're meant to be. With who they're meant to be with." He narrowed his eyes. "Though there hasn't been near enough drama for it to be the end of this."

"There's been drama," I countered. "More than enough of it. Maybe we're done."

He laughed. Actually threw his head back and cackled. "No, my girl, done is something we aren't, nor will we ever be," he said once he'd finished. "Especially you. You aren't one to live quiet, my girl. Not one to *love* quiet. It's comin'. Just make sure the causalities are other fuckers who ain't you," he ordered.

I smiled. "Of course. You taught me well."

He grinned back, full of melancholy that I'd never glimpsed on Steg's face. Every funeral, every injury, every battle, Steg was dry-eyed and determined. He was the face of the Sons of Templar, after all, and emotions meant weakness.

The Sons of Templar weren't weak.

But now, in the corner of the room, I was watching. Not weakness, but some other kind of strength.

"It's in your blood," he said. "Your daddy did the real work, raisin' a little girl who could outshoot me before she finished elementary school, instilling loyalty in you that almost made you throw away your own happiness for the club that your father taught you to die for. I just picked up where he left off. And even at seven, the job of raisin' you was done. Only thing I had to do was give you enough space, enough freedom to be, but enough direction not to get yourself killed." He squeezed my hand. "You're a good woman, Rosie. You're the heart of this club, just remember that. So making decisions to fill that heart up is never going to break the club."

His eyes went to Luke once more, whose eyes were on me, dancing with a playfulness that I didn't think would've been possible today.

Maybe wishes did come true.

For a time, at least.

CHAPTER NINETEEN

TWO MONTHS LATER

"Motherfucker is *dead*," I said as soon as I opened the door.

Just because it had been two months of what I could only call peace, that didn't mean I wasn't prepared for chaos.

I had expected it to be my own. I was okay with that. I was ready for that. Partly because I was used to it. Mostly because I had Luke at my side and felt all corny and cliché that with him, with us finally together, we could do anything.

It wasn't perfect. Life never was.

But it was something close to it.

We fought. A lot.

We also made up. A lot.

We were basically living together. Most of our time was spent at his place because it was bigger, closer to all my favorite restaurants and had more exciting surfaces to have sex on.

He had tried to get me to move in with him almost immediately after we'd gotten home from Amber. I'd said no. Not because of the normal reasons about it being too fast or that I needed to keep my independence or whatever bullshit women spouted when they were too afraid to make a dangerous decision.

Because no matter how much I liked the space and location of Luke's or the coziness and residency of my shoe collection, neither of them were home.

Now that I'd decided to jump in with both my Manolo-clad feet, I was going all in, in Rosie style. So we were looking for a home.

Together.

But I was not about to rush into where that new home would be. Like Cher said in *Clueless*, "You know how picky I am about my shoes and they only go on my feet." That was my attitude about our home. And also my shoes.

Luke was patient. "If this is going to be your home, your real one, your first real one, then take ten months to choose, babe. Take ten years. I've found my home. I'm holding it in my arms. So I'll wait for the perfect four walls and roof. As long as I fall asleep and wake up with you, the rest is just details."

Of course he just had to go all romantic. And I looked like an asshole for caring about the four walls and a roof. I loved him. A lot. But that didn't mean I didn't want the perfect house.

It was busy, house hunting, working together, hanging out with the family I'd missed greatly, and having all the sex. So busy that there wasn't time for too much drama. Or at least stuff that was out of the ordinary. Being in love with a man who you also worked with bounty hunting and such could be perceived as drama.

I perceived it as just another Tuesday.

But now drama was at my door. In the form of Polly.

With an eye so bruised and swollen that she likely couldn't see out of it.

"He did this?" I seethed, gently bringing her into my arms.

She didn't say anything, just sank into my embrace and sobbed soundlessly.

"Fucking *Craig*," I hissed.

I held her for a while, my anger growing. It mingled with my hurt, my immense pain at seeing another innocent girl battered at the hands of an asshole man. It would've hurt with any one of my sisters, friends or strangers. But Polly was different. She was the last of them. The last of my girls who didn't let the ugliness of the world tarnish the beautiful way she saw it. That didn't mean she didn't know sorrow, but she had this way of enduring it, not letting it make her hard.

Like Laurie.

Laurie had been broken and battered and murdered in the end.

Again, that sore spot that never quite healed and never quite would throbbed with that pain.

Because now it was Polly. I prayed it was the first time. That it wasn't any worse than it looked. And it already looked pretty fucking bad.

It didn't matter if it was one punch or five. First time or tenth. The mere act of taking someone who loved and lived so gently and then treating them so brutally was the ultimate sin.

And deserved the ultimate punishment.

I pushed Polly backward so I could gently frame her face and inspect the purplish red bruise steadily growing.

It was fresh.

Hours old.

"Are you hurt anywhere else?" I asked, using all my effort to keep my voice gentle. Looking at Polly, she needed gentle. She needed gentle hours before, but I couldn't change or control someone else's actions in the past. I could only control my actions in the present.

And my actions against them in the future.

She hiccupped. "No," she said shakily.

I nodded. "He didn't... do anything else?" I asked, praying to whoever was left to take care of this ugly world that the answer would be no.

She blinked, confused.

In her confusion, I found my relief. Because she didn't know what I was talking about, for a second at least. If it had happened, the worst, she would've known. Her body and mind would've been reminding her of it, not allowing her the momentary luxury of confusion.

"No," she realized finally, not knowing she'd already answered my question. "No, God, no. He just hit me," she whispered.

I grabbed her hand. "There's no *just*," I said firmly. "There's no spectrum of just a little bit of bad. Hitting a woman once or a thousand times is the same sin. I'm so sorry it happened to you, my Pol."

Again, she sank into my arms, sobbing loudly that time.

I really wanted to cry too. But I stayed strong.

For my friend. For my sister.

And for the coming revenge I would make sure I personally delivered.

"Thanks," Polly whispered, taking the mug of tea I offered her.

I hadn't even realized I had herbal tea. I found it stashed in the back of the cupboard, a remnant of Polly's temporary habitation.

"You sure you don't want wine?" I asked, sitting next to her. "Or tequila?"

She shook her head.

The quiet with Polly was almost as bad as the ever-worsening bruise covering almost half of her face.

Polly wasn't quiet.

She was never quiet.

She might've lived her life gently, but she did it loud.

And he took that from her.

I clenched my fist.

"You can't tell anyone," Polly whispered.

I snapped my head to her. "What are you talking about? Of course I'm telling people. Namely the crew I'll be assembling to make *Craig* a eunuch before we bury him in a shallow grave."

I wondered whether we could track down Heath. I knew he'd be the first in line to deal the killing blow.

His and Polly's relationship was complicated when I'd expected it to be simple. The girl lived for love. And even though I didn't believe in that shit, the way Heath looked at her, it was love.

I was certain there would've been a rushed wedding after seeing that look. I was right about the wedding, wrong about the groom.

And Polly, the girl who usually told Lucy and me everything about her current beau, down to his preferred brand of toothpaste, refused to utter a word about Heath and the looks.

He'd disappeared before the wedding.

Who could blame him?

"No, you can't," Polly said, roughly setting her mug down so the steaming liquid sloshed onto the coffee table. She snatched my hands. "Please."

I narrowed my eyes. "Please don't tell me you're going back to him."

She sharpened her own gaze. "Of course not. He lost me the second his hand turned into a fist." Her voice was strong, resolute.

So there was that.

"Well then, what's with the insane demand to keep something that is A, hard to hide, and B, something that needs to be dealt with a secret?" I demanded.

She regarded me. "You know what everyone thinks of me. Polly the romantic idiot. Head in the clouds. Clueless. My family's been in enough pain. I'm not causing them more. Not giving them another reason that they have to take care of me. They deserve to take care of themselves."

My heart hurt with her words, and the way the hurt in her voice told me she believed them. "No, babe. That's not what everyone thinks of you. You're the woman with a big heart, a bigger smile and strength to not let the world turn her natural beauty into inevitable cynicism," I said. "And your family will be in more pain if they know you went through this alone."

She blinked away her tears. "But I'm not alone. I've got you. Don't I?"

"Of course you've got me, idiot. You've got a lot more people though, babe. Trust me, this kind of stuff is easier to get through when you see how many people won't leave your side," I told her.

"Maybe," she agreed. "But this is the way I want to do it. And I'm asking you, as my friend, to respect that."

I frowned. "You're asking me to lie to everyone."

"I came to you because I knew you'd understand," she said. "Because you kept things from your family because you knew you had to. Because no matter what other people would've told you, you had to do it alone."

I chewed my lip. "And that was a mistake."

"Maybe," she said again. "But this is my mistake to make."

"Fuck," I hissed.

"Is that a yes?" she asked.

I glared at her. "Of course it is. But I'm not happy about it."

She nodded. "Thank you."

"I'm guessing we're hiding you out here for the foreseeable future?"

"Just until my eye heals enough to cover it with makeup." She reached for her tea, cupping it rather than using the handle.

"Well, that's normally a week, but we're surrounded by alpha males who can sniff out hidden injuries from a mile away. They're itching to pound on their chests and protect their women, so we'll make it one for general outings but two if we have to visit your brother-in-law."

"Perfect. I've just discovered *Riverdale* on Netflix, so silver lining!" she said, a little louder than the eerie whisper, sounding almost like her old self.

But I knew too well that she'd never be her old self.

I stood.

"Where are you going? We can start from episode one. I don't mind rewatching," she said.

"You're moving back in here, I assume?" I asked.

Her face turned sad. "If that's okay?"

"Of course that's okay, you little nitwit," I said playfully. "But you didn't come here with any bags, so I'll go get your stuff." I walked to retrieve my purse, the new Chanel that contained my favorite lipstick and also my favorite Glock.

"Rosie, you can't kill him!" Polly exclaimed, abandoning her tea again and adding to the lake on the coffee table.

I turned. "I know," I sighed. "At least not yet."

She put her hands on her hips. "Not ever."

I rested my purse on my shoulder. "Seriously? The asshole *hit you*. You're not going back to him, so what do you care?"

"I care because at one time, I loved him. A part of him, however small, however fleeting. I care because I'm married to him, despite him hitting me and definitely being an asshole. I care because no matter how shitty of a human being he is, he's still a human being. It's not up to me or you to decide the punishment for that. He'll have his sins on his soul. I don't want them on mine."

Somehow, even with the evidence fresh and throbbing on her face, Polly was still determined to believe the world wasn't about sin and punishment.

It was that determination that gave me pause.

"Please, for me," she whispered. "I know you operate under different rules than I do. And I would never judge you for that. Everyone lives their own life, and I understand yours. I respect it. But I can't live it. So please, Rosie."

I stared at her. "Fine," I grumbled. "I'll just get your stuff and I won't shoot him," I promised.

She smiled, big and bright and somehow free of the demons that should've been lurking there. "Thank you."

"Whatever," I muttered, walking out the door.

I'd promised not to shoot him. That just meant I had to get creative.

Unsuspecting, I'd opened the door to one of the gentlest humans I knew with a tattoo of violence on her face.

It was only fair that Craig got the same.

Or a version.

As soon as he opened the door, his face met the brass knuckles Gage had given me for Christmas.

Despite being what most people would call petite, I could throw a punch. Craig obviously could too, but he sure as shit couldn't take one.

The crunch of metal against bone was followed by a gurgled cry and Craig collapsing to the floor.

I stepped over his groaning body into his apartment, looked around.

"Nice place you got here," I said, dangling my gun from the hand that didn't have my brass knuckles on it.

He was still groaning.

"Pussy," I muttered.

I looked down at him. His cheek had opened up and blood was spurting all over his no-doubt expensive rug. His eye was already swelling.

"Oh, would you look at that," I said, standing over him. "You and your wife will match now."

"It was an accident," he groaned.

I bent at my knees so both I and my gun were in his face. His eyes radiated fear and cowardice.

"Oh, why didn't you say so? An accident? Well, that's okay, then. What'd she do? Not press your laundry right? Fuck up the eggs? She must've deserved it then," I said. Then I pistol-whipped him. "It was an accident when your mother got pregnant with you. That's the only accident here."

He blinked rapidly, holding his head and barely focusing.

I snatched the collar of his shirt. "See, you're stupid. Because you had the whole world in your hands and all you needed to do was treat her right. It's not hard with a woman like that, who'd rip her heart out of her chest for you. And she would've. But luckily, you showed your true colors early, so she didn't waste a huge chunk of her life with you. She's soft and tender, but she's not weak, so she's not going to blame herself or come back to you after you laid your hands on her. Luckily, she's too much of a good person to let me kill you."

I fastened the barrel to his forehead.

"Luckily for *you*. Not me. I would love to do it, trust me, but that would hurt Polly. And unlike you, I would never do that, even if it's doing the world a favor." I glared at him. "So here's what's going to happen, I'm going to get her stuff. You'll stay here, weak and crying on the floor, where you belong. Where you were stupid enough to think Polly would stay. You won't get up until after I leave. Then, when you're served with divorce papers, you will sign them, along with half of everything you own, even the stuff you've hidden in places you don't think anyone will find it." I pressed the barrel harder. "I'll find it. And if you're hiding anything from me, Craig, I'll hide your body so good only the aliens that take over our planet in a few hundred years will find your bones. Capisce?"

He leered at me. "You can't get away with it," he spat.

"Oh yes I can," I said softly. "You know I can. You know who Polly's brother-in-law is. You also need to know that the Sons of

Templar have her back. They're scary enough, but more importantly, *I've* got her back. And I know you think I'm a weak woman,
but trust me, you haven't seen shit. So be a good boy and don't
find out, 'kay?"

I waited for him to answer. I wasn't impatient.

I only moved the gun when he nodded once.

"Perfection," I said, dusting off my dress and putting my gun
and bloody brass knuckles back in my Chanel.

It was late before Luke got home.

He was away chasing a skip. Usually I'd be with him, but the
Golden Globes were on.

"You're not coming out because of some stupid awards show?"
he'd said that morning.

I gasped. "You take that back," I demanded. "It's *the* award
show. The one to start the season. Jen and Ange are going to be
attending. *Both of them.* Do you have any clue what that means?"

He stifled a grin. "None whatsoever, but I do take it back. It
totally makes sense to miss work for it."

I scowled at him, stifling my own smile.

He kissed me rough and hard. "Love you, babe."

I smiled full-on at that. "Love you."

He paused.

"I thought you were leaving," I said.

"Just takin' in the moment," he murmured.

"What moment?"

"The one where I get to kiss my woman goodbye, knowin' I'll
come home to her. Say three words that have been trapped in me
for decades. Just like to savor it sometimes. That feeling. The one
that tells me that life may be ugly and hard and violent, but it's
worth it for the fucking beauty of moments like this."

His stare was unyielding.

"I... we... you can't say things like that to me, Luke," I snapped. "Men don't say that in real life."

"Guess I'm dreamin', then," he said. He kissed me again, that time soft and tender. "Bye, babe," he murmured against my mouth.

"Yeah," I breathed.

I hadn't gotten to watch the Golden Globes, as it turned out. But I did have dozens of texts from Lucy telling me who she thought wore it better.

I got a pang looking at my phone thinking about how oblivious she was, thinking of dresses and feuds when her sister was sleeping away a broken marriage, a broken heart, and a very bruised face.

The door opened before I could contemplate whether I was being a good friend to one person at the expense of another.

"Honey, you're home," I chirped.

He was on me in three large strides. Granted, the apartment wasn't that big. Despite everything, I melted into his kiss.

It was far too short as he pulled back, face lazy and happy. That was until he zeroed in on my hand.

Brass knuckles were effective but they left marks. The force of my blow had broken the skin on a couple of fingers, and my hand was a light shade of purple in some places.

He snatched my hand. "What the fuck, Rosie? I thought you were staying home and watching the Golden Goes," he clipped.

I tried to snatch my hand back. It didn't work. "It's the Golden *Globes*," I corrected. "Everyone knows that. You're just pretending you don't know what it's called to hide the fact that you secretly watch the reruns and—"

"Rosie," he warned.

I fluttered my eyelids. "Would you believe me if I told you I tripped?"

His eyes narrowed. "Onto someone else's face, yeah. Who the fuck have you been fighting with?"

"The mailman," I lied. "He didn't deliver my shoes, even though it was overnight shipping."

"Rosie," he repeated.

I huffed. "Guess you're gonna find out anyway. Polly's moved in."

His eyes went hard. "What did the fucker do?" It wasn't surprising that he knew immediately that it had to do with Craig. He was a good judge of character and very protective over Polly.

"You can't tell anyone," I said first.

"What?" he seethed.

"Polly doesn't want people knowing about this."

He stared at me. "Secrets don't do well for people, babe. We know this."

I stared back. "I agree. But her mistakes were her own to make. Just like ours were."

He scowled at me in response, then gently kissed my hand.

"You're hurt. That makes it my responsibility," he murmured.

"I'm not hurt. Battle wounds don't count," I countered.

He eyed me. "You've got enough of those, Rosie."

I eyed him back. "You can never have enough."

He sighed and yanked me into his embrace, and I sank into it, letting the events of the day fully and completely wash over me now that I was safe.

We stayed like that for a long time. Though, forever wouldn't have been long enough.

"He hit her," Luke said when he pulled back, still keeping me in his arms.

"Yeah," I whispered. "How did you know?"

His thumb brushed the edge of my eyelids. "I can see it in your eyes, babe."

I sighed and pressed my head into his chest.

"You kill him?" Luke asked blandly, kissing my head.

"Polly wouldn't let me," I whined.

"You at least fuck him up?"

I nodded against his chest.

He stroked my head.

"We'll get him," he promised. "And we'll take care of her."

I pulled back. "I know," I whispered. My hand went down to cup him over his jeans. He let out a harsh breath and his eyes went dark. "But first I need to take care of you. And it seems my hands are injured. Do you think my mouth will suffice?"

My fingers worked at his belt and he grew underneath the denim.

His hand went to my breast, tweaking my nipple. "Oh fuck yes it'll suffice, babe," he growled.

TWO WEEKS LATER

"How do you feel after two weeks under quarantine?" I asked Polly, swinging my bags as we meandered down one of my favorite and mostly undiscovered vintage shopping spots in LA.

Polly smiled, pushing her heart-shaped shades to the top of her head. "Feels nice." Her smile disappeared. "But weird. I think I hate him, maybe. But I still miss him. Am I pathetic?"

I squeezed her hand. "No, babe. You're human. You're kind and loving. You don't let people go from your heart. That's not pathetic."

She squeezed back, pushing her shades back onto her face.

"So," I said. "Heath's back." I was going for a casual input into the conversation.

She stopped walking, right in the middle of the street. Some guy on his phone almost collided with her, then muttered insults under his breath.

I flipped him the bird.

Polly didn't notice him. "He is?" she whispered.

I nodded.

She swallowed visibly.

"Are you sure it's not him you really miss?" I asked gently.

She tilted her chin up. "I'm not sure about anything anymore."

I was about to make the most of that statement, to finally get the skinny on her and Heath, but someone decided to shoot at us before I could.

Assholes.

As soon as the blacked-out SUV with no plates screeched out from the corner, I was on guard. Then I saw the back window open and the glint of metal.

I dove on Polly a second before the shooting started.

I heard the first part of her strangled scream, the rest drowned out by the roar of at least one semiautomatic weapon.

It was a lull in the afternoon, which meant the street wasn't busy, but the people who were around screamed and ran. I covered our heads, hoping people wouldn't continue to be standing targets for much longer.

A sharp pain erupted in my shoulder, like a bee sting at first that grew more and more intense as the roar of bullets ground my teeth together.

And as quickly as it began, it was gone, the squeal of tires replacing the low boom of the gun. When it was apparent that the car was gone, people started crying, yelling, calling 911. I moved gingerly, aware of the fact that my arm was on fire, hot lava spilling from my blouse and down my arm.

My attention wasn't on my own bodily injuries as I focused on Polly's gray pallor and terrified eyes.

"Are you okay? Are you hit?" I asked quickly, running the one arm that was still working over her shaking body.

"No, no," she whispered, and then her eyes widened. "You are, Rosie. You're *shot.*"

I awkwardly stood up, dusting my skirt. "It's a flesh wound," I dismissed, then frowned at my sleeve. "I'm more worried about my blouse. This is vintage," I moaned.

Polly stood in front of me, regarding me in horror. "You're shot," she repeated. "And you're worried about your *blouse?*"

"Of course. The arm will be fine after a couple of stitches and hopefully some good drugs. Crepe silk, on the other hand?" I shook my head. "There's no ambulance for that."

She grinned weakly among the chaos around us. "You're crazy."

I grinned back. "The best people are."

Getting shot was like heartbreak. You saw people experience it in the movies, and in my world, more often in real life.

You know it hurts. You see it.

But you don't actually realize the fucking agony of it until it happens to you.

Heartbreak was obviously worse, because like for silk crepe shirts, there was no ambulance, no hospital for a break that incurable. Well, maybe there was, if you counted a fallen cop with great abs and an even better ass.

Who just happened to be storming through the ER, murder on his face and fear in his eyes.

I'd been rather blasé about the whole thing. It was a shoulder wound, for chrissake. I wasn't about to faint or cry like the other nitwit who got a graze on her shin. A graze. It only just broke the skin, wouldn't even need stitches. You would've thought it took the whole leg off.

No, I wasn't one to make a spectacle over something as asinine as a bullet wound. Not until I saw Luke's eyes. The utter terror in them. I guessed he'd gotten a frantic call from Polly, babbling about how I'd been shot. She'd been more upset than I had.

"Oh my God, oh my God," she chanted at my bedside once they'd stitched me up.

I squeezed her hand. "Babe, I'm okay." I frowned at her. "Don't faint," I commanded. Then I smiled. "They gave me morphine. This is aces."

She gaped at me, tears welling in her eyes. "Someone shot you. Someone shot at us."

I shrugged, ignoring the twinge that came with that. "It happens."

"It does not happen," she shrieked. "Hangnails happen. Bad hair days happen. Drive-by shootings *do not happen.*"

I narrowed my eyes. "Bad hair days do not happen." I frowned, patting my hair. "Not to me at least."

"This is my fault," she whispered.

"My hair is not your fault. It's those damn doctors messing it up," I snapped.

She looked at me, her eyes glassy. "No, this, the shooting. It's my fault."

It was my turn to gape at her. "You? No, the list of people who I've pissed off enough to try and ruin my shopping day by shooting me is almost as long as my shoe wish list. Trust me, this is *my* fault. Therefore I'm glad I'm the one lying here with the bad hair, not you." I paused. "Your hair looks great."

"I'm serious, Rosie," Polly said, face grim. "This happens the first day I'm in public after... you know who," she whispered.

I rolled my eyes. "He's not Voldemort. You can say his name, however bullshit it is."

"He's got connections, Rosie. Bad ones," she continued, wringing her hands.

I laughed. "I doubt it. Someone as cowardly as him does not have enough pull to organize a drive-by, especially in broad daylight."

"But—"

She was cut off by the aforementioned fallen cop, plus another man with murder in his eyes—his whole body, actually—following close behind.

I didn't think Polly was cut off by *my* murderous man. She was cut off by another.

Heath.

Guess he was back.

Couldn't fault the guy's timing.

"Holy fuck, Rosie," Luke all but yelled, pushing past a male nurse who was about to take my blood pressure.

His hands gathered my face with a gentleness that didn't match the rest of him. "You got shot," he whispered.

"So they tell me," I murmured.

"Baby," he rasped, his tone broken, defeated.

I put my hand on his. "I'm okay."

"You got shot," he repeated.

"But I'm *okay*," I repeated.

He wanted to say more, I could tell. He wanted to declare how he would protect me forever and how he'd failed in his job and how he was never letting me out of his sight. The usual things an alpha male said to his woman when she'd just been shot.

But we weren't usual. We were real. We were different. Different than the saint and sinner we'd once been. The cop and the criminal.

We were just Luke and Rosie now.

"We're going to kill every single person responsible for this," he declared.

I smiled. "Yes we are. We're well overdue for that kind of date night."

"Um, sir?" an uneasy voice interrupted.

Luke didn't turn. "What?"

"I've got to take her blood pressure." The nurse Luke had almost bowled over had finally gathered the confidence to speak, but fear saturated his tone.

It was strange, seeing the effect this Luke had on people. The Luke from before, Luke in uniform, in his saintly white hat, he put people at ease, made them feel safe.

That was his job, after all.

But this Luke, the one I'd torn the white hat away from and stained it with blood, he scared people, intimidated them. Just like animals in the wild could smell a threat, people could too. They could sense someone who didn't play by society's rules, smell when they weren't safe with them.

It was a mixture of pride and shame that curdled my stomach at that thought. Or maybe it was the cocktail of drugs on an empty stomach.

Could've been the bullet wound.

I doubted it, though.

Luke didn't answer or move. His eyes did a dance with mine, refusing to let them go. Then he pressed his forehead to mine, inhaling sharply, like he was testing the scent of my aliveness, making sure the stench of death wasn't clinging, hidden somewhere he couldn't see.

Satisfied, he moved back, though only slightly, still keeping a firm grip on the side of my neck.

The nurse stared at him for a moment.

Luke snapped his eyes from mine. "I thought you had tests to take," he snapped.

"I'm going to have to ask you move away, sir," the nurse said in a small voice.

"Don't care if you have to ask it or not, it's not fuckin' happenin'," Luke said.

The nurse paused, then awkwardly brushed past Luke to take my vitals.

I smiled, shaking my head. "You couldn't just play by the rules?"

He smiled back. "Been doin' that my whole life. Now that someone's taught me how fun it is to break them, I'm not going to play by shit anymore."

I grinned wider, tasting the sweetness of his smile, ignoring the sour of the thought that maybe it might backfire on me, this lesson I'd taught.

Maybe he'd turn into someone who resented me for taking those rules from him.

Maybe I'd turn into someone who resented myself for doing that.

CHAPTER TWENTY

They discharged me from the hospital a couple of hours after they made sure I wasn't going to die and then they'd have a lawsuit on their hands.

Well, I kind of discharged myself. They wanted to keep me overnight, but in the words of Cher from *Clueless*, "As if."

"They say you need to be here overnight, then you're fuckin' staying overnight," Luke clipped, trying to stop me from getting up.

I raised my brow. "Them saying that is a rule, and I'm pretty sure you said you're done following rules not two hours ago." The morphine was wearing off and my arm had started to ache. Not that I'd tell Luke that.

He kept his hand where it was, right over my heart, exerting gentle pressure. He flattened his palm so my heartbeat vibrated it slightly. His eyes found mine. "Not all rules," he murmured. "Any rules concerning your health and safety are nonnegotiable. Not when everything I am is attached to them."

I swallowed roughly. "I'm safe. With you, I'm safe, right?"

He gritted his teeth. "Of course."

"Then I need you to get me out of this hospital. I hate them.

They're not safe for me." My eyes glimmered with the words I didn't want to say, scared that if I mentioned Death, he'd hear. He lingered around these sterile hallways.

His eyes softened and his palm moved upward to my jaw. "Only if you promise *complete* bed rest."

I waggled my eyes. "I can totally promise that."

He narrowed his. "That's not what I mean. *Rest*," he said firmly, no hint of sexual innuendo in his tone.

I grinned wickedly. "I can rest with your head between my legs."

His face darkened. "I'll allow that," he rasped.

Unfortunately, that plan was ruined by my family.

You'd think with the commonality of shootings within the club, they wouldn't be dropping everything to break the land speed record to land here in LA almost immediately after we got home. Not for a mere shoulder wound, at least.

But apparently they did.

"Where is she?" Cade hissed, pushing at Luke before he could even answer.

"She's resting," Luke clipped, stepping back so almost the whole club could pile into my tiny living room, all of them with grim faces.

Well, not Gage. He was smiling.

But that didn't count because he was fucking insane. Drive-by shootings were like his Christmas. And he wasn't one to get all soft about something as simple as a flesh wound.

Cade's eyes ran over me, focusing on the bandage visible under my thin tank, resting there for a long time. They looked blank. Empty. Cold.

I knew different.

I knew he wasn't moving or speaking not because of fury. Well, it was certainly part of it, but I knew he wasn't because he couldn't. Because he was replaying everything that could've happened, trying to remind himself that it didn't. He was waiting to speak, to move, until he trusted himself to do it in the way the president of the Sons of Templar: California Chapter should do.

I winked at him.

It did what I'd intended, pissing him off enough to react. "Who the fuck have you pissed off now?" he demanded.

"We don't know this is Rosie's fault, so why don't you lay off?" Luke said, face and voice hard.

Cade turned his glare to him. "You're acquainted with Rosie, right?" he shot. "Of course this is her fuckin' fault."

Luke clenched his fist. "You better watch what you say about your sister being responsible for getting herself shot, almost fuckin' dying. That bullet was three inches shy of her heart. Think she's that eager to leave this fucking world?"

Luke's words carried silence with them. Silence in the men in the room who were presented with yet another death.

They didn't hold onto that for long. At least Cade didn't.

"You need to tell me what the fuck you're tangled up in. Right fucking now," Cade demanded, crossing his arms over his chest, obviously deciding to ignore Luke's presence altogether.

I wanted to cross mine right back, to make a statement. Kind of hard to do with the burning pain in my arm. "Why do you think it's me who's tangled up in something? It could've been an unlucky coincidence."

Cade gave me a wide-eyed look. "There are no coincidences when it comes to you. Especially when there's drive-by fuckin' shootings involved."

"He's got you there," Lucky muttered.

I silenced him with a glare.

The uneasy silence was broken with a loud banging on the door, which of course meant every male in the room whipped out a gun and just overreacted in general.

I rolled my eyes, pushing up from the sofa. "Chill, commandos. I ordered pizza."

Lucky was first to lower his gun and make his way to the door. "Great, I'm fucking starving."

Luke, who had all but arm-wrestled Cade to stand between me and the door, glared at me. "You ordered *pizza?*"

"Getting shot makes me work up an appetite."

"I'll give you two-point-five seconds to show me a pie or I'll shoot you," Lucky said from the door he'd just opened, obviously not to someone wearing a Domino's uniform.

Of course, that meant all guns were raised once more.

"I'm looking for Rosie."

I groaned.

The deep and irritated voice was familiar.

I stepped around Luke and Cade who both wore matching scowls when I managed to do so without either of them snagging me.

"It's okay, Lucky. I know him. You can let him in."

Lucky turned to raise his brow at me. "Okay, but I'm guessing he's an unexpected visitor, which means he gets no pizza," he whined.

He stepped back to let our newest arrival in, the men eyeing him warily, Luke with open hostility.

Well, everyone but Gage, who grinned at me. "I *knew* you coming back would mean I got to have some fun."

"Who the fuck is this?" Luke demanded.

I ignored that too. "Lucian, what are you doing here?"

"The team's dead," he said in answer, voice blank and somehow breathless. Not from the distance up our stairs after the elevator crapped out. He was a fit guy. Had been before, and now with the veins in his biceps pulsing and exposed by his Army-green wife beater, it seemed that he was more so.

Breathless from running. Not upstairs but obviously all the way from Venezuela. From some very bad fucking men.

I was a little breathless myself. Death was there, standing at Lucian's back.

Or maybe he was there all along.

"All of them?" I choked, remembering Arnie's declaration about winning back his childhood sweetheart once he'd gotten his shit together. Richie talking about how his dad was his best friend and they were going to go fishing when he finally stopped killing assholes.

Lucian nodded once. "They made us." His eyes went to my shoulder. "Fuck, they've found you." He stepped forward, as if to brush his fingers over my collarbone. Luke made short work of that stupid gesture, pulling my uninjured shoulder gently into him, positioning me so I was slightly behind him.

"You wanna keep that arm, I suggest you keep it to your fuckin' self," he growled.

Lucian looked from me to Luke, understanding. There was no anger, no jealousy from a lover who'd been pining for me. It wasn't like that with us, not really. We'd both used each other for different reasons.

"Not here to fight. I'm here to warn Rosie." His eyes went to the men scowling at him—apart from Gage, obviously—each with hands resting on their weapons. Cade was still holding his. "Looks like you don't need warning." His eyes went to Luke. "Or protecting."

"She's never needed protecting. She does a pretty fucking good job of that herself," Luke clipped. His eyes went to me. "Thought you said this shit was staying in Venezuela?"

I gave him my best wide-eyed puppy dog look. "Well I did think that. I don't know everything. I'm not Beyoncé."

"Someone needs to tell me what the fuck's going on. Now," Cade demanded, stepping forward.

"I'm gonna need to bounce," Lucian said. "I'm runnin' from one lot of guys with guns. Don't need any more on my tail. Looks like you're covered, Zee."

Cade lifted his gun. "You're not goin' anywhere."

Lucky moved swiftly to stand in front of the door, grinning

and winking at Lucian. "Sorry, bro, that's the way the cookie crumbles."

Lucian kept his mask on. He didn't scare easily and didn't look perturbed by the sheer weight of hostile glances focused on him.

"Lucky, let him go. He has nothing to do with this," I ordered.

"Do not fuckin' move, Lucky," Cade clipped.

Lucky moved his eyes from me to Cade. "Fuck," he murmured. "I can't figure out which one of you is less likely to kill me if I listen to the other one."

"I'm the one with the gun, and I'm your fuckin' president," Cade ground out.

"But Rosie stabbed me once for telling her that I liked her better with bangs."

I rolled my eyes. "It was a graze, harden up. And no one except J-Law looks good with bangs." Then I moved my eyes to Cade. "You're not going to get anything from him that you won't get from me. I know you need to throw your power around in high-pressure situations but also, don't be an asshole. Lucian was doing the right thing coming here. He risked his life for me, so how about you let him go on his way? We'll take care of this."

Cade gripped his gun. "Yeah, we fuckin' will."

There was a tense moment, and then Cade finally lowered his gun.

Lucky stepped back, looking relieved that he didn't have to make the decision.

Lucian turned to me. "I'm disappearing. You'd do well to do the same."

"I don't disappear," I told him. "I was kind of born to stand out. Plus, I don't run. I fight."

He didn't look insulted. "Then you're an idiot."

Luke stiffened beside me. "You just got lucky when Cade lowered his gun. You call her an idiot again, you won't be lucky anymore. And I won't lower mine, not until after I've used it." His voice was steel and full of promise.

"You can't fight this shit," Lucian said, speaking to the room. "Not even with a motorcycle gang at your back. They're bigger than that. You can't win."

"Well we don't lose, ever, so it looks like it's going to be interesting," I said.

Lucian shook his head. "Good luck."

Then he was gone.

"Pussy," Lucky muttered. "Running from a fight." He looked at me. "So you've pissed off a couple of drug dealers. We've handled worse."

I chewed my lip.

He regarded me. "It's worse, isn't it?"

I nodded. "Little bit."

Cade stared at me. "How much worse?"

I looked to Luke. He looked back.

"I thought you said you were gonna protect me," I whispered.

He laughed. "I will, but you don't need protecting. Your brother isn't going to hurt you."

I rolled my eyes.

"How much worse, Rosie?" Cade demanded.

"Quite a bit, I'd say."

Everyone swore.

"I *knew* you weren't done with the drama," Lucky said cheerfully.

And we weren't.

Not by a long shot.

After I told Cade, it was immediately decided that I was to leave for Amber and the safety of the club.

I expected Luke to argue.

He did not.

I didn't know who was more surprised, me or Cade.

"What? No spiel about how this is a job for the police or how you can look after me?" I demanded.

Luke regarded me. "Babe, you've *never* been a job for the police. And I'm not dumb. This is not somethin' for cops who get paid shit and have worse hours to deal with. They'll be bought off. The ones who aren't bought can't and won't do shit. They know they can't win." He paused. "I can look after you, but I'm not fuckin' stupid. This isn't a job for just me. This is a job for your family. You know better than anyone that any battle you fight is theirs too. And a few extra guns isn't gonna hurt. We've got a date."

"Um, now is hardly a time for a trip to Olive Garden," Lucky interjected. "Though those breadsticks are great."

"No, our date night consists of killing everyone responsible for shooting me and my whole team," I told him with a smile.

Lucky gaped at me. Then Luke. "Fuckin' hell," he muttered. "Me and Becky are going to have to do something crazy like rob a bank so you don't steal our thunder."

"We goin', then?" Cade demanded, ignoring Lucky.

I sighed.

Which brought me to now, sitting in church, telling the remaining brothers who hadn't come on the road trip and filling them on the extended version of "I pissed off some powerful Venezuelans."

"Jesus fucking Christ, Rosie!" Cade shouted, banging his fist on the table once I'd finished.

I leaned back, twirling one of my curls. "What? 'Cause I'm a girl I don't get to have some fun?"

Cade openly gaped at me. That was something. My stoic brother was famous for his murderous poker face. Never did he betray any form of human emotion unless he was around my sister-in-law or his babies. Then he was a big fucking teddy bear. Unless someone threatened them. He'd set the world on fire and not even blink if anything happened to them. And I'd hand him the match.

"I know you have a fucked-up idea of the concept of fun. I'm to blame for that, and I've accepted it. I get your version of fun is fucking with some gangbangers who sold drugs to kids. Or getting tangled up in shit with other chapters," he seethed. "I let you have that. We can clean that up, so you can handle that shit yourself. But international fucking criminals, Roe? You fucking serious? This can get you *dead*. Really fucking dead." His voice was shaking with fury that no doubt made prospects wet themselves.

I merely crossed my arms and rolled my eyes. I propped my boots up on the table, crossing one foot over the other ankle. "Don't know if you've noticed, but I'm alive," I pointed out.

He sighed. "Yeah, I've noticed the pain in my ass that means you're alive." He shook his head. "What is it with you and Lucy? You both got a pact to get murdered by South American crime lords?"

Lucky leaned forward. "You see, brother, it's like this. Some women, best friends and such, you know, when they spend a lot of time together, their... *cycles* link up." He screwed up his nose. The man who'd killed and tortured the people who raped his wife was grossed out by *periods*. "But that's *ordinary* women. We know these are not ordinary women, so that's their version of that." He held up his hands as if he'd solved the whole thing.

I tried to stifle my giggle, but it didn't work. Luke grinned and squeezed my hand.

Cade leaned forward on his hands. "You think this is funny, Rosie?"

"No, but Lucky is," I countered.

"This is serious."

I glared. "I'm aware. I'm not asking you to help."

"Don't be fuckin' dense. We're helping," Steg's throaty voice said instead of Cade. "That's not a question. First time you pulled a knife on one of our gun runners 'cause he insulted your shoes, I knew this day would come. Knew that the biggest battle we fought would not be because of your brother, or even Gage. It would be 'cause of you. We're ready, girl. No doubt about that."

"These are serious bad guys," I whispered.

Gage grinned. "So are we."

We declared war.

But the funny thing about war was it wasn't like the movies, where men shouting cries for family and country run toward the enemy, weapons raised, faces painted blue.

It was far more boring than that.

Keltan and the crew in LA gathered intel.

Luke pressed his contacts at the NSA for any high-profile Venezuelan nationals vacationing in the US of A.

There were no more drive-by shootings, explosions, not even a threatening note. An amateur would've thought they—whoever they were, exactly—had given up.

This was not our first rodeo.

"Migel Fernandez," Wire said, standing in front of a large screen, pointing to the image of a tanned, suave and—by the look of his suit—extremely rich man.

He wasn't unattractive, in that silver fox type of way. Trim, nice hair that had lashings of salt in the pepper, strong jaw. Not bad, if you ignored the fact that his suit was paid for by the trafficking, abuse, and torture of human beings.

"Businessman, very rarely seen in public. And when he is, he has a bigger entourage than the president," he continued, images covering the screen. They looked like grainy satellite images of a sprawling compound in the middle of the jungle, men in black, blurry but obviously security, scattered about the place.

"Not much is known about him officially," Wire continued. "Lot of legitimate businesses that keep up appearances. Clean, on the surface. Unofficially, he's one of the biggest players peddling human flesh. He specializes in attractive, young Americans. Preferably virgins, because they're worth more, you see. But he's not picky. He can cater to any taste, any kink. Nothing's off-limits." Wire screwed up his face. "Nothing."

His haunted eyes told me he'd seen something that he didn't even want to put on the screens in front of some of the most unshakeable men on the planet.

"He has contacts—customers, actually—in most governments around the world. Diplomatic immunity here in the States. Enough manpower to populate the army of a small country. Holds grudges. Is well known for exterminating anyone who crosses him, along with their entire family and known accomplices."

Cade looked to me blandly. "And *that's* who you've pissed off."

I shrugged. "Go big or go home, right?"

I saw Cade's face morph and his fists clench as he struggled not to yell at me. I could almost hear him counting it down in his head.

"This isn't Rosie's fault," Luke cut in from his place beside me. Which was where he'd been. Constantly.

It would've been annoying if I thought he was shadowing me because he thought I needed a knight. But it wasn't that. He knew I had a sword of my own. He just wanted to be near me, give me his sword too.

He'd braved the looks and glares and pointed comments whenever we were at the club. Most of them came from Cade.

Actually, all of them came from Cade.

We'd had conversations, and Cade hadn't shot him, which was his version of approval, but that didn't mean an almost thirty-year grudge would be settled in a handful of months. Cade wasn't wired that way.

Neither was Luke. But he was trying.

Cade settled his glare on Luke. "Rosie running off to Venezuela, putting her nose in shit where it didn't belong—like she always does—and deciding to throw stones at the biggest player in the human trafficking game without thinking he's gonna throw stones back *isn't* her fuckin' fault?" Cade questioned.

Luke's hand flexed on mine. "She was doin' the right thing."

Cade continued to stare. "The right thing would've been not fuckin' leavin' in the first place," he clipped. "I'm sure I've got you to thank for that one, so maybe it isn't Rosie's fault. Maybe it's yours. You wanted to destroy the club but it wasn't working the regular way, so you decided to try it different. Fuck my sister—"

"Stop," I hissed, slamming my hand down on the table.

Lucky jumped beside me, not expecting it. "Fuckin' hell," he muttered, placing his hand on his heart like an old lady might when someone cursed in front of her.

"Enough," I said quietly. "You continue that train of thought, you won't have a sister to push away anymore."

Cade's eyes flickered. "You haven't considered it?"

I tilted my head. "What? That Luke did some roundabout thing to push me away on the off chance I'd run, and gambled that it would be to Venezuela, where I would happen to stumble upon a human trafficking ring and decide to arm up?" I continued to glare at my brother. "And then he decided to quit the force he loved so much, move to LA to work with Keltan so he could organize Lucy to get stabbed so I would come home and somehow have the Venezuelan bigwigs try to shoot me on the street months later, all so he could destroy the *club*?" I asked, my tone dripping in sarcasm. "No, I haven't considered it, because I'm not that *fucking insane*, but now I know you're that fucking narcissistic. Could he not be here, standing up to the big, bad and all-powerful Cade because he, oh, I don't know, *fucking loves me!*" I shouted. "All you see is what you want to see. If you knew what Luke's done for this club—"

Luke squeezed my hand. "Baby," he murmured in my ear. "Easy. Don't say shit you're gonna regret."

I glared at him, hating that he was stopping my roll. Hating that he was right.

"There's a reason I left last year. A real reason," I clarified to the table. I eyed Lucky, who looked like he was going to start rattling off past transgressions. "Not because I felt like following Thirty Seconds to Mars across Eastern Europe. Not because I wanted to walk the El Camino, or party with some guy whose name I didn't remember," I said before he could. And maybe so I could put off saying the real reason I left. "I remember the name of this guy."

Lucky grinned. "Here we go."

I smiled back. Or attempted to. Then I sucked in a breath and looked above Cade's eyebrows as I spoke to the table. "His name was Kevin. We dated. I dumped him because I didn't like the way he spoke to me. Both with his words and his fists."

The second I finished my sentence, Lucky's grin disappeared. It would've been comical if the tone in the room allowed for it.

It did not.

Luke squeezed my hand.

I smiled weakly at him.

"Rosie—" Cade bit out, his form marble.

"Please, Cade, and all other furious males in the room—AKA every male in the room. Please do not interrupt story time," I requested. "There's plenty of time for yelling or breaking the furniture after I'm done." I went for airy because I didn't quite think I'd make it through otherwise. I knew I wouldn't make it through without Luke beside me.

"I didn't tell you because A, you had enough going on at the time, and B, because I handled it." I paused. "Or at least I believed I did. After I shot Devon, I came home. Kevin was there. Long story short, he was not happy about the breakup, or the very real castration threat I'd left hanging over his balls. He did not communicate this with words. He, to put it not quite delicately, beat the shit out of me."

Cade hissed out unintelligible words.

Lucky brought his fist down on the table so hard the wood cracked.

Steg hadn't moved a muscle, his eyes hard and shimmering.

"I'm just gonna preface the next part of the story by saying he did not rape me," I said, deciding not to tell them everything. I could tell my girlfriends; they could heal. These men couldn't, despite how strong they were, knowing that would leave a mark, so I protected them from that.

Luke squeezed my hand tighter that time, then brought it up so he could press his lips to it.

"He handcuffed me to the bed. With less-than-noble intentions. Before he could consummate those intentions, Luke arrived." That time *I* squeezed. "And he killed him."

The room paused. Everything. For a second, no one seemed to breathe, and a collection of eyes went to Luke. For the first time not in hatred or anger.

"Let's be clear here and say that he didn't technically *need* to kill him," I continued. "I'd managed to get him off me and chewing on his tongue. Luke could've done the 'cop' thing. Shot him in the leg. Restrained him. Cuffed him. Read him his rights. But he didn't. Because of me. He sacrificed everything he stood for because of me."

I looked around the room. At the men I grew up with. Who I considered family. My eyes lingered on Steg before landing on Cade.

"I'm not asking you to sacrifice everything you believe in," I whispered. "I'm not even asking you to kill for me. The opposite, in fact. I'm just asking you to do something for me. Let me be happy. Let me live with the man I love without the fear that the family I love will kill him. Because to be clear, ending this, ending him, that's me gone. One bullet will end two lives."

There was silence at the table for a long time.

The longest.

"Where'd you bury him?" Gage asked conversationally.

"Quarry that got shut down a few years ago, twenty minutes south," Luke answered.

Gage nodded. "*Nice.*"

I stifled my grin.

"He hit you and you didn't come to us?" Cade asked quietly. Only I could hear the hurt in his tone.

I softened my gaze. "I didn't need to," I said. "I know this club, know you. You've been determined to shield me from the worst of the worst, from all my Fuck-Ups. And I'll love you for that. Among other reasons, like your great taste in wives and cute kids. But I didn't need that shield that night. Luke was there. Luke's always been there."

My eyes moved to Luke, who was staring at me intently. "I'll always be here, babe," he promised.

There was a long pause at the table as everyone digested my words.

"Fuckin' hell, can we stop with the sappy shit?" Gage boomed. "We've established that Rosie is a badass bitch, so is it really a surprise that she's in love with a badass motherfucker too?" he asked the table.

I grinned.

"Can we please get back to figuring out how I'm going to get my killing in this year?" he continued.

The air around the table softened.

So did Cade's gaze, for a moment at least. Then it hardened again.

"Yeah, let's get to the killing."

CHAPTER TWENTY-ONE

ONE WEEK LATER

We were staying at Luke's house because Gage was at mine.

He'd offered to take back his old room at the clubhouse, but I knew no amount of disinfectant would clean out whatever had gone on there.

That and I was afraid.

Afraid of my own house.

The memories, the demons lurking there from that night. What happened. I was terrified that if I went back in there, it would all come back. He would come back: his touch, the invasion of my body. And I'd be reminded of just how easy it was.

I couldn't. And it made me realize that this was something I was going to live with for the rest of my life. It didn't make me weak; it would make me stronger. One day. And I knew Luke was right, I did have to talk about what happened. Staying silent, blaming myself when none of what happened to me was my fault, that was weak.

So I'd talk.

Eventually.

But right then, we were about to go out to dinner for Luke's parents' anniversary. We'd already done the official dinner with the parents a few days after we'd temporarily moved back to Amber.

I'd been nervous. Very nervous. It was funny, I never thought I'd care so much about something like that. But I cared about Luke more than anything. And he'd given everything to fit in with my family. I was terrified that I couldn't do the same, that his family wouldn't want me with him.

That couldn't have been further from the truth. His father had answered the door with a huge grin, taking me into his smoke-scented embrace.

"Ah, I'm so glad my boy's finally come to his senses," he chuckled as soon as he'd let me go.

I smiled. "I think it was me who had to come to my senses," I replied, glancing up at Luke.

Bill's eyes twinkled.

"Doesn't matter how you got here. Just matters that you're here." He looked at his son. "Finally."

And it went like that. I was welcomed. Into a slightly more conventional family than my own, but no less loving.

I wasn't nervous now. I was getting dressed, slipping into my brightest red dress.

It hugged in all the right places, though a little tight maybe. It was true what they said, happiness in relationships made you put on weight.

Luke hadn't gained a pound, the prick.

Then again, he was insane enough to go running. Every morning. Even on the *weekends.* To be fair, he made sure I'd gotten my workout before he left most mornings.

I didn't mind it, the fact that the zipper was a little more difficult to deal with. I remembered back when I first got home, when my clothes hung off me, when I lost all the curves I'd been so proud of. When I didn't recognize myself.

I looked in the mirror, running my fingers through my curls, letting them tumble wild down my back. My face was full, no gaunt cheekbones to be seen, which meant I had to contour again. Any use of more cosmetics was welcome to me. My eyes seemed brighter, more vibrant. I touched up my bright red lipstick.

Then I looked down, at the mingling of my numerous cosmetics products with Luke's lone tube of deodorant and bottle of after-shave. He didn't even gel his hair and it looked that good, the prick.

A glint of silver peeked out from behind my Chanel perfume. I was a magpie, so I was attracted to the shiny thing, my red-tipped fingernails fastening on it.

The steel was cold on my hands and the feeling crept into my fingers, upward so it was everywhere all at once. I fingered the lettering, seeing my warped reflection in the silver.

"Babe, are you ready to go?"

I turned. Luke was dressed all in black, slacks but no suit jacket. Black shirt, open collar.

Black.

What he was now.

And he looked good.

I'd never loved him more. Or hated myself, just in that moment.

"Babe?" he repeated, face contorted in worry. It changed when I turned and he saw what I had clutched in my hands.

"You don't wear this anymore," I whispered. "Because of me."

His eyes hardened. "No—"

"And you're not who you're meant to me because of me," I continued before he could speak. "You talk about killing people and you scare nurses and you don't care because I made you different. I *fucked up*. Biggest one of them all. Because I forgot who you are, who you're meant to be. The good person. The good man. I know I'm not bad or evil, but I'm not that good either. I'm somewhere in between."

"Rosie," he whispered.

"There are two kinds of people in this world, people who make mistakes and people who have regrets," I continued to babble. "The people who have regrets are the ones too afraid to do something as daring as live so instead they collect what-ifs like stamps, bundle them up and inspect them in the winter of their life." I paused. "Then there're the others, the ones who are too daring, who live maybe a little too much. Collecting mistakes and experiences and watching them on repeat with a smile on their face. Fuck-Ups may be hard to live with sometimes, but at least it means you've done something. Moved. It's no secret which camp I hitch my wagon to. What'll yours be?" I said it in a rush, a confidence radiating from my voice as faux as my fur.

He watched me, knowing the invitation behind my words. "I've got enough regrets to curse and inspect in the winter of my life, babe," he said. "But I'll be okay inspecting them if I've got a thousand summers with you. Making mistakes, maybe, but one I know I won't make is standing right in front of me." His hands fastened at my hips, yanking me close to him. "Maybe there was a time where I was that first type of person. Actually, there're no fucking maybes about it. I was. You were too. Because you lived wild and free, babe, that's true. But livin' wild when chaos is your normal is the same as livin' normal when you know nothing else. Maybe we both did the dance of regret with each other. I'm not gonna let us do that. Any mistake I make with you will be a treasure as long as I've got you beside me in the winter of my life."

"But—"

He took the shield from my hands.

"This badge." He fingered the shiny silver item that weighed so much more than the sum of its parts. "It used to be everything to me. There was nothing more important than this. What it represented. *Who* it represented. Me. The man I wanted to be. The man

I thought I needed to be. This badge used to be my reason for getting up in the morning. For *being*. My purpose." He paused, not really looking at me but at the same time staring into whatever was left of my soul. He was choosing his words carefully. "I was doing something. Something good, maybe," he continued. He didn't sound sure at the last part, like it was more of a question. Not to me, to himself.

I wanted to look away. I wanted to escape the stare of an intimate object, the blame that came with it, the guilt. The incredible guilt that followed me around the country and then out of it, which I knew I couldn't run from yet I itched to try once more. To escape. To do what I always did when the emotional going got a little too real.

I wanted to escape him too.

Even though every cell in my body rebelled against it, even though he held everything I ever wanted in his hands. Not the badge. Just him. I wanted to run. Not from him. *For* him. To give him back the life I'd stolen from him.

I wanted to trick myself that it wasn't too late for him to get it back, that I hadn't put it through the wood chipper like I had my own heart.

He seemed to sense my struggle, or at least my eagerness to escape. The lawman in him, I guessed. He knew when an outlaw was going to make a run for it. Instinct.

The silver clattered to the floor in a resounding echo and he was on me before I knew what happened. Before I could register just how pivotal that abandonment of that small piece of metal was.

His hands framed my face and his eyes searched mine. I couldn't bring myself to hide it. My utter love for him. The love that had started out as innocent and pure and had been warped, tangled into something ugly and brutal and nothing like the movies, yet I was loath to let it go. Even if it had already begun to destroy us.

Even if we had been goners the second I'd seen him on that curb at five years old.

His grip on me, both with his hands and his eyes, made it seem like he didn't want to let go either, even though it was bad for him. Even though I was bad for him.

"That badge *used* to be everything, Rosie," he rasped. "Who I wanted to be, my reason for being." His hands tightened at my face. "But fuck, baby, I didn't know shit about living for somethin'. *Breathin'* for something. Dying for something. Willing to kill for that something and still sleep at night as long as that something, *you*, is gathered naked in my arms." He yanked us closer together so no air separated us.

"But I'm not good," I whispered, my voice so small and vulnerable I didn't even recognize it.

He flinched. Full body. Like I'd struck him. Like the words actually hurt him to hear. "No, baby," he said, voice thick. "You're not."

"I'm not good," I repeated in a tone that belonged to someone rocking back in forward in a padded room wearing a straitjacket. That's who I was on the inside.

He nodded, not hearing the crazy in my tone, or ignoring it. "No. You're not." There was a beat, a palpable heaviness in the air at his pause. "Such a word doesn't even fucking scratch the surface of what you are. Labeling you as one singular thing would be a gross disservice to the magnificent creature that you are. You're so much fucking more than one side of two binaries, baby. You're strong. Stronger than most who wear badges, stronger than most who fight those who do. You're loyal. So fucking loyal I know you'd take a dagger for anyone you let into your life, and that list is fucking long and full of people who seem to brush with death too often for comfort. Know you'd do it for people you haven't even met yet. You'd take the blow for anyone who didn't deserve it just because you could. Because you would willingly and without fear be a shield for anyone. That scares the shit out me."

Fear, true fear, danced in his eyes at his words. It shook me to the core. Because it was that life-or-death kind of fear, when something happened to make you realize how fragile life really was.

"Every day, I have this bitter taste on the back of my tongue because I know you'll jump in front of a bullet without hesitation. Because of that thing you have inside you. That loyalty. Yet I love you for it. Your spark. Your fight. Your beauty. Not just on the outside, but the shit you got inside you. It's worth it." He glanced to the reflection of silver on the ground. "It was worth it. Giving it up. Whatever fucked-up me I was trying to be without you. I'd walk through fire for you, baby. I don't give a shit about the other stuff that kept us apart. That kept me from being a stupid bastard and burying my feelings so deep I hid them even from myself. That means nothing with you in my arms. In my bed."

His eyes searched mine, yet the vision wasn't crisp since mine were murky with tears.

"Which is where you're going to be for the rest of your fuckin' days, Rosie. And despite your penchant for taking bullets for those you love, there'll be a lot of them. Because you want to be the shield for people? Fine. But the thing is *I'm* your shield. And whatever shit you face, it's gotta go through me first."

"But I want to be your shield," I whispered, tears running down my face.

He wiped them away. "Okay, we'll be each other's," he murmured back. And then he took away any more words I could use as excuses or escapes and he kissed me. Reminded me of the one thing that mattered. The one thing I could control.

Not the bullet with my name on it. Or his.

But us.

And maybe it was going to be a big Rosie Fuck-Up. But it was going to be for life.

TWO DAYS LATER

"You've got to be fuckin' *shittin'* me," Cade spat, his shades directed to the parking lot.

Luke's own shades focused on Cade's glare, visible even beneath the dark glasses he wore, because he wore that glare in his entire body. Luke instinctively yanked me closer to him, obviously expecting a threat.

And he wasn't wrong.

My mother climbed out of a beat-up Camaro, her leopard-print heels hitting the pavement unsteadily at first. Then she righted herself, yanking off her knock-off sunglasses so we could see the streaks of makeup running down her face.

"My babies!" she screamed.

Yes, *screamed*. In the parking lot of a memorial.

Today marked a year to the day since Scott's death. I wasn't there for the funeral, which I was kind of glad of. I hated burying people. It was something we did for all the fallen brothers, but it meant a lot more to me, because I didn't get a proper chance to say goodbye.

Not just to Scott but to the person I was. To the demons I'd entertained after that day.

But there was my mother.

Screaming.

At a memorial.

Granted, it was a Sons of Templar memorial, so there would likely have been screaming at some point in the night once the bottles were empty and hearts were a little lighter. Or heavier.

But not now.

And not from her.

She went for me first, because I was always the easier one. I was always the one who forgot for a moment, that I was meant to be angry at the mother who abandoned me because I'd slowed down her party. Because I would always react as a little girl, even as a woman, I'd instinctively want my mother's embrace.

Wanted to pretend that she wanted it too.

But that time it was different. Because I was being held by someone who definitely wanted me, someone who wasn't letting me go.

Mom dropped her knock-off bag at our feet, arms open as if to hug me, glancing at Luke in a gesture for him to let me go.

Luke knew our story with Mom. Therefore, he did not let me go.

She awkwardly leaned in and kissed me sloppily on the cheek, her cheap perfume embracing me even though her body didn't.

"Oh, Rosie, baby," she cried, pretending that the moment hadn't happened when she leaned back. "I came as soon as I heard you were home, that you'd lost *another one*. This is just horrible. Horrible. I knew my babies would need their momma to get through this."

Cade snorted. Actually snorted.

All eyes went to him.

Not just because such a sound was foreign and never before heard. Gwen was gaping.

"Bullshit," he said. "You came because you're outta money, too old to get the attention you want, and too fuckin' washed up to hide your crazy from whatever guy is stupid enough to fuck you. You came back here because you've got nowhere else to go, not because we need you," he growled. "Clue in. You weren't here when we buried our father. When Rosie went to prom. Graduated. When she lost one of her best friends. When my daughter was born. My wedding day. My son's birth." He listed them off like bullets, aiming to hurt and maim the woman who birthed us. "We sure as fuck don't need you or want you," he spat. "You have any fuckin' respect for this club and for your children, you'll get back in that piece of shit and never come back here again."

Mom was gaping at him, with the audacity to look appalled. Hurt.

The truth did hurt. Especially when it was ugly. Especially when it showed you how ugly you were.

Mom wasn't. The years hadn't been kind to her, shown by the deep lines around her mouth and forehead, the makeup she slathered on sinking into the creases. Her eyes were a little sunken in, bloodshot. But she was still beautiful, under it. Or at least she had a shadow of something that told the world she used to be beautiful.

She dressed like she still was. She was slim, but more out of malnutrition than anything, her tight black dress molding over bones and tired flesh. It was much too short for a woman her age, even a woman who lived as hard and wild as she did.

Crocodile tears ran down her face. I was sure apologies, excuses, and tragedies were about to come spilling from her lipstick-smudged mouth.

They might have, had the barrel of a gun not settled in a deep wrinkle in the center of her forehead.

"You've got about thirty seconds to get out of here before I shoot you," Evie said, her eyes hard.

I blinked at her. Cade and Luke both stepped forward, as if to do something.

Evie wasn't worried. "You don't get to come and spread your poison upon these kids. Upon this day. You won't do it again. You may not remember how to be a mother, never were one. Nor a good person. But I'm sure you'll remember that I don't do empty threats. Today of all days. Death is visiting today. And he'll welcome another addition. I won't hesitate to give him one."

Evie wasn't lying. I knew that. She would shoot Mom, right there.

It felt strange to me that I didn't have immense panic at that thought. It was hurt. A lot of hurt. But not at seeing my mother killed in front of me. It was having a mother who put herself here. Took herself away from us, then put herself here.

She blinked at me, pleading with her eyes, expecting me to speak up, to fight for her.

Except that day I didn't feel like fighting. I hooked my hand into Luke's belt loop. He immediately turned, sensing my need, and took me into his arms, his body a barrier between me and my mother.

"They ain't gonna say shit," Evie croaked. "They got one true mother standin' here. It's the one holdin' the gun. I'll kill for them, and I'll kill for myself. So go, bitch, before I decide to spill your blood just to make this anything but the day we revisited the family we've lost."

Mom only had a sliver of hesitation, a painfully short amount, before she turned on her heel and left.

Evie didn't lower the gun until the engine started.

We all watched her leave.

Mom didn't look back once.

"I need a fucking drink," Evie muttered, turning on her stiletto heel and moving toward the clubhouse as if nothing happened.

"Me too," Cade said. He yanked Gwen into his side, giving me a look before following Evie.

I went to do the same when Luke stopped me, hands going to my face.

"What?" I asked, confused.

"Babe."

I waited. He didn't say anything else. "Babe is not an answer," I snapped. "I know you've taken to hanging around with men who think it is, but make no mistake, that's not gonna fly with me," I informed him.

"That was your mother," he said quietly, looking to where the Camaro had disappeared.

"No it wasn't," I replied. I jerked my head toward the clubhouse. "*That* was my mother. The woman who was wearing too much perfume and not enough clothes is just someone who gave birth to me and pops in when she needs a break from the party. And needs money, more often than not."

"Fuck, babe. I'm sorry," he murmured.

"I'm not," I replied. "Seriously. I may be damaged in a lot of ways, but that's not one of them. I don't have a hole where I'm meant to have a mother because I have them." I nodded back to the clubhouse once more. "They've given me more than she ever could have, even if she'd stayed. So I'm good. Don't worry about that. I'd be more focused on the crime lords out to get me," I teased.

He kissed me long and hard. "Fuck, I love you."

I grinned lazily. "I love you too."

"I'm thankful for her," I said to the fire.

Cade and I had gotten through the day. With each of the people who acted as our other halves beside us.

That was until Luke brought me into his arms, lips on my ear. "Think you and your brother need a moment?"

I leaned back, gaped at him for suggesting something I didn't realize I needed until right that second.

"I love you," I blurted in answer.

His eyes were oceans. "I love you, baby. To my bones," he murmured back.

Then he let me go.

Just like Gwen let Cade go when I wandered up to her.

Cade scoffed from his place across from me. "You're shittin' me."

I glanced at him. "Trust me, there're a lot of things I want to hate her for. I *should* hate her for." I took a pull of my beer. "She's a shitty mom and an arguably worse person. But she designed herself, you know? She majorly fucked up, don't get me wrong, but I think that's why Dad loved her. She saw through all the bull-shit of how people thought they were meant to be. She created herself for herself. She didn't follow any rules."

"Like bein' a fuckin' good mother," Cade spat.

I nodded. "Yeah, that. But if there's anything I got from her apart from great hair is that ability. That rebellion, I guess. Against that little part of every human that strives to be like everyone else for some illusion of safety that comes with unity. That's bullshit. She taught me, without even trying."

Cade regarded the fire. "No, kid. You did not get that shit from her. Or even Dad." His eyes met mine. "You got that shit from you. You were born with somethin' that no other human being has business having inside them before bein' able to speak. Born with chaos. Swear to God, I saw it the moment I looked into your eyes, a day old. Fuck, even as a kid, I looked at you and knew it."

I blinked away my blurry vision at the beautiful and heartfelt words coming from my brother.

"You're an exceptionally good man, Cade Fletcher," I whispered.

"Exceptional runs in the blood, just like trouble. Only thing we inherited from that bitch."

I screwed up my nose, trying to match the bitterness and hate in Cade's tone with the memories of my mother.

I couldn't.

In my fuzzy memories, she was the one smiling, dancing, laughing. Turning the music up so loud my teeth chattered. Letting me wear leopard-print cowboy boots with my ballet uniform. As I grew older and she visited less, those memories were all I had to cling to.

Today was my first real glimpse of the truth.

The ugly one.

"Was she really that bad?" I asked.

Cade's face softened. "Roe, no. She loved you. In her way. She just didn't know how to love herself, so she couldn't do it right.

357

She did you a favor by leaving. I don't like to think how fucked up you'd be if she'd stayed."

I grinned. "You mean even more fucked up?" I faked a shiver. "Me neither."

There was a long silence—well, immediate silence. The low hum of heavy metal and grumbled conversation carried from the wake that had now turned into a party.

"You okay, Roe?" Cade asked softly.

"No," I admitted. "Not at all."

"Yeah, me neither."

I looked over the shadows, past Death who was staring right at me, grinning that toothless grin, to my man. To Luke, holding his beer, chatting easily with the men who, up until a year or so before, he would've loved to have put in a prison. Now he partied with them.

He was doing that, and would be doing that forever.

For me.

And then Death wasn't in front of me anymore. He was still there, but behind Luke. Behind Luke's shield.

"But we will be okay," I whispered.

Cade's gaze was glued on Gwen. "Yeah," he agreed.

CHAPTER TWENTY-TWO

"She's turning into a little human being," I whispered, playing with Belle's long curls.

Cade had forbidden Gwen to cut them, so they were tumbling all the way down to her little booty.

"They do that," Gwen whispered back, smiling at her daughter.

She was beautiful, even as a toddler. Her green eyes, when they were open, were always sparkling, radiant against her tanned skin and dark hair. She had all of Gwen's beauty and softness with Cade's edge. All tumbled into a little girl.

"Cade's going to shoot *so many* teenage boys when she grows up," I said, giving her curls one last stroke before I stepped out of her bedroom.

Gwen followed me, shutting the door quietly. "Oh, I don't know, I think she's going to have him wrapped around her little finger when she's a teenager, considering she does already," she said, grinning.

I grinned back, happy that Cade had this to come home to, life and love and happiness to shake off that feeling of death. He had his family, the girls who he adored and his son who already worshipped him.

"You doing okay?" Gwen asked as she walked us to the living room littered in family photos. "You and Luke finally getting together, you getting shot, and your mom turning up in that way...." She handed me a much-needed glass of wine. "It's a lot for one person, even you, babe."

"Yeah," I said, sipping my wine. I thought for a second. "No, I guess I'm not, actually."

She sipped her own. "It's okay to not be," she said.

"Yeah, I know."

"Is it bad to say I'm happy for you?" she asked. "Despite being hunted by a human trafficking ring and all that jazz." She waved her hand. "But that's just another Tuesday for you," she teased. "But you and Luke, you're finally what you were both meant to be. You've got it."

I smiled. "Yeah, I've got it."

"Kind of feels like the ugliness of the world can't really get there, right into you, not when you've got him, right?"

I smiled. "I don't even want to punch you for saying something that corny because it's true."

She sipped her wine. "I know, and I don't even care about what an idiot I sound like. I'm a happy idiot with two beautiful children —who did not ruin my vagina, thank Lagerfeld—a husband who's hotter than Hades, and girlfriends Carrie Bradshaw would kill for."

And it was in that moment that Belle padded in, a toy bunny dangling from her chubby fingers, eyes thick with sleep. I grinned at my niece, knowing she would have some of her aunt's rebellion about bedtime, and about other things. The grin froze on my lips when I saw the man following her, pointing a gun to the back of her tiny head.

Gwen shot up, wineglass flying from her hand and shattering to the floor. She was about to run to her daughter when the man stopped, grabbing Isabella's arm so she dropped her bunny, but not tight enough to alarm her.

"Don't move," he commanded, voice flat. "Unless you want this to be your daughter's last day on earth."

I was standing by that point too, and both Gwen and I froze in absolute horror. Helplessness washed over me like acid.

Belle was still blinking away sleep, still not aware of the situation, thank God.

"My husband is going to kill you. Slowly. I'll make sure he lets me play with you first." Her voice was thick with fury and promise.

I was struck frozen.

"He won't, I don't think," the man said. "Not once we're done, at least."

"What do you want, asshole?" I hissed, fury and terror pulsating through me. "Whatever it is, you can have it. Let her go." Despite everything I'd been through with the club, laws we'd bent and broken, we'd never experienced this. We never hurt children.

He would die. If it was the last thing I did.

The empty gaze went to me. "So nice of you to ask, Rosie," he said with a familiarity that made my skin crawl. "It's you we want."

I stepped forward immediately, before he even finished speaking.

"Done," I said.

"Rosie, no," Gwen choked, torn between her need to get her daughter out of harm's way and her worry for me.

I ignored her. "Take the barrel of your gun off the four-year-old girl, motherfucker," I hissed.

For the longest and most horrible moment, I thought he wouldn't. I thought the finger resting on the trigger was going to squeeze and I'd watch the most sickening thing that could be done, a real-life nightmare. Something we'd never come back from.

Then the gun moved and I exhaled as it rested on me. I

snatched my beautiful little girl, sniffing her hair one last time before I handed her to Gwen, tears in her eyes.

"Rosie, don't do this," she pleaded, kissing her daughter's head.

"Tell Luke I love him. You already know I love you," I said.

Then the man snatched my arm roughly, pressed the cold steel into my temple and we left.

To Death, up close and personal, I presumed.

I wasn't knocked out.

Or blindfolded.

Which didn't mean good things for me. Generally when people kidnapped other people with the intention of eventually letting them go, they made sure no evidence could lead back to them. Hence the need for blindfolds and chloroform and such.

"You're one of Fernandez's men, aren't you?" I asked the silent man driving the SUV.

He hadn't spoken since he'd bustled me into the car and told me he'd come back and shoot Gwen and the children while I watched if I tried any "funny business." Yes, he said "funny business." It would've been funny if he hadn't been dead serious.

"The big bad crime lord really has to point guns at little girls to get who he wants?" I continued, fury turning my voice to ice. "I shouldn't be surprised, since he picks on defenseless girls, makes money off their suffering. He's a coward. Picking on people who can fight back isn't actually his style, is it?"

Silence.

"You've got a mother? Wife? Daughter? How do you think they'd feel about this shit?" I spat.

More silence.

"I'm going to kill you. One day. And I can't wait for that day to come, because you won't be feeling so fucking mute. You'll be begging for your life," I promised.

He didn't say a word.

I huffed, slamming my back into the seat and crossing my arms. Then my fingers snaked down to the knife in my boot, toying with the top of the handle.

I itched to sink it into the soft part of his neck. It would be easy. The car might crash, but the man who'd pointed a gun at my baby niece would be dead. Not a bad tradeoff. Then I remembered his promise. I didn't doubt that another spineless evil prick would replace him to carry that out.

I let go of the knife, accepting my fate. But far from peacefully or happily. I didn't want to die that day. There was too much to live for. How could it be the plan that everything I'd ever wanted was in my life and now my life was over?

"That's the way the cookie crumbles," I whispered, mimicking Lucky's words.

Maybe that's what happened. People died when they got every single thing they'd ever wanted. Because human beings weren't designed to get everything. Something needed to be taken away to balance that out.

I'd just have to make sure I went down with as much bullets and blood as I could.

We drove for a while, though I couldn't say for how long. I didn't even really take notice of what direction we went; I knew I wasn't getting out of this, so what was the point in marking landmarks?

I didn't want to die. I didn't want to give up, but I knew the world. Guys like Fernandez. If I fought, and won—which I could, if the odds were in my favor—then I'd survive. Luke would rejoice. There would be a reunion. Happiness.

But then five minutes, five days, five weeks afterward, there would be more blood.

And it wouldn't be the men, the ones wearing the patches, the ones ready for war. No, it would be those tiny humans with beautiful curls and cheeky smiles.

I thought of Lily's newborn. That content smile as Asher held her and her baby. Or Mia's little boys, one who'd tied up his preschool teacher for fun. Ones who brought love and light to Bull's eyes. The happiness that Bex had seemed to grasp onto, that Lucky had given her despite living through a nightmare I didn't know if I could've survived.

Of those women I may as well be shooting if I tried to fight.

Lizzie told me that I had to fight. Save myself. And she was right. But I already did that.

Luke already did that.

If it was just me and him, I would've fought.

To the death.

But my family was bigger than just me and Luke. And I had to shield them. Even if it meant the end of me.

Luke would understand.

<hr>

We were sitting in a large living room of some half-finished suburban mansion in a housing development that went bankrupt. Who knew why, though the fact that it was in the middle of fucking nowhere probably didn't help things.

Handy for people planning murder without those pesky witnesses, though.

It was sprawling and we were in the innermost room, the rest of the house crawling with armed men. Wire was right, this guy's entourage was excessive.

I was pushed down roughly onto a sofa, still covered in plastic. I wondered if that was because the furnishings were too premature or if they'd planned ahead.

Weirdly, I was devoid of fear.

I was full of anger, a lot of it. It pulsated through every part

SHIELD

of me like a living thing, urging me to run forward, throat punch one of the men at the door, snatch his weapon and start fighting.

I clenched my fists, willing myself to stay still, remember the people I was saving just by refusing to fight.

Luke's face popped into my mind.

I wasn't saving him by giving up.

My decision was damning him to a life of only breathing. Because that's what I would've been doing if I ever lost him. But I had no choice. He would understand.

He would forgive me.

Hopefully.

The door opened and the man from the photograph walked in. He was unassuming, not at all the picture of some sort of cruel evil villain.

Which was always the way. The absolute worst of humankind never looked evil. That was kind of the point.

"Rosie," he said, his smooth voice only holding a hint of an accent.

I smiled. "Misogynistic, murderous asshole," I greeted back.

His façade didn't flicker. "Ah, there's the spirit I've heard so much about."

He sat next to me on the sofa, bringing with him the scent of an expensive aftershave. I somehow expected him to smell like rot and decay and all of his evil deeds, decomposing on his soul from underneath his skin.

I wanted to shrink away from his proximity, but I stayed strong, jutting my chin out. My knife burned into my leg, begging me to use it, end it all now. But I guessed the man with the sniper rifle at the door wasn't just there for decoration, and I'd be dead before the knife found its home. Men like this didn't take risks unless they were sure they could come out alive. It was the way with cockroaches.

"I really don't want to hear the evil genius speech," I said instead of stabbing him in the neck. "If you'd just put the bullet in my head, I'd really appreciate it."

He paused, then chuckled throatily. "You think we brought you here to kill you?"

"Well I sure hope you plan on it, for your sake," I shot back. "Because you pointed a gun at my four-year-old niece. Came into my brother's home where his *children* and his *wife* sleep. Trudged your filth and evil into a good home. Scared my sister to death when she's had enough fear in her life." I paused. "She'll never forget that. Watching her baby girl almost get snatched from the earth, realizing she couldn't protect her. You did that. So yeah, I hope you're planning on killing me. Because if you let me walk out that door, I'll make it my life's mission to take down you and every single asshole you care about," I promised.

He didn't answer immediately, didn't look perturbed at all. Just regarded me.

The gaze was cold and uncomfortable. The stare of a being with nothing underneath his skin but a black soul. A true psychopath.

"I don't doubt you, Rosie. You seem to make quite sure to keep your promises," he said. "You caused a lot of trouble for me and my business."

I gaped at him. "Do you want an apology? So sorry, Doctor Evil, for foiling your evil plans to rape and enslave innocent women." Then I glared. "You're the most despicable person I've ever come into contact with," I whispered. "I hope when you die, it lasts for *months*."

"Well, you're not the only one who hopes for that, but I'm a stubborn man. I don't plan on dying just yet," he said, unbuttoning his suit jacket. "I'm not here to get you to understand my business. Most people have... trouble."

"Most people have hearts, that's why, motherfucker."

He raised his brow. "I came because I have a certain reputation to uphold. If people think they can interrupt my business without retribution, I have troubles, you see?" He sighed. "So retribution is necessary. Your team, they were easy. They didn't quite have the *complications* you do."

I tilted my head. "There should always be complications. Taking human life should never be easy," I hissed.

He shrugged. "Ah, but it is. You know this. In the right, or wrong, circumstances, it is easy. One of the easiest things on earth. But your family, they are powerful. So your life is not as easy to take. It would cause me more trouble, you see? I've had quite enough of trouble."

"So if you're not here to kill me, what are you going to do, slap me on the wrist?" I snapped, seriously doubting that was the case. The man had cut a man's hands off for fucking up his car detailing. True story. Wire showed me.

He looked at me a beat longer, then nodded to one of the men guarding the door, the one without the sniper rifle. He reached into his jacket and passed Fernandez a large brown envelope. He dumped the contents of the envelope and started laying photographs on the chipped coffee table in front of us.

My eyes were glued to the photos as soon as they landed on the wood. And they kept coming.

Mia chasing after Rocko, who was holding some kind of lit firework.

Cade in his bedroom, throwing a laughing Isabella into the air.

Amy and Brock holding hands as she scowled at him and he grinned wide at her.

Bex walking out of an NA meeting, Lucky bringing her into his arms.

Luke walking down the street, on the phone, grinning.

Evie sitting on the porch of her and Steg's house, smoking.

Ranger and Lizzie cheering on their kids at a soccer game.

And it went on.

"Your family is very large," Fernandez said pleasantly. "And very unique. Loyal. Strong, a lot of them." He tapped an image of

Cade, watching Gwen from a distance. Then on Luke's photo again. He moved the photo so it focused on Belle, running after her baby brother in their backyard. "And also very vulnerable."

"Don't you say another word if you want to keep breathing," I hissed, my voice small.

"I want to keep breathing very much," he said calmly. "I want everyone in your unique family to keep breathing. Which is why I'm here, having this chat with you."

"You're calling threatening babies a *chat?*" I hissed. "You really are a piece of shit."

"I'm not asking for your acceptance of my character, just your understanding of the situation." He stood up, straightening his jacket. "I'll leave you some time to think. You are my guest here, which means you will not be harmed." He looked to his guards. "In any way. And I will be back. Soon."

And then he was gone. I was left with all the photos of the people who made up my world, and the unsaid threat by a man promising to destroy that world.

CADE

Cade was frustrated.

They were getting nowhere on this Fernandez motherfucker.

Scratch that, they were getting a lot. A lot of things that made even Cade's stomach turn. A lot of things that haunted him, even after he'd put his children to bed, fucked his beautiful wife and she fell asleep in his arms.

Warm.

Breathing.

Her heart beating against his own.

But he lay awake for hours afterward, staring at Gwen's chest rising and falling, holding onto her. He lay awake and thought of that shit they'd found. The fucking atrocities. And he thought about Rosie being tangled up in that shit.

It scared him. She always scared him. The girl had no fear. She leaped, didn't look, didn't fucking think. Her courage wowed him. Her strength.

And she'd gone through shit the previous year and had done it without him. No matter what she said, he'd failed her. Because she'd been there every fucking step of the way when shit got rocky in his life. Got dark. When he thought he might lose Gwen. The baby. Rosie was there. The months he was without Gwen. Rosie was there. His wedding. His children's births. And every time after that. She was always there.

And he wasn't fucking there when she'd needed her big fucking brother.

The cop was.

Not a cop now, he guessed. But he'd always be a cop.

Cade would never like him. Too much shit went down for that to happen. But he fucking respected the shit out of the man. For what he did for Rosie. For standing by her. And he hadn't blanched at the various laws they'd broken in the process of trying to get Fernandez.

Cade was still uneasy about it, about showing Luke that shit. He may have been off the force, but he was still an outsider. But he made Rosie smile. Really fucking smile. And Cade would put all his shit aside for someone who made his little sister smile like that.

Who'd protect her.

He was sitting at church with him there, and it pissed Cade off that it didn't feel as wrong as it should've to have him sitting at that table with his brothers.

"I want something concrete," Cade growled. "I want something we can do to take this fucker down."

"Well, I've got a friend who knows a guy who can get his hands on some rogue nukes," Gage said, dead fucking serious.

Cade stared at him. "I can't believe I have to say this, but no fucking nukes, Gage."

Gage shrugged, carving at the table with his knife. "Offer's there. They're just going to waste."

"No nukes," Cade repeated.

He was about to continue when Gwen burst in the door, holding both of their children in her arms.

It was late, and she was meant to be at their place with Rosie. He immediately checked his babies for injuries. Nothing. But they weren't crying, and they should've been, being woken up and dragged to the club when they should've been sleeping. They should've been crying.

But they weren't.

They sensed something in their mother. Something that terrified them enough to keep them silent.

Cade was out of his chair before anyone could speak, Kingston in one arm and the other one around Gwen and Belle. He sucked in a breath, inhaling the smell of his family, just to tell his thundering heart that they were there, alive.

"Baby," he whispered. And fuck, he couldn't do anything but whisper, he was that terrified. It was like those shadows he'd been staring at every night had come to life and he couldn't breathe around them.

"They took Rosie," she sobbed. "They came into the house, they pointed a gun at Belle, and Rosie went with them. She knew they were going to kill her, but she went with them because they pointed a gun at our daughter."

Cade's blood went cold. Ice cold. Every part of him froze. He stared at his daughter. Took in her wide green eyes. Her little nose. Her red lips. The locks of her hair.

She's okay. She's okay and she's here and your world isn't falling apart. Keep your fucking shit together. For them.

Gwen stopped sobbing and her eyes went blank. "They pointed a gun at our baby, and now we have to kill them all."

LUKE

"They took Rosie.... She knew they were going to kill her but she went with them."

Luke heard nothing but that on a replay reel.

Twenty-three hours and thirty-six minutes. That's all he heard. He couldn't hear Rosie. He tried. Every moment that he sucked in ash instead of air and his heart shredded in his chest instead of beating, he tried to conjure up her throaty voice telling him she loved him.

Tried to remember the way her mouth tasted, the way her pussy tasted. The way she screwed up her nose when she was frustrated. How her smile lit up a fucking room whenever she was happy, which was a lot these days. How perfectly she fit in his arms.

He fucking couldn't.

It was as if someone had come and stolen away all of his memories of Rosie, just like they'd stolen her.

He barely kept it together. Fucking barely.

Cade was eerily calm. He'd been making orders, calling in markers to get in touch with someone who could tap into the fuck's location. Police came and went because they wanted every set of eyes out there looking for Rosie.

Luke barely noticed their glances at him, staring at the side he was standing on, the outlaw side.

He didn't see any of that. He just saw the last time he'd kissed Rosie.

"I don't like it." She pouted.

"What, me going to the clubhouse and trying to figure out how to kill the man stalking you while you drink wine?" His hands found her waist, then traveled lower to her perfect fucking ass. His cock hardened.

She smiled.

His cock hardened even more.

"No. Well yes, I like that because the menfolk are doing all the work."
She winked. "But I had plans for us tonight."

*Luke pulled her into him, smelling her perfume. Smelling her. "What
was that?"*

*She bit her lip and his cock twitched. Her lipstick was bright pink
today. Her hair was piled atop her head and she was wearing a bright
pink dress. Tight as shit and too short, but he loved it. Her heeled boots
were pink too. She was in a 'pink mood,' she'd said that morning after
he'd told her he liked her outfit. He'd actually showed her. By bending
her over the sofa the second she'd emerged from the bedroom.*

*He fucking loved that. Waking up to a different Rosie every day. But
the same in all the ways that mattered. He loved that she would never be
happy stationary. That to her, everything in her life was fluid, except the
people she loved. With Rosie, that was forever.*

*"Well," she said, "I was making room for some more of my clothes and
I found a rogue pair of handcuffs."*

Luke's cock pulsed again and he hissed out a breath.

*Her eyes flared. "Yeah," she whispered, feeling his cock pressing into
her stomach. "Now you get why I don't like it? We don't get to use them."*

*Luke yanked his mouth to hers, kissing her like he wanted to fuck
her: hard, rough, and with no mercy.*

She blinked dreamily when he stopped, her face flush.

"We're gonna fuckin' use them," Luke growled. "I promise you that."

*She smiled again. "I'll hold you to that, Crawford. And I'm thinking I
get to do the handcuffing."*

*She winked and sauntered away. He watched the sway of her ass, his
balls crying out to him to fuck her brains out. Now. But he didn't.
Because he had shit to do and she'd be there later on.*

But she wasn't. And now Luke might never get to fuckin' see
her bite her lip, watch her face flush after he kissed her. He
wanted to rip his own skin apart for how trapped he felt inside his
own body.

"Son."

Luke's head snapped up. He'd been sitting in a chair in church, on his own, head in his hands in a rare moment of stillness. He cursed himself for getting lost in that, even if it was for a few seconds. That was a few seconds he would never get back. That was a few seconds that could mean everything to Rosie.

His father stood in front of him, face unreadable. He looked very old all of a sudden. It was strange. He and Rosie had just seen the man and the lines on his forehead hadn't been there. He hadn't looked like that.

Luke stared at his father. "I failed," he choked out. "I swore, since that day in the car, I swore I'd protect her, and I fucking failed," he hissed, not caring that his father wouldn't remember the very day he decided to bring down the club to protect Rosie.

And now the only chance Rosie had was the club.

Luke's father walked in unhurriedly, clapped his son on the back. "No, Luke, you didn't fail her," he muttered. "You givin' up?"

"Fuck no," Luke said fiercely.

"Then you haven't failed her," Bill said firmly. "You know she don't need protectin'. You know she's strong. She's gonna be whole and well when you find her. You're gonna find her, Luke."

His father's voice was firm, but there was something beneath it. Desperation. Because Luke knew his father understood that if they didn't find her, he'd lose his son forever.

CHAPTER TWENTY-THREE

ROSIE

They kept me in that house for twenty-four hours.
Fernandez was true to his word. No one touched
me. They fed me. Gave me water. Bathroom breaks.
Very polite kidnappers, all in all.

But then again, they didn't need to starve me or beat me. Physical violence only went so far. They landed the deepest of blows without touching a hair on my head. Those photos worked better than anything else would have.

I got snatches of sleep, for handfuls of minutes. Then I saw Belle's beautiful locks, matted in blood. Gwen's sightless stare. Bex enduring more horrors. Bull meeting the Devil truly, without anything to bring him back.

But when Fernandez came back in, I was wide awake, ready.

"Ah, I'm glad to see you're looking so refreshed," he greeted warmly.

I glared at him.

"So you've considered my proposition?" he asked pleasantly.

"What do you want?" I hissed. "You went to all the trouble to kidnap me, surveil my family, threaten them. You've shown me how large your dick is, I get it. What's with the theatrics?"

"I hear you are a rather… unpredictable young woman," he said.

I snorted.

"I just need assurances that, on your next holiday, you do not choose to come to my country," he said smoothly.

"Ah, so you want to make sure your business isn't disrupted again," I spat.

He nodded once. "We are in understanding."

"Yeah, asshole. Congratu-fucking-lations."

He shook his head, smiling. "Unpredictable, brave, or stupid? I'm not sure which."

"Well you think on that real hard. Till your head explodes, even," I invited.

"Brave, I think," he surmised. "But brave or not, it's not you I kill if I hear of you being unpredictable again. I'll kill all of them." He nodded to the photos.

"I get it, Hannibal Lecter," I seethed.

He glanced at his hundred-thousand-dollar watch, bought with stolen innocence. "Ah, they should arrive soon."

I didn't answer.

"Your family is quite effective," he continued. "I didn't expect them to discover this location until later." His eyes moved over me with the first show of real interest since this thing began. It made me sick to my stomach. "Pity," he said. "But oh well. It has been a pleasure knowing you, Rosie. May we never meet again."

The sound of gunshots and frenzied yells echoed in the distance.

I glanced toward the closed door where the two men guarding it, lifted their semiautomatics, preparing to use them on whatever the source of the noise was.

I looked back to the monster in front of me, feigning disinterest. "That'll be my brother and my boyfriend here to pick me up.

It's the strangest thing, they don't approve of me going on unscheduled playdates with human traffickers." I shrugged in a 'what can you do' gesture. "I hope you're not too fond of your frontline men. I'd say most of them are already dead or at least maimed right now. But I'm sure you post them that way, least liked to most, for these very situations, no?"

His gaze didn't move to the door, didn't even flicker from where it was focused. On me. "You are a very strange woman," he observed, tilting his head in a way I didn't like. The way a cat regarded a mouse, deciding whether to play with it for a time or just not bother with the façade and eat it whole.

I didn't let my unease show. "Fuck you," I said with a smile.

The doors burst open, both Cade and Luke running point, side by side. Their eyes found me and their guns found the man in front of me. In any other situation, it would've been comical, among other things. My brother and his once archnemesis teaming up and pointing their guns at a common enemy instead of each other.

Brought together by me.

That was what I'd always wanted, wasn't it? Granted, the situation was a lot more fucked up than I'd planned.

But if it wasn't a major Fuck-Up, it wasn't Rosie.

Bull, Lucky, Gage, Asher, Dwayne, Brock, and Steg came in after them. Bull took care of one guard with the butt of his gun in a practiced and effortless jab. Gage, grinning and somehow covered in blood that I both guessed and hoped wasn't his own, plowed his fist through the face of the second guard. The crunching of bone traveled through the air.

I turned so my back was to Fernandez, a gesture of trust that I hoped wasn't another Fuck-Up that would land me in the grave. I made sure I stood in front of him, which meant in front of the guns pointed at him.

Both my brother's and Luke's eyes bulged in panic and fury.

"Rosie, get the fuck out of the way and over here. Right now," Cade barked.

I shook my head.

"Baby," Luke said. The softness of his voice was louder than Cade's furious yell.

It hit me every place it could. Every ounce of my being wanted to go to him. But that was selfishness. That would get some of my family killed, if I was lucky. All of them if I wasn't.

I wouldn't let one of them get hurt because of me.

Luke was right, I was their shield.

But I wouldn't let him die being mine, either.

"You've come to save me, I guess?" I asked with a false lightness that took everything in me to conjure. "The men riding in to rescue the damsel. You know, I love fairy tales as much as the next girl, but you also know I leave them where they belong. In the book. The one I never do things by. I don't need saving. I got this."

I didn't add that I was the one saving them. Both because I didn't think alpha males much appreciated such things being said to them at any moment. In ones such as this, I guessed it was much worse. Also because I was only saving them because I was the one who'd put them in this situation in the first place. Kind of a double negative.

"Rosie, this isn't the time. Get out of the fuckin' way," Cade clipped, losing patience. Not that he had much to lose anyway.

Luke was somewhat different. He regarded the situation with a lot more than the blind rage of my brother. I could see it, taste it, simmering around amongst the other, its particular brand more familiar to me than that of my own blood. Something else was working there, other than anger. He was putting it together.

You can take the cop out of the man....

"Fuck," he breathed. Then he lowered his gun, as if it weighed a thousand pounds.

His eyes never left mine.

"Crawford. What in the fuck are you doing?" Cade all but roared.

"I'm not pointing a gun at the woman I love," Luke said quietly. "And she said she's got this."

Cade gaped at Luke like he'd grown another head. "She's fucking *Rosie*. She ain't got shit but a boatload of trouble."

Luke's eye twitched. "I trust her. You should too." The words were forced out of him, just like his stationary stance. I could tell, more than anything, that he wanted to stride over, yank me behind his back and shield me from this. From everything.

But he knew he couldn't.

Seeing that on his face was worse than anything that could've been dished out in that room. So, like a coward, I stopped looking at his face and instead took the easy route, taking the wrath of my brother.

"Trust me, Cade, I know what I'm doing. For the club. For my family."

He glared at me, and continued to do so when, with an exaggerated sigh, Gage, of all people, was the first to lower his gun. Then Lucky, of course with a wink. Then Bull, with no expression because he was Bull. Brock shook his head with a shadow of a smile at the corner of his lips. Dwayne and Asher did it expressionless, and Steg was regarding me with twinkling eyes.

All of them, apart from Gage and Dwayne, had experience raising and using their weapons when their own women were in this exact situation. Or something very close. I knew they didn't lose a wink of sleep at night over those expelled bullets or lost lives. I knew they didn't because they had *it*. Their fairy tale. Or their violent, bloody, and painful version. The one they took out of the books.

This man had the power to take that away from them. I had the power to make sure that didn't happen. If I first swallowed my pride.

It went down easily when I thought of all of those happy ever afters that would stay intact. My beautiful nephew and niece who wouldn't have a family torn apart.

"Cade," I whispered, my voice little more than a plead.

He didn't move for a second, suspended in time almost. I knew it went against everything in him to lower his weapon. He considered himself my shield too. It was his job to protect me, and he took it seriously.

But I wouldn't let that mean he had to die for me like he would.

So I let out the breath I'd been holding when he lowered the gun.

The silence after that was toxic, suffocating.

A clap, harsh and ugly, cut through the air, and I turned to see the source of it.

"Wonderful. I see that one beautiful lady is all that is needed to stop any more bloodshed," Fernandez said, menace haunting his harsh accent. "So good, so good we do not have to engage in hostilities. It would have been... most unpleasant."

"We're going to go our separate ways now, aren't we?" I said, the words painful for me to utter.

"What the fuck?" both Cade and Luke growled almost simultaneously.

I glanced their way, but otherwise didn't acknowledge them. "No hard feelings now that we understand each other, right?" I asked Fernandez.

He smiled. Or stretched his facial muscles, showing teeth in the mimic of a smile. "Of course, my dear, we are understood. You keep your business and I keep my own and we... how you Americans say it? We cool?"

I did my own mime smile, all the while tasting battery acid climbing up my throat. "Yeah, we cool."

He nodded. "Well, I'll be going, then."

Cade's jaw twitched.

"Cade, let him through," I said.

"Are you fuckin' joking, Rosie?"

Luke looked at me, then Cade. "Do as she says."

"I'm not listenin' to a fuckin' cop when he tells me to let go of the man who *pointed a weapon at my four-year-old daughter's head in front of my fuckin' wife*," he spat.

"But your family are all alive, are they not? Surely you would like them to stay that way," Fernandez said blandly.

Luke caught Cade just before he lunged, Brock helping him to stop Cade from charging. He struggled with both of them, all logic gone from his eyes. Fernandez had just openly threatened his family. Cade's reaction was kneejerk and deadly.

"You're not listening to a cop because I ain't one," Luke hissed. "You're not even listening to me. You're listening to your sister who you need to fucking trust at this point in time. You know she loves your family with everything she has. You think she'd be making this call for anyone but them?" He had to yell over top of Cade's struggles.

Cade breathed heavily, wild eyes focused on Fernandez with a predator's determination. Then he moved to me, communicating a lot of things with that look. I tried to communicate back. Tried to tell him this was just a battle, that the war was ours.

He slackened in Luke's and Brock's grip, shaking them off. He focused on Fernandez. "This shit isn't over," he promised.

Fernandez smiled. "Oh, once you chat with your sister, I think you'll find that it is."

And then he walked forward. An uneasy moment passed when I thought that Cade might not move, might change his mind and blow them all away right there.

He stood to the side with a granite jaw. The rest of the men followed suit.

The second Fernandez was out the door, Luke was on me, shoving his gun into the back of his jeans and framing my face with his hands. I thought he'd talk first but he didn't, just plastered his mouth to mine. Not closed mouth. Not short. It was like he was sucking every part of me out to make sure it was all still there.

"He hurt you?" he demanded when he pulled back, eyes running over every part of my wrinkled but still intact outfit.

"No," I whispered.

His eyes met mine, fear, death, and love shimmering within them. "He had you for twenty-four hours, Rosie. *Twenty-four fucking hours*." He took my hand and placed it on his chest. "First time my heart's beat in twenty-four hours," he murmured.

"Rosie?" Cade's gruff voice demanded, breaking our moment.

Luke didn't move at first. His eyes roved over every inch of me, as if he had been away from me for years, decades, and he was trying to catalogue the changes that'd happened in his absence. Like a man deprived of water for almost long enough to kill him and then presented with a whole glistening lake of it. He pressed his lips to mine again, like before, hard and intense and most likely not appropriate for an audience.

I kissed him back. Fuck the audience.

I'd been deprived of water too. Of everything, really.

Then he let me go to reveal everyone standing around, like they didn't quite not know what to do with themselves since they weren't surrounded by bodies.

Cade's eyes went to Luke's firm hold around my shoulders. "Let her go, Crawford."

The grip tightened. "Not a fuckin' chance in hell."

I savored the feel of my safety for a second longer, inhaling deeply. Then I reached up to graze Luke's fingertips. "Luke," I whispered.

He glared down at me. "This is the first time I've had you in my arms in twenty-four hours," he growled. "During those hours, I was forced to entertain the idea that I might never fucking do this again. Or I'd have to hold the broken pieces of you, with nothing to put you back together with." His eyes went to Cade. "I'm sure with Cade's experience, he knows what the fuck he's asking and if the situation were reversed, he'd have the same response as me, which is *fuck right off.*"

My mind whirled at the deep of the emotion in Luke's voice, how it shook just a little, noticeably. He didn't care about showing these men that emotion. Mostly because he knew they'd all felt it before.

I squeezed his fingers. "Yeah, and I get it. I'm pretty darn pissed at my brother right now, but I owe him an explanation," I murmured.

Luke didn't move. "You can explain from here."

I touched his jaw. He gazed down at me. "I'll be two feet away."

He frowned as if the two feet were as wide as the distance between us months before.

Then he let me go with a tight face.

I kissed his jaw.

Then I stepped forward, expecting a lecture, a lot of swearing and yelling from my brother.

Instead, he yanked me roughly and tightly into his arms.

"Don't you ever fucking do that to me again," he murmured into my hair, kissing it.

I sank into his hold, clutching at the sides of his cut. "Don't really plan on it."

He kept a hold of me for a while longer, not seeming worried about time or witnesses. Then he let me go slightly, his hands going to my neck so I met his icy gray eyes. "Been scared a lot of times in my life," he growled. "Man enough to admit it. That's when the irreplaceable things in my life are taken from me. When I have to do nothing but think about how easy it is for fuckers to destroy me without touching me. You can take care of yourself. I know that." His eyes went behind me. "You've got a man who would die to make sure I don't live a nightmare of having a big fuckin' hole in my heart. That the club doesn't live with a big gaping hole where the soul of it was."

Tears ran down my face. "You're not going to yell at me?"

He smiled. "Maybe later. But Luke was right. You would give your life in a fucking second just so I could go to sleep with my family every single night. But you ain't doing that because if you do, I'm not sleeping easy for the rest of my days. I know that decision wasn't something you had a choice in. Hate it, but I know you're not givin' up. That's not my Roe." His eyes twinkled.

"Yeah, now that we're done with the sappy shit, you're gonna tell us we can kill them all, right?" Gage interjected, scratching an itch at the top of his head with the barrel of his gun.

I made eye contact with Gage and the three other personalities inside him, all anxious for blood.

"Eventually."

<hr />

It was safe to say the men were furious when they saw the photos and therefore the reason that deadly force was not what they could use to protect the people in said photos.

There was swearing, anger and a lot of "he's fucking dead." But then there was a reasonably rapid exit as the respective men went back to their families, to make sure a murderer was true to his words.

Death and revenge didn't mean shit if you were going home to an empty house with an empty heart. So we went home without revenge, but without any more holes in our family.

"Never been more scared in my life," Luke murmured against my head.

We were naked on the sofa. We hadn't even made it to the bedroom, our desperation to find peace in each other too chaotic to make things like proper horizontal surfaces seem important.

Nothing was really important but each other right then.

"Me either," I admitted.

He stroked my hair. "You went willingly, with him. Knowing

you might never come back. Never be right here with me again."
His voice wasn't hard or angry. It was soft, proud.

"You know I had no other choice," I whispered.

"I know, Rosie. You were protecting everyone, just like you always do. "That's what scared me the most, still fucking does. You have a choice like that, there's no hesitation, even though I know how hard it is to make. I'm not gonna beg you to not to make a choice that will take you from this world, take my world from me, 'cause I know that's never gonna happen. You're a warrior first, and you'll always fight. Just askin' you to let me be by your side while you fight."

That right there was what made us *us*.

He knew that my life was never going to be normal, that I wasn't normal. I needed action and I needed a man by my side, not in front of me, trying to protect me. I needed him to know that I could protect myself and not want to change me into something that made him feel more like a man and me less like a woman I was proud to be.

He was proud of the fact that I was strong, and he was man enough that it didn't make him look weak.

"I've got a strong woman. She can fight not just for herself but for everyone in her life, including me." He paused. "Me shooting Kevin that day, it wasn't me damning myself and saving you. It was you saving *me*. From the fucking bars I'd trapped myself in. You're so fucking strong, and that doesn't make me weak. It makes me into the best man I could ever be. Any man who would think different ain't a man at all." He kissed me hard and deep. "Plannin' on being a man, your man, till this world is done and the next one begins. After that too."

"And I'll be right next to you, fighting," I promised.

Sometimes in real life, the good guys didn't win, love didn't conquer all. Mostly because in real life, it wasn't as simple as creating good guys and bad guys. Sometimes the bad guys were the ones who did the most good. Or the good created the most evil. Most of it, the world—me included—was gray.

Love did a lot. Destroyed a lot. Put some of it back together.

But it didn't conquer all.

Four-point-five million people are trapped in forced sexual exploitation globally.

The shadow of Fernandez's threat still hung over our heads. We hadn't given up. That wasn't our style. We were playing the long game, which wasn't exactly our style either, but we were adapting.

We settled into routine, slowly gathering intel, slowly figuring out how to bring the operation down without a single drop of Templar blood hitting the ground.

It was going to take a while. A long while. Because Wire told us that he'd dropped off the face of the earth again, but he would almost certainly be watching us.

So we had to appear like things had gone back to normal while we looked for ways to end it.

Our version of normal wasn't exactly *normal.*

"You want to shoot him, babe, or should I?" I asked Luke.

Luke grinned. "Well, it is Valentine's Day. Consider it my gift to you." He gestured with his gun.

I smiled. "You get me the *best* gifts."

The boom of the gunshot ricocheted through the empty warehouse, the bullet finding its home just above the kneecap.

The man screamed.

"Remember that pain, my friend, the next time you think about breaking the restraining order your wife has against you and beating her so bad she can't walk for three weeks," Luke said. "If you do, maybe we won't be back to do the other one."

The man continued to scream.

I wandered up to Luke and kissed him while I waited for him to stop. "Love you," I whispered against his mouth.

His arms went around me. "And I love you, babe."

There was a lot of shit that stopped my life from being completely perfect, but those three words meant it didn't matter if it was or not.

LUKE

ONE WEEK LATER

"Rosie know you're here?"

"What do you think?" Luke sat down at the table that he'd thought he wanted to destroy. Strangely, it felt right, easy, slipping into the seat and looking around at the men of the Sons of Templar. "I value my fuckin' balls, so yes, she knows," he continued. "Told me she was 'sick of chattering like a bunch of women' and we were to call her 'when the action started.'"

Cade shook his head, grinning. "She never really was one for patience."

"Don't I know it," Luke murmured.

She was chaos, and he knew it. And he wouldn't have it any other way. There used to be days when he lived for order, structure. He thought that was him, that was right.

Fuck was he glad she proved him wrong.

"Might be a good thing she's not here," Luke continued. "Been talking to my contact at the state department. They're building a case against Fernandez. A case that's almost airtight. They just need some more info." He glanced to Wire.

"You honestly telling us you expect us to fucking *snitch?*" Lucky spat.

Luke regarded him. "Yeah, I know it goes against everything you stand for. Want to ride in with bullets and blood. But that leads directly back here. To your home. To your women. Make no doubt about it, we need to do this another way. A way that would never trace back to us, and the strong arm of the law would never lead back to men who would rather die than help out the law," Luke said.

"Damn fucking right," Gage muttered.

Brock eyed him. "I'm hoping you've got a plan once he's arrested? You're not asking us to be happy that he's getting three square meals a day and a warm bed behind bars?"

Luke regarded him. Then the table. "Of fucking course not. It's after that that the blood comes. We take the whole fucking operation down."

Cade smiled.

"Then maybe we can work something out."

And Luke knew they could.

They fucking had to. Because no way would he sleep easy knowing that fucker was sleeping, eating, breathing, fucking on the same planet as Rosie.

They'd get him.

And he'd die.

And Luke couldn't fucking wait for that day.

EPILOGUE

ROSIE

ONE YEAR LATER

I hate to say things like 'the end' and 'we lived happily ever after.' Because neither of those things would be true, even if I could see the future. I didn't have to be clairvoyant to know this wasn't the end. No way, no how. And I was smart enough to know that Luke and I wouldn't always be happy. Humans are never always happy. Even with the only person on earth they're meant to be with, there's going to be anger, pain, tears. But the joy, love, and laughter outweigh that.

But for the sake of it, it was the ending for the time being.

The ending, so far, had been soft.

Anticlimactic.

We got married about two weeks after we found the perfect house. A *home*. I didn't care about marriage, really. But I wanted Luke to be mine. Legally. If that was one law I'd stick with for the rest of my life, I'd be happy.

Our lives were still chaos. We were a husband and wife team who doubled as bounty hunters and beat up lowlifes for hire. So chaos was the nine-to-five. And we liked it that way.

But in each other, we found peace.

There were dramas. Cupid wasn't finished with the Sons of Templar, so there were *dramas*. Fucking big ones when we finally got Fernandez. And his death was proving to last a long time.

There were also other dramas. But they weren't our own.

We'd had enough.

To fill up one lifetime. To fill up three.

So we deserved this soft—kind of—ending, for the beginning was hard and full of pain.

There was still pain. Because you can't have life, can't have love, without it.

But that pain was bearable. Because that pain was meant to be. Because that pain was us.

ABOUT THE AUTHOR

ANNE MALCOM has been an avid reader since before she can remember, her mother responsible for her love of reading. It started with magical journeys into the world of Hogwarts and Middle Earth, then as she grew up her reading tastes grew with her. Her love of reading doesn't discriminate, she reads across many genres, although classics like Little Women and Gone with the Wind will hold special places in her heart. She also can't get enough romance, especially when some possessive alpha males throw their weight around.

One day, in a reading slump, Cade and Gwen's story came to her and started taking up space in her head until she put their story into words. Now that she has started, it doesn't look like she's going to stop anytime soon, with many more characters demanding their story be told as well.

Raised in small town New Zealand, Anne had a truly special childhood, growing up in one of the most beautiful countries in the world. She has backpacked across Europe, ridden camels in the Sahara and eaten her way through Italy, loving every moment. For now, she's back at home in New Zealand and quite happy. But who knows when the travel bug will bite her again.

Want to get stalking?
Instagram: anne.malcomauthor
Join Anne's kick ass reader group!

Here's some more ways to get in touch...

www.annemalcomauthor.com

annemalcomauthor@hotmail.com

ALSO BY ANNE MALCOM

WANT TO MEET ROSIE'S CRAZY FAMILY?

The Sons of Templar MC

Making the Cut (#1)

Firestorm (#2)

Outside the Lines: A Sons of Templar Novella (#2.5)

Out of the Ashes (#3)

Beyond the Horizon (#4)

Dauntless (#5)

Greenstone Security

Still Waters (#1)

Unquiet Mind

Echoes of Silence (#1)

Skeletons of Us (#2)

Broken Shelves (#3)

The Vein Chronicles

Fatal Harmony (#1)

Deathless (#2)